Praise for Will Weaver

BLACK DIRT, BRIGHT STARS

"With *Black Dirt, Bright Stars*, Weaver firmly establishes himself as the essential writer of prairie and pioneer literature. Weaver leaves no open wound unexamined or family bond escaped."
—Nicole Helget, *Stillwater* and
The End of the Wild, a New York Times Editor's Choice

"America's story is a story of immigrants, and Will Weaver's magnificent new novel is an important—and dramatic—reminder of that fact. *Black Dirt, Bright Stars* tells the story of a North Dakota farm family, immigrants from Norway and their descendants, and their struggles. They face not only the forces of nature but also the ignorance and prejudice of their neighbors. Weaver's characters are drawn with complexity and depth, and they are vividly presented. Episodes of their lives, harrowing and suspenseful, can also be read as important chapters in the nation's history, from the late 19th century to the present. Readers of Weaver's previous award-winning novel, *Power and Light*, will recognize characters from that narrative and will doubtless be pleased to renew the acquaintance, though *Black Dirt, Bright Stars* works just fine as a stand-alone book. This is a novel that deserves to be read and to be celebrated. It's a marvelous work of art."
—Larry Watson, *Montana 1948* and *Let Him Go*.

Power & Light

"... a consuming work of profound poetical depth and moral power.
A genuinely moving novel."
—Kirkus Reviews (2023)

Praise for his other novels and short stories

"Graceful writing that views America's heartland with a candid but
charitable eye."
—New York Times.

"Weaver writes with lyrical excitement and gritty power."
—San Francisco Chronicle

"Meticulously rendered writing with warmth, humor, and
compassion."
—Atlanta Journal-Constitution.

"Weaver is a backwoods pitcher with a 98-mph fastball."
—Los Angeles Times (front page).

"Compares with the best of Wendell Berry."
—Chicago Tribune

BLACK DIRT, BRIGHT STARS

CALUMET EDITIONS

Minneapolis

BLACK DIRT, BRIGHT STARS

Book 2, The Haugen Saga

WILL WEAVER

CALUMET EDITIONS

Minneapolis

For Rose

Selected Titles by Will Weaver

Red Earth, White Earth (Simon & Schuster)
A Gravestone Made of Wheat & Other Stories (Simon & Schuster)
Striking Out (HarperCollins)
Memory Boy (HarperCollins)
Saturday Night Dirt (Farrar, Straus & Giroux)
Sweet Land: New & Selected Stories (Borealis Books)
Power & Light (Calumet Editions)

"The arc of the moral universe is long,
but it bends toward justice."
Dr. Martin Luther King, Jr.

"Humbly I would add, it doesn't bend
on its own."
JB Pritzker, Governor of Illinois

Black Dirt, Bright Stars continues the Haugen Saga begun in *Power & Light*. As a sequel, this novel stands alone. However, your reading of it will be enriched by reading both books in order.

The Dakota Star

Vol. 18 Fargo, North Dakota
December 12, 1938. No. 362

Doctor Avoids Conviction On Sex Charge

On Friday, December 9th, in Fargo District Court, Robert McConnell, M.D., forty-one, long-time physician in Skye, withstood charges against him by a female patient. Miss Sally Haugen, twenty-two years old, a single woman also of Skye, accused Dr. McConnell of untoward sexual behavior while she was sedated in his office. Miss Haugen's complaint, the details of which are not suitable for this newspaper, was rendered moot when the jury failed to reach a verdict. The Honorable George Perrick ruled for a mistrial and set Dr. McConnell free. Gifford Bailey, attorney for Miss Haugen, was asked about the possibility of a new trial. "Justice was not served today," he said heatedly, "but there are no plans at this time."

Speaking for the doctor was his wife, Dolores "Dolly" McConnell, also his nurse and office manager. "We're happy that enough jurors saw the outlandishness of the girl's accusation," she said. "Now the doctor can get back to caring for his many patients back at home." Doctor McConnell is Skye's only physician and serves the greater part of Cavalier County, which stretches north to the Canadian border. The complainant, Miss Haugen, had no comment. Speaking on her behalf was her sister, Miss Jenny Haugen, seventeen. Admitting in courtroom testimony that she was instrumental in pressing for a trial "to seek justice for my sister and my family," Miss Haugen's final comment was, "This is not over. Not while I'm alive."

Will Weaver

Section One:
Slender Means

Chapter One
The Interview

Jenny waited for them to call her name. Across the lobby, winter sun lit the frosted glass of the main door. Shifting her boots on the cold granite floor, she was glad she had worn socks over tights. To the right stood a grandfather clock, pendulum still, the carved wood around its face a kind of headdress. She sniffed her hair, blew into cupped hands to warm them, and finger-typed on her lap... *The quick brown fox, the quick brown—*

"Miss Haugen?" A woman appeared. She wore a heavy sweater and her hair in a bun.

"Yes." Jenny stood.

The woman looked her up and down. "Follow me, then."

She trailed the lady's brown Oxfords down a hallway past milky glass windows with curving, black script. **Auditor. Clerk of Court. Assessor. County Attorney**. Beyond a counter, secretaries typed, their eyes tracking her like women who knit, whose fingers know the stitch. At the rear was the office of Arthur Olsen, Register of Deeds. The lady tapped on the door frame.

"What is it?" he said without looking up.

"Here's that young lady you asked after."

"Oh yes. Thank you, Thelma." Mr. Olsen waved Jenny forward and rose from his wide desk. Not tall, not short, not old, not young, he had thinning brown hair, a pleasant voice, resonant and low-pitched, and was broad-shouldered in a stiff-looking sport coat. "Nice to see you again, Miss Haugen."

"And you," she said. "Sir." His hand was warm and a bit damp. The office smelled of pipe smoke. To the side was a smaller desk with a black, Royal typewriter.

"We met last year on your visit here, but the name Haugen somehow rings a louder bell," he said.

"Haugen is not uncommon, I suppose."

"True. There are lots of Norwegians in these parts. And how are things up in the Skye?"

It was an easy joke about her hometown across the border in North Dakota and only a few miles from the Canadian border.

"Very well, thank you."

"You must have gotten up early for your drive."

"In my family, we always get up early."

"We're off to a good start already." Mr. Olsen grinned.

"I'll leave you two to it, then," Thelma said and clopped out of the room.

Mr. Olsen gestured to the smaller desk and the typewriter. "First things first, the typing test." He produced a pocket watch. "Shall we begin?"

"I'll need a moment to get settled."

"Of course."

Jenny sat, assuming the upright posture as recommended in the *Standard Handbook for Secretaries*. She wore a gray sweater over a white blouse with collar and a plaid wool skirt, a new outfit from Felderman's in Skye. White gloves were recommended for the "initial interview," but that seemed a bit much. She rolled a fresh sheet of paper around the rubber platen cylinder. Checked the ribbon spools left and right. Held both hands above the keys. Fixed her eyes on the test copy. "Ready."

In her side vision, Mr. Olsen raised his arm.

"Go."

She made the key bars fly. Their tiny faces popped against the paper like a drummer's tattoo. With her left hand she threw the carriage—a new line—then pressed on. The test copy advanced to a legal description of a land parcel. She understood the code, its numbers, periods, slashes, letters small and capitalized. She slowed to avoid errors. Into the halting rhythm came the faces of Sally, Dagmar, and Emil, her family back home, crowded in the smoky and dim cabin. At page end she spun in a fresh sheet of paper, then clattered anew, into easy text now, words only, confident enough to let the carriage bell ring, make a full line, make up time.

"Halt."

She threw up her hands as if the keys were hot.

Mr. Olsen took her pages and went to his desk and sat. Circled a word here. One there. Took his time. "Seventy-four words per minute with four errors," he said. "That's very acceptable, Miss Haugen."

"I need to spend more time on my numbers."

"We can continue our interview, then," Mr. Olsen said with a cramped smile.

Her armpits were slippery. The hard part was over.

Mr. Olsen began with general questions about townships, counties, and the general lay of the land. She was a farm girl. She knew about rods, acres, "quarters," the way land was organized in America. "We can thank Thomas Jefferson for that," she added. "The one-hundred-sixty-acre farm was enough land to support one family. That was his idea."

"True." Mr. Olsen leaned back. "I wish more people knew such things."

It's never useful to be a show-off, the secretary's handbook had cautioned. Your supervisor will not take to a girl who appears smarter than he is.

As the interview continued, she gained confidence. Mr. Olsen, oddly, lost his. At one point he asked her the same question twice, and rather than remark on his oversight, she found a different, correct answer. By the end his neck had flushed.

"I think I've heard enough, Miss Haugen," he said. He leaned back and made a tent of his fingers as if to find his comportment. "You're the same bright young lady I remember from your courthouse visit last year."

"I suppose I am."

"And your reference from our attorney friend, Gifford Bailey, was of the highest order. I feel confident you can do the job. When can you start?"

"Today?"

He smiled. "How about next Monday? I need to arrange a desk for you out with the other girls."

"Of course."

They shook hands.

"I'll walk you out."

As they crossed the lobby, he turned to her. "I meant to ask you about that business up in Skye."

"Business?"

"With the doctor? The charge against him by the young woman?"

"Yes, that."

"His trial in December was all the news in the Fargo paper," Mr. Olsen said. "Did you follow it?"

"My family did, yes."

"What did you make of it?"

She paused. "It was a horrible thing he did."

"Though he got off in the end?"

"By a mistrial," she said. "Which is quite different than a not guilty verdict."

"True. And unfortunate all around," Mr. Olsen said as they arrived at the front door.

She looked at him.

"I mean, I suppose now we'll never know," he said.

"We do know."

"Beg your pardon?"

"The trial with the doctor? That was my family. My older sister, Sally, was the one he raped."

"Oh dear." Mr. Olsen drew back slightly.

"He may be the town's doctor, but he's a horrible, lying person no better than a troll."

"A troll." Mr. Olsen's eyelids fluttered rapidly.

"Well, of course not a real troll." Jenny blushed. "Though it felt that way to my family. But we'll get justice someday. That's certain."

Mr. Olsen stared at her.

"I can see it's best I told you now," Jenny said.

"Yes." He stammered briefly. "Thank you."

"His crime was a great blow to my family. I'm trying to help them get back on their feet."

"I see." He cleared his throat. Glanced backward down the hall. "I like to have no distractions in the office. The girls talk when they should be working."

"Does that mean you can't hire me?"

He frowned. "To be honest, this all casts a shadow."

"Then I'm very glad I told you. Thank you for the interview."

"Miss Haugen, wait."

She stopped at the door, hand on the cold brass handle.

"That whole business didn't happen to you," Mr. Olsen said. "So, in the end, it shouldn't matter."

"If you're sure."

He stepped forward and put out a hand. "I am. See you Monday."

***

Outside the courthouse, in sharp January air, she exhaled a long white breath, then headed down the flights of steps. She had parked her brother Emil's Model T Ford street-side. Its electric starter groaned.

There was a hand crank if needed, but the engine caught. While it ran, she scraped frost from the windshield. As the glass cleared, the Polk County Courthouse of Crookston, Minnesota, emerged in reflection. A looming building with white columns and arched windows, it grew taller with each stroke of her scraper. She turned to look at her new home, of sorts. At the main door someone stepped away from the glass.

Before leaving town, she visited two rooming houses for working girls. The nearest one was her second choice, but walkable to her job. The room, with its own wood heater, was acceptable. Young women's stockings, darned at the heels, hung on fishline above the stove. "You'd share a bed," the landlady said. "Baths are once a week on Saturday. No male visitors."

"I'll take it."

"I'll need a dollar to hold it for you."

She filled out her information, then handed over a silver dollar.

Her route home was west out of Crookston and back across the Red River Valley. Like the name Skye, "valley" was a joke only to people from away. This farmland was as flat as a platter. Thirty miles wide and eighty miles tall, its northern edge touched the Canadian border. Today, only the occasional windbreak and the far-off smudge of gray grain bins broke its white plane.

In Grand Forks, she pulled into a Farmers Union filling station. Brought out the broom handle to stick the gas tank. A wide-shouldered young fellow wearing coveralls and a mechanic's beanie came out. Blond hair touched his ears.

"I can do that for you, Miss." He looked at her clothes.

"Thank you."

He took the rod, dipped the tank, and held out the stick. He smelled of oil and backroom, a flat scent like dirt and iron.

"Seventy-five cents will do," she said. After visiting the lady's room, she waited in the office to warm herself. A new Westinghouse calendar, January 1939, hung on the wall. A grinning boy flexed his arm while a little girl, doubtless his sister, squeezed his bicep, her expression wide-eyed and amazed.

The young man came through the door. "Five and a half gallons today."

She handed over three quarters.

He rang up the sale. "'She don't look like a farm girl,' I said to myself."

"Beg your pardon?"

"City girls don't like to check their own tanks. They don't want to get their hands dirty. Then I said to myself, 'Maybe she's a farm girl all dressed up.'"

She paused at the door. "She's actually a farm girl with a new town job."

"Here?" he said eagerly.

"*Nei*," she said.

"Dang. Just my luck."

She smiled. "Your luck might improve if you give your ladies' room some attention. It smells like a troll lives in there."

***

After Grand Forks, she left the main highway and drove west and north and west and north across snowy fields. Country roads laid out by farmers followed section lines. An hour later, her toes nearly numb, the home farm windmill rose above the cottonwoods. She steered up the snowy driveway toward the barn and outbuildings. Charred boards from the "new" house poked from the snow like blackened and broken teeth. Dag's Maytag washer, its wringer drooping like a broken jaw, stood in the snow. Across from it, the taller, Westinghouse refrigerator carried a shiny cap of ice. She stopped the car to stare. But beyond the burn site was the gray log cabin, the original immigrant hut, where smoke rose from the chimney.

Jenny tooted the horn.

Dagmar, her older sister, swung open the cabin door hardly before the sound had died. Sally, the middle sister, appeared tall over Dag's shoulder.

Jenny killed the engine.

"Well?" Dag shouted.

At the barn, Emil swung open the top half of the Dutch door.

Jenny held up two arms.

Dag did a little jig.

Emil took off his cap and touched the back of his head.

She headed into the cabin, which was overheated, close, and smelled of kerosene.

"Yes, I got the job."

"Now you'll go away." Dag caught Jenny and hugged hard. Dag was short and solid, Sally tall and lean.

"Crookston isn't that far." As near as she could be to the barrel stove, she unlaced her boots.

"It's in a whole different state," Dag said.

"Where will you live?" Sally asked softly.

"I found a boarding house. I'll room with three other girls." She took off her socks and tights and held her bare feet close to the stove. She flexed her toes, which were patchy white.

Emil's boots crunched snow, and he ducked inside. His odor— barn, snow, and old wool— washed over them.

"She got it, Emil," Dag said. "She has a job."

"How much they paying you?"

She told him. "And I'll send home what I can."

"*Vi kommer til å trenge det.*" He hung up his checkered wool jacket. "After the expense of the trial, things are tighter than a gnat's ass stretched over a rain barrel."

Jenny tugged his sleeve. "Things are always tight with you, Brother."

Dag turned to her pot of *suppe* on the little wood stove. Sally took her seat in the corner, out of the way, where she could see and listen. Emil warmed up close to the stove. He shivered and picked up his latest little troll carving. Leaned close to examine its rough-hewn face.

"How do you see to work on those?" Jenny asked and turned up the kerosene lamp.

"He could carve those little monsters in the dark," Dag said.

"I guess this one will be your going away present," Emil said.

Dag let out a single note, a kind of whimper.

"Things will all work out." Jenny got up and hugged her from behind. "You'll see."

Chapter Two
Boarding House Rules

She roomed at Schreiber's Boarding House with three other girls, two to a bed, the bathroom down the hall. Faded pink, floral wallpaper. Dark door trim painted over so many times as to round its edges. Dim light fixtures. They cooked on a hot plate and made endless cups of hot tea during the hard cold of January, during which they wore their clothes to bed and slept back-to-back. The airtight heater burned wood. Mr. Schreiber provided corncobs. The four of them took turns, every hour, feeding the beast, but by morning the fire went out and they could see their breath. More than once, as the cold penetrated the dark, Jenny dreamed she was home, outside in the night and searching for their old house. But she survived the month, and by the end of January, had sent ten dollars home.

Dag called her once a week, on Sunday evening. Emil had rigged the burned off telephone line to the little *hus*. The idea of Dag speaking to her from the dim, low-ceilinged cabin was too much to bear, and in her mind's eye Jenny transported them backward in time to their real house with its brown Chesterfield, treadle sewing machine, doilies, African violets, big radio, and the Maytag washer. Still, her brother and sisters had a roof over their heads, and she had a job.

Every Sunday evening at eight, Jenny waited in the downstairs hallway to snatch up the receiver before it made a full ring. Old Mrs.

Schreiber had ears like a deer. She came out from her quarters with an oven timer, set it for five minutes, then retreated.

"How's Sally?" It was always Jenny's first question.

Dag paused. "Passable."

"No worse?"

"She don't say much."

"Are you keeping warm?"

"We are," Dag said. "Emil's been getting up some of those dead cottonwoods. And Frau Meirs and the ladies came again with more things for the cabin. The boys at the lumber yard said they'd help us rebuild in the spring." Dag found a brighter tone.

"I have a regular paycheck now," Jenny said. "I'll help all I can."

"I'll be sure to tell Emil."

"How's he doing?"

Dag paused. "Getting up wood keeps him out of the house."

"I worry about him as much as Sally," Jenny said.

"He don't say much either," Dag said. "The trial took it out of him."

Jenny did her best to muster good news. Conversation to carry Dag away. She told her about the new job in the Register of Deeds office. The heavy ledgers with their fine penmanship. All the documents it took to own land. Nothing about the other office girls, Doris, Frances, and Opal, who seemed aligned against her, particularly Opal, unmarried and at least thirty. But much about her boss, Arthur "Art" Olsen. He was a medium sort of man in all ways, though he did have a nice voice. He had a slight limp, a result of polio, hardly noticeable around the office, though pronounced as he walked down the courthouse steps at day's end.

"Is he married?"

"No."

"That's probably why," Dag said. "The limp."

She did not mention that Mr. Olsen had nice hands. She had noticed them at once, sturdy fingers with clean nails, as he signed papers, or, when leaning close over her desk, he extended his index finger to a ledger line. Or that she liked his fresh aftershave. That he seemed like a clean man. That he lived in a small, brick house within walking distance of the courthouse.

***

On Wednesday, from the courthouse hallway, came a loud, laughing man's voice.

"Oh no," said Opal, touching her hair.

"What?" Jenny said.

"It's him," Frances whispered. She was the oldest of the girls, one who could type and talk and never miss a stroke.

"Who?" Jenny asked.

"Let her find out," Doris said to the other two.

Opal squeaked out a short, dry giggle.

"Well, well, who have we here?"

"Sam LaBonte," Frances murmured. She had the desk nearest to Jenny and was nicest of the three girls. "Pay him no attention."

LaBonte was short, middle-aged with broad shoulders, dark eyes and a shock of black hair beneath an impossibly dirty Newsboy hat.

"You there, Miss, with the curly brown hair."

Jenny focused on her typing.

"That's Jenny Haugen," Doris said. "She's new."

The other girls giggled.

"So, are you married, Miss Jenny?"

Jenny jammed her keys, reached into the basket to free them, and then typed on.

"Because if you're not, I have a strapping son you ought to meet," he said. "Though he'd need washing behind the ears."

Mr. Olsen came to his office doorway. "Sam, we'll have none of that talk." He came over to the counter to block LaBonte's view of Jenny.

"A pretty new girl. It never hurts to ask," Sam said. He leaned sideways to look further.

"It never hurts to pay your taxes on time." Mr. Olsen stepped sideways as well.

"I'll get to them," Sam said. "Just thought I'd look in and see if you folks are working hard or hardly working."

"We're quite busy here."

"Quite busy, yes," Sam said, leaning the other way for a last look at Jenny. "Yes, that's clear to see." He laughed again, a booming call, and left.

"We told you," Opal said to Jenny.

Mr. Olsen came over to her desk. "I apologize for that, Miss Haugen."

"It's no problem," Jenny said, and looked down to her work.

"Boorish behavior. I don't condone that in my office."

"I appreciate that, Mr. Olsen." She glanced briefly upward, then typed again.

He remained standing above her through two full carriage returns, during which she made the keys ratta-tat-tat.

"Your typing seems faster these days."

"I'm not sure of that." In fact, she practiced every night. It also helped to keep her fingers warm. One of her roommates had a typewriter, and they held contests—Distract the Typist was one—that always ended in hilarity and with Mrs. Schreiber pounding on the wall.

"What is your speed these days?"

"I don't really check." She lowered her voice. "Perhaps around eighty words."

"Eighty words a minute." Mr. Olsen turned to the other girls. "Who'd have guessed?"

They had no reply.

She continued to type. Eventually he went back to his office where he sat for the longest time at his desk, motionless. Across the room, the other girls murmured and purposefully did not look Jenny's way.

***

In February, Jenny had occasion to deliver a folder from Mr. Olsen to the county attorney down the hall.

"Something for a signature," she said to his secretary.

"Go on in, then." Her desk was positioned just outside the attorney's door.

Mr. Swanson had salt-and-pepper hair and an unlit pipe in his mouth. He frowned as he read aloud, pipe stem notwithstanding, from a book spread open on his desk. "What is it?"

"A signature, if you please."

He looked up to the new voice.

"I'm from Mr. Olsen's office." She handed over the paper.

He removed his pipe from his mouth. "The new girl. Miss…"

"Haugen."

"As in the Haugens from Skye?"

"Yes."

He sat back. "Art told me about you. Sit, if you have a minute."

"I'd best not." She glanced over her shoulder. The secretary, Carol, pretended not to watch.

"Well, a signature can take a minute, so you'll just have to." He winked.

She took a wooden chair.

He steepled his hands. "I followed your sister's trial."

"I see."

"I'm afraid it had no winners."

"I would agree."

"How is she doing, may I ask? Your sister and your family?"

"We're getting by, thank you. I've taken this job to help out."

Mr. Swanson leaned forward and lowered his voice. "Between you and me, I thought the bastard was guilty."

18

"He was."

"But mistrials happen," Mr. Swanson said. "We do the best we can, but then it comes to the jury, and we never know." He pushed aside the book on his desk, then scanned down the page she had delivered.

"Black's law books," she said, looking past him. "Gifford Bailey had them."

"Standard accessories in the business." He scribbled his name. "Such dry going I have to read the sentences aloud. Here you go."

She accepted the document, glanced over it, then turned to go.

"Do you have an interest in the law, Miss Haugen?"

She paused. "I did. Before the trial. But in the end, it left my family worse off."

"Still, it's where we have to start. Otherwise, we're back in the Wild West, wouldn't you agree?"

She took a moment. "I would agree that it's the place to start, yes."

***

At the end of the three months probationary period, she got a raise to a full sixteen dollars a week.

"Well-deserved," Mr. Olsen said. "You're one of my best girls." Yet in the open office area, in full view of the other girls, he twice corrected her about an exceedingly small matter.

"He's trying to show us all that he's not sweet on you," Doris said.

"I doubt that."

"We don't," Opal said and gave her carriage a hard throw.

On a warm day in mid-April, a couple of minutes after noon, Mr. Olsen paused by her desk. "Miss Haugen, I'm going to take my sandwich out on the steps in the sun. Would you care to join me?"

She glanced around. The other girls were already gone. "I suppose I could."

Outside they sat a few steps down from the front door… and well-spaced. Mr. Olsen had a tidy lunch box. She a peanut butter sandwich in waxed paper.

"My tulips are near to opening," he said.

"Spring is almost here."

"Usually, they're a full week later."

She nodded.

"I keep close track of when they bloom."

"I see."

They ate in silence.

"The nice thing about tulips is that they're dependable," he said. "They come up every year. The bad thing is that they lose their color over the years, and all of them end up yellow."

"I didn't know that."

On toward their three o'clock break, Jenny leaned across toward Frances's desk. "You could be right."

"Right?"

"About Mr. Olsen. I think he's sweet on me."

"We told you so."

"What should I do?"

Frances shrugged and kept typing. "You could marry him."

"Yes," Doris said. "Somebody has to."

***

On Friday Mr. Olsen invited her to lunch downtown.

"Downtown?"

"On Friday the café has a roast beef special."

"I try not to spend anything extra."

"I thought you might say that, but it will be my treat, Miss Haugen. You've been a good addition to the office."

She paused. "Well, I do have to go to the bank."

At the Prairie Café on Main Street, Mr. Olsen was of the same genial demeanor with the run-ragged waitress as the bank president,

Colby Hewitt, who stopped at their booth to say hello. As they waited for their food, which was quite slow in coming, he remarked, "It can't be an easy job."

"Being a bank president?" she said with a little smile.

He chuckled. "A waitress."

A young man paused at their booth. He wore a very modern tie and had color in his cheeks. "Hello, Art."

"Well," Arthur said. "Michael Clark."

Michael looked expectantly at Jenny.

"This is Miss Haugen, a new employee in the office," Arthur said. "I'm treating her to the roast beef."

"Hello there," Jenny said.

"Art's quite tight with his money." Michael had a bright laugh. "You must have caught him on a good day."

"Go on with you now," Arthur said. "Scram."

Michael laughed a quick, high note and moved on.

"Michael's in the men's church choir with me."

Over lunch she found that Mr. Olsen was quite conservative, believed that President Roosevelt was a "liberal," and that the New Deal was unfair to "those who had worked hard and saved."

"I see," she murmured.

"What are your thoughts on Roosevelt?"

"His WPA projects seem like a good thing. They put men to work."

"That's true," he said. "But enough about politics. I want to learn more about you."

Jenny glanced at her roast beef and gravy. Patted her lips with a napkin.

"For high school you came down to Grand Forks and boarded?"

"Yes."

"What made you leave the farm?"

"It's quite isolated up by the border." She reached for a bun.

"Your family must miss you."

"It's only my brother and two sisters on the farm. I'm the youngest. Our parents passed away."

"Sorry to hear that." Mr. Olsen moved the butter dish her way. "When did they come to North Dakota?"

"In 1906."

"Why Skye?"

"It had sufficient rocks."

Mr. Olsen stared.

"It's a joke in my family," Jenny said. "The story is that my father passed over the best farmland until he found a place where there were rocks. Like in Norway."

"A good one." Mr. Olsen chuckled and resumed eating.

"Though more likely because the land farther north was affordable," she continued. With some food in her stomach, she began to relax. "The best of it, down here in the valley, was taken, I'm sure."

"No doubt," Mr. Olsen said.

They ate in silence.

"It's pretty country up there," he said. "The Turtle Mountains. Canada not far off. Those rolling hills and trees to the west. I was up there once as a boy, before the war." He signaled the waitress for more bread.

"I do find it quite flat down here," she said. "I miss the trees."

"You know what they say about Norwegians who live in town?"

"No."

"They cut down the trees in order to name the streets after them."

She smiled.

"Elm Street. Maple Street," he continued.

"I'll pass that one on to my brother, Emil."

The waitress came and went.

"How long is the drive up to Skye?" he asked.

"In good weather, about two hours."

"Maybe this spring we could take a trip up there," Mr. Olsen said. "A Sunday outing. It would be nice to meet your family."

She coughed. Took a sip of water. "It's quite a long way."

***

In the third week of April, Mr. Olsen's tulips bloomed. He invited her to his house for a look and for Sunday dinner besides.

"That's very kind." She glanced around the office. "I'm afraid the girls will talk."

"Let them."

She paused. "I do miss Sunday dinners at home."

He picked her up at the rooming house. Mrs. Schreiber peeked from behind her curtain. They shook hands awkwardly, and off they drove. His face flushed as they drove.

His house was small, two-storey and red brick with similar houses close by. He parked in his garage, which fronted an alley, and then brought her through his tidy backyard with several flower beds, their contents marked with lettered stakes. Inside, the house smelled of roast beef. Her stomach growled.

"I guess I'm hungry."

"That's good. We'll eat soon." He took off his sport coat, the first time she had seen him without it, and hung it on a wooden hanger in the hall closet. In only a dress shirt, he was slope-shouldered and a bit pear-shaped. Ahead, the kitchen table was nicely set for two, including tablecloth and matching napkins with an old-fashioned pattern.

"I have to work on my gravy," he said, putting on a full-length apron. "Would you set out the beet and dill pickles and whatever else strikes you? They're in the Frigidaire."

His icebox shelves were jammed with jams, cheeses, sliced meats, bacon, and milk jars including one with heavy cream, along with apples, carrots, dried apricots, a box of assorted chocolates with tiny notes on its cover, a calendar of use, and a rating system.

"These look homemade," she said of the pickles. Little brown sprays of dill floated in the green brine.

"My own," he said. "I used to help Mother. Her pickles would snap like a rubber band."

"My sister, Dag, says it's all about the alum."

"Dag's right as rain," he said. "I certainly look forward to meeting her."

"You mentioned your tulips," Jenny ventured.

"Out front. Go give them a look."

She passed through his living room, dim and crammed with two Chesterfields, two armchairs, a treadle organ, and an oversized bureau desk, closed. Above the doorway sat three cuckoo clocks, ticking at different notes. To the side, away from direct light, stood a shelf of furry African violets with tiny pink blossoms. On the far wall hung a glass box with an American flag and some faded ribbons. Above the organ was a framed newspaper article, "Crookston Church Choir Wins Award," with Arthur centered among the group of twenty or so, young and old. She leaned closer. To his right stood the fellow from the café, Michael, the one who had said hello.

On the front steps she surveyed the street: the brick houses close together, Arthur's tidy tulips guarding the front steps.

"Yellow is just fine," she said. Back in the kitchen, she took a moment to let her eyes adjust.

Arthur sat at the table, staring.

"Mr. Olsen, are you all right?"

"Arthur, please. We're not at work."

He looked her up and down. "I've never been much the ladies' man, and now here I am, just turned thirty, and one has fallen out of the sky and landed in my lap."

"I beg your pardon?"

"I'm sorry. That came out oddly. I mean, here we are, you and me."

"What is it you're saying?"

He swallowed. "You're an attractive young lady, I'm a single fellow, and I'm wondering if there's a chance for us?"

"You mean, as beaus?"

"Yes."

"I suppose there's a chance for everything in this world, but…"

In the living room his cuckoo clocks dinged and peeped.

"Darn it, my gravy!" He hurried to the range.

It was the moment for leave-taking. She could easily walk home, but the table was set. They settled in for a Sunday dinner that Dag might have cooked—roast beef that fell apart in sheaves, mashed potatoes silky from cream, brown gravy (slightly dark and smoky), dill pickles, pickled beet slices, and dinner rolls with butter. For dessert there was cherry pie. She fanned her face. "Is this crust with lard?"

"It is."

"Not many men cook so well." Her cheeks were warm.

"My mother taught me," he said. "She worried that I'd always be a bachelor."

"Is she still with us?"

"Gone five years now," he said. "The extra furniture, clocks, the organ, the African violets… those were Mother's. I haven't had the heart to give them away."

"There's no rush, I suppose."

"That's my feeling."

"Your father?" She forked the last bite of pie, its plump, glazed cherry filling.

"Died in the Great War. Then it was just Mother and me."

"I noticed the flag and ribbons."

"Well not in the war," he continued. "Dad never made it to the front. Caught the Spanish flu and died in training camp. Not long after, I caught polio. Before that, my grandfather died young of a heart attack."

"That's bad luck. I'm so sorry."

He shrugged. "My mother always told me that Olsen men were jinxed. But here I am."

After dinner they worked together on the dishes in the small kitchen. He had a matching apron for her. Her face was dewy with heat from the range, from the heavy meal. She touched her cheeks. "I might have to sit down."

"Are you all right?"

"I think I've overeaten."

"Take the Chesterfield in the living room," he said. "I'll finish up here."

Soon enough he came in. "Feeling better?"

"Yes, thank you."

"I was happy to see you had an appetite." He drew the curtains partway.

She sat up straighter.

"Violets," he said. "They don't like much light."

"That's true. Dag grows them."

"They take a delicate touch."

They fell silent.

"Your treadle organ," she said. "Do you play?"

"Mainly the old hymns, Stephen Foster and the like." He settled onto a piano stool, round, with four claw feet gripping little glass globes. After pumping the treadle until the organ wheezed sound, he arranged some stops, then accompanied himself to "My Old Kentucky Home."

"You sing well."

"Thank you." He joined her on the Chesterfield. "The old songs are still a pleasure."

"Though I'm wondering about the line with 'the darkies.'"

"'Tis summer, and the darkies are gay,'" Mr. Olsen sang.

"Yes, that one. I wonder how they, the Negroes, must feel when they hear it."

Olsen blinked a few times. "I have to say I'd never thought of that."

"It came to mind."

"No, you're quite right," he said. "Perhaps that line belongs to an older time."

"I think so, yes."

"Another reason to admire you, Miss Jenny."

"And you, a professional man who's musical and can cook. I think your mother worried needlessly. Certainly, there's a woman out there for you."

"Is there a chance she could be you?"

Jenny paused. "That's flattering, but I can't put my job at risk."

"Of course, but—"

"My family depends on me. I have to put them first."

"I understand," he said. "Though what if arrangements could be made at work?"

"Arrangements?"

"So there would be no risk to your job."

She stared. "I'm not sure how."

"Leave that part to me. I have an idea."

"You seem to have many ideas, Arthur."

"You bring them out in me, Miss Jenny."

She let him slide across and give her a peck on the cheek.

***

The next week Jenny transferred to the County Assessor's office. It was livelier anyway and did not include Doris and Opal. The assessor, Norbert Smith, was older, pleasant enough and usually gone inspecting properties. This left the two main "girls," Dorothy and Mavis, both married, to run the office and show Jenny the ropes.

She and Mr. Olsen began to eat lunch together in full view of everyone. Around the courthouse he carried himself in a new, taller way. He was more jovial and took to humming. Jenny ate supper at his house at least two nights a week and always brought food home to her roommates.

One night, as the girls wolfed down leftovers, she murmured, "I don't know what I'm thinking."

"About what?" Gail asked.

"Giving Mr. Olsen encouragement."

"You must keep seeing him," Gail said immediately.

"Otherwise, we'll starve," Louise said.

"Shrivel up like raisins," Selma cried.

This resulted in a pillow fight and Mrs. Schreiber pounding on the wall.

Toward the end of May, when Jenny returned from her lunch with Mr. Olsen, Dorothy remarked, "It's only a matter of time."

"What is?"

"Mr. Olsen's going to pop the question."

Dorothy winked at Mavis.

"What gossips you are," Jenny said.

"You'll see," Mavis said.

Only a few days later, Thelma, the receptionist, came to Jenny's desk. "There's a young man asking after you."

"A young man?"

"If not for his uniform I'd have asked him to wait until break time."

"Oh dear," Jenny whispered to herself.

Chapter Three
The Handsome Visitor

Before heading to the lobby, Jenny slipped into the lady's room. Braced her hands on the sink. In the mirror she had color in her cheeks and heat all over. She patted her face with cold water, dried it, then smoothed her hair as best she could. Stepping out, she peered around the corner. It was really him. In blue uniform and narrow side hat—he was Canadian—Will Jamison stood by the grandfather clock. He had opened its door and set the pendulum in motion.

"I'm afraid it doesn't work," she said.

He turned. "That's a shame. Such a nice old clock."

She swallowed.

He smiled. Took off his hat.

"Your hair," she said.

"They shaved it. I suppose it will grow back."

"How ever did you find me?" she whispered. "I mean, I'm glad that you did."

"I called the farm," he said. "Your sister Dag told me where you worked."

She glanced over her shoulder. "Let's step outside," she murmured. They sat on the steps in the sun.

"I should have written that I enlisted," he said.

"I didn't know what to think," she replied. "You just disappeared."

"I'm sorry for that. I felt the call, and after that it happened quickly. When the world is heading to war, what use is a junior reporter at the *Winnipeg Free Press*?"

"Like work now for me," she said. "These last months have been hard times for my family. I have to be a grown up, not a silly girl."

"Our times together were silly?" he said. "The Winnipeg train? Our picnic in Cavalier? The day we saw your President Roosevelt in Grand Forks?"

"No, not at all," she said quickly.

"Though you're right. It is time to grow up." He looked far off.

"Where do you go now?"

"Back to England. I'm home on leave. I'm in pilot training."

"I hope it won't come to war."

"War is almost certain."

A car passed. The sun shone on its window glass.

"I really must get back to work," she said.

"May I see you tonight?" he asked.

"Yes."

"I have a room."

She turned.

"Sorry to be so forward," Will continued. "Life feels different now. Like there's not a moment to lose."

She did not touch him or lean his way. "Pick me up at my rooming house at six." She gave him the address.

As Jenny passed back to her desk, Thelma raised an eyebrow.

"A cousin," she said to Thelma, "from Canada."

"Certainly a handsome young man," Thelma replied. "This cousin of yours."

***

That night, in the Road Right Motel, she and Will Jamison broke the bed. Two legs collapsed, Jenny shrieked, and the whole bed tilted sideways such that they rolled partway onto the floor.

"Now we've done it," Will said.

Jenny, naked, panting and slick with sweat, laughed.

Someone in the next room pounded on the wall. "Have some goddamn decency."

"Go to hell," Jenny called back.

They made love three times. The first two times Will used a prophylactic. The third time not. "I only brought two."

She touched him. "That's poor planning."

"I'm probably all used up anyway."

She pulled him to her.

Later, they lay exhausted in each other's arms. Will rolled onto his side to face her. Toyed with her hair with his fingers, combed it from her eyes, ran his hands over her flushed, warm skin. "I don't know when I'll see you again."

"You're seeing me right now." She drew his long body close. Out of sight in his arms, her eyes burned and spilled over.

"I'll be sure to write," he said. "As often as I can."

Chapter Four
In Trouble

After Will Jamison's visit, Mr. Olsen's manner cooled. On their Sunday afternoon drive he had little to say.

"You're quiet today."

"Thinking."

"A penny for your thoughts?"

"They're hardly worth that."

"That's not true." She slid halfway across the wide front seat. Put a hand on his shoulder.

His grim look softened, and by the end of the drive he was mostly cheerful. They returned to his house where she, this time, drew the living room curtains and gave him a kiss. In a weak moment, she moved his hand to her breast. He flinched, then steadied himself and squeezed her breast rather hard.

She ate most nights at Mr. Olsen's house (he gave her a key), and she continued to put on a pound or three. Toward the end of July, she found herself in Arthur's bathtub (he was off at men's choir) looking down at breasts that seemed like those of another woman. She could lift them. They had weight. "Oh dear," she murmured.

Arthur noticed her new figure as well.

"It's your cooking," she said.

"A couple more pounds look good on you," he said. "And as we men would say, it's in all the right places."

She made an appointment with a woman doctor in Grand Forks, a no-nonsense lady in a white coat and hair pulled up under a mesh caul. After a short interview, the doctor stepped to a small sink and washed her hands, then dried them. She gestured at a table with stirrups. "If you'll lie back."

When Jenny was situated, the doctor touched her fingers to a round, open tin of Vaseline.

Jenny closed her eyes.

When it was over, the doctor rolled backward on her chair. "Your instincts are correct, Miss Haugen."

Jenny let out a breath.

"It is Miss Haugen, yes?" the doctor said.

"Correct."

As Jenny dressed, the doctor went again to the sink and washed. Afterward she sat with Jenny and took her hands. "Well, Miss Haugen, you have some decisions to make."

Hardly a week later, the office girls turned overly cheerful, then murmured to each other after she passed. She felt their gaze on her body. She began to see the courthouse—its doors and doorknobs, its windows and frames, the dark woodwork, the baluster and banisters, the grandfather clock, even the granite floors with their fine glints— in sharper focus. As if all was committing itself to memory. At the very end of July, on a hot day in Arthur's living room with the electric fan full on them, he played his organ. "'Tis summer, and the people are gay."

"Thank you for that, Arthur." She came over and stayed his hand. "We have to talk."

He swiveled on his stool. "What's on your mind?"

She swallowed. "I'm going to have a child."

He stared. "What?"

"I'm pregnant." She waited for his features to redden, his face to contort itself—for him to lurch upright and march her out the door. The clocks ticked. "Please say something, Arthur."

"It certainly wasn't me."

"It might have been, soon enough, the way we were going."

"It was this 'cousin' of yours, wasn't it? The handsome soldier."

She nodded.

"He certainly didn't fool *me*." Arthur went over to inspect his violets.

"It was stupid of me to lie to everyone."

"Who is he?" Arthur pinched off a dried flower.

"A boy. From my past. We were sweethearts."

He looked over. "Are you still?"

She paused. "He came to say goodbye."

"Goodbye for now? Or goodbye for good?"

"What does it matter?" She slumped into an armchair. "Certainly, it's over between us now. I can't continue at work. I'll have to give notice. Go back to the farm."

Outside, childrens' voices called as they passed on bicycles.

Arthur turned to her. "I'll marry you."

She looked up. "What?"

The cuckoo clocks paused their ticking. The little birds poked out from their doors and began to chirp.

"I said… I'll marry you."

"Because you feel sorry for me?" Jenny said. "That's hardly a reason to marry someone."

"Quite the opposite." He came across and stood before her. "I'm an old bachelor cripple who can't even let go of his dead mother's violets. I've never liked those damn things. When will I ever have the chance for a girl like you?"

"A girl like me?"

"A remarkable young woman with her whole life ahead of her."

"That's beyond kind, Arthur. But starting this way, what kind of marriage would it be?"

He shrugged. "Whatever we make of it."

***

At the end of July, Jenny and Arthur drove north to meet the family. West toward Grand Forks, then across the Red River Bridge into North Dakota, then northwest through farm country toward Skye. Arthur was in fine spirits.

"The farm's not much to see," Jenny said as they drew closer. "I've told you about the house fire. The new house isn't finished. My brother, Emil, can be intimidating. And be sure not to bring up Cargill or the banks."

"Thanks for all that."

"Sally is very quiet, but Dag makes up for it."

"I'm eager to meet them all." Arthur hummed as he drove.

Following her directions, he turned onto a gravel road where he slowed to less than twenty miles per hour lest flying gravel chip the Oldsmobile's paint. Finally, her stomach growling with hunger, they drew up to the driveway gate. She got out to roll it open.

"Does Emil have livestock?"

"Not anymore."

"Then why the big gate?"

"We've had trouble with strangers."

They came up the lane to a cluster of dusty white chickens. The rust-colored barn in need of painting. The gray, rough-sawn outbuildings. The little orange Allis-Chalmers. The burn site of the former house, now, with the snow gone, a black circle of trash anchored by Dag's charred Maytag. Nearby, the new house stood framed, roofed, windowless, the yellow wall studs bleached gray by the sun. Behind, as always, stood the little *hus*, tilted, low, gray, a worn path to its door. A thread of smoke rose from its chimney.

"Toot the horn."

Emil, holding a wrench, stepped out of the machine shed. He shaded his eyes. Dag, wearing an apron, came out of the little house. Sally appeared in the upstairs window of the new house, then stood to the side mostly out of sight where she could watch. Dag hurried across the yard, wiping her hands on her apron and smoothing her hair. Her round cheeks were flushed from kitchen heat.

"You must be Mr. Olsen."

"And you're Dagmar." He pumped her hand. It was Sunday, and he wore his wool sport coat with the very wide shoulders.

She looked him up and down. Smiled as best she could.

"I've brought you something," Arthur said.

"What? For me?" Dag waited as he produced a tray of African violets.

Dag touched her breast. "Why they're just like the ones I used to have. Before—"

"Jenny told me about the fire," Arthur said. "I thought these might cheer you up."

"That's very kind of you. Let me get them out of the sunlight."

Emil came across the yard in smudged coveralls and greasy cap, Emil who knew very well they were coming. Jenny forgot what an imposing figure he was: tall, lean, broad-shouldered, looming.

"This is my brother, Emil."

Emil bent down to give Arthur a close look. "*Snakker du norsk?*"

"I'm mostly Swede." Arthur leaned back but held his ground.

"A Swede. Trouble already," Emil said to Jenny.

"He doesn't mean it," Jenny said.

"That's a relief," Arthur replied.

The two men shook hands.

"Nice place you've got here," Arthur said.

"It will be nicer when the new house is done." Jenny gave Emil a nudge.

"Good help is hard to find," Emil said. "We had a couple of younger fellows, but they were as useless as tits on a boar."

"Show us the new house, Emil," Jenny said. "I'm eager to see the progress."

They turned. Sally stepped back from the upstairs window.

"Jenny told me about your bad luck with the fire," Arthur said as they walked.

"Wasn't bad luck. They burned us down." Emil spit to the side.

Arthur sneaked a glance at Jenny.

Jenny took his arm. "Let's head in."

Dag waited just inside the new house. A long table made of sawhorses and planks was set with plates and silverware and flour-sack napkins. "This will be the kitchen. We'll eat here today, the first meal in the new house."

"What fun," Arthur said. "Like a picnic."

"If the flies don't drive us out," Emil said.

There was a thump upstairs.

"Sally," Dag murmured. "She's working on her bedroom."

"I'll go up and say hello," Jenny said.

Arthur made to follow. Jenny stayed his arm. "We'll be down in a bit. You can meet her then."

She climbed the open, wooden stairs where the heat increased with each step. At the top were three doorways to three small rooms. Sally's south-facing room was cluttered with sawhorses, boards, a keg of nails, and tools. The ceiling seemed lower than their old house—only a few inches above Sally's head. A roughly framed bed with a straw tick sat in the corner, and by it a bench with Sally's suitcase, open. Her clothes hung on nails.

"My room." Sally wore a red headkerchief and work coveralls like Emil's.

"It's going to be perfect." Jenny hugged her sister, holding on extra-long, thinking of everything but saying nothing. Sally had not gained any weight and needed a bath.

"Do you sleep here?"

"Unless it's too hot."

"It seems like it might be," Jenny said, waving at the air before her face.

"You get used to it."

"Dag has dinner almost ready," Jenny said.

"I'll be along."

Happy to be back downstairs, Jenny helped Dag ferry food from the little house, which was sauna-hot from cooking, to the new house and the plank table.

"Emil, why not give Mr. Olsen a quick look around the farm while we get dinner ready."

"There ain't much to see."

Jenny tilted her head toward the door.

"Okay, okay," Emil said.

Dinner began at noon sharp without Sally, who pounded and sawed upstairs.

"She won't give up until she finishes her room," Dag said.

"A hard worker," Arthur said. "Like another girl I know." He put his arm around Jenny. Dag averted her eyes.

Midway through dinner the thumping and sawing sounds stopped. There was silence for quite a long time. Sally's boots appeared on the stairs.

"Mr. Olsen, if you would, when you meet Sally, please don't make a fuss?" Dag murmured.

"Of course."

They resumed chitchat. Sally took her place at the table.

"Sally, this is Arthur Olsen," Jenny said. "He's from the courthouse where I work."

Sally averted her gaze. "Hello."

"Pleased to meet you, Sally."

She looked to the bowls of food.

Arthur turned to Emil. "That orange tractor of yours, how many horsepower is it?"

Under the table, Jenny squeezed Arthur's hand.

The dinner proceeded smoothly, flies aside. Emil whacked them with a wire swatter.

"Soon we'll have windows and screens." Dag passed food and encouraged Arthur to tell them all about his job at the courthouse. He did not disappoint.

"Though I do miss my righthand girl." He gave Jenny a one-armed hug.

"Miss her?" said Dag.

"I've transferred to a different office," Jenny said. "Right down the hall. I was going to tell you."

"It became indecorous that Jenny work for me," Arthur said.

"Indecorous?" Dag stared.

Emil turned to her. "You got fired?"

"No, nothing like that."

Mr. Olsen beamed a smile at Jenny. "It might be time for our announcement."

Jenny gathered herself. "Arthur and I are engaged."

"To be married?" Emil asked.

"That's usually what that means," Jenny said.

"To him?" Emil said.

"Me," Arthur said.

"Well, well." Dag mustered a smile.

Emil raised a heavy eyebrow. "Ain't you a little old for Jenny?"

"She's not even twenty," Sally murmured.

"It might seem that way now," Arthur began, "but your Jenny is a remarkably mature young woman, and—"

"Arthur and I have had the talk about age," Jenny finished.

"Things gradually even out," Arthur continued. "When I'm, say, eighty years old, Jenny will be, what, sixty-eight?"

"Imagine that," Dag said.

"Yes, imagine that," Jenny murmured.

"Are you sure about this?" Emil turned to Jenny.

"Yes," she said.

Arthur took her hand.

Dag looked to Emil. "Well, that's that, then."

"If you have concerns," Arthur said, gaining confidence, "now is the time to air them."

Emil turned to Arthur. "Just one. If you ever mistreat Jenny, ever lay a hand on her in anger, you'll have me to deal with and there'll be a *hestepisk* involved."

"A *hestepisk*?"

"A horsewhip," said Sally.

Arthur's eyes widened. He managed a chuckle for Sally. "You know Norwegian too?"

"I know horsewhips." Sally gave Emil a look.

"That's enough," Jenny said.

"Just want to be clear." Emil snatched a fly from the air with his bare hand—dashed it to the floor.

"It's settled, then," Dag said brightly. "Shall we have our pie?"

After dessert and coffee, Dag and Jenny carried two baskets of dishes to the outside pitcher pump and washing table. Dag rattled on, weepy with pleasure. "Such good news. What a surprise. But I suppose it had to happen someday, you marrying and going away. Mr. Olsen seems nice. He's a little old but he seems steady."

"He is," Jenny said. "Both." In the sunlight she worked the pump handle.

"It's good that he has a courthouse job," Dag said. "He's not a man cut out for farm work."

"True." Jenny poured a half pail of water into Dag's pan.

"You seem so happy," Dag said as they worked. "You've gained a pound. Your skin is so nice. You're glowing."

Jenny, standing alongside the pump pipe with its spigot and little cast-iron belly, paused. "Yes, there's that."

Dag's gaze went up and down her. "Oh dear."

"I was about to tell you."

Dag let out a breath. "What a day it's been."

"Don't tell Emil," Jenny added. "We'll cross that bridge later."

Dag nodded. "Yes. *Den tid, den sorg.*"

They set to work on the dishes. Jenny washing, Dag rinsing and drying.

"Truth be told, I'm a little relieved," Dag said. "I wondered, you know, about Mr. Olsen. I mean, him being an older man and all. That part of marriage."

"He's old," Jenny said, and flicked soap bubbles at her sister, "but not that old."

***

Later, as they completed the long goodbye with the Haugens (Sally had disappeared), Arthur drove off with a toot of the horn.

Jenny let out a breath.

"A successful trip, I'd say," Arthur ventured.

"Yes."

"Dag's pleasant. Emil's as you warned me. And Sally, I couldn't tell what she thought of our news."

"You did fine by them all." Jenny glanced at her wristwatch. "Let's drive through town. I'll show you Skye."

On Main Street, she pointed out the dime store where she got her typewriter ribbons. The bakery. Felderman's Department Store. The library. Then the feedmill and the train depot.

"Turn here," she said.

He drove down Maple Street. "Nice houses here. Seems like a pleasant town to grow up in."

"Stop," Jenny said.

Arthur braked.

"There." She pointed to the tall house with its old-fashioned gables and wide front porch, the doctor's sign out front. "That's where it happened."

Arthur stared.

"Where the doctor raped Sally."

41

Arthur paused, gaze still on the house. "It seems so..."

"What?" A muscle pulsed along her jaw.

"Beyond the pale."

"'Pale,'" she muttered. "What does that mean anyway?"

Arthur glanced her way. "Just to be clear, I believe you."

"Thank you for that." She patted his leg.

They drove on and regained the main highway out of Skye. Arthur brought the Oldsmobile up to speed. She continued to look off at the fields.

"Your family has much to be hopeful about," Arthur said. "They have land. The new house is coming along. They have the old one to fall back on."

"It kept a roof over our heads. Not quite so fast through the corners, please."

"Sorry."

Jenny held onto the armrest. Kept her eyes on the highway ahead. "Emil always maintained the little house. He stored all our old things, the oil lamps and lanterns, after we got power and light."

"Aha." Arthur glanced her way.

"What?"

"The day you came for your interview? I knew I smelled kerosene lamp."

"Oh dear."

"No, no. I found it quite pleasing," he said. "It threw me back to my grandmother's house. I could hardly concentrate on our conversation."

"I see."

"That and you yourself, of course."

"Watch the road, dear."

"One thing," he ventured. "Horsewhips?"

She turned.

"Certainly Emil, or your father perhaps, never—"

"No. Not on us."

"That's a relief," Arthur said.

They drove on.

"I'm so glad we made this trip," he said and patted her leg. "Meeting your family, seeing where you grew up. I finally feel like I know you."

Chapter Five
Marriage

Jenny Haugen and Arthur Olsen were married on Saturday, August 13th, a fine summer day in Grand Forks, at a small park overlooking the Red River.

Dag and Emil arrived early. "Sally?" Jenny asked.

"She talked about coming," Dag said. "She was all shined up to go."

"At the last minute she wouldn't get in the car," Emil finished.

"Said she didn't feel well," Dag murmured.

"It would've been a good outing for her," Jenny said.

"Doesn't Emil look handsome?" Dag turned to her brother.

"He does," Jenny said with a smile. Emil was clean-shaven and wore a soft-shouldered wool coat and ironed dungarees plus his best black boots, ones he had made himself, and his fine summer hat—the one he had bought long ago in Fargo. Dag wore a new, light-yellow dress that she had sewn herself. "You both look nice."

"And you too," Dag said.

Dag had sewn a simple, white, bare-shouldered wedding dress for Jenny that already felt tight. With it she wore a white, store-bought hat but no ridiculous veil. Those days seemed past.

Emil looked up at the blue sky. "You got lucky with the weather."

"A good sign." Dag nudged him. "You head over there with the men, Emil. That's how weddings work."

"I wouldn't know," Emil said.

"Now you do," Dag replied.

Two of Jenny's former roommates at Mrs. Schreiber's came as bridesmaids, as did Betty Benoit, who worked for their trial lawyer, Mr. Bailey, who was officiating the wedding.

"I'm so pleased you could come," Jenny said.

"I wouldn't have missed it," Betty replied. The theme was yellow, which Betty met and then some with her bright-yellow trousers with a wide black belt, plus a sun hat with matching yellow band. "Where's Sally?" Betty asked, looking around.

"She wasn't able to come." Dag looked away.

"I was so hoping to see her," Betty said. "I think about her often."

"Thank you for that."

"How is she doing?" Betty asked.

Dag paused. "Okay. Just."

"But here we are," Jenny said.

"Yes, here we are." Betty took Jenny's arm.

Dag dabbed at her eyes.

On a perfect day in the upper Midwest, with wispy clouds in the high bluebell of the sky and warm sun in the little pavilion, the wedding proceeded. Michael Clark was Arthur's best man, and Jenny came forward on Emil's arm. Betty Benoit, seeing Arthur Olsen for the first time, looked at Jenny, then to the ground. The young Bailey girls, darling in their summer dresses and white anklets and black shoes, followed. One carried a bouquet of wildflowers, the other, the ring. Emil, tall and squint-eyed under his hat, handed Jenny off to Mr. Olsen, then leaned in to shake hands. Jenny drew a breath. She looked back to Dag who, ever so slightly, nodded.

***

They honeymooned southwest of Bemidji, Minnesota, in Itasca State Park, near the headwaters of the Mississippi River. Their cozy, log cabin had a smoke-browed stone fireplace, a kitchenette, and a small bedroom with a sturdily built bed, all of which smelled of old wood.

Arthur shivered. "It's a bit chilly in here. I'll make a fire."

"Let's keep the bedroom door open to warm it," Jenny said.

"It's going to take a while," Arthur said. "I'll go fetch more wood."

That night after supper, with the fireplace crackling, they had a nice kiss on the couch.

"I'll check the bedroom to see if it's warmer," she said. "Don't go anywhere."

He chuckled.

When she returned in her nightgown, Arthur was bent over, rearranging the logs with a poker.

"The bedroom is not toasty, but we'll keep each other warm."

He turned. Stood.

"What?" she asked.

"You're beautiful enough to be in a painting."

"And you're not an unhandsome man." She came across to the fire. Took him in her arms. "Sometimes I think you don't understand that about yourself."

"I don't have the confidence that other men have."

"Which is nonsense," she said. "It's a wonder that one of the girls in the office hadn't claimed you by now."

"I suppose I'm picky," he said.

They had a short kiss. "Shall we go in?" she asked.

"Go in and get comfortable. I'm going to grab one more log from the porch."

In bed, under the chilly, heavy blankets, she waited a minute. Two. There was thumping on the porch, then near the fireplace where the light flared brighter. Finally, he appeared in the bedroom doorway.

"What is it?" she asked.

"To be honest, I'm worried about your condition."

"Condition?"

"Your baby. Won't we upset it?"

"That's thoughtful, but no. My doctor told me as much."

There was a pause. "All right then." Arthur closed the door to a crack. Jenny heard rustling and a snap of suspenders.

"In the later months one has to be more careful, I suppose," she said, opening the chilly blankets for him. "But not tonight."

He slid quickly into the bed.

"You have on your Long Johns," she said.

"I wasn't sure."

"You're a kind and thoughtful man, Arthur, but those have to go."

They lay tight against each other, Arthur stiff as a fence post. His body, that was. The rest of him remained soft and warm. On his end, nothing seemed to be happening.

"I guess I'm still worrying," he murmured.

She moved his hand to her breast. "Please don't. And anyway, there's no pressure. We have the whole weekend."

"True," he said.

She closed her eyes. "If you like you could touch me." She moved his hand lower. Past her belly and down.

At her soft fur—at least she thought it was soft—his fingers flinched.

"Sorry," he said quickly.

"It's okay," she murmured. "You're doing fine. And you know what?"

"What?"

"I've always liked your hands. I noticed them the first time I met you."

"Thank you," Arthur said. His body seemed to loosen a bit.

"Many men don't take care of their fingernails. A woman likes a clean and tidy fellow."

"Well then," Arthur said, and concentrated.

"Like that, yes."

"You're sure?"

"I am." She let out a breath. "Just like that." She closed her eyes and thought of Will Jamison and the Road King Motel. Of the man who pounded on the adjoining wall. Of what her cries must have sounded like.

Afterward, with her hand, she gave Arthur relief. He groaned and fell back as sweaty as a workhorse after plowing.

"Are you okay, Arthur?"

"I need some practice, I guess."

"Well, that's what honeymoons are for."

They lay back. A mosquito needled somewhere in the dark. He turned to her. "Are you hungry?"

"I'm always hungry."

Humming, Arthur dressed and turned to the little kitchen where he made a second supper from food they had packed in a cooler along with an ice block. Afterward, they retired to the front porch. Close by the railing stood heavy pines with red-mottled bark and soaring tops, and in their deepening shadows she and Arthur drank tea. Afterward, he had a bowl of tobacco, which kept the mosquitos mostly at bay. At full dark, fireflies came out at the edge of the wood.

"As a boy I thought I could keep fireflies in a jar and have my own lantern," Arthur said.

"Did it work?"

"They died."

**

The next morning, they ate "The Lumberjack" breakfast special at the lodge, then took a narrow walking path to the headwaters itself, a sparkling stream that flowed over smooth rocks out of Lake Itasca and into the woods. They took off their shoes, and, holding hands, walked on the slippery rocks. The water was numbingly cold. Later that morning, Arthur took time to examine all the information and nature displays in Douglas Lodge, the grand old hall of Itasca State Park. He was especially curious about the Mississippi River. How it flowed north and east from the headwaters, not south like most people imagined. How it "wanted" to go all the way up through Canada to Hudson Bay but encountered a continental divide just north of Bemidji, which diverted its course eastward and then south.

"Without the continental divide there'd be no 'mighty Mississippi,'" Arthur said. "No barges and locks and dams. No Mark Twain. No New Orleans. Isn't that interesting?" He leaned close to the glass-sided diorama.

"Yes, dear." She needed a nap.

"Mrs. Olsen?" A young lodge clerk approached with a piece of paper.

She failed to understand that he meant her.

"That's us," Arthur said.

"I've been looking for you folks. I have an urgent message."

Chapter Six
Fargo

She and Arthur hurriedly checked out of their cabin, then drove south and west through the pine and lakes country toward Fargo.

"I'm terribly sorry," Jenny said again.

"Sally's in Fargo," Arthur repeated.

Jenny held onto her armrest. Her stomach felt woozy. "When Dag and Emil got back from the wedding, she was gone."

"What's wrong with Sally going to Fargo?"

"She must have taken the train," Jenny murmured.

"Why can't she take the train back home?" Arthur drove at the speed limit, no more.

"Because she's detained at the police station."

"The police station?"

"If you speed up a bit, I'll tell you the full story."

They had passed out of the forest at Detroit Lakes and into open country when she finished. "You know about Sally and the doctor. The trial in 1934. But Sally had a baby, his child, a little girl. She lives in Fargo with a family who took her in."

Arthur glanced her way, then back to the road ahead. "That's why Sally went to Fargo."

"To try to see her, yes. But the family forbids it."

He drove slower now, as if this news had added great weight to the car. "You might have told me some of this earlier."

"I should have." Jenny patted his arm. "I didn't want to burden you with so much information. My family is already a lot."

"So, the little girl would be about five years old by now," Arthur said.

"Yes. Rosalie is her name. A little red-haired one. We don't talk about her," Jenny said, "but she's always in mind, certainly for Sally."

"How did she come to live with the new family?"

Afer a pause, Jenny said, "Emil gave her away. To them."

Art looked sideways for long moments.

"The road," Jenny said.

"Sorry." Arthur drove on.

"Those were difficult, complicated times," Jenny said. "Let's not go back there. Not today."

"Okay," Arthur said. "And anyway, it doesn't change anything between you and me."

"Thank you for that."

"Though it's a shame we didn't have another night in our little cabin," he added.

"I'll make it up to you, dear."

He chuckled and accelerated, a man now on a mission, the captain of his Oldsmobile. As they sped on through the bright, full green of a Minnesota summer day, Jenny glanced behind, then to Arthur, then to the highway ahead. What if this moment was the happiest of their lives together, which might be long? She made a sound.

"What's that?" Arthur said.

She put a hand to her mouth. "Perhaps pull over."

He barely made it to a stop. She barely got the door open before spewing eggs and bacon bits, the Lumberjack special, onto gravel.

"I must be a little car sick," she said.

"Take your time," Arthur said. "Get it all out." She bent low again. He came around and steadied her, afterward offering her his clean, white handkerchief.

***

At the police station in downtown Fargo, Jenny hurried inside. Beyond a tall counter, managed by a deputy, Sally sat in a chair as if on school detention.

"Sally," Jenny called.

"We're here now," Arthur said.

Dressed as a working man with cap and coveralls, she looked up as if she was expecting them.

"Your sister was pretending to be a city worker," a deputy said. "She was lurking in the neighborhood near the Rossi residence. Some neighbors thought her behavior was odd, especially since she was talking to the little Rossi girl, so they called us."

"Hello, Arthur," Sally said evenly.

They shook hands.

"I'm sorry for all this," Arthur said to the officer.

Jenny gave him a surprised look.

Sally looked up to Jenny. "I saw her," she whispered. "I talked to my little girl."

"Which is the problem." The deputy pushed back his hat. "Mr. Rossi gave me the background dope, including a copy of the legal agreement, which says no contact with the birth mother. Do you confirm that?"

"Yes," Jenny said.

Arthur turned to Jenny.

"We could have put her in the slammer," the officer said. "But Mr. Rossi didn't want that, though his wife thought differently. She was upset."

"We thank Mr. Rossi, and we thank you," Jenny said.

"We had to do paperwork on your sister," the officer said. "Which means the incident is on file here. If it happens again, we'd have no choice—"

"I'm sure it won't," Arthur said. "Right, Sally?"

Sally stayed quiet.

"Come then," Jenny said.

"Don't forget this." The officer retrieved a broom from the corner. Handed it to Jenny. "She had it all planned."

As they began the nearly four-hour drive north to the home farm, Sally, in the back seat, watched out her window. Arthur turned on the radio. The stations all carried farm news.

"Let's find some music." Jenny took over the radio dial. Low on the band, one station carried swing music. "How about Glen Miller?"

"Fine," Arthur said. "Enough with grain and cattle prices."

In the back seat Sally had leaned sideways and was asleep.

***

They arrived at the farm late afternoon. Emil knelt by his Allis-Chalmers, fixing a front tire. Jenny tugged Sally's sleeve. "We're here."

Sally sat up, groggy.

Arthur killed the engine. Let out a breath.

Dag came to the front door of the new house and hurried to the car. Emil, stone-faced, stood up.

"You made it," Dag called.

"We did." Jenny got out and stretched as if this was any old trip back to the farm.

"I'm sure you're all famished," Dag said. "Supper's ready."

"I could eat," Sally said. She watched as Emil came across the yard toward them.

"I fed your chickens," Emil said.

"Enough?"

"Go and check."

"I will."

As Sally headed across the yard, Dag whispered, "When we got home from the wedding she was gone. We didn't want to bother you on your special night, but when she didn't show up…"

"We're glad you did," Jenny said. "I told you to always call."

After a pause, Arthur said, "Yes. Call any time."

"How did it go in Fargo?" Dag asked.

"Arthur was a lifesaver."

"Oh Arthur, we can't thank you enough." Dag wrapped him into a Dag-hug.

"No need of that." Arthur patted Dag's shoulder as he extricated himself. "Sally's family now."

"What about the next time she runs?" Emil said.

"Maybe she's got it out of her system," Arthur ventured.

"You don't know her," Emil replied, and spit.

When they were seated for supper, Sally sat erectly, head up as if all was well.

"Well. We're all together again," Dag said.

"Isn't that nice," Jenny said.

"I wish we were a praying family." Dag's lower lip came out, and her eyes threatened to spill.

"*Takk Gud* we're not." Emil eyed the mashed potatoes.

"Maybe Arthur could give a blessing," Dag said.

"My pleasure." He closed his eyes and set forth on the "miracle of family" and the "bounty of the earth" and "promise of eternal life through Jesus."

Emil gave Jenny a side look.

She averted her eyes.

Dag glared at them.

"Amen," Arthur said.

"Thank you, Arthur," Dag said. She turned to Emil. "See? That didn't hurt."

They moved the bowls and dishes around the table: roast chicken, gravy, green beans, pickled beets, fresh-baked buns with Dag's perfect, lightly toasted egg-white glaze. Forks clinked on plates.

"So much progress." Jenny looked around the new house.

"At least we can cook here now," Dag said.

"When will you get power and light again?" Jenny asked.

"No rush," Emil said. "The old lanterns work fine."

"Soon would be nice," Dag said, with a glance at Emil. "I miss my radio."

"More chicken anyone?" Sally stood up with the bowl.

"Fill the gravy boat too," Emil said.

"Please," Dag said.

"They won't say 'please' the next place she goes," Emil said.

Sally had no reply.

"If you run off to Fargo and they catch you again, you'll be working in a kitchen with bars on the windows," Emil continued.

"Enough, Emil," Jenny said. "Please."

"Jail or the State Hospital in Jamestown," Emil said with a shrug. "It will be one or the other."

"Here you go." Sally handed Arthur the gravy boat.

"Jenny rescued it from the old house," Dag said to Arthur. "It's a little smoky."

"It works just fine." Arthur poured pale gravy.

"Don't say we didn't warn you," Emil said to Sally.

"Maybe you should put bars on my window upstairs," she replied.

"We'd never do that," Dag said immediately.

"And while you're at it, why not a padlock on my door?" Sally continued. "Lock me in."

"Have we told you about Itasca State Park?" Jenny asked.

"No, we'd love to hear," Dag said.

"Arthur?"

Revived by the food, Arthur presented the Haugens with facts about the park, established in 1905, and Douglas Lodge, the Mississippi headwaters itself, how the river "almost headed north" but for a little-remarked continental divide, and how some of the giant red pine each contained enough board feet to build an entire house.

"Imagine that," Dag said.

"I believe there's pie?" Jenny said.

"There is." Dag stood.

Arthur glanced at his watch. "I've been rattling on. We have a long drive home."

"You could stay the night," Dag said. "Emil could make room in the *lille* house."

"We can make it home before dark," Jenny said. "The days are long now."

After apple pie and coffee, and as Arthur and Jenny made to leave, Dag got weepy again. Aside, she said to Jenny, "I'm so happy for you. It was a beautiful wedding. And Arthur's such a steady one. Just think, your whole lives ahead of you. Sometimes I think of what might have been for me and Walter."

Jenny hugged Dag hard—squeezed the breath from her. "Call if you need anything. Day or night."

They trailed down the steps and into the yard. Sally disappeared upstairs. Arthur settled into the driver's seat. Jenny turned to her family for a last goodbye.

"Maybe we should lock her in at night," Emil said.

"We'd never do that," Dag replied. "Shame on you."

"We do it with the chickens," he said. "It's to keep them safe."

"She's not a chicken," Jenny said. "Sally's your sister."

"You don't have to live with her," Emil replied.

"It's true, I don't." Jenny's voice caught. She hugged Emil, which felt like holding an oak beam.

He patted her back. "We'll do our best."

"I know you will."

Finally, she and Arthur were off in the Oldsmobile. At the far end of the driveway, though she had promised herself she wouldn't, Jenny looked back. Emil was heading across to the barn. Dag remained, arm upright in a wave, like a statue.

Once on the main highway, Arthur's eyes went squinty. He drove on, gripping the big steering wheel as if it might come loose.

"Are you okay?"

"That big meal did me in," he said. "It's been quite a day, to be honest."

"I can drive."

Arthur pulled over on the spot, and they made the switch—the first time he had let her drive him anywhere. He leaned back in the passenger's seat. "I think my nerves gave out."

"It's been a long day," Jenny said.

"I used to worry that my life was overly quiet," he murmured.

"Rest," Jenny said. "I'll get us back to your house."

Arthur closed his eyes.

"Home," Jenny said. "That's what I meant."

He was already dozing.

Chapter Seven
Cleaning House

At the end of August, Jenny gave notice at the courthouse. One certainly couldn't have a public job while in an obvious family way. This spared Mr. Smith from having to let her go. He seemed relieved and briskly shook her hand while keeping his gaze at shoulder height and above. On her last day, the office girls brought out cupcakes for the afternoon break. There were small gifts, mainly kitchen-related items, including potholders and an apron. It was a nice, ten-minute going away party.

At home on Monday, she sat in the crowded, dim living room. Made a list. Afterward she turned to the house, starting with the furniture. During her first days home, she convinced Arthur to get rid of one Chesterfield, an armchair, a library table, two end tables, and three lamps. She inquired about the cuckoo clocks. "Three seems like a great plenty."

"Oh heaven's no. I love my little cuckoos."

She inquired also about the pump organ. How much, really, did he play it? This was also a bridge too far.

She turned to his clothes, ridding his closet of the stiffest, most pungent sport coats. The oldest of them had thick, handmade shoulder pads. "Mother," Arthur explained. "She always nagged me about standing straightly." After the sport coats went two pairs of shoes, several pairs of long johns, and several shirts worn at the collars. Arthur had no real objections to a review of his clothes, "so long as he had enough to wear to work." The local Salvation Army was happy to receive what Jenny had brought.

After going through his closet, she turned to the kitchen, especially the cupboards and dishware. Who needed sixteen teacups and saucers? Three black, number eight iron fry pans? Arthur did, it turned out. Discreetly, she disappeared some chipped glassware, a cracked platter, and several coffee cups.

In the second week, after the house was less cluttered, she cleaned. She addressed the windows (filmy from cooking oil) with vinegar water and newspaper. The wallpaper with a light Borax solution (her white rags came away brown). The porcelain sink stains with Fels Naptha (she succeeded only in dulling them). She brought the kitchen linoleum to a shine with Johnson's Glo-Coat wax. "No rubbing, no buffing! Just apply and let it dry!" it read. Which was not true. It still needed polishing.

The postman came each morning around ten, and she tried not to be the woman at the window. As if he was aware of her longing, a letter came from Will Jamison. Dag had forwarded it inside a new envelope and stamp, bless her. After "Dearest Jenny" much was blacked out. She held the thin, airmail parchment up to the light, but the dark stripes were absolute. In his man's cursive, not flowery but clear, he wrote that "things were heating up," that his squadron was "on move," and that she was "so often in his mind." He closed with "All my love." She added the letter to his others, now a thin stack of them tied with red yarn, and hid them in the least likely place Arthur might find them, her underwear drawer. She could not bring herself to write back to Will. To explain her new life. He would blame himself—be distracted, which could be dangerous. And how, if his squadron was on the move, would her letters ever find him?

After the house was brightened, and space made for more of her things, she turned to the lawn and Arthur's flower beds. She weeded, trimmed, and thinned—the orange day lilies had taken over—and brought the beds under control. She pushed the heavy mower across the small square of grass at near trotting pace in order to spin its blades at high rpms. Fragrant green shavings flew. At the end of a full day's work in the sun, when Arthur came home from the courthouse, she took him to see the front yard. "What do you think?"

He stared. "I rather liked working in my flowers. Now what will I do with my spare time?"

The next morning, she dropped Arthur off at work and headed home... to Skye.

***

Passing the Crookston city limits sign and entering the widening landscape, the open fields, she let out a breath. Leaned back in the seat. After Fisher she slowed at East Grand Forks, then crossed the Red River Bridge into North Dakota. For no reason, she honked her horn.

In Grand Forks she braked at the stone arches of the fairgrounds, but could not bring herself to turn in. It was where she and Will had heard President Roosevelt speak ages ago—had seen him close up. She thought of driving past the high school where Mr. Gatzke was likely framed in the first-floor window of the principal's office, fretting about this year's class of '39. How was it possible that she had been a high school girl only last year?

***

Dag waved and waved from the porch at the sight of Arthur's Oldsmobile. Sally peeped out from behind the chicken coop. Jenny killed the engine and got out. "I'm home."

"What a surprise," Dag called.

Sally held up an arm, then came across the yard. Jenny went to greet her first.

She hugged Sally, who was ever leaner and with hair ever shorter.

Sally drew back. Stared at Jenny's face, her middle.

"What?" Jenny said.

"You're going to have a baby." Sally's voice was scratchy from lack of use.

"I am," Jenny said. "I came to tell you."

Dag joined them and said to Sally, "I should have told you."

Sally turned. "You knew?"

"Yes. And now we all do."

"Except Emil," Jenny said.

"He'll soon be in for lunch," Dag said.

Sally clutched Dag's arm. "Why didn't you tell me?"

"I'm sorry," Dag said. "It was just—"

"We didn't mean to leave you out," Jenny said.

"With everything going on," Dag continued, "I suppose we thought it best to wait."

"Everything?" Sally replied. "You mean me?"

"No, not just you," Jenny said. "Emil, Arthur, all of it."

"Why do you lie? Why do you keep things from me?" Sally pulled away from Jenny's hand and headed back across the yard.

"Oh dear," Jenny said.

Dag shrugged. "Welcome home."

Things did not improve with Emil.

"A baby? *Herregud!*" He drew back.

"Yes, *Onkel* Emil."

"What about your job?"

She touched her belly. "A woman can't work if she's pregnant. Not in a public job anyway."

"If a woman can and if she wants to," Emil said, "I don't see why she shouldn't."

"It's just the way it is, Emil," Dag said.

"Sally worked all the way up till it was time," he added.

"Life is different in town," Dag said.

"I can still send a few dollars home every month," Jenny said. "Arthur won't mind."

"I won't take Arthur's money," Emil said.

"I could take a job," Dag said. "Mrs. Lyle at the café is always pestering me."

"No," Jenny and Emil said at the same time.

Across the yard, there was a thud—a kick or something thrown hard against the backside of the barn.

Emil turned to Jenny. "We've got our hands full here."

***

After noon dinner, Jenny drove Dag to town for shopping. Sally wouldn't come.

At the grocery store she pressed Dag to buy more than flour, cheese, and the usual staples. "These Idaho peaches will be out of season soon." Jenny held a plump, furry one to Dag's nose.

"I suppose we could get a couple to eat fresh."

Jenny set about choosing a half dozen.

"I don't can anymore," Dag said, "My canning jars all got melted."

"Maybe it was a sign," Jenny said. "There's better variety in the grocery stores now. It's not like you have to keep a year's supply of food at home."

"I'm not sure Emil would agree."

They moved on. Paused by a near empty shelf of oranges. They were small and a bit sunken. Dag sniffed one. "Navel oranges are all done for the year. I so wish we could get good oranges in the winter."

"That'll happen someday," Jenny said.

They turned down the candy and confections aisle.

"Well, well." A heavy-set woman drew up. She had sharply colored brown hair and carried a wire basket.

"Oh dear." Dag tugged Jenny's sleeve to turn her around.

Jenny brushed off Dag's hand. "If it's not Mrs. Robert

McConnell."

Dolly McConnell brought her basket to the front. Held it before her. It carried enough candy for Halloween. "Dragged yourself back home, have you, Miss Haugen?"

"It's Mrs. Olsen now. And I'm just visiting, not that it's anything to you."

"Considering what your family put the doctor through, it's probably best you don't live here."

"Are you threatening me?"

"It's you who threatened us. Every town needs its doctor."

"You might think you've gotten away with it," Jenny said. "And you may think we're done with you—"

"Come." Dag pulled Jenny's arm.

"Everybody knows your sister is crazy," Dolly called after them.

Outside, Dag looked over her shoulder as she steered Jenny along. "That's why we don't often go to town."

Chapter Eight
Library Card

After a long and nauseated weekend at home (she had thought that part of her pregnancy was over), come Monday morning she was happy to send Arthur off to work. After tidying up the breakfast dishes, she sat in the living room. Tried to read. Arthur had a dusty shelf of books, including four volumes on growing African violets. Several old novels by Kipling, Arthur Conan Doyle, Jack London. *Concerning Children* by Charlotte Perkins Gilman, author of *The Yellow Wallpaper*, the spine of which seemed unbroken. Two children's books by Edith Nesbit, *The Railway Children* and *The WouldBeGoods*. Both dated and inscribed to "Little Arthur." On their pages here and there were his crabbed attempts at printing. Square letters, mistakes lined out, then started again as if the story books were his own blank pages to write on. Where was his mother? Who let their children write in their books? She culled several, excluding those with Arthur's handiwork, then boxed them for a trip she had been meaning to take since arriving in town.

Crookston's tall white Carnegie Library, like most across the Midwest, had a flight of granite steps up to round columns and a lamppost by the main door. Inside, the librarian and her desk faced the front. She was not old, thirty at most, and had pleasant features with an upturned nose and bobbed hair.

"I have some books to donate," Jenny said. "If you take such old ones."

"We do indeed." Her nameplate read "Miss Klapperich."

"They're dusty in more ways than one."

"There's a book in the world for everyone," Miss Klapperich said. "Even ones on African violets."

Jenny moved on to browse the shelves. Lifted this book. That one. Restored each.

"Is there a book in particular?" Miss Klapperich had come unnoticed behind Jenny.

"Just looking. Hoping one will strike me."

"Of course." She seemed disappointed not to be of use.

"In high school I once tried to read all of the *Harvard Classics*, but it was foolish," Jenny said. "Maybe something less taxing."

"A novel? A history?"

"Perhaps a history."

"I have the book for you," Miss Klapperich said.

They walked among the shelves, Jenny speaking in low tones that a library demanded, though Miss Klapperich, with a pleasing, easy laugh, seemed unconcerned.

"Try this one," she said. "Most people think he was only a poet."

Jenny settled into an armchair with a biography of Lincoln written by Carl Sandburg. A ripple of nausea spread through her. She held her belly. Burped. She gave Sandburg a short half hour.

"No luck?" said Miss Klapperich.

"It feels a bit much right now." She handed back the biography.

"We have magazines and newspapers on the far rack."

"Do you have the *Skye View* from North Dakota?"

"No, but if you have a few days, I could get you a copy."

"I have many days."

"Skye was all in the news last year." Miss Klapperich scribbled a note to herself. "The trial of that doctor. If you're wanting to read about it, we have older issues of the *Fargo Forum*."

"Not that. I'm from Skye. I like to keep up."

"From Skye? Well then, you must have followed the trial."

"And while I'm here, I'd like to apply for a library card," Jenny said.

Miss Klapperich paused. "Of course."

Jenny sat to fill out a form, then returned it.

"You're her." Miss Klapperich smiled.

"Her?"

"Art Olsen's wife."

"I am."

"We all wondered when he would meet his match."

"We?"

Miss Klapperich colored. "The ladies in my book club. We're quite the gossips."

After her first visit, Jenny came weekly to the library. Edith Klapperich usually had a *Skye View*. Jenny always read it, though not straightaway. First came the *Fargo Forum*, *The Minneapolis Star*, and *The Winnipeg Free Press*, all for news of the war. The Battle of Britain was ongoing since late summer of 1940. She pored over the articles, seized upon any announcements of success in the air war against the German Luftwaffe. Only afterward did she turn to her hometown paper.

In October of 1940, in the "Goings On About Town" column, she read about Doctor and Mrs. McConnell hosting a Sunday afternoon coffee for the new pastor.

In November, the *Skye View* featured the doctor in a front-page article about his charity work for the Turtle Mountain Indian Reservation, where at a drum ceremony the tribal leaders honored him with an eagle feather and turtle shell.

"The bastard."

"Excuse me?" A woman in a chair nearby glared.

"Sorry."

"There might have been children nearby," the woman said.

"But there weren't, were there?"

The woman looked away.

After that she avoided the *Skye View* in favor of *Life*, *Time*, and *The Saturday Evening Post*. The baby preferred she not read at all. By Christmas it was a gymnast, turning somersaults. By early February, a football kicker. By March, a rolling, tumbling cannonball.

After a doctor's visit, the cheerful nurse walked Jenny back to the lobby where Arthur waited. "All's well, Pappa."

"That's good to hear," he said.

"If I were to bet, I'd say it's a boy," the nurse said. "And a big one."

"Just so it's healthy," Arthur said.

Chapter Nine
Baby John

On February tenth, 1940, in the Crookston Hospital, second floor, John William Olsen, seven pounds even and over twenty-three inches long, was born.

"You and Arthur didn't waste any time," Emil said.

"Hush," Dag said. "He's a bit early. Wanted to get a start in this world." Dag, Emil, and Sally had arrived at the hospital the day after the birth, and now crowded the room with its white, iron-spoked bed where Jenny rested with baby John. Sally was wan and clean enough in a blue work shirt and long pants, but smelled like a chicken coop.

"Could we crack a window?" Jenny murmured. "So warm in here."

Emil went over. Tugged on the handle. "It's painted shut. Why would they do that?"

"Don't make a fuss," Dag said. She found a small towel and fanned Jenny and John.

"He's certainly a healthy one."

"He is."

"His hair is so light, but I think he takes after you more than Jenny," Dag said to Arthur.

"We're just glad he's healthy." Arthur sat in a chair by the door. The Haugens sat close around the bed.

"Keep fanning, if you would," Jenny said. "It's close in here."

"What happy days." Dag dabbed at her eyes.

Emil rustled the newspaper that he had pinched from the hospital waiting room. "*Bortsett fra krigen.*"

"Hush, Emil," Dag said. "We're not talking about war today."

"Well, we're going to be deep in it soon. Roosevelt has the draft now. You know where those boys are going."

"Somebody has to hold back the Krauts," Arthur said.

"Too late for that," Emil said sharply.

"Would you like to hold him?" Jenny asked Sally.

"Maybe later," she murmured.

"Emil?"

"I'll hold *småen.*"

"He's not that little," Dag said.

"Jenny will show you how," Arthur said. "We wouldn't want to drop him."

"I ain't gonna drop him," Emil replied.

Her lying-in was six days, at least two too many, though it left time for visitors. Some girls from the courthouse came by, as did Edith Klapperich with a friend who might have been her twin. They had the same short hair and quick laugh. And then it was home to Arthur's house.

***

The spring of 1940 was a haze of short nights and day naps when she could. There were three letters from Will Jamison, mostly blacked out, the handwriting tilted sharply forward, as if for speed, as if written against a wind. The last was July 20, 1940. After that, silence. Which was a kind of relief. He had moved on, perhaps met an English girl, and, after all, she was Mrs. Arthur Olsen, mother of John Arthur Olsen, an ever-hungry, seldom sleeping, red-faced little man.

Her first evening out alone was with Edith to her ladies' book club, where she was the youngest attendee by far. Edith, at twenty-nine, was next oldest, and after her the other women's hair shaded gray to bright white. The oldest lady, Minnie Long, a widow, was eighty-nine and tonight hosted at her home that was long on doilies, African violets, and knit throws. There was one for every chair.

The ladies were pleased to meet "Mrs. Olsen herself."

"New blood is good for us."

"You'll bring down our average age by ten years."

"So important to hear what modern young ladies think these days."

The first order of business was to vote on the upcoming books. As their "professional" reader, Edith nominated Huxley's *Brave New World*, Hurston's *Their Eyes Were Watching God,* Fitzgerald's *Tender Is the Night*, and Mitchell's *Gone with the Wind*. Margaret Mitchell won going away. After that, they turned to tonight's book, Dale Carnegie's *How to Win Friends and Influence People*.

"Such good advice throughout," said Mrs. Long.

"It seems to be much about taking personal action."

"And trying to be a better person."

"That's something we can all agree upon."

Discussion veered off to the book's connection to the Scriptures, and how much of what Carnegie said was already in the Bible— many of the same messages just rearranged for a more pleasing tone.

"It almost seems like stealing," Jenny said.

The ladies looked at her.

"From the Bible, I mean," Jenny said. Her cheeks warmed.

"Well, no harm in that," one lady said.

Edith turned to Jenny. "What did you think of the book overall?"

Jenny paused. "I liked the advice on how to become a better person. Though to me the book seemed written for men. Salesmen, generals, politicians and the like."

Ina Fenske spoke up. "What about that spot where the piano teacher—"

"Babette," Miss Klapperich said.

"Where Babette convinced her student to trim her nails without having an argument about it? That's good advice for mothers with daughters."

"Yes," Jenny said. "But later in the book he brings in Napoleon and Tolstoi. They had nagging wives, or so Carnegie says, and therefore it was perfectly fine for the men to take lovers and go off on their own."

The ladies stared.

"Like every unhappy marriage is the fault of the wife," Jenny finished, and shrugged. "That hardly seems fair."

"Well, well, aren't you the young suffragette," one said.

"I suppose I am."

"You who married Arthur Olsen and moved into his house."

The ladies giggled.

"He's never said so," Jenny replied, "but I think Arthur found the pickings in town rather slim."

"Shall we have our cookies now?" Edith said quickly. After the book club disaster, Edith rang on the telephone to apologize and dropped by with several new books. She took immediately to John and came regularly after that, sometimes with Sara, her woman friend.

"He's the handsomest baby ever." Edith swayed with him in the rocking chair. "That blond hair, those cheeks, those long legs. He's perfection."

"He is." Sara leaned close.

"You three seem comfortable," Jenny said. "I'm going to step into the kitchen and tidy up."

"Do," Edith murmured.

Jenny stayed in the kitchen as long as she could, trying, for a few minutes, to forget that she was now a mother and a wife living in a home not her own, and that was not going to change for years to come.

Chapter Ten
The Letter

In October, an oversized envelope from Skye arrived at the house. There was a brief note from Dag (not much new on the farm, and Sally "fair"). Inside was another letter, sealed, and postmarked from Winnipeg, Manitoba. The penmanship was fine, rounded cursive, certainly a woman's hand.

Dear Miss Haugen:

I am writing to you on behalf of my son, William Jamison. I regret to tell you that his plane was lost in the air Battle of Britain on August 17, 1940. Neither he nor his plane was found.

I am his mother, Evelyn. He had spoken fondly of you, "the American girl on the train," and said you and he had spent some "brief but wonderful" times together. You must have meant a good deal to him because, following his instructions, I am enclosing a cheque for half of his military death benefit. I do not know the full extent of your relationship with my son, but I have always trusted his judgement.

As you might expect, our family is broken by our loss. Further communication with you might well only complicate or increase our grief, so it's probably best to leave things here, at least for now. My husband and I trust that you will use this money wisely and in a manner which would honor the memory of our son.

Very sincerely,

Mrs. Wallace (Evelyn) Jamison

Jenny, rocking a fussy little John, had hoped to be presentable when Arthur returned from work.

"Has something happened?" he said straightaway.

"It's been a long day."

"You're crying."

"It happens after childbirth. Some women get the blues."

He came over, chucked John's chin. "Let me take him."

"Don't you want your whiskey?"

"That can wait."

"Thank you. I might have a short nap."

Arthur hoisted John up and patted out a good burp.

"Well," she said.

"You have to have the touch, right Little Mister?" Arthur rubbed John's back.

"You're a natural father, Arthur."

"But I'm not his father," Arthur said and turned away.

Jenny took a deep breath. "Yes, that was terribly clumsy of me, Arthur. I'm sorry." She wept again.

Chapter Eleven
Land

The next day, after Arthur had gone to work, Jenny took the letter from Winnipeg—took all of Will's letters outside and burned them. Let their ashes fall among the lilies. Later, she bathed, put on a clean day dress, and had a chicken roasting when Arthur came home from work.

"Smells good in here. Looks like you and Little Mister had a better day?"

"We did," she said. "And some good news in the mail."

"How's that?"

"A check," she said.

"A check?"

"As you know, I've helped my family a good deal."

"To a fault," Arthur said. He poured himself his glass of whiskey.

"It's for five hundred dollars."

"Well. Emil's paying you back?" Arthur raised his glass. "That's a miracle."

"I took it to the Farmers State Bank and started a savings account."

"That's not our bank."

"I was thinking that two different banks for us might be good. In case the Depression ever returned. If there were more bank failures, that sort of thing."

"Now you're sounding like your brother."

"I suppose you're right."

"But it's not the worst logic," Arthur said, "and I suppose it is your money." He drained his glass.

"They needed your signature," she said. "Apparently, we women can't manage money on our own. So I signed for you."

Arthur raised an eyebrow.

"That's the nice thing about a small town and a husband with a good reputation," she said. She patted his arm. "Another drop before I put away your bottle?"

Arthur held out his glass. "I guess I have no objection to making it your account. As long as you don't go wild with the money."

"I won't. It's nice to have a nest egg. I do miss my paycheck."

"We're getting by fine." Arthur tipped back his head, then went to the sink to rinse his glass.

"I ran into Mrs. Albrecht down the street. She takes in young ones. She fell in love with John."

"I'm sure she did." Arthur wiped his glass.

"I think I'm the type of person who needs to get back in the swing of things," Jenny said.

He held it up to the light. "And a boy needs his mother."

***

With the war check (what else could she call it?) she sent money to Emil to help finish the new house. Gave Sally and Dag some "pin money." Made the final payment to Mr. Bailey for the power and light loan on the home farm (last year felt a lifetime ago). The rest she hoarded.

In January of 1941, Dorothy from the assessor's office took sudden medical leave for an ongoing female issue of some kind. Mr. Smith, the assessor, called Jenny wondering if there was "any chance" she could fill in a couple of days a week.

"I could manage," she said. "But I'll have to talk to Arthur."

"Of course," he said.

"Out of the question," Arthur said to Jenny that night. "I won't have my wife be one of those women."

"What kind of women do you mean, Arthur? There are many mothers who would like to work, and their families could use the money."

"We are getting along just fine," Arthur said and drained his after-work whiskey.

Across the living room, John, eleven months and a speed-crawler, veered toward the plant stand and brought down Arthur's African violets. Arthur swore, John cried, and Jenny leaped into action. Arthur took his whiskey bottle and stamped down the basement stairs. When he returned a good while later, Jenny had restored the violets and had supper cooking, John on her hip.

"I'm sorry I swore," Arthur said.

"You're forgiven." She stirred the gravy.

"I'll take the boy," Arthur said.

John wailed at that.

"If you could walk him around while I finish supper," Jenny said. "Thanks."

Later, as they ate, with John quiet in his bassinet, Arthur said, "I suppose we could try it for a spell. See how it goes."

"She'd even feed John supper," Jenny said. "You and I could eat in peace."

"Like before?" Arthur said. He did not look up from his plate.

On Monday, she returned to the courthouse two days a week. Then three. Doris took an early retirement to deal with her health, and by spring Jenny was back to full-time, in the same desk as from before Baby John. "Courthouses, if anything, like tradition," Arthur said.

The assessor's and the treasurer's offices adjoined. As the spring tax deadline approached, Jenny thought to look at Arthur's tax statement. His house was valued at three thousand dollars, had no bank lien, and was solely in his name. Of course, it was current with its taxes, unlike some in town. After the tax deadline passed, the Crookston newspaper, like most towns, printed its yearly list of delinquent taxpayers, or the "list of shame," as the courthouse secretaries called it. The names included Samuel L. Labonte Auto Repair (no surprise there), plus a couple of people whose names raised eyebrows ("I hear they're getting divorced," Arthur said). There was also an eighty-acre parcel of farmland that belonged to a man and a woman with different names.

"Who are these people?" Jenny asked.

"Ah, those two," Arthur said. "Ellen Larsen and Harvey Hendrickson. They're brother and sister. She's married… he never did. They inherited some land jointly, but they can't agree on the time of day so neither of them pays the taxes. If they don't watch out, it's going to go forfeit."

When Arthur was not looking, she wrote down the addresses, Ellen locally, Harvey east a few miles near Oklee.

On Saturday, while Arthur watched John, she drove off to grocery shop and run "errands." Ellen Larsen lived in a fine, big house on Pleasant Avenue with a view of the Red Lake River and answered the door herself.

Jenny introduced herself. "I work at the courthouse."

"Oh dear. I suppose it's about the land."

Jenny stood straighter. "It is, yes."

"Well, come in, then."

Overstuffed with antiques, the house had hardly a place to sit. Mrs. Larsen made Jenny a cup of tea. "We have a renter on shares, but I don't like him. I think he cheats us. Or else Harvey isn't giving me my money. Harvey's supposed to pay the taxes."

"Though he hasn't been."

"Sounds just like him," Mrs. Larsen said.

"I was thinking," Jenny said, as if it had only now occurred to her, "if the land is such an aggravation, perhaps you might want to sell it?"

"Our renter has been pestering us to buy it. But, like I said, he rubs me the wrong way."

"I'd be interested in buying it."

Mrs. Larsen blinked. "What would a young woman like you do with farmland?"

"I'm from the farm. I miss it," Jenny said. "Maybe someday my son might like to farm."

"I see."

They took a sip of tea. Jenny glanced around. "Your living room is very comforting. I like how you've saved the old things. My job as a girl was to clean the lantern glasses every morning."

***

It took two weeks and several phone calls to Harvey Hendrickson, with Jenny as the intermediary. The brother and sister finally agreed that selling the land might be simpler than fighting about it.

"Us buy land?" Arthur said at the supper table. "We're not farmers."

"As an investment," she said. "I have my nest egg in the bank, but the bank pays hardly any interest."

"I'd be wary of taking it out of the bank."

"At least come with me to look at the land. When's the last time you've been beyond the city limits?"

The next day she drove Arthur north of town to see the eighty-acre parcel, which was table-flat and empty in all directions. Four gray Butler grain bins stood near the road. They got out of the car. She picked up a peat-dark clod of dirt. Sniffed it.

"There's nothing out here," Arthur said.

"That's a good thing. No trees to farm around. No rocks to haul."

Arthur scratched his head.

"There's a farmer who'll rent it," she said, "so already there'd be income."

"But a lien on my house?"

"Short term," Jenny said and took his arm as she looked across the field. "I've looked closely at the calculations. Talked to a banker. Interest rates are low… just over 4 percent. He thinks it would be a good investment. As he said, 'They don't make more land.'"

Arthur squinted across the empty field. Patted her arm. "Sorry, dear. I'm just not one for risk."

They drove back to town in silence.

The next day, she met again with Ellen Larsen. Who called Harvey. When he answered, Ellen handed the receiver to Jenny. They agreed on a down payment and a contract for deed.

"I don't mean to pry, but why is it you and your brother don't talk?"

Ellen pointed across the living room. "The butter churn. When our folks died, I got the churn. He said mother promised it to him, but that's not true. She'd always promised it to me."

At the bank on Friday, the loan officer, a pale young man wearing a bright tie, looked over her papers, which were signed by Ellen and Harvey. "A contract for deed, a down payment, which you've made, and a five-year term for the balance."

"Yes."

"The price per acre is right. Land value is still depressed from the war, plus you have a renter."

"Yes."

"So, what do you need from me?"

"If things go well, nothing. If they don't, some help with the payment at the end."

"Art is okay with this, your name only on the deed?"

"We've talked it over thoroughly."

"Well, I know Art." The banker shuffled the papers one last time. "He'd be good for this in any case. I see no reason not to back you up. Though to be clear, if things don't work out, the bank will be next in line for the land."

"I understand."

***

At home afterward, Arthur crossed his arms at her news. "I'm afraid you've made a big mistake."

"I hope not."

"We agreed you wouldn't go wild with your money."

"I don't think I have," she said.

"Time will tell, won't it?" He snapped open his newspaper. She set about making his supper.

Later, when John was fully asleep, she put on her robe (only) and came to the living room. Sat with Arthur on the couch. "I hope you won't stay angry with me." She let her robe slack open in the front.

He glanced down at her breasts, then away. "I'll get over it."

"Maybe I could help change your mood." She took his hand. Put it inside her robe. "It's been a while."

"I try not to bother you."

"It's not a bother," she said. "It's what married couples do."

He swallowed.

"But if you're not in the mood."

"I can certainly *be* in the mood." He put down his paper. "You go on in, and I'll be right there."

She gave him a peck on the cheek, then headed down the hall. It was their little routine, and she imagined that every marriage had one. Arthur first went to the bathroom, took several minutes to wash up. She heard water running and then he came into the darkened bedroom quite ready. They had to move fast—he didn't last long— and he much preferred her on her stomach, face down. Which was fine. Tonight, as always, she closed her eyes and thought of Will.

Chapter Twelve
The Renter

Her renter was Arnie Schmidt, who farmed a quarter section a mile up the road. Schmidt was a short, barrel-chested man with a German accent, a ruddy face, and a spray of veins across each cheek. He had a pungent but not unpleasant man-smell about him and was not happy to meet Jenny. "We had hoped to buy that eighty," he said, arms crossed. His wife looked on from the porch. "That pair, Ellen and Harvey, were hard to work with."

"I'm a farm girl," Jenny said. "I guess I spoke their language."

"Maybe it was my language," Schmidt said. "Maybe she didn't like the Deutsch."

"I'm sure it's not that," Jenny said. "And anyway, I'm happy to rent it to you as before."

"Well, that's *some* consolation."

"Same arrangement?" Jenny said. "Two thirds, one third?"

They shook hands. His was a real hand, with a wide palm and thick fingers. And their rental arrangement was the standard in farm country: two thirds of the crop to the renter, one third to the owner, who also paid the taxes. Shared risk, shared reward.

With land taxes due in October, the summer was make or break. Early on, rain came when needed, and the heavy soil held moisture through dry spells. The wheat thickened, shaded green to yellow. As the weeks turned toward the long days of *midsommar*, Jenny visited her field every Saturday, sometimes stopping by the Schmidt farm to remind them of her presence. Her ownership. In late July, she and Herr Schmidt again stood at field's edge.

"The crop looks good," Jenny remarked.

"Looks can be deceptive." Schmidt clucked his tongue. "Wheat can look great in the field but then doesn't weigh out." He bent and stripped off a handful of kernels.

"Wheat should run sixty pounds to the bushel, right?" She stood alongside him. He smelled of vinegar today. She did not mind that either.

"Good wheat, *ja*." He sniffed the wheat and was about to toss it.

She cupped her hands. He poured the kernels into them. She sniffed the damp kernels, then popped one in her mouth. Pinched it between her front teeth. "Firm. Good kernel." She spit it away.

He turned her way. "You know things."

"I told you, I'm a farm girl. Learned a lot from my big brother." She laughed and scrunched up her eyes, saying, "Very big brother."

He glanced toward her car. "Why is it your husband never comes along with you?"

She shrugged. "He's a town guy."

"*Eine mädchen* like you, if I was him, I'd want to know where you were at all times." Schmidt winked.

"I'm not sure I'd like that," she said. "I'm a pretty independent girl."

He looked her up and down. Swallowed as if about to say something.

She checked her watch. "Call me when you're going to combine. I'll come out, and we'll see about that yield." She winked at *him* this time.

***

Two weeks later, after several hot drying days, she and Arnie and little John stood field-side. A John Deere combine harvester, green and turtle-shaped, came toward them pulled by a smaller tractor. A yellow corona of dust floated behind. To the side, tracking just out of the dust, came a smaller John Deere, pulling a wooden, high-sided wheat wagon. The combine's chattering sickle cut the wheat, the wheat fell under the turning paddle wheel, then rode the slatted canvas into the belly of the combine to its shaker and sieves. Chaff and wheat straw spewed from the rear.

"We'll be lucky to get twenty bushel per acre," Arnie said.

The combine grew larger in a drumming clatter of chains, sieves, and fanning straw. John ducked behind Jenny.

"Nothing to be afraid of, boy." Arnie reached around Jenny and patted his head.

John leaned away from *him* too.

The combine noise reached crescendo at the turn. Then the rig swung back downfield and stopped. The trailing wagon pulled alongside. The tractor driver pulled a rope, and pale wheat pulsed from the auger.

"The combine's grain tank holds thirty-five bushels, yes?" Jenny said above the noise.

Schmidt gave her a sideways glance. "Right again."

"The field is eighty rods long. He's stopped twice to empty. I think it's running better than we think."

Schmidt pursed his lips. "We'll see."

The combine receded downfield, John began to fidget, and she took her leave. She drove north along the field, slowly, to show Schmidt she was in no hurry, and as well to see if John would fall asleep in the rear, which he did. Across the road was a farmstead with a nice, big, white house and a wide front porch. Rust-colored chickens ranged across the open yard. A woman hung clothes on a line.

Jenny turned into her driveway. A cluster of wild roses, the pink, thin-petalled kind, hugged the mailbox post. She killed the motor and carefully eased out and closed the door. The woman stood up by her clothes basket.

"Hello," Jenny called. She walked over. "I'm your new neighbor."

The woman wore a blue kerchief over windblown sandy hair. The clothes on the line were men's, including an olive brown wool shirt with a wide collar and large breast pockets and a matching pair of pants. A serviceman's clothes. "New neighbor?" she said.

"Jenny Olsen. I bought the eighty across the road."

"You yourself?" She looked Jenny up and down.

"Yes."

"Well, we heard somebody from town bought it."

"That's me," Jenny said with a smile.

"We thought it might go tax-forfeited," the woman said, not smiling. "We had our eye on it, but with our son in the army now, things are kind of up in the air." A shadow passed through her eyes.

"I didn't get your name."

"Olive. Olive Wagner."

"Do you know the Schmidt family?" Jenny glanced back at the combine, the wagons.

"Yes."

"Arnie, he seems nice."

"Nice enough," Olive said.

"Looks to be a good farmer."

"The Schmidt fellows know their wheat," Olive said.

"I'm renting the land on shares," Jenny said, "so I hope things turn out."

Olive Wagner's gaze went to the field and the combine.

"Can I help you with those sheets?" Jenny asked.

With clothespins in their mouths, and the corners of the white sheet in hand, Jenny followed Olive's lead. They got them pinned without a single sheet touching the grass. Two women, sunshine and breeze, the smell of clean sheets.

"Olson with an 'o'?" Olive Wagner asked.

"Olsen with an 'e'," Jenny said. "My husband's family was Swedish."

"And yours?"

"Haugen. My parents came over from the Stavanger area."

"Closer to Oslo for mine," Olive said.

They finished hanging the sheets.

"Are those Rhode Island Reds?" Jenny asked.

"They are," Olive said. She turned to her flock.

"We had Buff Orpingtons," Jenny said.

"They're nice," Olive replied. "A gentle breed."

The combine, louder again, passed near the road. "Schmidt said the wheat's going to run around twenty bushel per acre," Jenny said.

After a pause, Olive said, "Seems like it would be more than that."

"I thought so too. I've pitched my share of bundles."

Olive Wagner nodded. "I'll keep an eye on your field, and him."

"Thank you."

"Otherwise, you have to go on trust," Olive said. "Sometimes we women are too trusting, if you know what I mean."

Jenny glanced to the army outfit airing in the breeze. "Your son's in the service, you said."

"Billy, yes." Her gaze went to the upstairs window of the farmhouse. Centered below the sharp peak, its curtains were closed. "He didn't have to go. There's the draft now, since last September, and there's a farm exemption, him being an only son. But he got it in his head he had to go. He's home from his basic training."

"After that?"

"Something to do with tanks and Patton's army."

Jenny nodded.

"Your husband?" Olive said. She glanced at Jenny's ring hand.

"He's older, plus he had polio."

"Lucky for him," Olive said.

They were silent.

"It was good to meet you," Jenny said. "I'll come back next Saturday."

"I'll be here," Olive said. "I'm not going anywhere."

***

The next Saturday afternoon she returned to her farmstead to inspect the Butler grain bins, five hundred bushels each in capacity, three of which were full. The fourth was half full. On the ground was spilled wheat, a half bushel at least. She found a grocery sack in the car and rescued most of it.

Afterward she stopped at Olive Wagner's place. She was in the garden. Her clothesline was empty.

"I rescued some spilled grain," Jenny said. "Your chickens might like it."

"They will… thank you. Can you have a cup of coffee?"

They sat and chatted on the porch. Olive said, "Schmidt hauled some grain home to his place."

"I see."

"Three wagon loads."

"That's good to know," Jenny said evenly. "I'm sure he's honest."

"But you never know," Olive finished. She went inside and returned with a small piece of paper. On it was the day and time when each wagon passed by. "Keep it."

Her next stop was Arnie Schmidt's farm. It was late morning, and their kitchen smelled of cabbage. "You're around so much, you should move out from town," Arnie's wife said. She was stockier and ruddier even than her husband.

"Maybe I will someday," Jenny said.

"Well, farming is feast or famine," Arnie said. "Mostly famine this year." He gestured for her to sit at the kitchen table, then brought out his notebook. "Like I said, it could have been a better year, but we'll take what God gives us."

"*Gott sei dank*," his wife said.

"You don't mind hearing a little German, I hope." Arnie lowered his voice—leaned forward to peer through the window as if there might be spies—then chortled.

"German doesn't bother me," Jenny said.

"You never know, these days," his wife said. *"Wir sprechen zu Hause nur Deutsch."*

"Any way," Arnie said, "we were able to mostly fill those bins on your place."

"And I heard you hauled some home," Jenny said.

Arnie blinked, then coughed. Glanced at his wife. "Yes, yes, we did."

"Olive Wagner mentioned it," Jenny said. "She and I were having coffee."

"I see," Herr Wagner said.

"She has time on her hands," Jenny said. "Keeps track of things."

"Yes, well, three wagon loads, as it turned out," Arnie said. "I didn't want to overfill that last bin of yours. In the end, the wheat ran thirty-five bushels."

"That's good news all around."

"Though prices are down this year." Arnie reclaimed his pained face.

"We're lucky the government has price supports in place," Jenny said. "Otherwise, it would be under a dollar fifty per bushel. Which is what they're paying today at the elevator."

"You're right again, *meine mädchen.*"

Arnie's wife raised an eyebrow.

With his big fingers around a pencil, Arnie leaned in to do the final figures. "For your third of the crop, this is what we're looking at, then."

Jenny leaned closer. "That seems right."

"You could have done that in your head," Arnie said. With an ink pen, the old-fashioned kind with a nib, he made out the check. "Me, I need to see numbers on paper."

"I'm glad this went well," Jenny said. "It's nice to know we can trust our neighbors."

"If we can't trust our neighbors, what's the use?" He boomed out a laugh as he handed over the check.

"*Danke sehr*," Jenny said.

"*Bitte.*"

Back in town, Jenny's first stop was home to look in on John, who was still napping. She showed her check to Arthur, whose eyes widened. "Well," he said. "Forgive me for being skeptical about your little land venture."

"You're forgiven." She gave him a peck on the cheek. "And thanks for baby-sitting."

"I think I'll have my whiskey early today."

With her wheat check she paid her land taxes and set aside the rest. On October sixteenth, the day after real estate taxes were due, Jenny ate her sandwich with the girls from the auditor's office. Listened for who, again, was late with their taxes.

Chapter Thirteen
War Parade

Behind her new life in Minnesota as a young wife, mother, and now landowner, was, always, the home farm. Sally. Dag. Emil. On Friday, the Fourth of July, 1942, a bright and humid morning, Jenny drove up the farm lane and tooted the horn. The beginnings of a front porch were underway, though only the upright studs and wooden floor so far. With Emil there was no rush.

"We were worried you wouldn't come." Dag wore an apron and had a daisy of white flour on her pink, right cheek. "The war and all."

"I've saved my gas coupons, plus it's a long weekend." Jenny wiped Dag's cheek. Gave her a hug.

"Must be nice to have a day off." Emil stepped up to accept his hug.

"You could take one. It wouldn't hurt you," Jenny said.

"It must have taken a full tank of gas to come all this way," Dag said.

"She can't stop fretting about the rationing," Emil said.

"First gas, now sugar. How will I bake?" Dag answered.

"I can trade gas for sugar any day," Emil said, "but she don't listen to me."

Dag looked toward the Oldsmobile and said, "No Arthur?"

"He's tied up with men's choir, Rotary Club, and the parade in Crookston."

"And the boy?" as Emil called John.

"He's coming awake." They peeked inside the car. John was stirring in his little blanket bed on the floor. Jenny lifted him out into daylight, making him squint.

"That white-blond hair," Dag said, taking him from Jenny. "Where does that come from?"

"Norway," Emil said.

In the upstairs window, a face moved out of sight behind the curtains.

"How has Sally been?" Jenny asked.

"Average," Emil said. "And not on the high side of average."

They were all seated at the kitchen table, John having some fresh bread sopped in cream and brown sugar, the adults having coffee, when Sally finally came down the stairs.

"There you are," Jenny said.

Sally wore long pants and a long-sleeved shirt even in the heat—a man's shirt, one of Emil's that Dag had altered. She had lost more weight, her face was drawn, and she had done something to her hair. Chopped short and combed back above her ears, it shone with oil. She accepted a hug from Jenny.

"Would you like to hold John?" Jenny asked. "He's been fussing a bit."

"Maybe later," Sally said. Her voice was thin. Her face softened as she stared at John.

"I'll hold him," Emil said.

"Let's go see your Uncle Emil," Jenny said.

John blinked and blinked, John whose sleeper would soon smell of barn and tobacco. She handed him over to his uncle.

"I was thinking," Jenny said, as she settled in at the table. "We should go to town for the parade."

Only John replied, a short burbling.

"Together. Like we used to," Jenny continued. "After all, it's the Fourth of July."

Dag glanced at Sally. "We hadn't planned to."

"I'll go with you," Emil said, rocking John as if he were a natural father.

"Sally?" Jenny said.

"No," she said, with a look to Emil. "I might run off."

Emil made no reply.

"It's settled then," Dag said. "Sally and I will stay and watch John. You and Emil go to town. It'll be a nice outing for you."

***

"Fancy car." Emil ran his hand across the high, steel dashboard of the Oldsmobile as Jenny drove.

"Arthur thinks a heavier car is safer on the highway."

"A Motorola radio too."

"Give it a try."

Emil figured out the two knobs, then turned the needle sideways across the band of numbers. There was mostly static, or stations that played John Philip Sousa and patriotic songs.

"War music." He clicked off the radio.

"It *is* the Fourth of July, and we *are* at war," Jenny replied.

"A damned shame that we got sucked in," Emil said.

"But Pearl Harbor. And now the Germans have taken Norway," Jenny said. "We have to do something."

Emil turned to the passing fields. "I thought about going back home. Picking up a rifle."

"You're too old," Jenny said and patted his arm. "Besides, you have *us* to worry about."

Arriving in Skye, Jenny turned down Maple Street. Emil looked toward it beforehand, as if he knew she would turn. The doctor's neighborhood was quiet. Everybody was at the parade, and his tall-peaked house with cupolas came into view. A shiny black car sat in his driveway, nose out and gleaming. Its radiator grill arched upward to an eagle hood ornament, bullet head lamps and teardrop turn signals

91

perched on curving fenders, and a wide running board stretched below the double doors. The long car sat tall on white sidewall tires.

"He has a new Packard," Emil said. "Look at that thing."

She slowed. "It's monstrous."

"He drives it around like he's the king of England," Emil said.

She glanced at Emil. Drove on. They parked down by the feed mill—there were cars everywhere—and she and Emil joined the throngs walking toward Main Street. Kids pulled at their parents' arms to hurry them along. No one looked twice at Jenny and Emil.

"We all could have come," Jenny said. "Like a family."

"Sally won't go to town no matter what," he said.

On a bandstand a polka band thumped away, and below it people sat in rows of folding chairs as they waited for the speeches and the parade to follow. On the platform near the musicians sat a lineup of local dignitaries. Doctor McConnell wore a plaid tartan jacket and a stars-and-stripes Uncle Sam cap. He stared out at the crowd with a steady, pleased smile.

"The bastard is the mayor now," Emil muttered.

Seated in the front row of spectators was a plump, brown-haired woman with a small, fidgeting, rusty-haired boy. His square forehead drew Jenny's gaze. It was certainly young Martin McConnell, who'd be six now, and his mother, Dolly, who had colored her hair even darker. Martin kept swiveling his head, a jerky, suspicious glance at other kids who, not stuck with their mothers, might have an advantage when it came to positions for the parade and the candy toss. He tugged, then jerked roughly at his mother's arm until she gave in. People close by her smiled and made "boys will be boys" gestures. Martin leaped from his seat and rushed off.

"And now let's hear from the mayor hisself," a man said. This received a good round of applause. Doctor McConnell rose, using a cane, and headed to the microphone.

"Limp, you sonofabitch," Emil muttered.

"We gather today to celebrate Independence Day," the doctor began in his commanding voice, "but in the shadow of a grave threat to America and our very freedoms."

Jenny's stomach clenched. "I can't bear the sight of him."

Emil, jaw set, watched the doctor.

"I'll meet you down by the post office for the parade," she said. She eased out and made her way through the crowd and toward Main Street. In the post office window was an army recruiting poster—"Uncle Sam Needs You!" Beside it, a smaller poster—"Have You Joined Your National Ski Patrol? Do You Speak Norwegian, Swedish, German or Finnish? Our Private Work is Financed by the War Department." A smiling soldier stood on skis and poles in snow, a rucksack and rifle on his back, white mountains behind.

Ahead was commotion among some boys. Martin McConnell stood near other, bigger boys who commanded prime curb space.

"First come, first served, bub."

"My pappa's the mayor," Martin said.

"He can go to hell."

Martin put up his fists.

"None of that, you boys," Jenny said.

Martin glared up at her.

"There's a good spot right over there," she said to him. "I'll show you."

Martin followed her, then raced ahead to claim a spot as if she might take it first.

"Mine!"

"Take it. Now you're all set," she said.

He ignored her after that.

She stood alongside him. "Is your father really the mayor?"

Martin nodded.

"He must be a very important man."

"More important than anybody in the world," Martin said. He peered down the street. At the far end, the flag carriers, the floats, the

93

old cars were gathered. Martin had dull eyes more gray than blue. There was yellow matter in the corner of one. His ears were not that clean either.

"How old are you?" Jenny asked.

"Almost seven," he said without looking.

"Want to know a secret about your father?"

He turned.

She bent down. Whispered.

Martin stared.

"Do you know what that means?"

He shook his head sideways.

"When you get home, ask him." Jenny stood again. "Or your mother, for that matter."

He stared up at her.

"Don't forget," Jenny said cheerfully.

The boy narrowed his eyes. "Are you a witch?"

"Yes."

"I'll kill you." Martin put up his fists.

"You can't kill witches. They live forever."

He frowned, his forehead bunching.

"Oh look," Jenny said. "The candy wagon."

Martin spun to look. He shaded his eyes. "I don't see nuthin'." When he turned back, the witch was gone.

***

Jenny joined Emil for the parade. Down Main Street came the colors, their red, white and blue folds limp on this hot and wind-still day. Everyone stood. Men (except Emil), doffed their hats. Behind the flag bearer came the town bagpiper, an old Scotsman named McCurdy. He claimed that Skye was named for the island "back home," though others believed that the town name came, way back, from a misspelling. After the piper came the high school drum corps, and after them a gaggle of young men in civilian clothes, marching in step and carrying wooden, dummy rifles. People clapped wildly.

"They're going into the service," said a heavyset woman beside Jenny, tears in her eyes. "That's my son, David, front row on the right."

"Too bad for him," Emil said.

The woman stared.

"He means the war," Jenny said. "Too bad it had to happen."

The woman gave them a long look, then blinked. "You're them Haugens. The ones who put the doctor through that trial."

"That's us," Emil said.

"And we'd do it again," Jenny said. She pulled Emil away, down the street to a better vantage point.

Following the young soldiers-to-be came the World War I veterans seated on a hay rack on wooden chairs. In the baking sun they sat erect in heavy, olive-wool uniforms buttoned to throat. Several had an empty sleeve or pant leg pinned up. Following the soldiers of the Great War came a black, steam-driven Hart-Parr tractor, rumbling and clanking on iron lugs booted with rubber caps so as not to damage the street, its steam whistle giving off ear-biting shrieks. Then came a color parade of freshly washed tractors: John Deere in bright green, Farmall and Massey Ferguson red, Case in bright orange, Minneapolis Moline in yellow, most steered by a grinning boy or two on their father's knees. Next came the downtown merchant floats, wagons and low trailers trimmed with toilet paper flowers, and waving girls who tossed candy to the wild kids, including Martin McConnell, who scrambled for it and jostled with the other boys. Then the local body shop entry approached, a badly dented Plymouth coupe on a trailer—"We Meet Our Customers By Accident!" Bringing up the rear, as if to remind everyone of the order of life, was Victor Sipe, pipe in mouth, behind the wheel of his black hearse.

"That's it," Emil said of the parade.

"In the nick of time," Jenny murmured. The woman they had spoken with now stood with two other ladies. All three stared across at Emil and Jenny.

***

On the drive home they passed the city limits sign. Emil said, "Maybe I should run for mayor."

"That's a great idea," Jenny said. "You're so popular you'd win going away."

Emil's shoulders heaved in silent laughter.

Jenny drove on. "They can all go to hell, for all I care."

Emil glanced her way, then nodded. "But it's hard here for Dag. I feel bad about that. I have to be with her when she does her shopping in town."

Jenny turned his way. "Ever think about moving?"

"Moving?" Emil stared at her.

Jenny shrugged. "Away from Skye."

"Pappa got us the land. I finished paying for it. It'd take an earthquake for me to move," he said.

"I couldn't imagine living over in Minnesota, but now I do. It's not so bad."

Emil looked out over the wheat fields.

"Threshing soon?" Jenny asked.

"Another couple of weeks." He rolled down his window. Ditches held the dried, flat spice of wildflowers—black-eyed Susans, lupines, goldenrod—and the passing hedge-end of the wheat field carried a yeasty scent. "If I can raise a crew."

"I'm sure help is hard to find."

"With the war, there ain't an able-bodied man to be found. Eddie was the last one, and now he'll be gone too."

"I might have to come back and shock wheat."

"You were good," Emil said. "You could keep up with the boys. Though nowadays there are hardly any binders and bundles to

96

fool with. It's mostly swathers and pull-behind combines. The old threshing machines are parked."

She drove on. "With the war, I sometimes worry about living in town."

"War or hard times, it's good to be on the farm," he said. "We hardly noticed the Depression. We always had food."

"I put in a Victory Garden."

"If it don't grow, you can always come home."

She turned onto their road.

"If things get tight, I mean," he said. "We'll take you in. The whole family."

The landscape blurred. She dabbed at her eyes, then patted Emil's arm. "I'm sure that won't be necessary, Brother. But thanks."

"I can always use the help." Emil reclaimed his gruffness. "We could even put Arthur to work."

Jenny shrugged. "He could drive a tractor."

"Maybe," Emil allowed.

"I was kidding."

They tried not to laugh.

She drew up to the driveway gate. Emil got out to open it. Waved her through.

At home Sally was sitting close beside the Chesterfield to make sure John didn't roll off.

"How was the parade?" Dag asked.

"You didn't miss much," Emil said with a glance to Jenny. He headed over to scoop up John.

"Did you see anybody we know?" Dag asked.

"Just the usuals," Emil said.

***

At the McConnell house in Skye that night, following supper, Dolly massaged the doctor's stump while Martin sat on the living room floor eating chocolates.

"Save some candy for tomorrow," his mother said.

Martin ignored her.

"You already ruined your appetite for supper," his father said.

"You hardly ate anything," his mother added.

Martin shoved another chocolate in his mouth.

His father stared and pointed directly at Martin and said, "One more and I'm coming over there."

Martin matched his father's gaze and pushed out his lips. Quick as a rat, he darted across and snatched his father's wooden foot.

"Martin—bring that back this instant," his mother called.

"No," Martin said without expression. He settled back by his candy and ate another chocolate.

"Martin, damn you."

"Robert, don't swear at him. He's your son."

Martin watched them as he chewed.

"What are we to do with him?" Dolly said. "He doesn't mind me. Doesn't mind his babysitters, the ones that will come anymore. How's he going to get by in school this fall?"

"Ha ha." Martin pointed at his father. "You're a rapist."

Chapter Fourteen
The Packard

The following Saturday night Jenny handed a list of instructions to Arthur. All week she had been agitated, restless, which always happened after a trip back to the home farm. Her life in town was under-equipped. A garage without tools. A kitchen drawer without knives. "I'll try not to be long."

"Scrap drives are important for the war effort," Arthur said. "Don't worry about me and John."

"His bottle is on the stove."

"You already went through that," he said. "Go. Have fun with the ladies. And don't forget your grease."

She headed to the Oldsmobile. Its gas gauge read exactly three-quarters full. She started the engine and drove off slowly, then at the west edge of town pulled over and killed the engine. She felt underneath the steering column for the speedometer cable, then unscrewed its collar. Pulled out the skinny, square-cornered little finger that turned the numbers of the odometer.

Back at the wheel, she eased up to highway speed in order to save gas. Passing the city limits sign, she tossed out the tin of bacon grease, which bounced and spattered behind, then turned on the radio. It was, after all, Saturday night. Rolling its dial through war music, past "We're Going to Slap the Dirty Little Jap" and "There's

A Gold Star in Her Window," she found some decent country and western. Turned it up loud.

Crookston receded in her mirror. She caught a glimpse of herself and smoothed her hair. At seven p.m. the high sun ahead lit the highway heading west. These were the long days of summer, when daylight held until after ten p.m., and all things seemed possible. The Oldsmobile ate up the miles. Oncoming sunlight heated the interior, and the fabric of the empty passenger seat gave off a wooly odor. She rolled down the window part-way and sang along with the radio. "All I want is you, just you."

In twenty minutes, she slowed over the Red River bridge and entered Grand Forks, North Dakota. Continuing west toward the rough, cowboy side of town, she bumped over railroad tracks, passed bars and a sprawling stockyard that she smelled well ahead of time. She had been here once long ago with Emil. He had brought a cow that couldn't calve, and afterward they had eaten hamburgers at the Circle J Bar & Grill. Its light still flashed, weakly, inside a neon lasso. She turned in and parked. Nearby, a horse trailer thudded and rocked. A horse whinnied.

Inside the Circle J, a red and yellow jukebox played "When the World Has Turned You Down." There was plenty of seating beneath a thin blue haze of cigarette smoke. She took a stool at the bar. A fellow in a cowboy hat stared at her. A man in a seed cap lifted a cigarette with a corn-picker hand. It had missing and twisted fingers. He took a long draw as if to show her, straight-away, why he remained on the home front.

"What'll it be?" asked the bartender.

"Beer?" she said.

"Bottle or glass." The bartender was a squat man with a bent, boxer's nose and a dirty towel over his shoulder.

"Glass."

He waited, then pointed to the taps. "I don't read minds, lady."

"Millers."

"The high life, eh?" said the man with the corn-picker hand. She ignored him.

"Say, sugar," said the cowboy on her left. "Are you rationed?"

"Tone it down, Bob," the bartender said.

Bob hunched his shoulders. Lifted his cigarette.

"So, what brings a lady into a joint like this?" The bartender set her beer on a stained coaster.

"I'm looking for some help."

"Help is hard to find these days."

"I'm sure it is." Jenny glanced at the other men.

The bartender polished a glass. "What kind of help?"

"The kind a lady can't do by herself."

"Can't or won't?"

"Both."

"Like, what, handyman work?" the bartender said. "Again, I don't read minds."

She lowered her voice. "There's a man who has done my family a great wrong."

The bartender waited.

"We tried the law, the courts, but they let us down."

"That kind of work. Talk to Joe." He nodded toward the rear of the bar.

As the man with the corn-picker fingers slid closer, Jenny pivoted off her bar stool and, beer glass in hand, headed back to the pool table. A lone man leaned over to line up a shot. He was small-framed and lean with sinewy arms. He wore a cap pulled low across his forehead. In side profile, he had a square, clean-shaven jaw. He glanced up at her. His cross-eyes shocked her.

"What?" he said.

"Just watching. If you don't mind."

He missed his shot. "I mind."

"You're Joe, right?"

"And you're bad luck." He lined up another shot.

"I suppose pool is harder than it looks," she said.

He straightened. His left eye wandered as if shy about meeting her straight on. "You never played?"

"No." She fixed her gaze on his left, steady eye. His nose leaned a bit to the right and had a dent in its bridge. The rims of his ears were cauliflowered. Thick.

"Do you know what Mark Twain said about pool?" He moved to line up a shot.

"I'm sure I don't."

"'Proficiency at pool is a sign of misspent youth.'"

"You must be a reader," Jenny said.

"My mother was. Me, not so much." He squinted at his next shot.

"The bartender said you might be able to help me."

"I don't do yard work. I don't do carpentry. I don't do plumbing."

"None of those."

"What, then?"

"There's a man. A very bad man."

"Lots of those around." Joe eyed his shot. Sank the eight ball. "I'm one."

"I'm sure not as bad as this one."

He straightened and pointed toward a booth.

She sat across from him. He turned to favor her with his steady eye. On the wall above was a war poster, "Save Your Cans and Pass the Ammunition." A row of beer cans, laid horizontally, shrank into bullets, an ammunition belt that fed the machine gun of a square-jawed GI. A spear of fire blazed from the muzzle.

When she finished her story, Joe leaned back. "This bastard's the town doctor?"

She nodded.

"What is it you want done to him?"

She lowered her voice.

"That's all?" Joe laughed. "Seems like a lady's husband could do that for her."

"My husband's not that kind of man."

He drained his beer. "Up and back to Skye, that's a trip."

"I've got gas coupons. I'll pay your expenses plus twenty dollars."

He shrugged. "It's not like I'm real busy."

"Half now, half when it's finished."

"How do you know I won't stiff you?"

"When I read about it in the Skye newspaper, we'll meet here again. I'll pay you the other half."

"You've got this all figured out."

"I'm the kind of woman who likes to have a plan." She took a ten-dollar bill from her purse. Slid it his way.

His good eye looked her up and down. "Cash on the barrelhead is fine. Though there's other ways a woman can pay a guy."

She drained her own beer. Grimaced at the taste. "What would that make me?"

"A fun gal?"

"Pool looks fun."

They headed to the green felt table. Joe racked the balls. Removed the frame in a delicate lift that left a perfect triangle of shiny, colored balls tight against each other. He instructed her how to hold the stick. "Don't try to kill it."

On the break, she got two balls in, one striped and one solid.

"Now you got to choose," Joe said. "Stripes or solids."

"Solids." She got one more in, then stepped aside.

Joe lined up his shot. Sighted down his nose.

"May I ask, were you a wrestler?"

He sank the orange number thirteen. "Some. But Midwest Golden Gloves champ, 1939, welterweight." Walking around the table, he lined up his next shot. Drilled it.

"Do you still box? Fight?"

"Fight. The Saturday night fights, right?"

She nodded.

"And no, I don't. The doc says I got to take care of my good eye.

I can't fight, the army wouldn't take me, so here I am."

"Playing pool with me."

He gave her a quick grin, then bent to his shot.

"I never got your last name," she said.

"Tully."

"Tully. It suits you."

"You suit me." He stroked his cue. Missed the shot.

"I'm married, remember?"

"My bad luck never ends."

She lined up her shot. "Well, Mr. Tully. If your trip goes well, I'll have more work for you."

***

When she arrived home, Arthur was reading the newspaper. The house was quiet save for the radio on low, playing classical.

"How'd it go with John?"

"He was a little fussy, so we had a bath together."

"That's nice."

"After that he didn't miss you in the least."

She came across and gave Arthur a peck on the cheek.

"You smell smoky."

"Many ladies use cigarettes nowadays."

"A bad habit," Arthur said.

"Well, they can't sit around and smoke their pipes like men, can they?" Jenny unbuttoned her smelly dress.

"You're certainly in a good mood."

"Isn't that what these scrap drives are really all about?" she said. "To give us ladies on the home front a sense of purpose? I doubt that it's really about the grease or the aluminum." She stepped out of her dress, tossed it to Arthur. He caught it.

"It is indeed," Arthur said. "Every little bit counts—"

"—said the lady as she peed into the ocean." Jenny headed down the hallway.

"Have you been drinking?"

"Maybe." She let her slip drop to the floor.

"Well," he said. "You're in a good mood."

"I am indeed. In the right mood. If you don't mind a smoky lady."

He glanced at the clock.

"Unless it's too late," she said.

"No. You get started. I'll be right in."

"I thought you just had a bath."

"I did. But I have my little routines."

***

Two weeks later, a thin envelope came for Jenny. It was postmarked Skye, North Dakota, with her name written in Emil's hand. She had forgotten what good penmanship he had. Inside was a clipping from the *Skye View*, a headline article and photo below. "Doctor's Packard Burned, Vandals Sought." The charred Packard slumped on melted tires. The heat had scorched a black corona across the front of his garage.

When Arthur came home from work, Jenny had a pot roast in the oven, John in his pajamas, and the grease can set out.

"By the way, dear," she said. "I have scrap drive again tonight."

Section Two:
The War Years

Chapter Fifteen
1943: "Why We Fight"

On a warm, humid day in August, Jenny huffed and puffed up the granite steps, which seemed steeper each trip, and through the tall doors of the Carnegie Library. At the front desk, Edith smiled.

"Look at you."

"Moo."

"Nonsense, you look fine," Edith said. "How much longer?"

"A couple of weeks or so."

"A second child. Arthur must be over the moon."

"He is."

Edith pointed past Jenny. "We have a new reading chair for you to try."

"That sounds fine," Jenny said. "The wooden ones aren't a good fit these days."

"Come," Edith said, her voice gay.

The new armchair was blue and well padded, with sturdy, covered arms plus a shiny brass plaque across the back.

"'Reserved for Mrs. Arthur Olsen'," Jenny read. "What in the world?"

"A recent donation to the library," Edith said. "By a certain local man."

"Arthur."

"Over the moon," Edith said.

Jenny eased into the chair.

"If you need anything, just wave and I'll bring it," Edith said.

"There is a book I've meant to try again," Jenny said. "*The Great Gatsby.*"

"Fitzgerald. I'll get it for you." She returned shortly. "If you're having trouble with his novels, you might try his short stories."

"I'm determined to finish this one someday."

When Edith was gone, she opened the novel carefully. After a few pages, the sentences blurred, lifted, floated away. In their place came Will Jamison, his hat brim pulled low the first time she saw him on the train, the lap blanket over their legs, his kisses, how her lips burned as she flew off the train at the Joliette siding where the wagon waited, the red light of his train shrinking away in the snow. She refocused on the text, skipping along, looking for whatever would stay with her.

> " I saw that I was not alone—fifty feet away a figure had emerged from the shadow of my neighbor's mansion and was standing with his hands in his pockets regarding the silver pepper of the stars. Something in his leisurely movements and the secure position of his feet upon the lawn suggested it was Mr. Gatsby himself, come out to determine what share was his of our local heavens."

"Dear Jenny, are you okay?"

Jenny started. Edith was close at hand. "I'm not entirely sure."

Edith handed Jenny a hankie, lilac-scented, and she dabbed her eyes.

"Is it the novel or…?" Her gaze fell on Jenny's hand resting atop her belly.

"A bit of each." She handed back the novel. "I think I'll stick to newspapers for now. These days I just don't have the mind for much else."

"Don't get up. I'll bring you some."

Because of paper shortages, the *Skye View* was published once a week, and noticeably thinner. In compensation, it carried bolder headlines, especially the August 11th, 1943 issue. "Kennedy Son Hero in The Pacific!" She glanced through the article, which did not add up. Young Captain Kennedy had rescued his men, yes, but had allowed his PT-109 boat to be run over by the Japs and sunk in the first place. Below it was a smaller article about the Allied campaign in Italy, "a slog." She turned to the Skye local news, which included upgrades on the jail, a forecast of good wheat harvest, plus an article on prostitution on Portage Avenue in Winnipeg. She skipped forward to *Goings On About Town.*

> On Sunday, August 9, Doctor and Mrs. Robert Mc-
> Connell hosted an afternoon social in honor of the
> new school principal and his wife, Mr. and Mrs.
> Elwood Grant. Mr. Grant, M.A., comes to Skye by
> way of Grand Forks, where he was rector at Red
> River Academy, a private school for boys. Known as
> a strict disciplinarian, he is thought to be a breath of
> fresh air when it comes to running a tight ship in the
> elementary grades. The previous principal, Mr. Arse-
> nault, resigned abruptly this spring following a "no
> confidence" vote by the school board. Lemon cake, a
> specialty of Mrs. McConnell, was added to fresh lem-
> onade and chipped ice, completing the social event of
> the week!

"Him," Jenny muttered. Martin McConnell, the doctor's unruly young son she had seen at the war parade, this was all about him.

"Beg pardon?" Edith looked up from her desk.

"Nothing. Sorry." Jenny turned the pages, then, at the end, went back to the article on social life in Skye. Wrote down the name Elwood Grant.

On her way out, Jenny paused at Edith's desk. "I just remembered. I need to make an appointment. May I use the library's telephone?"

"Of course." Edith vacated her chair. Headed across to her reshelving cart.

From her purse and the emergency fold of her wallet, Jenny took out a scrap of paper with a phone number. Dialed the Circle J Bar in Grand Forks. After several rings someone picked up. There was juke box music and noise behind.

"Is Joe there?"

"Tully? He's always here."

***

That Friday night at supper, Arthur said, "There's a new movie at The Grand. *For Whom the Bell Tolls* with Gary Cooper."

"A war movie?"

"Yes, after the Hemingway novel."

"Have you read it?"

"No. It's something about soldiers holding a bridge in Spain."

She remained quiet.

"Going to the movies, spending a little money, is a way to support the war effort—keep our economy healthy," Arthur said. "Isn't that what your man FDR says?"

"It is."

"I've already arranged for a babysitter," Arthur said. "And the theater is air-conditioned now."

She left the dishes. Readied herself. Arthur, the most punctual man in the world, dawdled, and the cuckoo hands approached seven p.m. before they finally drove off. The Grand Theater, on Second Street, was only three minutes away, and there was a line at the ticket window. Edith Klapperich and Sara were close to the front. "Yoo-hoo," Sara called. Both waved for Arthur to bring Jenny forward.

"Really, it's not necessary," Jenny said.

"We insist," Edith said.

"Yes. Certainly. By all means." People in line gave way to the greatly pregnant Jenny on Arthur's arm.

"Well, I'd be happy to get off my feet."

There were claps on the back for Arthur from the men, and a friendly jostle or two. This summer, the heavier with child she was, the more Arthur escorted her out and about, and the more convivial he was in public. He seemed to her like a politician.

In the cool, darkened theater they settled into their seats. A Donald Duck cartoon played—"Donald Gets Drafted." Arthur chuckled throughout. After that, a war announcement. "A skillet of bacon grease is its own little munitions factory!" said a commanding, male voice. "Every year two billion pounds of waste kitchen fats are thrown away, enough glycerin for millions of rapid-fire cannon shells. Making a roast? Don't throw out those lovely puddles of grease drippings. Save them for our boys on the front line."

Arthur turned her way.

"I know, I know," Jenny said. "I try to save it." On screen, the shiny fat made her stomach clench.

Next came a newsreel—"Why We Fight: The Battle of Britain." She drew a breath. Looked to her lap. The lead-in was like cartoon music, a rising swirl violin, then Lowell Thomas with his deep and dramatic voice. His pauses. Behind his narration was the bumblebee drone and the mosquito whine of plunging airplanes, the concussions of shells. Her supper, roast beef and potatoes, rose in her throat. Her forehead warmed. She tried to think of other places, other things. Will Jamison filled the horizon of her mind—the first time they met, on that freezing train to Winnipeg. Their first kiss. Their last kiss. The first time they made love. The last time. The broken bed at the Road King Motel. Their woolen picnic blanket under the tree in the country park. Gold finches fluttering above in the green crown like diamonds. All of it a reel, a film of her own in which she and her own handsome soldier were the stars, and the world turned their way.

"And that, my fellow Americans, is why we fight," Lowell Thomas concluded. A clicking, flapping sound, then brighter light. She opened her eyes. People in seats around chatted or dug in bags of popcorn. The newsreel was only something to sit through until the movie began. The melted butter on their popcorn smelled rancid.

"Are you okay?" Arthur asked.

She gripped her armrests as the movie began. Gary Cooper fell in love with Ingrid Bergman, but the bridge, always the bridge, called him. She lost track of the story. Concentrated on holding back waves of dizziness. Thirty minutes into the movie, as another fight for the bridge began, she puked.

***

At the hospital, Arthur paced. "I should never have taken you to the movies."

"The baby has to come sometime." Nurses eased Jenny into a wheelchair.

Another nurse steered Arthur to the waiting area. "We'll take it from here, Mr. Olsen."

At sunup the next morning, Roland Arthur Olsen, a stubby, thick chested, nine-pound boy was born. It was a hard birth.

"Did I swear?"

"A blue streak." The nurse blotted Jenny's face with a cool washcloth.

By late morning she was in a room with Roland and ready for Arthur, who hovered outside.

"Come have a look, pappa," the nurse called.

Arthur hurried in and bent low to look. "He looks just like me," he said with wonder.

"He's all yours," Jenny said. "Take him away. I need to sleep."

***

Four days later she arrived home from the hospital with the baby to find a full house. Lined up on her living room couch were Dag, Emil, and Sally. "Surprise," Edith Klapperich said from the kitchen.

Even Sally smiled.

"Well." Jenny steadied herself at the kitchen counter. Luckily, Arthur carried the baby. John stumbled forward to hug Jenny around the legs.

"Mama, Mama," he said with his big, John smile.

"We came down to see *babyen*," Emil said.

"And help out," Dag added. "I brought supper."

"Go see your uncle," Jenny said to John.

Emil held out his arms.

"Can we see the new one?" Dag came forward to peek under the blanket. Emil and Sally followed, with Edith leaning in from behind.

Roland's face was red, and his eyes were puffy and shut.

"Looks like he went ten rounds with Jack Dempsey," Emil remarked.

"Really, Emil," Dag said.

"That's your brother," Emil said to John and tickled him. John laughed and struggled to get away. Emil held him upside down, with more laughter and horseplay.

Edith served coffee and a plate of cookies.

"Anything new in Skye?" Jenny asked.

"Not so much," Emil said.

"There was that school business," Dag remarked.

"School business?" Jenny asked.

"A new principal," Dag continued. "Fellow by the name of Elwood Grant. He came hardly a month ago. Bought a house... moved in. Was supposed to bring his family from Fargo, but he just up and quit."

"Didn't even take his furniture," Emil added, while balancing John. "Left everything and high-tailed it back to Fargo."

"I wonder why," Dag said.

"Something spooked him, that's for sure." Emil gave Jenny the briefest of glances.

After Dag's fried chicken, brought from the farm, Jenny wanted only to go to bed. John was flushed from wild play with Uncle Emil.

"Too much excitement." Dag clucked her tongue at Emil and took John to the couch. She cooled his face with a damp washcloth. "Shall I read to him?"

"Please do," Jenny said.

John found *The Little Engine That Could*.

"Things look under control," Edith said. "I'll slip out now."

"There's no hurry," Emil said.

Edith colored slightly. "You all need your family time."

When Edith was gone, Emil turned to Jenny. "We thought Sally could stay on a few days."

Jenny looked up. "Stay on?"

"Here. To help out," Emil said.

Jenny blinked. "That's very thoughtful," she began, "but—"

"Give you and Arthur a hand around the house," Emil added.

"Well now." Arthur turned to Jenny.

"We have neighbors," Jenny said. "Millie and Chet. Millie's pretty helpful." She took Sally's hand. "And Arthur's Rotary auxiliary women said they'd fill in with cooking."

"No sense having strangers in the house when you can have family," Emil said.

Dag paused her reading to John. "It might be good for everyone."

"Not in book," John said.

"You've got it memorized."

"He does," Jenny said.

"I believe Dag's right," Arthur said. "Having Sally here for a few days might be just the ticket to get you back on your feet."

Jenny paused. "Of course," she said to Sally. "We're happy to have you."

Emil stood. "I'll get her bag."

***

On his first night home, Roland ate every three hours and preferred to be walked about afterward. Groggy, sometime toward morning Jenny carried him into the kitchen just as Sally came in the front door. She wore her long nightgown.

Jenny squinted at the clock… 4:46 a.m.

"Some fresh air," Sally said. "I wasn't sleeping."

"Me neither," Jenny said, rocking Roland. "He's a hungry one."

"If he was on a bottle, I could feed him and you could sleep."

"He will be soon enough," Jenny said.

She dozed some in the armchair with Roland, until the smell of bacon awoke her. Arthur was in the bathroom, humming as he shaved, and Sally was at the stove, cooking. Arthur emerged, dressed for work and smelling of Old Spice.

"I hope we didn't wake you." He stooped to give her a kiss.

Even John was up, on the couch paging through a book.

"Breakfast is ready," Sally called.

"Bacon," John said to his Aunt Sally.

"When I'm here, you can have it every day," Sally said.

"Not every day," Jenny said.

Arthur was pleased to eat a "good breakfast," as he called it, and soon enough, in fine spirits, left for work.

After which it was Sally, Jenny, and the boys.

John turned Arthur's newspaper to the comics section and squinted at the pictures. "Can you read to me?"

"She will later," Jenny said. "It's going to be a hot one today. You two might want to head outside and play some before the sun gets high."

"Can we go to playground?" John asked eagerly.

"Sure," Sally said.

"It's about a half-mile," Jenny said. "I could drive you."

"That's not far," Sally said to John. "We'll walk."

"Take the red wagon," Jenny said.

And soon enough the two were off, leaving Jenny alone with her little prize fighter. Roland was slightly yellow, a bit jaundiced, the doctor said, so, on his orders she sat with him on the porch steps in the sunlight. Let it shine on his soft pink skin.

Millie Arneson came out onto her porch. "Look at you," she called. "Always quite stylish and wearing a day dress." Millie came across the lawn.

"Meet Roland Arthur Olsen," Jenny said, holding him up.

"He looks like a keeper."

"There's coffee inside," Jenny said. "I've reused the grounds, but it's still coffee."

"When the war is over we'll have good coffee again," Millie said.

They sat in the sunlight and chatted. Roland fussed a bit, but tolerably. Jenny turned him over, like a fish, to warm his backside.

"Look at those legs and shoulders," Millie said. "He's going to be a wrestler."

"That's what my brother says," Jenny said, rocking the baby. "Uncle Emil."

Millie took a sip of her coffee. "Have they gone back to North Dakota?"

"Yes. Though my sister Sally is staying on to help out."

"I see."

"You've never met Sally," Jenny said.

"Not really." Millie was briefly silent. "How long will she stay?"

"A few days at least. We'll see how things go."

Millie cleared her throat. Looked off across the fenceless yards. "I should mention. Sally was out in your backyard early this morning."

"Yes," Jenny said. "I was up with Roland and saw her come in."

"She took a pee."

Jenny turned.

"Chet saw her," Millie continued. "He's an early bird. Likes to listen to the radio and hear the war news. He said there was a farm boy from north of town killed in Italy. Anyway, Chet was making coffee when he looked out the kitchen window and there was your sister taking a pee on the lawn."

"I see."

"'She just hiked up her gown and squatted,' he said."

"She's not used to town life, I suppose."

"I don't mind that Chet saw her," Millie continued. "But I wouldn't want my boys to see that."

Jenny had no answer.

"This is town." Millie gestured to the houses around, to the neighborhood. "You can't just pee anywhere."

***

Sally and John came back from the playground a long time later. Jenny expected John to be faint with hunger, but he was lively and pink-faced from too much sun.

"I was just about to come look for you."

"We walked to the gas station," Sally said.

"I had peanuts," John said.

"I let him turn the crank on the coin box," Sally said. "He thought we should have gotten more peanuts."

"The Holiday Station?" Jenny said. "That's a long way."

"We had the wagon," Sally said.

"Can we read?" John asked Sally.

"Sure."

"He'll wear you out with his books," Jenny said.

Sally shrugged. "What else is there to do in town?"

That afternoon John took a long nap, and while Roland snored in his bassinet, Jenny showed Sally around the laundry room, especially the new, square, side-by-side GE "Filter-flo" washer with matching drier.

"I never knew they had pink washing machines," Sally said.

"That was Arthur," Jenny said. "He wanted me to have the newest style."

She showed Sally the settings, the Fingertip Selector buttons, how to add detergent. Sally nodded but stayed back.

"They're foolproof," Jenny said. "Once the clothes have rinsed and spun, they go into the drier." She swung open the round door. Held it open like one of those tidy housewives in the newspaper ads.

Sally nodded.

"Would you like to try a load of your clothes?" Jenny asked.

"Maybe tomorrow. I should get busy in the kitchen."

Jenny had a glass of milk while Sally laid out red potatoes for peeling.

"I hope you'll take advantage of town life," Jenny said. "The new washing machine, the bathtub, toilets. I've come to take indoor plumbing for granted."

Sally glanced her way.

"We're on the city sewer. No septic tanks to worry about. In the bathtub, you can use all the hot water you want."

Sally began to peel potatoes.

"Remember how Emil always bothered us about that?" Jenny said. "How much hot water does a person need?" she said in Emil's voice.

"I could try the tub," Sally said. "But I don't want to get too used to it."

Jenny didn't say anything about the peeing incident, nor did she mention it to Arthur. The whole thing… Chet looking out the window, Millie with her overly cheerful laugh, her not wanting her boys seeing "that." All of it stuck in her craw like a week-old donut. John had taken to waking up at night from bad dreams about trolls. "He's far too young for such stories," Jenny said to Sally. And the guest bedroom and the house itself had begun to smell barny, like Sally. Her cooking "help" was bacon every morning for breakfast and scalloped potatoes and ham for supper. Arthur gradually took over supper duties.

***

On the morning of Sally's sixth day, there came a knock on the door.

"I'll get it," Sally said.

Millie drew back from Sally, who towered over her. "Sally, I was thinking you were off with John."

"No."

"Well, as it turns out," Millie said, "I came to talk to Jenny."

"If you want to take your walk now, that would be fine," Jenny said.

When Sally and John were off, Millie said, "It happened again."

Jenny shifted Roland to her other arm.

"I saw her do it this time," Millie said. "Peed right on your lawn."

"I don't think it hurts the grass."

"Soon she'll be peeing in broad daylight," Millie said.

"I've thought about it," Jenny said, "and here's how I see it. If you don't like Sally peeing on the lawn, our lawn, then don't look out your goddamned window."

"I beg your pardon?"

Baby Roland wailed.

"I'm sorry." Jenny began to rock Roland.

"I should think so."

"Sorry that I frightened you, little man," Jenny cooed to Roland.

"Well then." Millie stood. "Chet says that if this continues, we might have to talk to the police."

Jenny turned to her. "*Dra til helvete!*"

"What does that mean?"

"Figure it out." When Millie was gone, Jenny sat a long while rocking Roland, then called Arthur at work.

"Is everything okay?" he said.

"Sally has to go home."

***

Arthur took the next day off from work to drive Sally back to Skye, which would be faster than waiting for Emil. Jenny, between nursing Roland and watching after John, made them a big lunch for the road.

"Did you take your pills?"

"Yes."

"Do you have your ration book for gas?"

"Yes."

"Emil will give you gas for the trip home," Jenny said. "Don't let him 'forget.'"

"I'll be late for supper," Arthur said, "what with the lower speed limit now."

"Okay. I'll be waiting." Jenny gave them both a hug.

After Arthur and Sally left, it was just fussy Roland and whiny John, who was sad that Aunt Sally had to go.

"Park," he said.

"We can't go to the park," Jenny said. "We have baby Roland now. I have to watch him."

Which set John to wailing.

Which in turn set Roland to wailing.

On toward noon, dizzy from hunger and lack of sleep, Jenny saw Millie Arneson sitting on her porch having a cigarette. She stepped out. "I'm sorry," she called across.

Millie exhaled without turning. "*Dra til helvete*," she said. "I figured out what that means."

"I was exhausted."

Millie nodded.

"And anyway, Arthur took Sally home so you won't have to worry about our damn grass anymore." She went back inside and let the door slam.

She was trying to make a sandwich, nurse Roland, and tend to John when there was a tap-tap on the door. Millie let herself in. "You go sit with Roland, and I'll finish lunch. Then, if Little Man will sleep, I'll take John for an hour, and you can have a nap."

Jenny began to sob.

With Millie's help, the three of them rebounded that afternoon. Jenny was able to put in a hot tuna dish for Arthur, who dragged in after six.

"How did it go with Sally?"

Arthur went straightaway to the cupboard for his glass of whiskey. "It was a long day."

Chapter Sixteen
The Wagner Farm

The farm boy killed in the Italian campaign was Olive Wagner's son, Billy. "Oh no." Jenny put down the local paper.

Arthur looked her way.

"The Wagner boy."

"Yes, I heard."

Jenny took a breath. "We should go to the funeral."

"Okay, we will," Arthur said. "It's patriotic. You don't have to know a family to support them."

Billy Wagner's memorial came in September. There was a casket, though it was empty, or "mostly so," as someone whispered. Olive Wagner did not once look directly at the flag-draped coffin with Billy's army photo atop.

After the service, and the procession to the cemetery, and the taps, and the rifle volley, there was lunch back at the Lutheran church basement. Arthur was surprised that Jenny wanted to stay for all of it, and more than happy to escort her and his two boys through the lunch line. He steered John and carried Roland on his shoulder, his family on parade. There were ham buns, red JELL-O, marshmallow salad, cookies, brownies, black coffee. As people got food into their bellies, the sound volume in the basement rose, and the tragedy of the day receded before a cheerful buzz. The Arnesons came over to say hello. Chet avoided eye contact, and they moved on soon enough. At one point Olive Wagner sat alone, holding her coffee in both hands, staring into the cup. Jenny went over.

"Who's this?" Olive touched Roland's fat, little cheek.

"My new one."

"Congratulations." Olive's sandy-colored hair was newly shot with gray, and her eyelids hung reddened.

"Thank you."

They were silent.

Olive looked across the church basement to her husband, standing with other men, including Herr Schmidt. "How can men do that?" she murmured.

Dennis Wagner, a slim, wiry man in a stiff-looking suit, glanced back to his wife, then turned reluctantly to the other fellows. The farmers had ruddy faces, sun-tanned up to their cap lines, and bone-white above. Arnie Schmidt laughed at something and clapped Dennis on the shoulder.

"Talk to each other like nothing has happened," Olive finished.

"I suppose we all have our way of dealing with things."

"Dennis and I are moving to Seattle," she said. "There's work in the airline plants, plus the winters are mild. They say a person can grow roses all year 'round."

"Well," Jenny said. "That will be a change."

"Yes," Olive said emphatically.

The hum of voices and clink of silverware continued.

"May I ask," Jenny said, "what will become of your farm?"

"Arnie Schmidt wants to buy us out." Olive glanced at the men. "He and Dennis have been talking."

Jenny looked to the men, then back to Olive. "I'd be interested in buying it."

Olive turned. "You yourself?"

"Yes."

Olive blinked, then held her gaze on Jenny. "Why shouldn't you?"

"It's good land," Jenny began. "And you've kept the house and yard so nice. Those rose bushes by the mailbox are so pink and fragrant."

"You could move out of town," Olive said. "Your boys would have some room to breathe." Her eyes went to the baby. "They get big before you know it."

Herr Schmidt looked across at Jenny and Olive Wagner, who sat close now. His smile slipped.

"Though I don't want to create trouble for you with Dennis," Jenny said. "If you've already been talking with Schmidt."

"I'll take care of that," Olive said, turning away from the men. "It's time we women did more for each other."

"I feel badly even mentioning the farm today."

"That first time when you stopped by," Olive said, "when you helped me pin the sheets… and Billy was asleep upstairs? Do you remember?"

"Of course."

"Dennis was combining, and he could have used Billy's help with the wagon, but I told him to rest, catch up on his sleep. Truth be told, Billy was never much for farming. I think that's why he enlisted, to get away." She looked to the glass block window at the top of the basement wall, its watery light.

"I'll go to the bank tomorrow," Jenny said. "I don't think there'll be any trouble. Whatever price per acre you think is fair."

Olive looked once more to the men, then squeezed Jenny's hand and released it. "It's settled then."

Chapter Seventeen
The Christmas Radio

The war occupied world news that fall, and Jenny's boys and the Wagner farm occupied her on the home front. Arthur was cool to the idea of owning "still more land plus a house to keep up." But he could not argue with the rental income. One of Arnie Schmidt's sons and family moved into the Wagner house the day after Olive and Dennis left for Seattle, and they were prompt with their monthly check. The first snow came early, in mid-November, a signal of quieter days ahead.

"On the farm, the first snow was always a kind of relief," Jenny said.

Arthur looked up from his newspaper. "How so?"

"It meant that the biggest work was over," she said. "The planting, the growing, the harvesting."

"I hadn't thought of snow that way," Arthur said and returned to his reading.

The flu at Jenny's house put off a big family Thanksgiving. "Let's look ahead to Christmas," Dag said over the phone. "We'll make it extra special."

On Christmas Day the weather cooperated for Emil and the sisters' trip down to Crookston. At the toot of a horn out front, John rushed to the window. "Uncle Emil!"

Jenny took in a breath. "Indeed, it is."

"We can do this." Arthur gave her a brief, one-armed hug.

There came clumping on the porch, boot stamping, and suddenly the house was full.

"Merry Christmas," Arthur called from the kitchen.

"You need an apron like Arthur's," Dag said to Emil. "I should make you one."

"I don't need no apron," Emil replied.

Sally wore pressed dungarees and a new, wide-knit red sweater.

"Don't you look nice," Jenny said.

"Hello everyone." Sally's voice was surprisingly clear.

"I knitted her a new sweater," Dag said. "An early Christmas present."

"The arms aren't long enough," Emil said. "Nobody's got longer arms than Sally."

"The arms are just fine." Jenny gave her sisters a hug.

"Smells good in here," Dag said.

"My turkey needs some time," Arthur replied.

"We've got all day," Emil said and made a quick lunge to scoop up John, who shrieked with joy.

Dinner came together slowly but steadily, each dish a part of the main. Dill pickles (selected, baby cukes no bigger than a thumb). Beet pickles (really, pickled beets, though the former name had stuck long ago). Baked acorn squash, small ones cut in half and with a shiny basin of butter and brown sugar. Dag's dinner rolls with a perfect, brown tan across their crowns, that broke open warm, flaky, and white. And the turkey itself, Arthur's burnished masterpiece, stuffed with homemade dressing, little cubes of dried bread suffused with juice and spices (perhaps a bit long on sage). Gravy, pale in its narrow boat, and which, before stirring, carried a glassy sheen.

Left on his own, John turned on the radio. General Eisenhower's voice filled the room. The new allied commander in Europe sounded like every other farmer from the Midwest.

"Turn that off, please," Jenny said.

Arthur stepped over. Paused to listen.

"Now," Jenny said.

Arthur killed the radio. "Ike will get it done over there."

"Should leave it to the Brits," Emil said. "They're ready to fight a war, and we're not."

"Hush, you fellows," Dag said. "We're not talking war and politics today."

"If you don't talk about them, they just keep happening," Emil replied.

Arthur bristled. "We need to trust our elected leaders."

"They're bought and paid for," Emil said. "Cargill, the Rockefellers, Carnegie, and the rest of the rich men." He turned sideways to spit, then remembered he was inside.

"Carnegie gave America libraries," Jenny said.

"Libraries are the least those crooks should do for us," Emil muttered.

"Shush." Dag shook a long-handled spoon at Emil.

John laughed at Aunt Dag's spoon, and conversation turned back to the day at hand. To family life.

For dinner, Jenny and Sally sat with John and Roland at the kids' table, and Dag waited on everybody. Midway through the meal, Roland fussed—he was four months now—and Jenny excused herself to feed him. In the bedroom with the door closed, she nursed him. Beyond was the clink of silverware, voices, a sharp trill of laughter from John (likely something Uncle Emil had done). Roland gurgled, then went back to work at her breast. She touched his cheek. "You're never going to war," she whispered. "You or John."

In the kitchen, John warbled with laughter.

"Emil, that's a bad thing to teach him," Dag said.

"Yes," Arthur said, voice muffled. "We don't want any bad habits."

When Jenny returned with Roland, John said immediately, "Uncle Emil drank the gravy."

"It was empty," Emil said of the little boat. "I just tipped it up to get the last drops."

After pumpkin pie and ice cream there were presents. Surprising everyone, Sally said, "I'll be Santa."

Dag looked at Jenny. Sally began to distribute gifts.

Emil had carved trolls for the boys, never uglier and more detailed, right down to warts on their chins.

"Big one for me," John said, and hugged it.

"And the little one for baby brother," Emil said. "He can keep it in his crib."

"If it doesn't give him nightmares," Arthur ventured.

"They're your best work," Jenny said.

"I made myself a new *kniv*," Emil replied.

Jenny's Christmas present from Emil was his old *tollekniv*, the wooden handle sanded and varnished, the small blade honed like a razor, and with a handmade sheath. Its thick grip fit her palm as if made for her hand. "Thank you, Brother. Just what a lady needs."

Arthur chuckled.

"Don't lose it," Emil said. "Or let the boys get after it."

"I'll keep it in my purse," she said. "It's the perfect size."

After presents, and when the string and wrapping paper were gathered up, Emil and Arthur went for a smoke out on the porch. Sally headed upstairs with John to play with his new toys. In the kitchen, Jenny and Dag worked on the stack of dishes.

"Sally looks and acts so much better," Jenny said.

"She does, yes." Dag didn't look up from the sink.

"But?"

Dag turned. "Remember that winter when she was working on her plan for the new chicken coop, and wouldn't tell us?"

Jenny nodded.

"*Eg aner ugler i mosen,*" Dag said. "I think she's up to something again."

Jenny patted her arm. "Well, today was wonderful."

"It was," Dag allowed.

That evening, after Emil and her sisters had left for Skye, and when Arthur and the boys, spent, had gone down early, Jenny made herself a plate of leftovers. What with a full house and all the commotion today, she hadn't eaten much. The kitchen table, bare, clean, and long with its extra leaves, was not right for one person. She drew up a rocking chair close by the radio. Turning the needle across the numbers, she paused on the British Forces Broadcasting Service. The BFBS ran a repeat broadcast of Edward R. Murrow's "Orchestrated Hell," which described, with sound effects, a Royal Air Force bombing raid over Berlin. She quickly moved the needle. Passing through dead spots and Christmas carols, she stopped on the Voice of America. "The allies are turning the tide," said the announcer, and gave details of the various United States' Corps arriving in the European Theater and then news of the Red Army's offensive "pressing Hitler on the East." She rolled the dial back the other way, landing on "Silent Night." She leaned back, closed her eyes, and, in the quiet house, heard the song as if for the first time.

Chapter Eighteen
On the Run

Sally wasn't sure they knew. About the calendar. What she had marked on it. Today was March 31st. Dag was in charge of the kitchen calendar in the new house and liked to turn the page on the last day of the month. Emil preferred the morning of the first day of the new month.

"Why be in a hurry?" he said, as always, at the end of the month. They were at breakfast.

"I'll take care of the calendar. You take care of your tractors and fields," Dag said.

"You could get up at midnight and turn the page," Sally said to him. Emil didn't reply.

"In fact, I think I'll turn it right now," Dag said with a glance to her brother.

"When you turn it early, it's like we're losing a whole day." Emil snapped his fingers. "Gone. Just like that."

"Fine by me," Dag said sharply. "I'll be happy to be done with this month and this whole winter."

Sally watched Emil from the side of her eye.

Dag stepped over to the 1944 Farmers Union calendar, with its black-lettered days and red ones for Sundays. She lifted the page. Leaned closer.

"What?" Emil said.

"Nothing," Dag replied quickly.

Sally took a sip of her hot cocoa.

Emil squinted, then got up and went over to look at the calendar. He stared at it, then returned to his place.

Dag turned away. "More coffee?"

"I'd take a splash." Emil did not look at Sally.

After she poured, Dag glanced out the window. "Looks like it's going to be sunny."

"Not so cold either," Emil said.

"We'll get out today, get some fresh air," Dag said to Sally. "Do us all good after these long days inside."

So now they all knew, and nobody spoke about it. The mark, the square, drawn around April 15th. It was her little girl's tenth birthday.

As the first days of April turned toward mid-month, Dag and Emil watched her ever closer. Watched her like the red tail hawks that floated high above the chicken yard, heads cocked, always spying, marking everything that moved. On April 15th, Sally did her daily chores. Came in for lunch at straight up noon. Late that night, floorboards creaked outside her door, then went silent. It was Dag. Sally pretended to snore.

She let the following day pass too. Did her chores. Carried water. Helped Emil clean wheat seed for planting. She scooped shovels-full into the old, red Clipper fanning mill with its belts and pulleys and clattering sieves and little gas motor. With a bandana across his nose, Emil sprinkled the wheat from a bottle of clear liquid labeled with a skull and crossbones, seed treatment against smut. Afterward they loaded sharp-smelling gunny sacks into the pickup.

"If you take the tractor and seeder, I can drive the pickup out to the field," Sally said.

He looked.

"Save you from having to walk back," she said.

"Okay."

She drove behind him in the dust of the tractor and grain drill. At field-side they filled the grain hopper. She leveled off the seed while Emil checked the fill tubes, greased the discs. Then he was ready to plant.

"I'll take my truck keys."

She handed them over. He kept them in his pocket by day. Under his pillow at night. The coil wire to the tractor engine he kept behind a loose board in the machine shed. She had eyes.

She waited until planting was done a full week later. The next Saturday, when Emil took Dag to town for groceries, she packed a big lunch and some clothes, fresh socks especially, then found the tractor's coil wire. At the gas tank she filled the tractor with fuel, and also a spare gas can, which she strapped behind the iron seat. After choking the carburetor, she pressed the starter button. The engine caught, and she drove down the lane to the township road and then south.

In road gear, the tractor's speed blew back her cap. She caught it. Jammed it lower across her forehead. Chilled air from the ditches and their melt-water flowed over her. She buttoned her shirt to the throat, and her jacket as well. Pulled her cap brim still lower.

She passed fields with men planting. A tractor, a grain drill, a pickup, a wagon. The same as Emil. Everything everywhere was the same. The men looked up, gave short waves, then turned back to their work.

South of Hoople, her tractor surged and sputtered. She pulled over, added fuel from the spare can, drove on. This time she took the township roads toward Larimore. The route, the map, was in her head. By two p.m., the tractor's engine again huffed and stuttered. She pulled off the road at a small flowage, a culvert and some Cottonwood, and parked the tractor out of sight. She adjusted her shirt, tightening the band across her breasts, then gathered up her satchel and headed back to the road. Set out walking. When the sound of a vehicle approached from behind, she turned and stuck out her thumb.

That night she slept in a corncrib south of Hillsboro. She wormed down into the ear corn, pulling the crackly husks about her until only her face was visible. In the morning, she walked fast to warm up. Kept her face to the south, the low red sun warm on her left cheek.

***

On Sunday morning the phone rang. Arthur picked up, then handed it to Jenny. "Emil."

"Oh dear," she said.

"She's on the run," Emil said.

Jenny listened. "Why didn't you call me yesterday?"

There were a few seconds of uncomfortable silence. Jenny could feel Emil struggling.

"It was late. By the time you got here it would be dark. Figured it could wait till morning."

She knew arguing wouldn't do any good. "Let me talk to Arthur. I'll call you back." Carefully she replaced the receiver.

"What?" Arthur said.

She turned.

"You have to go," Arthur said.

"Are you sure? Can you handle things here?"

"I'll call your friend, Edith, if need be. Go."

Jenny left within the hour. On a chilly day with broken clouds, she pressed the speed limit past black fields, some seeded, some not, and arrived at the home farm two hours later.

"We were in town," Dag said, twisting her hands. "Our Saturday shopping. When we got back, she was gone."

"She took the tractor," Emil said.

"I thought you—"

"She must have seen where I hid the coil wire."

135

"There's food gone from the ice box," Dag added. "Her coat, hat, boots too."

"And a gas can," Emil said. "Enough to get her most of the way there."

"She's going to Fargo, we're sure," Dag said. "Her little girl turned ten last week."

"Every April I worry," Jenny said.

"She was acting funny last week," Emil added.

"We watched her close," Dag continued. "But after April fifteenth passed and she didn't act up, we figured we were in the clear."

"She fooled us," Emil said.

"The main thing now is to find her," Jenny replied.

She drove them south on gravel toward Fargo.

"She won't take the main road," Emil said. "She's too smart for that."

"There were maps under her mattress," Dag said.

"Anything marked on them? Roads? Towns?"

"No," Dag said.

"What's top speed on your tractor?" Jenny asked.

"In road gear, maybe ten or twelve miles per hour," Emil said. "With our town trip, and waiting for you, she has several hours on us."

"I hope she can stay warm," Dag said.

Dust billowed behind Arthur's Oldsmobile as Jenny sped south through Hoople. Past the turnoff to Ops. On toward Inkster. Ahead and all around were empty fields and the road ahead.

Jenny slowed.

"What?" Dag asked.

"On the tractor it would take her all day and then some to get to Fargo."

"She's taking the train," Emil said suddenly. "From Grand Forks."

Jenny turned east at the next crossroad, and within a half hour they arrived in Grand Forks and headed to the depot.

"Look for the tractor," Emil said. "She won't park it close up. It'll be hid somewhere."

There was no orange tractor. And no sighting of Sally boarding the afternoon train to Fargo.

"Are you sure?" Jenny said to the clerk behind the window. "Quite a tall woman. Thin. Short hair."

"Wearing trousers and a man's cap," Dag added.

"Nobody like that," he said. "Why? Is she in trouble?"

They returned to the Oldsmobile. "*Vi må tenke på dette,*" Emil said. He lit a cigarette.

Dag began to sniffle. "What good does thinking about it do? We have no idea where she is."

Emil exhaled a thin stream of smoke.

"I'll take you home," Jenny said. "For now."

"We need a bite to eat," Dag said. "We can think better on a full stomach."

Back at the farm, Dag made cold ham sandwiches and coffee after which, and following some debate, Jenny and Emil drove to town to the sheriff's office. It was manned by a young, thick-shouldered deputy, the weekend guy, who doubled as jailer. He took notes on a yellow pad.

"But this is not a complaint," he repeated.

"No," Jenny said.

"She took your tractor, but she didn't steal it."

"She didn't steal it," Emil said. "We're family."

"She's a runaway," Jenny said. "That's what we mean to say."

"How old is she?"

"Twenty-eight," Jenny said.

The deputy leaned back in his chair. "Let me get this straight. She's an adult, she lives at home, she took the tractor, and you're not charging her with anything."

"That's right," Emil said.

The deputy put down his pencil. "I should call the sheriff. See what he says."

"What about Lars Torgerson?" Jenny said. "We know him and he knows Sally."

The jailer shrugged. "He's chief deputy now. That would save bothering the sheriff."

They drove to the east side of Skye, a newer neighborhood with smaller houses. In his yard, Lars Torgerson was playing ball with a toddler.

Jenny stopped the car. Got out.

"Jenny. Emil. Long time no see." He wore a baseball cap.

"It's about Sally," Emil said. "She's on the run."

"Yes. Bud gave the gist of it on the phone."

A woman came out to the front step. She was short, not unpretty, and quite pregnant. "Everything okay?"

"No problem," Lars called.

"Supper's ready soon."

After Jenny filled in the details, Lars glanced toward his house, then wrapped an arm around his little boy. "Run to Momma. I'll come soon." The little boy grabbed the ball and headed off.

"What do we do?" Jenny asked.

Lars pursed his lips. "Well, Bud was right. She hasn't broken any laws."

"Yet," Jenny said. "There's the 'no contact' matter in Fargo from her little girl's family."

"That would be a problem," Lars said.

"We don't want to see her in jail," Emil added.

"We don't." Lars bit his lower lip. "So, we've got to find her."

"Thank you," Jenny said.

Lars looked to his house. "We were supposed to go to my wife's folks' place in Saint John for Sunday dinner, but I'll tell her we've got a missing person. I'll make some calls and try to round up a search party."

"*Tusen takk*," Emil said.

"We'll meet at your farm first thing in the morning," Lars said. They turned to go.

"I'm glad you came to me," Lars said. "I would have wanted to know."

Back at the home farm, Jenny stopped the car. Emil and Dag got out. She did not.

"Could you stay the night?" Dag asked. "It's too late to drive home."

Jenny let out a breath. "Let me call Arthur and see how things are with the boys."

On the home phone in Crookston there was no crying or wailing. John laughed at something.

"Things are just fine," Arthur said. "Your friends Edith and Sara are here. We've had our supper and they're doing dishes."

"Hello Jenny, hello!" they called in the background.

"We haven't found Sally," Jenny said.

"Oh dear," Arthur said.

"We have a search party lined up first thing in the morning."

"Then you must stay on," Arthur said.

"That's why I called," Jenny said.

"We'll be fine," Arthur replied. "Don't even think about us."

"I'm lucky to have you."

"Don't get all weepy on me," Arthur said. "You've got a big day ahead of you."

That night she slept in Sally's bed. Buried her face in Sally's pillow. Took in the woody scent of her hair.

***

Two pickups and a car arrived at the farm just after sunup and the searchers assembled by Lars. One man limped, one had an eye missing, another, a corn-picker hand.

Dag clucked her tongue. "Odds and sods," she murmured.

"It's easy to forget about the war," Jenny replied.

"Beggars can't be choosers, I guess," Dag said.

"*Nød lærer naken kvinne å spinne,*" Emil muttered.

Jenny turned his way. "A naked woman must learn to spin?"

"Pretty good," he said and tugged her sleeve.

Dag's lower lip trembled.

"Buck up now," Jenny murmured. "We're going to find Sally."

In one of the pickups a dog barked, then finished with a long, mournful note.

"I brought my coon hound," one of the men said.

"Please, not a dog," Jenny said to Lars.

"The goal is to find her, right?" he answered. He waved the group into a circle. "Listen up, everybody. I've called down to the sheriff's offices in the counties south of us. Walsh, Traill, Grand Forks, and Cass. The fellows there are on the lookout, and as of now so are we. We'll take different roads in five vehicles." He gave them the gathering points, the time to meet. "Any questions?"

They shook their heads.

"We'll find her," Lars said and touched Jenny's arm.

And so, at eight a.m., the convoy left the farm.

Jenny rode with Lars in the sheriff's car. Emil and Dag came behind in Jenny's Oldsmobile. One by one the trailing cars and pickups branched off to other roads.

Lars glanced in his rearview mirror. "One of these days we'll have two-way radios in our cars."

"That would be useful," Jenny said.

"Like telephones in the home," Lars said. He winked at Jenny.

"With Emil it was like pulling teeth," she replied, "but he couldn't do without it now."

"He's something, your brother."

They rode along in silence.

"Someday it would be nice to talk," Lars ventured, eyes straight ahead. "About Sally. About everything that happened."

Jenny looked his way.

"There was no time to say anything during the trial, and never a good time after," Lars said. "Life just sort of went on."

"Though not so much for Sally."

"That's the hell of it," Lars said and looked her way.

***

Their convoy gathered at the sheriff's office in Grafton, the county seat of Walsh County.

"Anything?" Dag asked quickly.

"Nothing," Lars said.

The other drivers shook their heads.

"She's on the township roads," Emil said. "She's smart."

After checking a map, they fanned out again driving south and west.

Their first break came at the police office in Larimore. An Allis-Chalmers, empty on gas, was found in a windbreak south of town.

Lars headed there, fast. A deputy sheriff's car waited. Emil and the Oldsmobile pulled up behind.

"That's it," Emil said as they walked toward the poplars. "That's my tractor."

"It was covered with branches," a fellow in a seed cap said. "If I hadn't turned that way, I'da never seen it."

"She's on foot," Lars said.

"We'll catch up with her quick, now," a fellow said. "Shall I get the dog?"

"Unless she caught a ride," Dag replied.

They turned to Dag. Who shrugged.

"Dag's right," Jenny said. "Anyone would stop for a person walking. This is North Dakota."

They drove on, scanning the trees, what few there were, and the ditches. There was no sign of her. Jenny checked the map. "If she got a ride, it might be all the way to Northwood, which looks to be about ten miles. There's nothing else out here."

Lars nodded and turned east.

In Northwood, a town of seven hundred built around a looming grain elevator, they stopped to inquire at the gas station. A woman clerk said yes, a pickup had dropped off a tall man, who had used the bathroom, then set out walking south.

"Which bathroom?" Jenny asked.

The woman stared. "Why, the men's... I think."

"How long ago?" Lars asked.

The woman shrugged. "An hour or so."

Emil stared across at the grain elevator, at the railroad tracks behind. "She might walk the rails. They're headed southeast toward Fargo."

"She likes railroad tracks," Jenny added.

"She walks them to find things," Dag said. "Not if she wanted to get somewhere and could catch a lift."

Lars nodded. He directed two of the cars to head east. "We'll head south."

A few minutes down the road, he suddenly leaned forward to peer through the windshield. Well ahead, a quarter mile, a figure walked briskly with long strides. At the sound of the cars, she turned as if for the prospect of a ride. Her hand came up to shade her eyes, and in the same motion she bolted down the ditch and across the field.

"That's her," Jenny called.

"My God," Lars said, "I've never seen anyone run like that."

"She has long legs," Jenny replied. "You'd better step on it if you want to catch her."

By the time Lars braked to a stop, Sally had disappeared behind a long windbreak that ran west. A half mile further on lay the only heavy cover, a wooded area along the Goose River.

"If she gets in the trees, it'll be hard to find her," Emil said.

"Bring the dog," Lars called.

"Please," Jenny said.

"Do you and Dag want to wait in the car?" Lars said. "Stay warm?"

"Maybe I will," Dag said. She turned away so no one could see her face.

They fanned out on each side of the windbreak, the dog meandering, sniffing. Once it bayed and surged forward. A rooster pheasant blew upward, chortling and brilliant, then glided across to a dry slough and the drainage ditch. As the men pressed on toward the woods, Jenny lagged back. To the left, or south, a dry slough narrowed toward a big culvert and a graveled, township road that ran overhead. She back-tracked and walked along the edge of the cattails. Their dry, winter-killed blades stood dense and head height. A faint trail of broken fronds led through them.

She plunged into them, leaves crackling, the wafer-thin leaves sharp on her hands and face. In the thickest of the mess, her forward motion was like swimming. Furry cattail heads broke off, their seeds floating in the late sunlight like a haze of insects. She spit them out. Kept going. The cattail slough turned to mud, and the trail of broken stalks revealed boot prints. Their stride was impossibly long, as if a giant had walked there. Gumbo sucked at her shoes, which grew enormous and heavy. She pulled herself along, cattail clump to cattail clump, their leaves biting at her cheeks.

The dense growth petered out into sluggish flowage that disappeared into a concrete culvert, its mouth wider than tall, big enough for a person to pass through. She stopped at the entrance. The pipe breathed cooler air. A tangle of blackened tree limbs mostly blocked the gray eye of the far end.

"Sally?" Her voice echoed in the tube. Water dripped.

After long moments, a soft voice said, "What?"

"It's time to go home."

Far off, the bloodhound bayed once.

"I just wanted to see her. She's ten years old now."

"I know. And you'll see her someday."

"You don't know that."

Jenny paused. "I suppose I don't. But I've come to think that nothing happens unless we try. And today, you did."

"Look where it got me."

"Something will come from this," Jenny said.

"When?" Something splashed, as if Sally had pitched a stick.

"I can't say. But life never goes on all bad or all good."

"So, I just wait?"

"That's part of it, I think."

"How long do I wait?" Sally asked. "My whole life?"

"Not that long," Jenny said. "I promise."

Stooped, muddy and hatless, Sally emerged. Jenny took her hand and led her to the car. Dag hurried to meet them, weeping for joy. She hugged Sally and did not let go.

"Your shoes," she said to them. "Your pants, your skirt."

"We don't care about our shoes or clothes," Jenny said.

"True. We don't," Dag replied. "We'll get you new ones at home."

Back by Arthur's Oldsmobile, they ditched their shoes.

Sally looked around at the pickups and the sheriff's car. "I'm in trouble, I suppose."

"You haven't done anything against the law. We were worried, that's all."

Jenny shivered, then started the engine to warm the car. She honked the horn to signal the men, then sat in the back seat with her sisters.

"We're getting Arthur's upholstery all muddy," Sally said. "He'll be mad."

"*Den tid, den sorg,*" Jenny replied.

"And your face," Sally said. "Your cheeks have little cuts."

"Those cattail leaves were sharp," Jenny answered. "I'm not as tall as you."

"You look a fright," Dag said and touched Jenny's cheeks.

"Thanks a lot," Jenny answered.

"I have a clean hankie in my purse and some water I brought for Sally," Dag said.

Jenny closed her eyes as Dag tended to her face. "Ouch!"

"Hold still."

"Where did you sleep last night?" Jenny asked Sally.

"In a corn crib," she said. "I burrowed down in the ears. Covered myself. It wasn't so bad."

Dag let out a whimper as she dabbed at Jenny's cuts.

The three sisters were sitting arm-in-arm in the back seat when the men arrived. Jenny cranked her window down halfway.

"*Takk gud*," Emil said, and let out a breath.

"Where did you find her?" Lars asked.

"In the culvert," Jenny answered.

"Like a troll," Sally said, not meeting anyone's gaze. "That's where they live, under bridges. Underground."

"You're not a damn troll, Sally," Emil said. He opened the door and knelt close by his sisters.

"Emil's right," Lars said. "We know who the real troll is." His voice broke.

"It's okay now," Jenny murmured to him. "She's safe."

Lars took a moment to compose himself, then turned to the gathering of men. "All done here, boys. Thanks for your help. You can head on home. We got a happy ending."

***

At the farm, Dag and Emil had returned ahead of Jenny's car. Dag took charge of Sally. "I have water heating on the stove. Let's get you into the tub." While Sally was soaking, Dag washed Jenny's face with castile soap, then dabbed her cheeks with rubbing alcohol.

"That stings."

"We have to do it," Dag said. "We don't want an infection."

"Jenny's tough," Emil said.

"What's Arthur going to say?" Dag murmured as she worked.

"That's the good thing about him." Jenny's voice caught. "He never minds when I'm gone. Whatever trouble I bring home, he's quick to forgive."

"You're lucky to have him," Dag said.

"I am. I am."

Dag patted her face dry and put on more salve.

"I must look a fright."

"A bit," Dag said. She held up a hand mirror.

Jenny sucked in a breath. "Lucky I've got a husband," Jenny said. "I'd scare off any man, now."

"Stop that. You always thought Sally was the beautiful one. You're just as pretty."

"I don't even have shoes for the trip home," Jenny said.

"You can borrow a pair of mine," Dag said. "And you need to get some food in you. Emil? Set out that cold chicken and some bread."

"I am a little hungry," Jenny said. She helped Dag and Emil finish laying the table.

"If you could wait just a minute, Sally will be out of the tub and then we can eat together," Dag said.

They listened. There was no sound beyond the bathroom door.

"We should check on her," Jenny said.

She and Dag went to the bathroom door.

"Sally?"

"It's open. I don't care anymore."

Jenny followed Dag inside. Sally's knees rose up sharply from the short tub. She lay back with a washcloth over her eyes, her breasts floating in the soapy water like white flowers of lily pads. "What do you want?"

"To make sure you haven't drowned," Jenny said.

"Ha," Dag said. "That's Emil's line."

"Remember how he always nagged us about using too much hot water, or taking too long in the tub?" Jenny said.

"He still does," Sally said.

"He's getting supper on for us," Dag said. "Sit up. We'll wash your hair."

Sally obeyed. Dag poured a pitcher of warm water over her head. Jenny soaped her hair, then Dag repeated a pour and rinse.

"Done," Dag said.

Sally stepped out and accepted a towel.

"I'd forgotten," Jenny said.

"What?" Sally said, her voice muffled underneath the towel.

"How beautiful you are. With your frame, you could be in the magazines."

"It's true," Dag said. "A model for the Monkey Ward's catalogue."

"You know what happens to those catalogues," Sally said.

"What?" Dag replied.

"They end up in outhouses."

Jenny glanced at Dag.

"It's going to be okay," Dag said to Sally. "We're all home now."

Soon they all gathered at the table. Sally's clean, short hair fluffed above her ears, and her bathrobe softened her angles. They sat in their usual order, Sally between Dag and Jenny, Emil nearest the woodstove.

"How are the boys?" Dag asked Jenny.

Jenny brought them up to date.

"John's going to be a ball player." Emil passed the bread. "He can throw a kittenball like a boy twice his age."

"You never know how children turn out," Dag said. "What they'll do, where they'll go."

"Like me?" Sally asked.

"No," Dag said quickly. "You turned out just fine."

"That's not true," Sally said, but bent to her food.

They took their time eating. No one hurried. Midway, Jenny let out a breath and leaned back in her chair. Checked the wall clock.

"Could you stay the night?" Dag asked. "It will be very late by the time you get home."

"I should get home. It's been a long day."

"I can make up a nice bed on the Chesterfield," Dag added.

"You should stay," Sally murmured.

After a pause, Jenny said, "Okay. I will. Let me call Arthur first. Collect," she said to Emil.

"Just call him," Emil said.

"Big spender," Jenny said, with a wink to her sisters.

Dag giggled. Sally hunched her shoulders to hold in a laugh.

Arthur was happy to hear from her, and happy that she was not driving at night. "It's so terribly dark up there in farm country."

"Kiss the boys. I'll be home in the morning."

After a cup of hot cocoa, and after Sally had gone up to her room, Jenny fell onto the Chesterfield in her clothes.

"I can find you a nightgown," Dag said.

"I'm too tired." She let Dag cover her up. Put more salve on her cheeks.

"It's so nice being together again," Dag murmured. "Like a real family."

***

Jenny awoke to moonlight through the lace curtains, a veil of black and white hanging on the breath of the house. Midnight, only. She lit a stick match and then the table lantern. Went to the door. In the yard, the Oldsmobile gleamed under a big, pinkish moon. Nearly full, it dimmed the stars around. She crossed the silvery yard to the outhouse where, door open, she peed.

Back in the house, she lay under her blanket with eyes open. The moonlight crawled the floor with impossible slowness. She turned face into the Chesterfield. It carried a faint scent of kerosene. After long minutes of trying to get comfortable, she sat up. Lit the lamp again. At the table she wrote a note. *I couldn't*

148

sleep, so will head home. I'll drive carefully, don't worry. It's nearly a full moon, anyway. Love, Jenny. Leaning in, she blew out the flame.

In the car, she eased the door shut and started the engine. She waited for an upstairs lamp to come on. The windows remained dark. Leaving the headlights off, driving easily by moonlight, she headed down the lane. The trick to driving in full dark without headlamps was to look a few degrees aslant, follow the ghost road in the side of one's eye. Tonight, under the round, pinkish moon, she needed no such help.

Reaching the blacktop, she pulled out the headlight knob. The yellow beams pitched forward weakly in the moonlight. "Who needs you?" she murmured. She pushed in the knob, then drove without headlights at highway speed along the washed, illuminated fields. Why not, as Emil might say, save the battery?

Some miles south, a car approached, its oncoming light at first a single eye, then separating into two. At the last moment she pulled her headlamp knob. The approaching car swerved—a flinch of surprise—and the driver let out a long blast of the horn.

She laughed and drove on.

***

The closer to home, the faster she sped. Arthur and the boys were doubtless sleeping. He did not snore, another matter she took for granted about him. She would ease into the house, then into a warm bed and a warm body to hug. Maybe she would forget her nightgown. Give Arthur a middle-of-the-night surprise. It's how things worked best with him—unplanned and quick.

At two a.m. the streets of Crookston were quiet. The grain elevator rose up tall and square-sided, its tin shining. Beyond loomed the white dome of the courthouse. The only traffic light was green, though it turned yellow and then red as she approached. She braked briefly, looked both ways, then drove through.

Arriving at her street, she parked in the alley before their garage and eased out without slamming her car door. No reason to wake up Chet and Millie, who were nosy enough as it was.

Slipping into the house, she thought to go upstairs—check on the boys. Down the hall, a blade of light showed beneath their bedroom door. Arthur was still up. Though her surprise would not be complete, a warm tide, a flush of love, passed through her. She unbuttoned her blouse on the way.

The door was locked.

"Arthur?"

A grunt. Sudden thudding. Silence.

"Arthur?"

"One moment."

Finally, the door opened to Arthur, wrapped in a sheet. Behind, the bed was rumpled, the room rank-smelling.

"You're home." Arthur was red-faced and sweaty.

"Is there someone here?" She clutched her blouse shut.

After a long beat of silence, from the below far side of the bed, like a prairie dog peeping from a hole, rose a face. It was the young man from the church choir, Michael Clark.

"I'm sorry," he whimpered. His shoulders were bare.

"As am I," Arthur began, his face crimson. "I've long been meaning to explain some things."

Jenny looked from Michael to Arthur and back. "I've been such a fool."

Arthur raised his hand as if to say more. His eyeballs rolled back white, and he followed his hand forward, tipping full length, face down, nothing to break his fall, with a thud that jolted the floorboards.

"Arthur?" Jenny tried to roll him over.

"Art?" Michael hurried over, clutching a sheet about him. He, too, smelled strongly.

"Help me turn him."

On his back, Arthur's tongue lolled out, and his eyeballs remained white. She shook his face. "Arthur?"

"Do something," Michael called.

She shook him. His head lolled.

"Please," Michael said, his voice cracking.

"Shhh." She took up his wrist and closed her eyes.

"Well? Is there a pulse?"

"I'm not sure. I think he's had a heart attack." Her voice broke.

"Arthur!" Michael cried. He pulled his arms to lift him upright.

"Please. The boys are sleeping." She leaned closer and held his limp wrist to her ear.

"Anything?" Michael said.

"Shhhh." She listened long moments, then shook her head. "Nothing."

"We have to call someone," Michael said, his voice cracking. "The doctor. The police."

Jenny let down Arthur's arm. Smoothed the hair on his chest. "Oh Arthur, you old fool."

Michael pulled on his clothes. "I'll call."

"No." She buttoned her blouse all the way.

Michael stared.

"I mean… and say what to them?" she finished.

Michael turned back to Arthur and his open, staring eyes.

"We need to think this through, Michael," Jenny said. "Put your clothes on. We need a plan."

Chapter Nineteen
The Blue Magazine

When the police, and then the coroner, arrived, the bedroom windows were open for fresh air, and Arthur lay on the floor, dressed in pajamas, his eyes closed. The bed, tidied, had one side turned down. Michael, fully clothed and with hair combed, waited in the living room.

"I came home and found him," Jenny said. "I called Michael Clark, they're friends from church choir, and then you."

Frank Rezac, the Crookston police chief, a big man with hooded eyes made heavier by the early hour, nodded. He stayed out of the coroner's way, his gaze slowly traversing the room. The coroner touched the back of his hand to Arthur's neck. Worked Arthur's fingers. His wrist. "Warm. No rigor mortis. He's died within the hour."

"I knew I should have come home." Jenny's voice quavered. "I was up in Skye visiting my family. I didn't want to drive in the dark. But then I got worried about Arthur and the boys, or maybe just lonesome, so I got up in the middle of the night and drove back."

Michael appeared in the doorway. "It's not your fault."

The police chief and the coroner stared. "What?" the chief said.

"Surprising him, he means," Jenny said. "It was likely Arthur's heart. I had to keep after him to take his pills. His grandfather died young of heart trouble."

"How old was Art?" the coroner asked.

"Thirty-six." Jenny and Michael spoke at the same time.

"Finally found him a wife, had his boys," the coroner said. "Then boom." He snapped his fingers.

"Art was a good man," the chief said. "All for the town."

Michael wept. Jenny steered him back to the living room. Her legs felt numb and heavy.

***

The church parking lot overflowed. The pews were packed. Jenny, escorted by her family, wore black. She had thought of wearing a widow's veil to cover her beat-up face, the fine red cattail cuts on her cheeks. She wondered if there would be scars.

Sally held John's hand. In his school clothes and polished shoes, he was never a handsomer lad. Emil carried Roland (already too heavy for Dag) on his shoulder. From this new height, Roland looked around the church wide-eyed and pleased. The six pall bearers included Colby Hewitt, bank president, Norbert Smith from the assessor's office, and three men from the Chamber of Commerce, Rotary, and the Elks Club. Sam LaBonte was Jenny's choice for the last slot. Shined up and shaven, he wore a yellowed white shirt, an old wool tie, and one of Arthur's sport coats. On his side of the casket, Sam walked stiffly and straight, carrying his weight as if Arthur were a president or a king. She dropped her head. Stared at her hands. Tried not to think.

The sermon ran long and Emil fidgeted. Afterward Edith Klapperich declaimed a poem. She chose A. E. Housman's "To an Athlete Dying Young," which she presented from memory and with the passion of a stage actress. In the moment of silence following, it seemed possible that Arthur once had been a star athlete. The pastor forgot what came next and had to check the program.

"Are you holding up?" Dag murmured.

"I'm okay," Jenny said. She sneaked a look at her wristwatch.

They went out from the church, Jenny first behind the casket, to swelling organ music. Once outside, it was straightaway to the cemetery for the burial. Emil drove Arthur's shiny Oldsmobile. The cortege, led by Frank Rezac in the chief's car, red cherry flashing, turned into "the stiller town," as Housman wrote, of Greenwood Cemetery. They passed a small, fieldstone building.

Dag shivered. "I hope I don't die in winter."

Jenny shushed her.

"What do you mean, Aunt Dag?"

Emil glanced back at John. "If you croak in winter, they keep you in that shed until the ground thaws in the spring. Then they bury you."

"Okay," John said easily.

"There'll be lunch afterward," Dag said quickly to John. "Are you hungry?"

"Yes," he said immediately.

"I could eat," Sally murmured.

Jenny covered her mouth, but the laugh escaped.

***

Two days after the funeral, Chief Rezac stopped by the house. He pushed back his hat. "I wanted to see how you're doing."

"My sisters are here for a spell," Jenny said. "They're helping with the house and the boys."

"That's nice," the chief said. "That's what family is for."

"Coffee?" Dag called across.

"Had mine," the chief said. "Too much gives me indigestion."

"Can we play outside?" John called to Sally.

"Get your coat."

Dag came over to take Roland. "We'll all go out so you and the chief can talk."

When the house was quiet, Chief Rezac cleared his throat. "I wanted to ask you a little more about the night Art died."

"Okay."

The chief shifted on his feet. "Your next-door neighbors, Chet and Millie, mentioned there was a car parked down the street."

"Yes?" Jenny said.

"All evening, they said. It was still there when I arrived."

Jenny waited.

"I know the car," the chief said. "It belongs to Mike Clark."

Jenny let out a breath. "Please sit."

The chief took off his hat, moved a toy, then sat on the edge of the Chesterfield.

"I came home unexpectedly," she said. "In the middle of the night."

"Okay."

"When I found the two men together, at first I didn't understand," Jenny said. "Then it hit me like a lightning bolt. Arthur was a homosexual. I had been fooling myself ever since we married."

The chief stroked his chin. Took his time before speaking. "We always wondered a bit about Arthur. But then when he married…"

"Wait here." She went to the bedroom and returned with a magazine. "I've been trying to figure things out, think of what signs I had missed. I found this in Arthur's closet."

The sheriff took it. "A blue magazine."

"All men and boys," Jenny said. "The writing, what there is of it, is in Swedish."

The chief set the magazine face down. "When you found the two men together, Arthur was still alive?"

"Yes," Jenny said. "I'm sorry I misled you."

The chief pursed his lips.

"He fell over right before our eyes," Jenny said. "It must have been the shock of being caught."

"After he died, did you or Mike Clark move the body or in any way try to conceal what had happened?"

"Only to put on his pajamas," Jenny said. "It seemed like the least we could do."

The chief nodded. He stood, and after a pause said, "I'll take the magazine. You won't see it again. And I believe that's that."

"That's that?"

"I see no reason to add any of this to the report."

"And Michael Clark?"

"I'll speak privately with him." The chief put on his hat.

"I can't thank you enough." They shook hands.

"Art was all for our town," the chief said. "Nothing changes that."

Section Three: The 1950s

Chapter Twenty
Growing Family

On May 12, 1956, a warm bright Saturday morning, Jenny loaded the station wagon. She and the kids were overdue for a trip up to Skye. Every month or so, Jenny drove to North Dakota to check on Emil, Dag, and Sally at the home farm. "Or so" had grown, as the years passed, to six weeks, and sometimes two months. She did the best she could by them. No news was good news. She had her job and her boys—and now a girl.

Angel Tully, eight, a slim-faced girl with black hair and blacker pupils, sat on the porch steps in her baggy sweatshirt and baggier pants. She liked clothes with many pockets. Angel was Joe's daughter, Joe from the Circle J Bar in Grand Forks. She now was staying "for a while" with Jenny and family.

"I don't want to go." Angel folded her skinny arms firmly across her chest.

"You have to." Roland, quite the mechanic at age thirteen, leaned under the upraised hood of the Ford as he checked the oil.

"I know how to stay home alone," she answered.

"Then stay home."

"Roland." Jenny leveled a pointer finger at him. "And don't wipe oil on your jeans."

Roland muttered something as he let the hood drop.

"Roland swore," Angel said.

"No, I dint."

"That's enough, you two." She didn't mind the bickering between Angel and Roland. It was an improvement from a year ago when Angel arrived with her father and her suitcase. She had stayed in the car while Joe came to the house. "It's a lot to ask," he said. "But with me going away, and her mom like she is…"

"She'll be safe here," Jenny said. "It's the least I can do for you."

Today Roland bugged out his eyes at Angel. He had a stocky upper body, heavy in the shoulders like his father, Arthur, though with Haugen hair, thick, like his Uncle Emil's.

"Anyway, there's no room for me in the car," Angel replied. "All the boxes and stuff."

"You'll all fit," Jenny said. "It's why we have a station wagon now."

"Why do you bring them so much stuff?" Angel asked. "Are they poor?"

"They're not poor," Roland said sharply.

"I just like to," Jenny said. "They're family. All I've got."

"We're family." Roland gave a side eye glance at Angel.

"And anyway, we'll be back home for supper."

"That's hours," Angel said.

"So, we'd best get going," Jenny said cheerfully.

"See?" Roland replied.

"John," Jenny called. John was in the backyard playing catch with Butch Arneson, the neighbor boy. It was full, green spring, and the two were fools for baseball. Whenever a mitt and a ball were involved, John was deaf. Today he came running—so fast that his cap flew off. His lank, dandelion-yellow hair caught the sun. He raced back to retrieve his cap, then paused to heave the baseball a remarkably long way back to Butch, who caught it without moving a step.

"Strike." John came laughing up to his mother. Twirled her around. "I get to drive, right?"

"Maybe," Jenny said.

"He'll crash the car," Angel said with alarm.

"Never," John said. He grabbed Angel by the wrists and gave her a full out, full circle swing. Angel's scream fell between fear and joy.

They left at exactly nine a.m. The goal was to arrive at the home farm in time for noon dinner, if not before. Driving north, a few miles past the city limits, Jenny pulled over.

"I know how to drive too," Roland said to Angel.

"I doubt that."

"I do."

"Hush," Jenny said.

As Jenny and John changed seats, Jenny turned to Angel. "John's a good driver." This was not entirely true; he was easily distracted. However, in the general area of parenting, she had learned that sometimes saying so, made it so.

"Keep your nose in your book," Roland said. "That way you won't have to look."

John settled in behind the wheel of the Ford Ranch Wagon. Gripping the wide hoop, he looked through the windshield, north. "One hour and we could be in Canada."

"Another time," Jenny said.

John brought up the rpms.

"Remember," Jenny said, "clutch out slow, then—"

With a lurch and chirp of the tires, they were off.

North of Crookston, winter wheat blushed green on the higher cheeks of the fields, "high" being relative on this flat sea of farmland. First was a short detour to check on the land Jenny owned, though locally it was still called "the Wagner farm."

"Turn here," Roland said.

John braked. "The fields and roads all look the same."

"No, they don't," Roland replied.

"Slow down a bit," Jenny said, which brought a groan from Angel. As they drew near her fields, Jenny rolled down her window.

Flat as a cutting board, her two hundred and forty acres stretched east to a skinny line of willows. The Schmidt family had planted their own fields first, but by squinting in the same fashion as night driving, she made out the faintest, green fuzz of wheat.

"Are we there?" Angel asked.

"We're not even in North Dakota," said Roland.

"This is land that I own," Jenny explained. "We live in town, but I rent out the land and house to another family." Two shutters hung askew. The lawn was mowed. There was a swing-set.

"Why can't we kick them out and live here ourselves?" Roland asked.

"I like living in town," John said. "It's close to school and the ballfield."

"If we lived out here, you could have your own ball field," Roland said.

"I'd never want to live out here," Angel said.

Jenny checked her watch. "Let's keep going."

John accelerated sharply, and the loaded station wagon groaned forward. Gravel chattered in the wheel wells, and soon they regained the blacktop.

As they rolled north John looked at birds on wires, at tractors in the fields, at ducks on the ponds. Everything was of interest to him.

"Eyes on the road," Jenny said.

At Warren, they turned west to Oslo and the Red River, which constituted the border between Minnesota and North Dakota.

"The Red River of the North," Jenny said to Angel. "Do you know why they call it that?"

"No." Angel did not look up from her book.

"Because it flows north," Roland said.

"That's right," Jenny said. "It wants to go all the way to Hudson Bay in Canada."

John drove with one hand now, as if he had been driving all his life.

"We're going across the river." Jenny glanced back at Angel. "Into a different state."

Angel looked up briefly.

"Ready?" John called. Bridge planking rumbled beneath the tires.

"Do you feel any different?" Jenny asked.

"No," Angel said.

"Sort of," Roland said.

"I always do," John said.

They drove north on Highway 29, then north and west through farm country as if climbing a giant staircase. At 11:46 a.m., with Angel slightly car-sick, they reached the home driveway.

"We're here," Jenny said. The mailbox leaned south. Sunshine had burned off the galvanizing along the top. Rust bled down the sides.

Angel peered out.

"This is where I grew up."

"We know, Ma," John said easily.

"But Angel doesn't."

"True, Ma." He stopped at the gate. Closed and padlocked, it hung stiffly from its post, a railroad tie. Gray weathered boards made up the wide face of the gate, which traveled on a skinny iron wheel relieved from an old dump rake.

"See those long boards? Those are from the old railroad snow fence." She pointed across to the field to the railroad tracks and a wooden fence that paralleled it. Some of the old boards had come loose. Others were missing. "When I was a little girl, the snow fence caught the blowing snow and made drifts as high as a house. We skied on top them."

"That must have been fun," John said.

"They were so high we could see all the way to Montana."

"Really?" Roland said.

"No. But that's what your Uncle Emil said."

Jenny produced the padlock's key from her purse, got out, and unlocked the gate. The iron wheel crunched across gravel as she pushed it open, after which John pulled forward. With the same scraping sound, she closed the gate behind. Clicked shut the padlock.

"Are we locked in?" Angel called.

"I have the key." Jenny held it up.

"Uncle Emil likes the gate locked coming and going," Roland said.

"Why?" Angel said.

"That's just the way he is," John said.

They drove up the lane. Ahead, around a bend in the driveway, the windbreak of pines had grown taller, which made the new house look smaller still. Which it was, a third smaller than "the new house" that had burned in 1938. This one looked much the same—narrow and tall with a sharp roofline. Across from it the little *hus* leaned impossibly south, saved from tipping by brace posts. A worn path led to its door. Across the yard, the barn was weathered and square-backed, its front repainted red. Behind the barn, corral posts remained but carried no fencing. The livestock, Toby and Brownie, were long gone. Weeds, mostly bull thistles and "pigweed," grew in the corral dirt. Three faded, squat, gray Butler grain bins formed a line beyond the old wooden granary. And in place of Sally's grand coop, the one that had burned in 1935, was a much smaller one, the tar paper on its sides held down by vertical strips of wooden lath. A half dozen chickens ranged across the yard, herded by a big, dark rooster. The yard-light pole remained. No wires came or went.

"Why don't they have electricity?" Angel asked.

"Uncle Emil doesn't like it," Roland said.

"How could anyone not like electricity?" Angel said.

John tooted the horn.

"Can I stay in the car?" Angel asked.

"That would be very impolite," Jenny said.

"Will Uncle Emil let me drive the tractor?" Roland asked.

"Maybe. For sure he'll give you a ride."

"I brought my ball and mitt. I'm going to practice pitching," John said.

"You're always playing baseball," Angel said.

"You're always reading," Roland said.

Dag came out on the porch. She had put on weight over the years, though maybe her red-checkered cooking apron made her look wider.

"Hullo," Dag called gaily. "Are the children along?"

"Of course," Jenny called. She hugged Dag. Sally and Emil were nowhere in sight.

"I drove all the way," John said.

"Well, I'll be," Dag said. "And you're a foot taller, I swear. It's been so long."

"Come on," Roland said. He opened the car door for Angel. "You have to get out."

"Is that Miss Angel?" Dag peered in. "So nice to see you again."

"What do you say, Angel?" Jenny said.

"Hello." Angel remained in the rear.

"You are such a pretty girl," Dag said. "I have fresh cookies in the house."

Angel emerged and stood close beside Jenny. John and Roland were already off.

"Jenny mentioned you're quite the reader," Dag said.

Angel hunched her shoulders and looked down to her book.

"We'll get some food in her, and she'll feel better," Jenny said.

"Dinner will be a while," Dag said. "Let's go into the house and get you a cookie to tide you over."

"Boys," Jenny called. "Help bring in the boxes."

"Boxes?" said Dag. "Now what?"

"We've brought you a few things," Jenny said. "Plus a new outfit for Sally."

"You spend too much on us," Dag said.

"Nonsense."

"After we unload these, can I go find Uncle Emil?" Roland asked.

"He's in the machine shed," Dag said. "But don't turn your back on that rooster."

The rooster was a big, handsome fellow with a high red comb and flowing black cape; dangling, crimson wattles; and a rust-colored body and high-arching, black tail feathers. Strutting on yellow shanks with spurs, he bobbed his head as he herded a group of hens.

"I'm not scared of no chicken." Carrying a tower of boxes, Roland headed to the house.

Jenny and Angel followed Dag up onto the porch, which sagged a bit these days, and then into the house.

"It smells good in here," Jenny said.

"Saturdays I bake, like always," Dag said.

Angel looked at her work.

"Here's your cookie," Dag said.

Angel's eyes went to the orderly rows of cookies, cooling.

"You may have another when you're done." Dag steered Angel toward the couch. "Sit right here. Stretch out if you like. It's where Uncle Emil takes his naps."

Angel sat, then hunched her shoulders. "It stinks."

"Angel," Jenny said.

"But it does," Angel said.

"I suppose it does smell a bit, though not so bad as it used to," Dag said, "now that the livestock are gone."

"You'll be fine," Jenny said to Angel. "Eat your cookie and read your book while we get dinner ready."

She slouched behind her book. The kitchen disappeared from view.

Chapter Twenty-One
A Noise Upstairs

In the farmhouse, Angel listened to the adults with one ear as she read. Across in the kitchen, Dag and Mrs. Olsen, who wanted Angel to call her Jenny, talked on. Gradually, their voices softened to a faraway murmur. *The Borrowers*, which the librarian lady had picked out for her, had words such as "decanter" and "wainscot" and others she didn't know. India was a faraway country, and England was across the ocean but not quite so far away as India, but the book had just enough drawings to explain the story. A hallway held a tall grandfather clock with the tiny door beneath it, from which the little people, the Borrowers, came and went. Another of old Mrs. Driver, the cook, reaching up to light the lantern on the wall, a sconce, while wearing her apron over her long dress and button shoes. Another one of young Kate at an easel practicing her painting while Mrs. May crocheted. In this book they said "whilst." The pictures were not really pictures. More like outlines in black and white, but they clearly showed the worrisome life of the Borrowers, who, dressed ever so nicely, lived in their space beneath the floorboards.

Angel started at the tug on her sleeve.

"Sorry, dear. I didn't mean to frighten you," said Dag. "Would you like your other cookie now? I'm afraid my chicken isn't quite done."

"Yes, please." For a moment Dag was Mrs. May, come to ask her if she might like tea.

"That's a polite girl," Dag said.

Angel returned to her book.

"We're going outside to round up the boys and look at the garden," Jenny said. "Will you be all right here?"

"Of course she will," Dag said.

***

Sometime later Angel put down her book. Cocked her head. A sound. A thump somewhere in the house. She held aside the lace curtain. In the yard, a little orange tractor "putt-putted" in a wide circle with Roland at the wheel, sitting between Emil's legs. Dag and Jenny clapped soundlessly. Roland grinned and steered. To the side, John pitched his white baseball against a target on the side of the granary.

She went to the kitchen and put four cookies in her pockets, then arranged the spacing in the rows of cookies to disguise the missing ones. She looked about the empty living room. The lantern on the wall, with its curved, elaborate holder reaching up like an arm and a hand to hold the glass bowl of oil, was just like the wall lantern in *The Borrowers*. And there were doilies, too, on the little tables, and rag rugs, and furry-leafed violets in the window with the dimmest light.

She walked to the stairway. Its narrow, cupped wooden steps led up. She started up, stepping softly, as quiet as a Borrower, until she reached the top. There, almost in a circle, were three doors to three rooms. She turned the knob of one door. Behind was a narrow closet hung with very old dresses that smelled of mothballs. The dresses were very long.

She tried the next door. It was a bedroom. On a small stand beside the narrow bed, tightly made, was a swan-shaped ceramic water pitcher and a water glass. Below, peeking out from the bedspread, was a tin chamber pot with a white ball handle. Across, stood a small dresser. She eased open the drawer. A lady's underthings, large size. Across from the bed was a low, box-like dresser of sorts with a fitted cover that zipped up the middle. Its hem reached exactly to the floor. Glancing behind—the house was still quiet—she drew down the zipper. Inside were thin wooden shelves, the whole thing made of peach crates. Centered was a picture of a woman in a car with no top. A convertible. The woman smiled for the camera. She was pretty, and the man with her had dark, wavy hair combed back, smiling with big white teeth. He held up his hat, white with a dark band. Near the photograph sat a bowl of hair pins and two very old-looking lipstick tubes. Angel opened one. It smelled of roses. She sneezed, then zipped the coverlet and stepped away. It was a room for a governess, a sad room because governesses never married.

She eased open the door to the third room. It smelled like the Chesterfield, only stronger, like pee. A narrow window looked out on the yard. In the narrow opening between the curtains, sunlight struck through like a knife.

"Hello there."

Angel jumped back. A tall person stood in the shadows. Not man or woman, wearing a woman's head kerchief but dressed in a man's shirt and pants and boots. "Are you my little girl?"

"No."

The person reached out a long arm. Long, bony fingers clamped on Angel's arm and pulled her toward a hug. She broke loose, thumping down the stairs and out onto the porch—ran toward the sound of the tractor and adult voices.

The big rooster came from nowhere.

Angling toward her at full speed, yellow legs a blur, kicking up dust, thick neck out-thrust, it charged. She shouted at it and drew to a halt. The rooster fluttered upward, kicking his clawed feet and spurs at her face. She swore at him, then ducked and ran. The rooster followed, its short legs churning double-time.

Roland came running, shouting, kicking at the rooster. John too. He threw his baseball—a direct hit. The rooster tumbled, shook off the dust and readied himself for another charge. Roland crouched in front of Angel. Emil came running, swearing, kicking at the rooster.

"That's it for you, mister," Emil called. "The last straw."

The rooster retreated, bobbing its head. Emil stepped over to the machine shed.

Jenny pulled her aside, saying, "Are you okay?"

"Yes. He didn't scare me."

"Dag warned us. I didn't think he was that ornery."

Emil returned with a long-handled shovel. He advanced on the rooster, which weaved and bobbed his head like a boxer. Emil swung. The rooster fluttered into the air—hopped over the blade.

"Strike one," John called.

"Club him, Uncle Emil," Roland shouted.

Emil swung again and this time banged the rooster full on. It sprawled in the dust, then regained its feet, dragging a wing, still full of fight.

"Come, Angel," Jenny said.

She shrugged off Jenny's hand. "I want to watch."

"Leave that to Emil and the boys." Jenny took her arm and headed them toward the house. "You were running. Is everything all right?"

Angel pointed to the high window. "There's a man upstairs."

"You went up there?"

"Yes."

Jenny stopped. "You shouldn't snoop. It's not polite."

"I was just looking around."

"That wasn't a man. It was Sally, our other sister," Jenny said. "There are three of us."

"It was a man," Angel said.

"Sometimes she looks like a man," Jenny said as they continued toward the house. "It's just the way she dresses."

Angel tilted her head to the single, upstairs window.

***

Noon dinner included boiled potatoes with butter, roasted chicken, gravy, pickled beets, dill pickles, white buns over-glazed on top with a brown shine of butter, green beans, and birthday cake of lemon meringue with browned curlicues of white frosting.

"I've never seen a girl eat so much," Dag said happily.

Sally's chair remained empty.

Angel looked up the stairway. "Doesn't she eat?"

"Sally often waits until later," Dag said.

"She's shy," Jenny added.

"Don't worry, she'll eat when everybody's gone," Dag said.

"Why?" Angel said.

"That's just the way she is," Roland said.

"All people are different," John said. "Like Roland. He's *really* different."

Angel laughed.

"None of that, children," Jenny said.

Dag kept the food moving. Toward the end of the meal, she excused herself. "I'll check on Sally."

They watched Dag go up the stairs. For long moments no one said anything.

"I heard there's a new grocery store in Skye," Jenny said.

"Yes. But I like the old one," Emil said. "And anyway, we don't go to town much. Ernie Sitz brings our groceries. I give him a list every week."

"He's the mailman," Jenny explained to Angel.

Upstairs, Dag's voice was muffled.

Angel looked at Jenny, who turned to Emil. "Did Roland do all right on the tractor?"

Emil's gaze remained on the stairway as he said, "He's getting the hang of it."

"Next summer maybe I could come and stay for a while," Roland said.

"Now there's an idea." Emil turned to Roland and smiled. "I can always use the help."

"Can I, Mom? Can I?"

"We'll see."

Dag came downstairs. "Aunt Sally says to go ahead without her. Light the birthday cake candles, Emil."

"Do the match thing on your overalls," Roland said.

Dag clucked her tongue. "You shouldn't teach the boys those tricks."

"It don't hurt them none." Emil stood and produced a stick match from his shirt pocket and gave it a lightning fast rub up and down his pant leg.

Angel squinted but didn't lean away.

The match head smoked, then flared yellow. The boys clapped. Emil lit the birthday candles one by one.

"I can light a match that way too," Roland whispered to Angel.

They sang "Happy Birthday." Jenny blew out the candles in one breath and then they dug into their cake.

Angel finished first. "Can I go to the car now?" She looked to the stairway.

"No," Roland said.

Jenny shrugged. "Don't see why not. You can read in the back seat."

Angel took her book and went out.

Roland turned to his mother. "We're not going home yet. We just got here."

"That's true." Jenny ruffled Roland's flat-top. "Though I like to get back before dark."

Outside, a door slammed on the station wagon.

"If you're done with your cake, maybe Uncle Emil could give you boys another tractor ride."

Roland beat John to the door, and with a crash and clatter on the front porch, they were gone. Emil followed, leaving just Jenny and Dag at the table.

"Whew," Dag said.

"Yes. The kids tend to fill up a room."

"Angel is quiet but nice," Dag said.

"Yes."

"And such a reader."

"Maybe to a fault."

Dag looked over.

"I think it's her way of escaping the life at hand."

"Well, who knows what she's been through."

"There's that, yes."

"Do you take her to visit her father at the prison?"

"No. It's a long drive, and he thought it would be too tough on her seeing him there."

"And her real mother?"

"She drops by once a month or so. Doesn't stay long. Usually smells of alcohol."

"At least she did what's best for her daughter."

"That was Joe's concern. It's why he asked me to take her in."

"Wasn't there anyone else?"

"Her grandmother on Joe's side, but she's infirm."

"How long will he be in for?"

"Ten years. That's with good behavior. He's been in prison before."

Dag clucked her tongue. "How do you know him again?"

Jenny turned away. Scraped a plate. "He has worked for me on several occasions. Odd jobs."

After they finished the dishes, Jenny went upstairs. Sally's bedroom door remained closed. Jenny knocked. "It's me."

No answer.

Quietly she tried the knob. It didn't turn. "I brought some things for you. Some pants and a new work shirt. Summer-weight so you'll be cool."

No answer. She put her ear to the wood. At length she said, "I'll call you. We can talk on the phone. Everything's fine with the kids.

And it sounds like you surprised Angel. I'm sorry she was snooping. She's a nice girl."

There was no reply.

"Anyway, we'll be heading home soon," Jenny said. "I'll wave to you from the yard." She left the bag against the door.

Downstairs, Dag had a pained look. "Sally hasn't been good lately."

"I guessed that."

"She doesn't keep herself clean anymore," Dag said. "Emil thinks she might have to go somewhere." Her voice faltered.

"Go somewhere?"

"Some place where they care for people like her," Dag said.

"People like her," Jenny said. She looked out the window. The tractor came by, Roland driving and Emil and John standing on the drawbar.

"You don't know how it is for us," Dag said. "Day to day we don't know how she's going to be."

Jenny took Dag's hand. "Let me think on things. When I get back home, I'll talk to a doctor. Someone."

"We need to do something," Dag said, "and soon."

***

On the way home, with John driving, Roland went over the story again about "the damned old rooster."

"That's swearing," Angel said.

"It is. No swearing, please," Jenny said.

Roland glared at Angel.

"But thanks for saving Angel," Jenny added.

"I could have outrun that old rooster," Angel replied.

"No way," Roland said. "He'd have pecked your eyes out."

"That's enough. It's over and done," Jenny said.

The car rolled on.

"What's wrong with your sister?" Angel asked Jenny.

"She's crazy." Roland made a cork-screw motion around an ear.

Jenny turned to the back seat, and in one motion grabbed his shirt at the throat.

"What?" he cried.

"Don't ever say that." She shook him once, hard.

Roland shied backward, as if she might strike him.

"Gees, Mom," John said.

His mother stared. "I'm sorry, Roland. I didn't mean to do that."

Roland set his jaw and turned to look at the fields.

At length, Jenny turned to Angel. "Sally has had some bad luck in her life. Some hard times. But she's not crazy."

Angel nodded, then turned to the fields as well. "Like my mom."

Chapter Twenty-Two
The Phone Call

At the Olsen's house that night, Jenny arranged for Angel to have her bowl of ice cream in bed. It was her reward for "being a good girl on the trip." From the first night she had stayed there, she had slept on the far side of Jenny's bed. John and Roland had their rooms upstairs. Jenny said this sleeping arrangement would have to do "for now." But her back was warm, and she was closest to the door.

Tonight, Angel arranged her pillows and settled back to read more in *The Borrowers*. In the living room the radio played, a baseball game. John groaned at something. "Clack-clack-clack" went checker pieces on the board. "Got you," Roland said.

"Dang it."

"You have to pay attention," Jenny said with a laugh.

"I was," John answered crossly.

Angel remembered Jenny turning off the light and lowering her pillows. Her last, drifting thoughts were of *The Borrowers* story. The most important character in a book always had the most adventure, and today, from the rooster attack, that was her. A telephone jingled far away. Mrs. May didn't have one, so maybe it was the doorbell, perhaps a delivery boy with a telegraph about the war.

She awoke to the bedroom light and Jenny, fully dressed, sitting on the bed and stroking her arm. The librarian lady stood in the doorway, smiling oddly.

"Angel, there's been an emergency," Jenny said. Her voice was funny. A note off. "I have to go help Emil and Dag and Sally. Miss Edith will be here with you tonight, and I'll be back much later."

Angel stared.

"I brought a couple of books you might like," the library lady said. "In the morning we'll look at them."

Angel nodded.

The library lady and Jenny had a quick, hard hug and then Jenny was gone.

"Did you like *The Borrowers*?" the library lady asked. "My favorite character was Ariety. She's quite brave, don't you think?"

John could hear voices coming from the living room. "What happened?" John asked Jenny. "Just tell me."

"Something with Aunt Sally. An accident. I have to go."

***

Her drive was not to Skye, but the Grand Forks Hospital. Sally was coming by ambulance. Dag and Emil followed in the truck.

Jenny arrived just after midnight to an empty parking lot by the emergency entrance. The waiting room was empty but for an older woman with puffy red eyes, wearing a housecoat. Her eyes went to Jenny's feet... her bedroom slippers.

"You too?"

"Sorry?" Jenny said.

"My husband. He had a heart attack, they think."

"I hope things work out." She took a seat away from the lady, where she could see out the window.

In the next hour, time overflowed the waiting room, the parking lot. Three times Jenny stepped outside to look, then had to come back in so as not to freeze. The third time she returned the older lady was gone.

At almost one a.m. a flashing red cherry and headlights approached and turned in. Emil's pickup followed. She hurried out.

A garage-type door opened, the ambulance rolled inside, and the door came down.

Emil and Dag stepped out.

"She tried to hang herself," Dag said.

Jenny wrapped Dag in a hug.

"Upstairs in her room," Emil said. "But it didn't work. She was too tall." He choked a sound that, in another time, might have been a laugh.

"I heard the noise," Dag said. "I called for Emil. He ran up and cut her down."

"Had to break her door open," Emil said.

"It's always locked," Dag added.

"Come," Jenny said. "Get warmed up."

In the waiting room, she brought Dag and Emil a paper cup of coffee from the squat glass pot.

Emil grimaced at the taste but took a long swallow.

"You tell her the rest," Dag said to him.

"What? Please," Jenny said.

"Sally couldn't breathe right," Emil said.

"From the rope." Dag's voice carried an unnatural calm.

"We didn't want to take her to the doctor," Emil said.

"Not to him," Dag said. "Not McConnell."

"So Emil had to open up her windpipe," Dag finished.

Jenny stared.

"I used one of Dag's knitting needles." Emil, too, spoke evenly and without blinking.

"Once Emil got the hole in her throat—it wasn't even that big—her color returned, just like that." Dag snapped her fingers.

"The ambulance fellow said we probably damaged her voice box," Dag said. "She might never talk right again."

"But she's alive," Emil said without expression.

Jenny went to them. Gathered them in her arms and did not let go. Dag's shoulders heaved.

"We've worried about this," Emil said. "That she might try it."

"Last week she butchered all her chickens," Dag said. "Just chopped their heads off."

"We should have known what that meant," Emil said.

"We should have known more, sooner," Dag said.

"I've been remiss," Jenny blurted. "I've left it all to you."

"Don't," Dag said quickly.

"Dag's right," Emil added. "We can't any of us blame ourselves."

"She's alive," Dag said. "Now we go forward from here."

Chapter Twenty-Three
A Place For Sally

Sally's Grand Forks doctors, after attending that night to her home-made tracheotomy, recommended that she remain in their secure ward at least a week for evaluation. Not for the surgery, but for "the other."

"This gives us some time to make a plan," Jenny said. It was the wee hours at the hospital, and Sally was "resting comfortably."

Dag looked to Emil. "We can't bring her home until she gets better. It's too much."

Emil nodded.

Dag lowered her gaze.

"There's no shame in saying that," Jenny said.

"She needs something different than us, than the farm," Emil said.

"I'll speak with the doctors tomorrow," Jenny said. "They'll have some ideas."

Emil and Dag headed back to Skye that same night—or rather, morning. As Jenny saw them off from the hospital parking lot, the first, purple light rose in the east.

In two days, they returned to Jenny's house. Dag stayed on with the children. Jenny and Emil drove west toward Jamestown, North Dakota, to check out a facility there.

They didn't talk much. The green, flat land west of Fargo dulled and began to undulate. Low, dry, tree-less hills rose up and fell away.

"You couldn't pay me to live out here," Emil said.

"What are those white rings about the dry sloughs?" Jenny asked.

"Alkali," Emil replied.

***

The North Dakota Hospital for the Insane, now called "The State Hospital," squatted on the south edge of Jamestown. Built in 1893, its four storey, brick wings stretched wide and rampart-like. Marshes and lowland of the James River lay behind. But for a water wheel, the hospital might have been a textile mill.

The tour attendant, a plump woman wearing a square-shouldered brown dress, carried a heavy ring of keys. "We're quite proud of our reforms." She waved for Emil, Jenny and the small group to follow her through the rear door. Of the six visitors, none wanted to be first. Jenny nudged Emil forward. "Especially how our residents make use of themselves," the lady continued.

Out back were vegetable gardens. Patients in blue coveralls raked or weeded or tended to plants. Attendants, wearing all white, stood around watching. The guide paused, held up a clipboard. "Let me read to you from a new report by Dr. R. O. Saxvik, one of our state health officials. 'Gone are the cages, strait jackets, leg irons, stern guards, malnutrition, windowless seclusion rooms, unorganized departments, the sixty-hour work week, the naked despondent patient on a back ward, the odors from wards crammed with untidy and helpless men and women, the tuberculosis patients in disorganized treatment areas, the neglected surgical problems, and the bedlam of disturbed units.'"

Emil glanced at Jenny.

"I read this to all families considering us for a loved one," the guide said, as if speaking to Emil. "It's important that you all know how much things have changed for the better in our business."

Emil looked around, then upward to the windows. Here and there a person looked out without moving. "Could we see up there?" he said. "Where they live?"

"I'm afraid not." The guide's smile slipped. "Patients like their privacy. Routines are important. Do you folks have a dog? A pet of any kind?"

"No," Jenny said.

"If you did, you'd understand about the importance of routines," the guide said. "Pets, the retarded, and even the fully insane all do better with consistency. The same things every day."

Emil turned to Jenny.

"We thank you for your time," Jenny said. She nodded toward the exit.

"There's much more to see," the guide replied.

"We've seen plenty," Emil replied.

Leaving the parking lot, they were silent until the stop sign.

Jenny braked. Glanced in the rearview mirror.

"Would be a cold day in hell before Sally comes here," Emil said.

"I agree." She turned onto the highway and brought the Oldsmobile up to speed. "There's another state hospital, closer to me, down in Fergus Falls. It's next on my list."

"That's in Minnesota. We'd have to pay there."

"*Den tid, den sorg*," Jenny said. "For now, she's safe in the Grand Forks hospital. You and Dag can go home until we know more."

"It's planting time. I should be in the fields."

"Then you better rest while you can. Tip your seat back. Have a snooze."

"You won't run off the road?" Emil said.

"I promise."

Emil laughed and leaned back. Let his eyes close. Within a half mile he was slack-jawed and snoring. She reached over and lowered his cap bill to keep out the sun.

Chapter Twenty-Four
Fergus Falls

That same week Jenny took another day off from work and drove, alone, south to Fergus Falls, Minnesota, a good-sized farming town of twenty-five thousand. Its State Hospital, built in the 1890s, looked like a German castle. She had read up on its history; she was not prepared for its size. Three turret-like towers, sharply peaked, the middle one tallest, soared in front. Two-storey wings, patient quarters, stretched right and left, with gable windows to break up the roofline. The circular drive brought her past tidy, landscaped grounds to the front steps. From the window arches and elaborate stonework it was easy to imagine hitching posts for big horses with ribbons in their manes and black carriages behind.

She parked. Craning her neck at the towering façade, she headed inside.

The foyer was high, light, and airy with polished granite floors and the faint smell of vinegar. She followed bronzed wall signs and their arrows to "Admitting," a spacious waiting room with counters before nurses and secretaries who worked behind.

"I'm here for the tour," Jenny said. "Olsen. I called ahead."

"The next one starts in ten minutes," said a cheerful, youngish, very tidy fellow in white. "Have a seat."

Eight other people waited, all couples of various kinds. The nearest woman, about Jenny's age, sat most certainly with her mother, who was very pale and kept bobbing her head.

"Hello there," Jenny said.

The daughter nodded once. The mother shied behind her daughter, then peeked over her shoulder. "It's okay, Ma," the daughter said.

At two p.m. sharp, the tour began.

"Fergus Falls State Hospital was built on the Kirkbride design," the guide began as he walked. "That would be Thomas Story Kirkbride." The young man wore all white, and his rubber-soled shoes chirped. "Thomas Kirkbride believed in what he called 'moral treatment.' Since hospitals for the insane were often for people with no place else to go, Mr. Kirkbride believed that they should find peace here, a retreat from the world, and a restorative atmosphere." He paused for effect. "Here, rich and poor alike are treated with dignity and respect."

The guide reminded Jenny of Arthur's Michael Clark.

"What would all that cost us?" asked a man in the group.

"If your loved one is indigent, and a resident of Minnesota, nothing," the guide answered. "It's your tax dollars at work."

"Our Bob, we can't handle him at home anymore," a woman blurted. She began to sniffle.

"We have treatment and care for every level of need," the guide said. "After our tour you'll each speak with an admitting staff member to discuss your situation. Shall we move on?" The guide pivoted sharply and pointed forward.

The group passed through the rear door. "Mr. Kirkbride's design provides comfortable living quarters for a curative effect, 'a special apparatus for lunacy,' he termed it, though we don't use that word anymore." The guide waved them along. "Most of all he believed in the therapeutic effect of sunlight and fresh air." As they stepped outside, he held out his arms to tidy gardens, barns, and stretching fields.

"It might as well be the farm," a man said to his wife. He had a sun-browned face.

"It *is* a farm," the guide answered. "We have six hundred forty acres. Many of our residents come from farms. They're happy to have work which is known to them. Corn, grain, hay, milk cows… we're self-sufficient like any farm."

"Do you have chickens?" Jenny asked.

"Do we ever." The guide pointed to a long, low building just like the one Sally had designed from a Murray McMurry Poultry catalogue. "Would you like a look inside?"

"Not necessary, thank you."

"Let's move on then. Across, you'll see our greenhouse, the funding for that thanks to FDR and Federal Relief Programs. Over there you'll see our grist mill, and alongside it the bakery. We make all our own bread. Perhaps you can smell it?"

The same fellow with a weathered face scratched the back of his neck. "A person could live here."

His wife turned to him. Stared.

"Many people choose to," the guide said. "Our population at present is about two thousand five hundred. We're a village all ourselves."

In the long vegetable gardens people hoed, weeded, raked.

"You'll note that our residents don't wear the same color clothes or any kind of uniform," the guide said.

"Why is that?" someone asked.

"They're not convicts," the guide replied. "In fact, here, it's our staff that wears a uniform."

After the tour, Jenny met with a no-nonsense woman in a side office.

"Fill out this checklist," she said. "It's a list of behaviors, good and bad, plus any particular skills your loved one would bring to our community."

Jenny accepted the clipboard. The behaviors were in alphabetical order. As she worked quietly, a faint clicking came from somewhere across or down the hall. A sewing machine. A sash rattling in a light, uneven breeze. "Ticka-ticka. Tick-tick." Upon reaching the line for Nervous Breakdown, Jenny paused. "My sister tried to commit suicide."

"That box is further down."

Jenny finished. Handed over the pages.

The woman scanned the sheets without expression. "Graduated high school. Held a job."

"She's quite smart."

"We have two general types of residents," the woman said. "Those who are retarded and those who are not, but troubled."

"She's troubled."

"When was the suicide attempt?"

"A week ago. She's in the hospital now in Grand Forks."

"Did something precipitate it?"

"A crime against her."

"Recently?"

"Twenty-three years ago."

The woman leaned back. Her features softened.

Jenny told her the whole story, at first haltingly, then in a stream. "She was never the same."

"Nor was your family."

"That's correct."

The woman pushed a small blue box of Kleenex her way.

"Thank you. I'm fine." In the end, she took one.

"We do have a room for your Sally," the woman said. "Since she's from North Dakota she'd be an out-of-state resident. It would be pay as you go."

"I understand."

"Here are our rates." The lady handed over a sheet.

Jenny scanned down the page. "Oh dear."

"The state of Minnesota is strict about non-residents."

"I'll have to talk to my brother and sister about the cost. May I call you?"

"Don't wait too long," the lady said. "Our rooms go quickly."

They shook hands. In the hallway Jenny paused. Cocked her head. She returned to the office doorway. "May I ask, what is that tapping sound?"

"That? I don't even hear it anymore. It's our telegraph."

"Telegraph?"

"We have our own little office. You'd think the telephone would have killed off the telegraph, but it's surprising how it hangs on. It's hard to find operators. Nobody trains on the telegraph anymore."

Jenny stepped inside. "We'll take that room for my sister. Where do I sign?"

Chapter Twenty-Five
Check-In

For Sally's checkout from the Grand Forks Hospital, the staff dressed her in clothes that Jenny provided. A dark blue skirt, white blouse, and a lightweight, gray wool sweater. Jenny had bought a new ensemble from underwear to outer, including a fine scarf for her neck.

"Fresh clothes for a fresh start," she said.

Sally did not react. Medication had hooded her eyes.

"We're all here," Dag said loudly.

"You look all shined up." Emil filled the doorway.

"Doesn't she, though?" Dag said.

Two male attendants, dressed in white, one on either side of Sally, walked her out.

"She goes in the back seat," one said to Emil. "Someone should sit on both sides of her so she can't get at the door handle."

"Be sure to lock the doors," the other said.

Emil and Dag put Sally between them. The attendants closed the doors. Emil and Dag each pressed down the lock button.

"Best of luck to you folks," one of the attendants said.

Before starting the engine, Jenny turned to Sally. "We're not going home today."

Sally had no reply.

"We can't take you home just yet." Dag's voice cracked.

Emil's jaw moved but nothing came out.

"You have to get better first," Jenny said.

"We've found a place for you until then," Dag finished.

"A different hospital. More than a hospital. A way better one. You'll be staying there for a while," Jenny said.

"Until you get back on track," Dag said.

Sally looked out her window. "I don't have a track." Her voice came in a low wheeze.

"The good thing is, you'll be closer to me." Jenny put the car in gear. "I can see you every weekend."

"And we'll take care of things at home," Dag said.

"At least I don't have chickens," Sally muttered. "Emil would have starved them to death."

***

The day was bright, the sky high and blue as they drove south toward Fergus Falls. Farmers worked their fields. At every tractor, Emil turned his head.

"Funny how just a hundred miles or so makes such a difference," Dag said.

Emil had no comment.

Sally stared through the windshield.

"How about some music?" Jenny said.

"That's what we need," Dag said.

Jenny turned the dial.

"There, that station," Dag said.

Jenny paused the needle at "Some Enchanted Evening" and Perry Como.

"Remember that day we got power and light?" Dag said. "When the radio came on and scared Emil?"

Emil again had no comment.

"And Walter," Dag said. "He was such a good dancer." She looked out the window. "We used to park his car out in the field and dance in the moonlight to the radio. We had such plans."

Jenny felt Emil's gaze on the back of her head.

"Maybe something a little more modern?" She rolled the dial to "Heartbreak Hotel."

"Elvis," Dag said. "Wouldn't he be something to see?"

"How about peace and quiet?" Emil said.

Soon after the radio went off, Sally dozed, leaning on Emil's shoulder. A half hour later she snorted, straightened. "I have to pee."

"Bad?" Jenny replied.

She nodded.

"We can stop in Halstad," Jenny said.

Halstad, population three hundred fifty, had one gas station and two pumps with round white heads. Inside the dim back room a man pounded on a tire.

"We'll go in with you," Dag said.

"I can pee by myself."

"I have to go too," Jenny said.

"It's around back," the attendant said. "You'll need a key." He wore a Bardahl beanie and gray coveralls.

"You might as well fill," Jenny said. "Regular."

The fellow wiped his hands on his pants.

With Sally between them and Emil not far behind, they headed around and behind the building. The attendant, hand on the nozzle, watched.

Behind the station were a few scattered houses and a street that petered out at a gap in willow trees with a glint of the Red River behind. Northwest were open fields. Sally took it all in before stepping inside the restroom.

"If she runs, we'll never catch her," Dag whispered.

There were sounds behind the door. Water running.

"How you doing in there?" Dag called.

Sally came out.

"Okay," Jenny said, and took her arm. "We can keep driving now."

"You said you had to go," Sally said hoarsely.

"Let's get you situated in the car first."

"You thought I'd run away," Sally said.

"You've done it before," Emil said.

In the front office of the station, Jenny paid for the gas.

"What's wrong with her?" the fellow said.

"Who?"

"That lady you took to the bathroom."

"Nothing's wrong with her, and what's it to you?"

When they were back on the highway, Sally dozed off within a mile. She tilted over against Dag this time, who, though crowded, didn't move. She nodded to Jenny and pointed down the highway. "I'm okay," she mouthed.

Sally slept until Jenny parked at the Fergus Falls State Hospital and turned off the engine.

"We're here," Emil said.

Sally sat up fully and blinked. Peered out.

"This is the State Hospital in Fergus Falls," Jenny said.

"It's where you'll be staying for a while," Jenny added.

"Until you get back on track," Emil added.

"You already said that," Sally murmured.

"You need to get away from the farm for a while," Dag said. "That's what Emil means."

"Everybody, wait here," Jenny said.

Inside, it took several minutes to round up the two required attendants. Jenny paced. She went to the door and looked out at her car. The windows of the Oldsmobile remained rolled up.

"Here we are," a cheerful nurse said. "I'm Eleanor and this is James."

James was a giant Black man with a wide mouth and round eyes.

"How do?" he said cheerfully.

"James will escort Sally inside," Eleanor said. She wore all white down to her shoes, and her hair was pulled back into a tight ponytail.

They all shook hands. James's palm was big and warm.

"Your sister do okay on the drive?" James had a smooth, rich voice. On his shoulder he carried a leather strap with a buckle.

"Quite well."

"She fight you?"

"No." Her eyes went to the strap.

"My little helper," James said. "Sometimes, when they realize where they going, we need to restrain them."

"Here we are," Eleanor said.

At the car, Jenny opened the rear door halfway. Emil peered up at the nurses.

"This is James and Eleanor," Jenny said. "They've come to get Sally."

Emil unfolded himself from the back seat. "Emil Haugen." He put out a hand to James. The two men were the same height, which, with Emil, was a rarity.

"Mr. Haugen." James pumped his hand. "That's one fine Oldsmobile."

"Hers." Emil nodded to Jenny. "My little sister's."

Dag stepped out the other side. Stood close in order to block the open door.

"That's my other sister, Dagmar," Jenny said.

"You all family, then?" James said. "That the way it should be. All together." He bent to look inside. "You must be Sally?"

She hunched her shoulders.

"It's okay," Jenny said. "James is a nice man."

"Could you take my hand?" James said. "It's big but it's soft."

"It is," Jenny said.

After long seconds, Sally's long, pale arm came out.

James eased her up from the back seat. Took her arm in his. "We gonna take you inside and get you all situated."

Jenny looked to the pavement beneath her feet. Ants moved along a fine crack where they had pushed up grains of sand.

Their world below, her world above. Her knees felt weak. Dag took her hand.

"I'll get Sally's bag." Emil went to the trunk.

With Sally between the two attendants, they all headed up the steps. Inside, Sally looked up at the high foyer. Sunlight struck through the upper glass and lit the space around with the brightness of an examining room.

Sally leaned down. Touched Jenny's cheek… its pink, raised lines. "Look what I did to you. My little sister."

"Did what?" Jenny said.

"No one notices those marks," Dag said.

"I do," Sally whispered. "I should disappear. Never come back."

"You're not disappearing," Jenny said and held her sister.

"We have something to show you, Sally," Eleanor said.

She led Sally past several offices to a door that said "Telegraph."

They crowded into a windowless office with two desks and two telegraph terminals. An older, pale fellow wearing a headset listened, then began to tattoo his finger on the transmitter key. "Ticka-ticka. Ticka-ticka."

"I've heard that you know Morse code," Eleanor said.

Sally nodded, her eyes on the man's dancing finger.

"We need some help here sending and receiving telegrams. Would that suit you?"

"Yes," Sally whispered.

***

Leaving the hospital, Jenny was okay until the stop sign at the end of the driveway. She braked and put her forehead on the steering wheel.

"It was the right thing." Dag patted her shoulder.

"It had to be done," Emil said.

"We couldn't go on the way we were," Dag said softly.

Jenny lifted her head. She gripped the wheel. The car idled.

"Maybe we need something to eat," Dag offered.

"I guess I haven't eaten much today." Jenny turned toward downtown Fergus Falls.

"DairyLand." Dag pointed to a bright red building with white trim and a peaked roof. "That could be good."

Jenny parked in the lot. Let out a breath.

"I'll go check it out," Emil said.

In the car, Dag stroked Jenny's hair. "The people were nice there. James, he was so friendly. And the telegraph office. That was a sign."

"Of what?"

"That our luck is changing."

Jenny looked at her hands on the steering wheel. "I don't believe in luck anymore."

"You need to get some food in you," Dag said. "Everything will look better."

Emil returned to the car and settled into the front seat. "I couldn't get in."

Jenny looked across to the restaurant. "Was it full?"

"There was no door."

"What?" Dag said.

They squinted across. A young couple walked up to a side window. It slid open, and a man in a white paper hat leaned out.

"I think you walk up there and order your food," Jenny said.

"What in the world?" Dag said.

"Let's all go this time," Jenny said. "We can do it."

Afterward, they ate their hamburgers and fries and milkshakes in the car.

"Tasty," Emil said.

"Very," Dag said.

"A dollar seventy-five for the three of us," Emil added. "That ain't bad."

"I wish we had a DairyLand in Skye," Dag said.

"The only thing better is if they'd bring the food out to your car," Emil replied.

"I don't think that will ever happen," Dag replied.

"It might, someday," Jenny said. She was feeling better.

"Think of it," Emil said. "You could eat in your car and not have to talk to anyone."

"Just your kind of place," Jenny said.

Emil's shoulders rose and fell.

"She's right," Dag said.

When they finished, she and Emil delivered their paper trash to the DairyLand can. Back at the wheel, she squared her shoulders, took a breath, and started the engine.

"Let Emil drive," Dag said. "You drove all the way here."

She glanced his way.

"I could drive us," he said.

"You stretch out in the backseat and have a nice rest," Dag said. "I'll sit up front and help."

"I know how to drive," Emil said.

"You look at things too much," Dag said. "Every field, every tractor, you crane your neck."

"Shall we do this or not?" Jenny said.

With a good deal of fuss and door slamming, they all rotated positions. Emil settled in at the wheel, then adjusted the seat for his long legs. Jenny lay back in the wide, rear seat. Above the Oldsmobile's roof was a pale, curved sky.

"Close your eyes," Dag said.

She did.

"I'll get us home," Emil said.

"You won't run off the road?" Jenny murmured.

Emil huffed out another laugh and put the Oldsmobile in gear.

Chapter Twenty-Six
The Follies

The next week she focused on the children and work. Angel's library books were due, so on Thursday after school they headed to the Carnegie. While Angel browsed, Jenny told Edith all about the trip to Fergus Falls.

Edith hugged her. "I don't know how you do it. Your job. The boys, and now Angel. You're burning the candle at both ends."

"I need a wife."

Edith laughed brightly, which brought a glare from Angel.

"Oh dear, now we've annoyed her," Edith whispered.

"I've never seen a girl so much about rules," Jenny said.

While Edith attended to another patron, Jenny passed along the newspaper rack, each volume secured by a portable wood rod. She hesitated, then took up the *Skye View*. The front page, far right, carried a headline with the article below:

Local College Boy to Star in Musical

Martin McConnell, son of Doctor and Mrs. Robert McConnell, will perform in this spring's "Flicker-tail Follies," the well-regarded variety show produced at the University of North Dakota, Grand Forks. This year's Follies celebrates thirty-one years of showcasing lively and talented students, and has gained nation-wide fame. Life Magazine (May, 1950) wrote: "Of all the springtime college musical shows that bounce around the country, none kicks up more excitement than the University of North Dakota's Flickertail Follies. Named after a spunky little gopher who flicks his tail when he runs, the show consists of a series of competing vaudeville acts." The Follies are sponsored by the University's professional journalism fraternity, as well as other social clubs. Awards are given for both fraternity and sorority skits. However, as written in Life, "The combined acts, put on jointly by sororities and fraternity groups, seem to hold the most fascination for everybody." Mr. McConnell is a member of Chi Sigma Kappa fraternity. According to proud mother Mrs. McConnell, Martin, now a senior, will star in "Modern Mother Goose Land," "Roman Holiday," "Ivy League Envy," and "Rhythm in Warpaint." "The doctor and I will be front row to cheer him on," she said.

Jenny glanced about, then took the newspaper behind a bookcase. She took out her Christmas gift from Emil, the *kniv* she always carried in her purse, and drew its blade lightly about the article, then slipped both into her purse.

The following weekend, on Saturday night, Edith arrived as Jenny dressed.

"Back here."

Edith appeared in the bedroom doorway. "Don't you look nice!"

Jenny turned left, then right to the mirror. "A hat, do you think?"

"Definitely."

Jenny found her gray felt cloche.

Edith stepped close to tilt the small brim just right. Tucked up a strand of hair behind Jenny's ear. "Who's the lucky fellow?"

"No one," Jenny said.

"Well, why shouldn't there be?" Edith replied. "You're only thirty-six, and never prettier."

"Yes, well, I used to be prettier." Jenny touched her cheeks. The cattails scars had subsided, but in full light their pale, fine stripes remained.

"Nonsense. You need to get out there, get yourself on the market."

"Market," Jenny said, and adjusted her hat lower. "That never had the right ring to it."

"You know very well what I mean." Edith tipped Jenny's hat back to where it had been. "They say just when you give up, or are least expecting it, that's when it happens."

"Well, not tonight. It's a college program. A family I know has their son in it."

"Take John along. He needs to start thinking about colleges."

"He's only sixteen," Jenny said. "And anyway, it will be a quick trip. I won't be late."

"I'll be here. We're going to make popcorn."

***

The university in Grand Forks lay across the highway from the fairgrounds where FDR had spoken in 1937. Jenny slowed her car by the stone arch gates, then turned south toward the campus of undistinguished, red-brick buildings. Hemmed in by narrow streets and tight-together houses, the west side of the campus ended at English Coulee, a narrow, sluggish river below tree-lined banks.

On Sixth Avenue she drove past Cambridge, Harvard, Oxford, and Princeton Streets. Chi Sigma Kappa fraternity house stood at the far end of the street. The two-storey residence was the shabbiest of the row, its cornices crumbling from inferior yellow bricks. An upper, white shutter hung askew. Its flat roof had a railing all around, and music played from the open front door. On the front porch, a garbage can overflowed with brown glass bottles. She checked her wristwatch. Drove on.

Central High School Auditorium, an FDR and WPA project, buzzed a full half-hour before showtime. Grabbing a program, she found her way upstairs to a balcony seat. Below in the grand hall, the velvet curtain remained closed. Before it, front row center, sat the doctor and Dolly. His red hair had faded to gray. Dolly's hair remained Clairol brown.

The Flickertail Follies program cover carried bold orange, yellow, and black intertwined hands, suggesting a coming together of the races. Local sponsors included the Silverman and the Straus clothing stores, Hotel Ryan, Wong's Café, and Whitey's Café.

In "Modern Mother Goose Land," Martin McConnell was listed in Ensemble. In "Ivy League Envy," he was listed in Residents. In "Roman Holiday," he was listed far down among Citizens. For "Rhythm and Warpaint," he appeared in the "Me Makum Pow-wow" number among Various Braves.

"Starring… right," Jenny muttered. A woman to Jenny's right glanced her way.

The show led off with "Modern Mother Goose," an all-male cast of college boys dressed as toddlers and infants, all dancing wildly to a Bill Haley song. The story was something about no longer jumping over candlesticks but instead rocking around a giant clock. Martin McConnell wore an oversize diaper plus a giant pacifier in his mouth. He staggered as he danced as if trying to keep up with the bigger kids who all knew how to "bop." The audience laughed and cheered. Dolly McConnell clapped wildly.

The second act, "This Is the Follies," combined boys and girls in some manner of sketch about the show itself. The third, "Parisian Portraits," was all sorority girls in a skit about café life in Paris, complete with French berets, striped shirts for the waiters, and exaggerated accents. Some of the girls were quite pretty and appeared to know how to speak French.

The curtain closed, and, following thudding and clattering behind, the velvet folds rose on "Rhythm In Warpaint." An Indian teepee and a fake-stone fire ring lay before a painted backdrop of mountains. The maiden Red Wing came out to applause. Wearing a headband with a single, upright chicken feather along with a fringed leather vest, she yodeled her song to the hills. From beyond the "mountains" came the beat of a drum and the answering song of her Brave. Their reunion was a dramatic, long embrace. Pow-wow dancers streamed in to celebrate their love. Martin McConnell, now wearing red face paint and a feathered headdress, staggered as he hopped and stamped. The audience laughed. His mother did not clap this time. Martin McConnell was clearly drunk, as likely were other of the fraternity brothers who, hand to mouth, whooped and careened about the two lovers. The curtain fell. The audience stood for a loud ovation.

At intermission, people around Jenny stood to stretch and chat.

"You have someone in the show?" asked the lady in the next seat.

"Me? No." She kept her gaze on the McConnells.

"Nor do we, but we attend every year," the woman said. Her husband smiled.

"I see," Jenny murmured.

"It's so encouraging to see such up-and-coming young people," the lady continued. "So lively and talented, their whole lives in front of them."

"Excuse me," Jenny said.

On the main floor, which was crowded and not brightly lit, she slipped among the chatterers until within earshot of the McConnells. "Well, college boys will be college boys," Dolly said to another lady. They laughed. The doctor did not.

"Our Martin? We're not sure," Dolly said. "He has many interests, right Robert?"

"Perhaps too many."

Dolly chuckled.

"They'll find themselves," the other woman said. "They all do."

"And your son?" Dolly asked.

"He's off to Harvard for medical school," the lady said.

Dolly paused. "Isn't that remarkable."

"With Charles, not so much," the lady said. "He's always known what he wanted to do. Why, way back in grade school—"

"Pardon me," Dolly said. "I must visit the ladies' room."

Jenny turned away. Dolly passed, grim-faced, unseeing. The doctor took up the chat, mainly nodding now and again at the talkative lady. Tilting her hat down a bit and peering as if to look through the crack in the velvet curtain, Jenny eased close enough to smell his pipe. His aftershave.

"I'm a physician myself."

"Well, that's fine. Where do you practice?"

"Up in farm country. The Cavalier area."

"I see. Well, the small towns need their doctor."

Heat coursed through her. His neck was the same, the thick trunk of it, the prominent artery. The flush of warmth dampened her armpits. Her hand went to her purse, to the *tollekniv*, its handle stubby and smooth in her palm.

A bell dinged. The auditorium lights blinked.

"Here I am." Dolly approached.

"The nick of time," the doctor said.

Jenny let out a breath. Averting her face, she headed up the aisle. In the dimming lights, Dolly gave her a smile and nod in passing, then blinked. In the side of her eye Jenny saw her swing around and stare. Jenny continued to the exit, through the lobby, and out the door.

In her car, she sat for long moments without starting the engine. Checked the time. Looked left, then right.

At the Fifth Street and Demers Avenue stop sign, she turned west on University Avenue. Drove back to fraternity row. She parked across from the Chi Sigma Kappa house. The street was deserted. No music, no motion, no one anywhere. The world had emptied itself.

The wooden steps, cupped and worn, led up to a creaky porch. She eased open the tall door, stepped inside to the stale stink of beer. To the side was a kitchen and dining room. Scatters of plates and half-eaten food lay on the wooden tables. To the other side was a mail area and posterboard with pinups, including Marilyn Monroe, her page battered at the edges with staple holes through her belly, but her back still arched and her smile bright. The mail slots listed "Martin McConnell #16."

She paused to listen, then headed up the stairs and down the hall. At room #16, she eased open the door. Wrinkled her nose from the smell. A double room, two rumpled beds, unmade. Two desks, one piled with books and papers, the other with beer bottles, cigarette butts, some *Playboys*, and letters all to Martin McConnell. One from the Dean's office. One from the registrar. "No-show in class." "Probationary period." An official letter from the fraternity itself, Chi Sigma Kappa. "Past due room and board due immediately." To the side, as if recently delivered, was a stapled essay entitled "The Battle of the Bulge: A Turning Point in World War Two. Written By Martin McConnell." A penciled note paper-clipped to the back read, "Here's your paper for old Schnabel. Now at least you can graduate. You owe me your big bulge, hahaha—Nancy."

"Who are you?"

Jenny drew up. From the bed across, a bleary-eyed college boy rose from a mess of blankets and pillows.

"I'm… Martin's mother. Is he here?"

"What time is it?" the boy mumbled.

"Eight-thirty."

"Shit. I missed the show." The boy fell back and covered his head. He began to snore. Jenny gave a last look around, took the history paper, and left.

***

With the sun down behind, she drove east toward the high crown of dark over Crookston. It was almost ten p.m. She'd promised Edith she would be home by nine. She sped up, passing two cars in a row. An oncoming car gave way and flashed its headlights.

At home, a police car and an ambulance sat in the driveway. Chet and Millie stood outside with Edith and an officer. They looked up as she braked sharply and rushed forward.

"What's happened?"

"There you are," Edith called.

"You're Mrs. Olsen?" the officer said.

"She is." There was accusation in Millie's voice.

"Please, tell me what happened."

"Everything's okay," Edith said. "We just had a little excitement."

"Excitement?"

The ambulance man, dressed in white, came down the steps. "He's fine now."

"John," Edith said.

Jenny hurried inside. John sat on the couch, pale-faced, Roland and Angel on either side. Spilled popcorn littered the floor along with a small pool of vomit.

"Mom," Roland said, and hurried over.

"Whatever?"

"We were just goofing around." Roland's voice quivered.

"John choked," Angel said. "Roland and him had a popcorn eating contest."

John smiled wanly. "Sorry, Ma."

"Miss Edith called the police," Angel said. "We didn't know what else to do. John was turning blue."

"The policeman shook him and then gave John a big clap on the back, and it all came out," Roland said.

"My God," Jenny said.

"I'm fine, Ma."

"We were lucky she was here," Angel said, and looked to Edith.

"Yeah, Mom," Roland said. "Where did you go, anyway?"

Chapter Twenty-Seven
The Help

The next day after work, Edith showed up unannounced. "I'm so sorry about last night," she said. "I thought it would just be a routine evening. A little television. Some popcorn."

"I'm glad you were there."

"It seemed like a harmless game. They were tossing popcorn, catching it with their mouths."

"I should have been home," Jenny said.

Edith pursed her lips. "May we talk?"

"Let's sit on the porch."

After they settled in, Edith took her hand. "I worry. About you."

"Me?"

"I know what you've gone through with Sally. Taking her to Fergus Falls must have been impossibly hard. But now that she's situated, it would seem like you could let go a bit."

"Let go?"

"Focus on yourself and your family a bit more."

"What are you saying?" She withdrew her hand.

"No, no. You're a good mother. But over the years I've seen how Sally's trouble has troubled you. And Dag and Emil too."

Jenny nodded. "It has, yes."

"I've always been happy to help," Edith began. "But I feel like there are things you're not telling me. Like this event in Grand Forks that you went to all by yourself."

"Oh Edith, you're a far better friend than I." With that, she told her about Flickertail Follies. That she knew the McConnells would be there. That she got close to the doctor (though she mentioned nothing about the knife in her purse). That afterward she went to the fraternity house.

Edith stared wide-eyed. "You took the boy's history paper?"

"Yes. The one he didn't write."

"Oh dear. You must return it."

Jenny shrugged. "Can't. On the drive home I rolled down the window and let the pages fly. He was cheating. He doesn't deserve to graduate. The whole McConnell family deserves nothing—less than nothing."

Edith took her hand again. "This proves it."

"Proves what?"

"That you must talk to someone."

"I'm talking to you right now."

"Not me. A professional person. A minister, though I know you're not much for church. A doctor. Somebody."

"What would that change?"

"Nothing in terms of what happened to Sally. But it might change what will become of you."

Jenny did not meet Edith's gaze.

"You can't go on this way," she said. "You've got your children, your job. You've too much to lose."

Jenny had no comment.

"Promise me?" Edith pressed.

***

On Monday she took her last sick day from work and drove the twenty miles back to the Grand Forks campus. At the medical school building, she followed signs to the Psychology/Psychiatry Department.

A secretary, a tidy older woman with the erect posture of a librarian, looked up. "May I help you?"

Jenny stepped up to the high counter. "I'd like to speak with a doctor."

"Just to be clear, this is a medical school, not a clinic," the woman said.

"Of course," Jenny said. Her eyes went to the departmental sign.

The secretary lowered her voice slightly. "If you have personal problems, whether they be marriage issues, female trouble or the like, there are counselors in private practice that we recommend."

"Yes," Jenny said. "That's what I'm looking for. A counselor."

The secretary produced a small, three-ring binder. "Here you go."

Standing at the high counter, Jenny turned the pages.

"I've included their photographs," the secretary said.

Jenny turned the sheets. Pages one through five featured unsmiling white-haired men in white coats.

"People find that helpful," the secretary continued.

Jenny turned the page to Lurelle Stokes, Ph.D., a narrow-faced, smiling Black woman in a white coat. Jenny paged on (three more older men), then backward. "Tell me more about Doctor Stokes."

The secretary blinked. "She's from Georgia. Her husband is in the military. He's up here working on the new Grand Forks Air Force Base west of town. The Cold War, you know."

"I've heard."

"Doctor Arvid Johnson comes highly recommended." The secretary's gaze fell again to the binder. "I could call over to the clinic and check his schedule."

Jenny flipped to Arvid Johnson, a narrow-faced man with a pointy white goatee.

"I think Dr. Stokes." She closed the book. "Could you call her office?"

"I could," the secretary said, "if she had a phone."

Within the hour, in downtown Grand Forks, Jenny climbed the stairway of the Masons' Professional Building. The worn carpet smelled of chemical cleaner. On the second floor, a "Dr. L. Stokes" sign pointed down a dim hallway to the right. She passed a dentist's office. Behind the door came a high-pitched whine. Next door was a polished brass name plate: "Lurelle Stokes, Ph.D., Counselor."

She tapped.

Inside, radio music died.

The door opened.

"Hello there." Dr. Stokes wore a white coat, was tall and thin. She had wide-set eyes and ironed hair, plus a gap between her upper front teeth that broadened her smile. "May I help you?"

"I'm Jenny Olsen."

They shook hands. Her fingers were long and strong.

"A secretary at the medical school recommended you as someone to talk to."

"Recommended me? Well, glory be. Come in."

Her office was small, clean, and uncluttered. On the wall hung two framed diplomas: a Bachelor of Arts in Philosophy from Tuskegee University and Doctor of Psychology from Emory University. Below the diplomas were family photos, including one that looked very old: a field of white cotton, a faded shed, and before it a weathered Black couple in straw hats beside a pair of horses and a wagon.

"My grandparents," she said.

"Those look like Belgians."

"They were, indeed," Dr. Stokes said. "You must be from the farm."

"I am." Jenny filled out a card with her address and phone number and then they chitchatted. Dr. Stokes spoke a full beat slower than people in the Midwest. There was honey in her voice, and she enunciated like a schoolteacher. Soon enough she said, "So, Mrs. Olsen, may I ask what brings you here today?"

Beyond the wall, the dentist's drill continued.

"I'm here to talk about a crime."

"Go on," Dr. Stokes said.

"One for which there was never any justice."

Doctor Stokes nodded. "When did this happen to you?"

"Not to me. To my sister."

Doctor Stokes blinked. "I see." Her gaze flickered to Jenny's cheeks, then across to the photograph of her grandparents.

"This is what you do, yes?" Jenny asked. "Talk about family troubles?"

"Indeed, it is," Dr. Stokes said. "Though if you don't mind, may I ask you about your face?"

"You may," Jenny said.

"It's part of my protocol," Dr. Stokes explained. "Whenever I see any injuries, no matter how small—"

"My little scars, you mean?"

"I have to ask about them," Dr. Stokes finished. "There are people who, for various reasons, inflict injuries upon themselves. Though in my far back African culture, yours would be called beauty scars, and quite nice ones."

"Thank you for that," Jenny said dryly.

"But some young women these days have a compulsion to cut themselves. It's a manifestation of some great pain they're in."

"Cattails," Jenny said. "That's how I came by my beauty scars. Running through a swamp searching for my sister, who had run away. Do you know how sharp cattail leaves are?"

"I don't, and thank you," Doctor Stokes said. "We can move on."

In the next few minutes Jenny gave Dr. Stokes the short version of the Haugen family trouble: Sally's visit to Doctor McConnell, the ether, the rape, the baby, the trial, arson, Sally's mental decline, her suicide attempt, and the trip last week to the State Hospital.

"My goodness, that's a lot." Dr. Stokes briefly clutched Jenny's hands. "I'm so sorry for your troubles. But you've done the right thing. You've reached out to someone."

"Thank you, I guess." She gathered herself. On Dr. Stokes's radio, softly, as if far away, a woman sang low and slow.

"So where would you like to begin?" Dr. Stokes took up a notepad.

"That's pretty much it." Jenny took up her purse. "How much do I owe you?"

Dr. Stokes blinked. "I beg your pardon?"

"I promised someone I'd talk to a professional person about this matter," Jenny said. "And now I've kept that promise."

There was silence. The dentist's drill had stopped. Dr. Stokes cocked her head at Jenny. "Have you and I gotten off on the wrong foot?"

"Why, not at all."

"Maybe it's that infernal drilling next door," Dr. Stokes said. "I wish that old fart would retire."

"Not the drilling or you," Jenny said. "I'm very pleased to meet you."

"Well, that's a relief."

Jenny fished out her wallet.

Dr. Stokes waved her off. "Today was us getting acquainted. Working through troubles like this can take time. If you want to continue, we'll discuss my fee schedule. She reached for her business card and handed it to Jenny. "You may call me any time, day or night."

Jenny tucked the card in her purse. She cocked her head to the woman singer. "That radio station, is it WMAQ out of Chicago?"

"It is indeed." Doctor Stokes leaned over to turn up the sound.

"That sounds like Nina Simone."

"I believe you're right," she said.

"Sometimes at night when the house is quiet, I listen to Daddy-O Daylie."

"He's on very late," Dr. Stokes said. "You must like jazz."

"I never sleep a full night. All jazz sounds much the same to me, but it's calming," Jenny said. "When my mind keeps turning. When I—"

At the door came a tap-tap, then shuffling. Dr. Stokes's face took on a pained look. "I believe my next patient is here."

"Of course." Jenny moved to leave. "I was finished anyway."

"I don't think so," Dr. Stokes said with her gap-toothed smile.

They shook hands. "Good day, Dr. Stokes."

"Good day, Mrs. Olsen."

In the hallway, a young woman, quite pregnant, turned away to hide her face.

Chapter Twenty-Eight
House Call

She put Dr. Stokes's business card in her dressing table drawer, and, that summer, devoted herself to kids. Angel was more lost than usual in her books. Jenny enrolled her in swimming lessons at the public pool. Angel hated it. Saturday-swim was a battle, but Jenny held the line. In a big surprise to the kids, Jenny bought a television. Evenings, the boys watched loud episodes of *Gunsmoke*, *Wyatt Earp*, and *The 64,000 Dollar Question*, John's favorite, along with the *Saturday Night Fights*. After school, Angel watched *Lassie*, but never gave herself fully over to it, and always had a book within reach. Her favorite program was *Queen for a Day* on NBC. She watched wide-eyed as John and Roland laughed at the ladies, one by one, sharing their sad problems.

"This is not a good show." Jenny stepped before the television. "Let's find something different."

"Is it real?" Angel asked.

"Those stories? We don't know for sure," Jenny said. "That's the problem with television."

"How do you get on the show?" Angel asked.

"You have to have something bad happen to you," Roland said.

Angel looked to Jenny.

"And be married," Jenny said. She touched Angel's hair. "At least that part of the show is real—we hope."

"Wyatt Earp is real," John said.

Roland turned sharply. "He is?"

"No, you knucklehead."

Angel laughed.

"Enough, or we turn it off," Jenny said.

Mainly Angel read in the bedroom, and the main way to get her out was a trip to the library. As a reward for the morning swimming lessons, Jenny took her every Saturday afternoon. Angel had recently gained "upstairs privileges" from Edith, who these days had the first streaks of gray in her hair. Angel could now look at grown-up books, and Jenny, reading in the great room, could keep an eye on her.

Killing time those Saturday afternoons, Jenny tried not to read the *Skye View*. She was not always successful. In the middle of August, "M. McConnell" was cited for reckless driving and speeding. It was the briefest note buried at the bottom of the police report.

"Bastards," she muttered.

Faces in the library turned.

They left soon after, Angel pretending she and Jenny were not together. As they passed the front desk, Edith said, "Angel, I need to speak to Jenny."

"I certainly hope so." She kept walking.

Jenny handed back the newspaper. "Please don't let me read the *Skye View*."

"Speaking of, I noticed that someone clipped an article."

"Sorry," Jenny said.

"I might have to restrict your privileges," Edith said.

Jenny smiled. Edith did not.

"I won't do it again," Jenny said.

"By the way, Angel wanted to check out this book." She handed over a heavy volume.

"*Families and Mental Illness: A Psychological Study*," Jenny read.

"I told her she could read it if she wanted, but it was quite adult and boring," Edith said. "I've ordered some brand-new books for girls, and she'd be first to have them."

That night, when the kids were asleep, Jenny took out Lurelle Stokes's business card. Stepped up to the black wall phone.

"Who is this?" Dr. Stokes said immediately, as if it might be a crank call.

"Mrs. Olsen. Jenny Olsen. Awhile back I came to your office."

"Of course, yes."

"I'm wondering if we could talk?"

"Yes," Dr. Stokes said. "I was hoping you might call someday."

Jenny paused.

"That's to say, I've been wondering how you and your family are doing."

"That's very kind," Jenny said.

And so they talked, at first about Sally and how she was doing at the State Hospital. Dr. Stokes steered the conversation around to the children. To "home life," question after question.

"That's pretty much it," Jenny said at length.

"Three children, a full-time job, no husband, and the home farm to worry about," Dr. Stokes said. "I can see why your mind turns at night."

"I suppose it is a lot."

"Tell me more about Angel. I'm not clear on how she came to live with you."

Jenny paused. "Her father is in prison. He used to work for me. Her mother is often missing in action, a drinker, I think. I'm looking after Angel until things improve for her family. Which might be awhile."

"What if I came by your house sometime? A social call. I'd like to meet the boys and Miss Angel in particular."

"That's very thoughtful, but it's too much to ask."

"To be honest, the weekends get a bit long. Caliste, my husband, is always on duty over at the air base. I'm happy to get out of the house."

"In that case, I'd be happy for a visit," Jenny said.

"Well then."

"Goodness," Jenny said. "It's after midnight. How long have we been talking?"

"A while." Dr. Stokes's voice thinned as if she were stifling a yawn.

"I shouldn't have called so late."

"Nonsense," Dr. Stokes said. "Day or night, remember?"

After they hung up, Jenny stepped out onto the lawn for a breath of air. A spray of stars, their pinpricks dulled by the streetlight, hung overhead. Chet and Millie's house was dark. So was the neighborhood around. She went to the middle of the yard, hoisted up her nightgown, squatted and peed.

***

The next Saturday, Lurelle Stokes parked her car out front. Jenny came onto the porch. Dr. Stokes waved, then headed up the sidewalk.

"What a nice neighborhood. So neat and tidy."

"It is."

"And please call me Lurelle."

Millie Arneson came onto her porch. Pretended to fuss with a plant.

"And neighbors close by," Jenny said.

Lurelle smiled. "And a front porch. I so miss those from Georgia."

"We can sit out if you like. The kids are off various places. Angel's at swimming lessons, but she'll be home soon."

Across, Millie lingered, watching from the side of her eyes, then went inside. Her kitchen curtain moved slightly. Jenny waved to the curtain.

Jenny brought coffee and a small plate of cookies to the front porch.

"I've been thinking about your family situation," Lurelle said.

Jenny listened.

"There's Angel," Lurelle said, "and there's you and your sister's trouble."

"That's pretty much it."

"Regarding Sally, there's a novel, *Crime and Punishment*, that came to mind."

"By the Russian fellow."

"Dostoevsky, yes," Lurelle said. "Do you know it?"

"I tried to read it in high school. The family where I boarded had a library. But it was too much. I couldn't keep track of the characters."

"Russian novels are challenging that way," Lurelle said. "The characters' names keep changing, nicknames on top of nicknames. But it's no loss you didn't finish because at the bottom of things, it's an objectionable story. Two women are murdered by a young man, yet it's the man that Tolstoy rattles on about for the rest of the book, his fear for the man's soul."

"I see."

"But the title is useful," Lurelle said. "Crime and punishment. As if one follows the other."

"It doesn't," Jenny said sharply.

"Correct," Lurelle continued. "So, when it happens to us—a great injustice—how do we go on living a good and useful life?"

Down the street, two kids called to each other and rode their bikes in a tight circle.

"That photograph on your office wall," Jenny said. "Your grandparents and their horses. That first time we met, when I said the word 'crime,' you looked at it."

Lurelle took a sip of coffee. "My grandfather's back had bullwhip scars. You could feel them through his shirt."

"But he went on," Jenny said. "That's what you're going to tell me."

"He did go on."

"That was rude of me," Jenny said. "I'm sorry."

Lurelle smiled her forgiveness and checked her watch. "How long until the children come home?"

"A half hour or so."

"Let's do something truly useful. Do you have flour and lard?"

On toward noon, car doors thudded. John had his driver's license now. There was hubbub, laughter, a half-shriek from Angel and then footsteps thundered on the porch.

"I win." Roland mostly fell inside the kitchen, then drew up at the sight of Lurelle Stokes.

"You must be Roland." She held up a hand whitened with flour.

Roland's eyes bugged out. He bolted.

"Roland. Come back here," Jenny called.

"Gees!" John exclaimed. There was a collision on the porch, after which John, looking over his shoulder, came into the kitchen. "What's eating Roland?" He turned to see Lurelle Stokes.

"Hello. You're John, I'm guessing."

"John, this is Doctor Stokes. A new friend."

"Miss Lurelle, you can call me," Lurelle said. "I'd shake hands, but…" She held up her white palms.

"Pleased to meet you, Miss Lurelle." John tossed his baseball glove atop the refrigerator as usual. "Smells good in here."

"Biscuits," Lurelle said. "You're just in time."

"Did it go okay at the pool?" Jenny asked.

"No problem," John said.

"Try a biscuit," Jenny said.

"Put butter on it," Lurelle added.

"Holy cow," John said as he chewed. His gaze went to the biscuit pan.

Angel dragged in. She had been hanging her towel and suit on the clothesline. She had wet hair and was always crabby after swimming lessons.

"Why is Roland hiding in the garage?" She stopped at the sight of Lurelle Stokes.

"You must be Angel," Lurelle said.

"This is my friend, Doctor Lurelle Stokes," Jenny said.

"Miss Lurelle is fine."

"Ever so pleased to meet you." Angel curtsied.

Lurelle let out a pleased laugh. "And I, you, Miss Angel. Such fine manners. Miss Jenny speaks so well of you."

"She does?"

"Of course I do."

"She says you're an especially good reader."

Angel shrugged. She looked to Jenny. "I should change."

"First take a biscuit out to Roland," Jenny said. "Tell him if he doesn't come in, that's all he gets. One."

Angel, pleased at this task, headed out with a buttered biscuit.

"I'm sorry about Roland," Jenny said.

"We'll make up," Lurelle said.

Soon Angel came back with Roland, who mumbled a hello and accepted a second, buttered biscuit from Lurelle.

"That's better," Jenny said and ruffled Roland's crew cut.

"I'll head in now," Angel said.

"I've heard your side of the bedroom is looking quite nice," Lurelle said. "Decorated and everything."

Angel nodded.

"Would you show it to me?"

"I suppose I could."

When Angel and Lurelle disappeared down the hall, Jenny pushed her pointer finger right between Roland's eyes.

"I was surprised, that was all." He leaned away. "I didn't mean nothing."

"Anything," Jenny said.

"It's not like any of us knew about your friend," John said.

"True," Jenny said. "But now you do."

"Can she teach you how to make biscuits?" John asked.

"You can only hope."

The boys were still hungry, so Jenny rationed the biscuits and made them a proper sandwich. Down the hall it was quiet. After the boys headed back outside, Jenny tapped on Angel's bedroom door.

"Come in," Angel called.

Angel sat back on a nest of pillows on the bed alongside Lurelle, who held a book.

"I'm starting *The Borrowers* again," Angel said. "Miss Lurelle said she hadn't read it for a very long time."

"I'll be in the kitchen," Jenny said. "Don't let her wear you out."

Lurelle returned to the book. "Everything they had was borrowed," she read, dropping her voice into lower tones. "They had nothing of their own."

Jenny paused outside the door and listened.

"Despite this, my brother said, they were touchy and conceited, and thought they owned the world," Lurelle read. "They thought human beings were just invented to do the dirty work—great slaves put there for them to use. At least, that's what they told each other. But my brother said that, underneath, he thought they were frightened. It was because they were frightened, he thought, that they had grown so small. Each generation had become smaller and smaller."

Jenny was finishing the dishes, with Roland and John back inside for "one last biscuit," when Lurelle and Angel finally came out.

Roland's eyes widened.

"Don't," Jenny mouthed.

Angel walked into the kitchen as if nothing about her had changed.

"Well, don't you look nice," Jenny said.

"Miss Lurelle did up my hair."

"We had a fine time braiding it," Lurelle said. "My sisters and I always did each other's hair."

"You must miss your family," Jenny said.

"Terribly."

After Lurelle and Angel finished their late lunch, the family saw her off.

"Boys? Miss Lurelle is leaving."

Roland reappeared. He stuck out a hand, though bent away as if Miss Lurelle's fingers might be burning hot or freezing cold. "Pleased to meet you, Miss Lurelle."

"And I you, Master Roland."

"Can you teach Ma how to make those biscuits?" John asked.

"I can."

As Lurelle drove off, Roland cocked his head. "She's nice."

Jenny remained on the sidewalk as Lurelle's car receded. A cloud passed. Sunlight in the neighborhood dimmed as if a shade had been lowered.

"Yoohoo." Millie waved from her porch.

"Damn," Jenny muttered. Millie came across the yard before she could escape.

"I noticed you had a visitor."

"Yes."

"Did you hire some help?" Millie continued. "If so, I'm looking too. I just can't seem to keep up with my housekeeping these days."

From inside the house came the voices of the children—a commotion, some small matter, Angel laughing as if she had bested Roland. "Yes," Jenny said. "We have help."

"Does she do windows?" Millie asked.

Chapter Twenty-Nine
Louis Armstrong

For the rest of the summer and into fall, Jenny saw Dr. Stokes twice a month at her office. She did not directly address Jenny's fixation with the McConnell family but approached it by focusing on "personal well-being" through "daily choices," including strategies on how not to think about "certain things." Every other visit, Jenny brought Angel. On her first meeting, Angel saw the trap that had been set and refused to talk. Rather than wheedle Angel to talk, Dr. Stokes did her hair.

Miss Lurelle also made the occasional "drop-by" house call, always on the weekend. From this combination of office and home visits, Angel became less withdrawn, though she was most outgoing when it was the three of them, together. At the beginning of September, Lurelle called to invite Jenny and Angel to a special event.

"Louis Armstrong is playing a concert in Grand Forks," Lurelle said. "He and his band are coming a couple of weeks from now."

"Louis Armstrong in Grand Forks?"

"My thoughts exactly," Lurelle said. "It'll be good for the town, and I thought you and Angel might like it too. The whole family."

"I'd love to," Jenny said. "Let me check with them."

"Wouldn't it be late when we got home?" Angel asked.

Jenny mustered her cheerful voice. "At least think about it. You don't have to decide now."

As Tuesday, September seventeenth approached, Louis Armstrong was a hard sell.

"Tuesday night is *Gunsmoke*," Roland said.

"I have baseball," John said.

"Baseball? I thought that was over."

"Baseball never sleeps, Ma."

Jenny laughed as John gave her a twirl.

"I have a new book," Angel said.

***

Jenny drove west toward Grand Forks in the late afternoon sun.

"This is so exciting." Edith wore a blue pillbox hat and a patterned, collar dress, long and swingy in the skirt.

"You look nice. And smell good too."

Edith blushed. "One doesn't get to see Louis Armstrong every night."

"That's what I told the children."

"They're young," Edith said. "Not their kind of music either."

"I hope they'll do all right alone."

"They will," Edith said. "I told them no popcorn."

They crossed the bridge over the Red River and into North Dakota, then continued west through town.

"I have to show you something," Jenny said. "We have time."

She slowed by the fairgrounds. "Racing Saturday night!" read the sign over the stone arch. The gate was open, the ticket booth empty. She drove in.

"When I was in high school, my class saw President Roosevelt speak here," Jenny said.

"Lucky you," Edith said.

"Sort of," Jenny said. "I slipped away from my class to meet a young man, a reporter, who wanted to get a close-up photo of Roosevelt."

"Oh my. A young man."

"Will Jamison, from the *Winnipeg Free Press*. He got the photo, but it was of Roosevelt in his wheelchair, which was not the kind of image his handlers wanted in the newspapers. His bodyguards caught us and took away the film. The president called me over and told me not to hang around reporters. 'They're a bad lot,'" she said in Roosevelt's tinny voice.

Edith's mouth hung open. "Why haven't I heard this story before?"

Jenny shrugged. "It's a bad habit in my family. We hold back."

"What else don't I know about you?" Edith teased.

"That's all you get today," Jenny said.

They walked over to the grandstand. Two fellows were working on the tall, wire-mesh fence that protected the spectators from crashing race cars. She walked up the wooden steps of the bleachers. Edith followed.

"Well, a little more," Jenny said. "My class sat right here."

"It must have been amazing," Edith said.

"It was."

"You ladies are a few days early for the races," one of the men called.

"We like to get a good seat."

He grinned. Pushed back his hat. "Anything we can do for you?"

"Not really," Jenny said.

"She was here some years ago," Edith said. "She saw Roosevelt speak."

"Roosevelt?" the second fellow said.

"The president," Edith said.

"Right over there," Jenny said. "There was a platform stage built just for the occasion. This whole grandstand was full and then some. October, 1936."

"Before my time," the first fellow said.

"Me too," said the other.

***

Lurelle Stokes lived in university housing on the west side of the campus. Jenny drove past red brick buildings, including the library, class halls, and fraternity houses, then on to a quiet street with identical small white houses. All very plain. No front porches.

Look for the red geraniums.

And there they were. Lurelle out front, tending to them. She looked extra tall and slim in her blue dress and white collar as she watered the bright bank of ruby blossoms. Two empty, metal lawn chairs sat by the front door.

Jenny tooted her horn. Lurelle waved. From inside the house, a Black man came to the front door. He paused behind the screen, then receded as if dissolving.

"You found me," Lurelle called.

"And I've brought a friend," Jenny said.

"I see," Lurelle said, with a faintest tint of disappointment in her voice.

Jenny made the introductions. Edith and Lurelle were both tall and willowy and leaned toward each other to shake hands.

"Such a nice neighborhood," Edith said.

"Thank you." Lurelle looked down the street. "We have housing over at the air base, but it's so empty and flat I can't bear to live out there."

"It *is* the prairie," Jenny said.

"Here I have neighbors," Lurelle said. "Most are faculty or graduate students. I'm not either one, but the university was kind enough to accommodate me. Maybe they needed some color."

"Your geraniums are very bright," Edith said.

Lurelle laughed and steered them inside. "Come meet the colonel."

The house smelled of fresh cigarette smoke.

"Caliste?"

They waited in the living room. The house was quite compact. Lurelle's husband had disappeared.

"Would you like an iced tea?" Lurelle went to a battered, white Frigidaire with round shoulders.

Presently an unsmiling, square-shouldered man appeared in the hallway. He had the build of a wrestler.

"Miss Jenny, this is my husband, Colonel Caliste Broussard. Caliste, Mrs. Jenny Olsen and her friend, Edith Klapperich."

He nodded. "Ladies."

"Caliste," Edith said. "That's a distinctive name."

"Cajun," Lurelle said. "Caliste is from New Orleans."

"That's right." His accent was stronger even than Lurelle's.

"New Orleans," Jenny said. "How did you two meet, may I ask?"

"In college up north."

Which brought a smile from Lurelle. "He means Atlanta."

Caliste's mouth softened ever so slightly. "Seemed way north at the time."

"Then Grand Forks must feel like—"

"The end of the world," Lurelle finished.

Caliste did not smile.

"The air force thought they needed Caliste at the new base," Lurelle said, "so here we are."

"Will you come to the concert tonight?" Edith asked.

"I'm not much for Louis Armstrong." Caliste patted his shirt pocket. Found a pack of Old Golds.

"Why, who couldn't like Louis Armstrong's music?" Jenny said.

"It's not so much his music." Caliste lifted his silver lighter.

"Would you mind smoking outside, dear?" Lurelle said. "This living room is so small."

"Sure." Caliste let his lighter snap shut, then took a bottle of beer from the refrigerator, and the newspaper, and headed outside.

"There's this thing among Black folks about Louis Armstrong." Lurelle lowered her voice.

Jenny and Edith waited.

"Many think he doesn't speak up enough," Lurelle continued. "About the way things are for us. Like right now, what's going on down in Little Rock."

"The school segregation matter," Jenny said.

"It's a disgrace," Edith added.

"'I don't talk no politics… I jess blows mah horn,'" Caliste said from outside.

"Oh dear," Lurelle murmured. The window screen was open to the yard below.

The women fell silent.

"When you finish your tea, we could go any time," Lurelle said.

***

They were ninety minutes early for the concert.

"Let's drive past his hotel," Lurelle said. "See if we can spot him."

"I'm up for anything."

Edith giggled. "Me too."

"I think he and his band will be one of the first Negroes to stay at The Dakota," Lurelle said as she drove downtown. "I hope things go all right there."

The Dakota, the largest hotel downtown, had a squarish, undistinguished front and was quiet streetside. Lurelle parked nearby.

Jenny and Edith followed Lurelle through the revolving door and into the lobby, which was quite grand, with a high arching ceiling, chandeliers, plus a wide banner: "**Welcome Mr. Louis Armstrong and his All-Star Band**!"

"Well, that's a good sign," Lurelle murmured.

A bellboy, speaking with a young man who carried a note pad, noticed Lurelle. "Are you all with Mr. Armstong's group?"

Lurelle paused. "Yes, I am. Along with my assistants."

"Hello there," Jenny and Edith said at once.

"How may I make your stay better?" the bellboy said, tipping his cap.

"This is such a fine hotel, so large, that I've completely forgotten his room number," Lurelle said.

The bellboy looked them up and down. "Or, like Larry here, maybe you just want to meet Mr. Armstrong?" He winked at Jenny and Edith.

"Young man, I'm afraid you've caught us," Lurelle said.

The bellboy shrugged. "Well, Mr. Armstong's a nice enough fella. And I was just going to take Larry up for a brief visit."

"I work for *The Grand Forks Herald*." Larry stepped forward and shook hands with them. "I'm trying to get an interview before the show."

The bellboy glanced back to the main desk. "If you promise not to stay long or be a bother, I'll take you all up together."

"We promise," Lurelle said.

In the elevator, the bellboy pushed the button. "Besides, he shouldn't mind seeing another... I mean someone... you know."

"A friend from down South?" Lurelle finished.

"Yes." The bellboy reddened. "That's what I meant."

Mr. Armstrong's door was cracked open. The bellboy tapped. There were voices, the smell of cigarette smoke.

"Room service."

"And then some," a taller Black man said as he eyeballed the hallway group. "Come on in, then."

The bellboy rolled in the cart. Lurelle's group followed.

The room, windows propped open for air, was crowded with musicians, all Black men in suits and ties. Their hair shone with pomade. One wore sunglasses. Another carried drumsticks. A guitar leaned in the corner, and a saxophone case, lined with ruby velvet, lay open on a bed. "Mr. Armstrong is shaving," said a big-boned, big-bosomed woman. She had a wide mouth and a supple voice.

"Keep an eye on things, Velma," said the tall musician. He nodded to the musical instruments. "We gotta eat too."

"Hello there," Velma said to Lurelle.

"I'm Dr. Lurelle Stokes, and these are my friends, Jenny and Edith. Welcome to North Dakota."

"Thank you. Velma Middleton," the woman said. "But I don't know as anyone called for a doctor."

"I'm a counselor," Lurelle said. "That kind of doctor."

"I'm Larry Luebenow," said the young man, "from the local newspaper."

"A head-shrink." Velma ignored the young man. She laughed heartily. "Lord knows this band could use one some days. All those miles. All of us packed together in the bus."

"Truth be told, we were just hoping to meet Mr. Armstrong," Lurelle said.

"And I'm hoping to get a quick comment for *The Grand Forks Herald*."

"Mr. Armstrong don't do no interviews before a concert," Velma said.

"Any small word would do," Larry said. "Wouldn't take but a minute."

"Is that my supper?" The raspy voice from the bathroom was unmistakable. Louis Armstrong emerged, wiping his face with a towel and wearing a Hawaiian shirt and walking shorts. He had skinny legs for such a barrel-chested, big-faced man.

"Yessir," said the bellboy.

"And a local sister and her friends just come to say hello," Velma said to Louis.

"Hello sister," he said, giving Lurelle a quick handshake. He nodded to Jenny and Edith.

"I'm from *The Grand Forks Herald*."

"Is that the lobster I ordered?" Armstrong asked.

"Yessir," the bellboy said, "the finest one we had."

"We a long way from salt water, son." He lifted the cover.

"Just a quick comment or two, Mr. Armstrong?" Larry said.

"Okay, okay, but I got a show tonight." Armstrong looked Lurelle up and down. "Sister, you'd better have a bite of supper with me. You could stand to gain a pound. You too," he said to Edith, who laughed.

"Me, I can't gain an ounce," Lurelle said.

"Some gals got all the luck," Velma Middleton said.

The reporter seized the moment. "Mr. Armstrong, you're a famous musician. What musicians do you like?"

Armstrong shrugged. "Bing Crosby, I suppose."

"Do you know each other?"

"Somewhat. Not like we're brothers."

"Which of his music do you like?"

"Most all of it," Armstrong said. "Crosby, he a smooth cat."

After a couple more questions, the reporter paused. "I wasn't supposed to ask you anything like this, Mr. Armstrong, but I'm wondering about your thoughts on Little Rock, Arkansas. Those girls trying to go to school."

"They's three boys with them too." Armstrong looked at the reporter squarely for the first time.

"Yessir, that's right," the young man said. "Central High School."

"Say, ain't we playing Central High School here tonight?" Armstrong turned to Velma.

"Yeah, Louis," she said. "Same name."

"I'm wondering if they's any colored kids go to school here?"

"Yes," Lurelle answered. "With the air force base here now, there's a few of us folks around. Their kids all go to public school."

"You see?" Armstrong turned to Velma as if she was the one who had asked the question. "Colored kids can go to school up here, but down south? Noooo."

The reporter set to scribbling.

"Down in Little Rock, they got the National Guard ring-round the school to keep our kids out," Armstrong said, louder now.

"President Eisenhower met with Governor Faubus three days ago," the reporter began. "He's trying to—"

"Eisenhower?" Armstrong interrupted. "Eisenhower is a mother-fucking plowboy. He ain't got guts enough to help those kids."

Lurelle's eyes widened.

"It's getting almost so bad a colored man hasn't got any country," Armstrong continued. He went to the window and looked down at the street. "The government, they want me to go to Russia. A goodwill tour, they call it. But the way they treating my people in the south, the government can go to hell."

The reporter scribbled faster.

"Louis," Velma said, "you better eat your supper now." She turned to the reporter and said, "Don't print all that, son."

"You should be with me on my tours down south," Armstrong said to the reporter. "It's Jim Crow all the way. We'd be travelin' Green Book if I weren't so famous."

"That's true, Louis, but you got to eat," Velma said, steering him toward his supper.

"Everywhere I go they always big on singing 'The Star-Spangled Banner,'" Armstrong said, "but here's how I sing it."

Lurelle's mouth fell open at Armstrong's version, half of which were swear words.

"You can't get all riled up, Louis," Velma said, "not before a show."

"I ain't riled up. I'm just telling it like it is."

"Thank you so much for dropping by." Velma herded the guests out. "Mr. Armstrong needs to eat."

Outside, in the hallway, the reporter murmured, "Holy Cow."

"Me too," Edith said. "Louis Armstrong spoke to me."

"Could I get your names?" the reporter asked.

Lurelle looked at Jenny and Edith.

"Not for the article. Just in case my boss at the paper doesn't believe me."

"You can use mine," Edith said.

"She's a librarian," Jenny said. "Everybody believes a librarian."

Afterward, the four of them went down the elevator. The reporter walked away. He had resumed scribbling.

"Well," Jenny said. They stepped out into the early evening sunlight of First Avenue. "Now you've got something to tell Caliste."

"I do indeed," Lurelle said.

At the Central High School auditorium, a space as fine as a small opera hall, a plaque at the door gave the details of its construction.

"Roosevelt and WPA," Jenny read.

"We should bring that program back," Edith said.

They headed in to claim their seats. The crowd grew.

"I think all the Black folks in North Dakota are here," Lurelle whispered. "All fifty of them."

"They should be sitting up front," Jenny said.

"They're here," Lurelle said. "That's the main thing."

"It's progress," Edith said.

The evening featured the Louis Armstrong people were expecting, the big-eyed, jovial, balloon-cheeked horn man singing all his hits, though he hardly ever made eye contact with his audience. At his smallest comments, the crowd went wild with applause. As he launched into "When You're Smilin'" the packed auditorium let loose a howl. Around Jenny, the spectators leaned forward, eyes alight, smiling, their gaze locked on Armstrong.

The concert was not long, and that was probably a good thing. She worried that people might injure their hands from clapping. But the night was something they all would take home and remember, an hour in a world that was still wonderful.

Outside, on the street, Edith said, "I feel like I never want to go home."

"Me neither," Jenny said.

"We'll go back and sit on my porch and have a lemonade," Lurelle said.

At the Stokes.s house, the living room light was on, as was the porch light. Lurelle parked. Nobody stirred to get out.

"I wish Caliste could have heard what Mr. Armstrong had to say," Lurelle said.

"You mean about Eisenhower?" Jenny replied.

Lurelle nodded.

"I've a feeling he'll be able to read about it in the paper," Edith said.

On the porch, as their chairs scraped, Caliste came to the door. "Just us," Lurelle called across.

"How'd it go with old Armstrong?' He lit a cigarette. Leaned in the doorway.

Lurelle paused. Looked to Jenny and Edith. "I think you had to be there."

The three women laughed.

Caliste stared.

"But don't worry, dear," Lurelle said. "If you bring us all a lemonade, I'll tell you everything."

"Yes, why not join us?" Jenny said.

"Make it a party," Edith said, and twirled once before sitting.

Caliste looked at the ladies. "I think now I should have gone."

***

As Jenny and Edith drove back to Crookston, a bright full moon rose up before them.

"Don't you love a big moon?" Edith said.

"Such a romantic, you are."

"Yes, well." Edith looked out to the fields.

They drove on. "That time I met Roosevelt?" Jenny said. "There's more to the story."

"I knew it," Edith said immediately.

"The young reporter? We were lovers. Everywhere—on the Winnipeg train, in parks, in his car, in the Road Kill Motel. We broke a bed there."

Edith drew in a breath. As they drove, she told Edith almost everything.

"Oh my. Lucky you."

"He enlisted in the air force in England and was killed in the Battle of Britain in October of 1941." They arrived on Jenny's street. She killed the engine and the lights.

Edith took her hand. "But you had love."

"I did. Nothing or no one comes close to him. That's why I don't put myself out there. 'On the market,' as you say."

"And I thought you were the perfect, grieving widow. That it was all about Arthur. You were Andromache, and he was Hector."

Jenny turned.

"The Greek plays," Edith said. "The wives were famous for grieving their heroic husbands."

"Arthur was no Hector," Jenny said.

Edith tittered.

"That didn't come out quite right," Jenny said.

"But it's true," Edith said. "You and Arthur weren't exactly a perfect match."

"Agreed."

"Well, I had love too," Edith said. "But then Sara went back home and married her high school sweetheart, for Heaven's sakes."

"She was nice," Jenny said. "I liked her."

"I probably was just an experiment."

"I don't think so," Jenny said. "You two seemed very happy."

"We were." Edith sniffled.

Jenny pulled her over and hugged her. "You'll find someone again."

"I doubt it. Not in this town."

"You wait. Just when you think it won't happen, it does. That's what you told me."

Edith leaned in and gave Jenny a long, hard kiss on the lips.

Jenny, startled, gave her a brief kiss back, then extricated herself.

"Oh dear," Edith said. "Now I've ruined everything." She burst into tears.

"Don't be foolish. You haven't ruined anything. In fact, maybe the opposite."

"The opposite?"

"You've reminded me that I could use a man on occasion." She touched her lips. "I haven't had such a good kiss since before the war."

"Thank you. I guess. What a night." Edith wiped her eyes. "By the way, I think Lurelle is more fond of you than you know."

"Whatever do you mean?"

"You know what I mean. And anyway, I'm the expert in these matters."

"What a silly goose you are."

"And meeting Louis Armstrong," Edith continued. "The concert. A full moon coming home. Thinking about Sara, which always makes me blue."

"Are you blue a lot?"

Edith paused. "I suppose I am."

"Maybe you should talk to someone," Jenny said.

Edith turned.

"A minister, though I know you're not much for church. A doctor, a counselor, a professional person."

"Maybe you're right."

Jenny smiled.

Edith's eyes widened. "You're a horrible, horrible person."

Jenny laughed. "Out with you. Scram. I have kids to check on."

Chapter Thirty
The Greyhound South

For Jenny's family, the nineteen-fifties closed on a high note. Sally's accommodations in Fergus Falls seemed to suit her. John finished up his baseball scholarship at Moorhead State College and caught the eye of professional baseball scouts. Roland had become a champion high school wrestler. And Jenny had become Angel's legal guardian despite not having a "man in the house." This designation came in part thanks to Arthur Olsen, whose name still commanded respect in the courthouse and about town. With her family in order, Jenny at last had some breathing room, as Lurelle called it. Some time to think about herself.

She took Lurelle up to Skye to see the home farm and to meet Emil and Dag. Emil took to Lurelle right off, Lurelle who could talk horses, implements, and farming. The two left on a tractor ride to see his crops, Lurelle sitting on the iron fender with one hand on Emil's shoulder to steady herself.

"I'm so ashamed of myself," Jenny said at the kitchen window, dabbing at her eyes.

"Why-ever for?" Dag said.

"Emil and Lurelle," she said. "I wasn't sure if they'd get along. You know."

"She's nice," Dag said. "But so thin. Is she well?"

"I'm not sure," Jenny said. "She doesn't talk about it."

"In any case, she reminds me of Sally. Both so tall. Those long arms."

Which set them both to sniffling.

"And you?" Jenny said. They were alone. They did not have to whisper. There was no one upstairs.

"I find myself doing things I haven't done for years." Dag picked up her sewing basket. "I'm making doilies again."

Jenny touched the white circle. "They're exactly like the old ones."

"I didn't think I could remember the pattern."

"I can see my Christmas present."

"Now you've spoiled the surprise."

"And Emil?" Jenny asked. "How is he?"

Dag raised her shoulders and let them drop. "Every time we go to town, he drives past the doctor's house," she said. "We stop to look. If I'm not with him and he's gone a long time, I know he parks there. One night I saw him leave with a whole gunnysack of salt. What would he do with that?"

***

Angel, fourteen, still carried a reserve, a skepticism of most everything—though, surprising everyone, she finally took to swimming. Jenny dropped her off at the pool, and, wearing black goggles and a tight rubber cap, Angel swam lap after lap by herself. She had friends at high school, though none who came for a sleep-over, nor was she invited to any. Unlike any girl in her school, she wore her hair in tight, wound-up braids, Miss Lurelle style. Her grades in English and history and music were perfect, less so in math and sciences. For her birthday, Jenny bought her a radio. She hoped to hear teen music issuing from behind the bedroom door. Buddy Holly, Chuck Berry, Connie Francis, Richie Valens, The Everly Brothers. Instead, there was classical music from a small, public station in Fargo.

"Give her time," Lurelle said. "She's only fourteen."

Jenny's children grew ever bigger. Roland, in high school, wrestled at 185 pounds. John was as tall as his father had been. But Lurelle withered. By the end of 1960, she was as skinny as a pitchfork and walked stiffly, slightly stooped, as if into an invisible wind. Her hair had thinned, her eye sockets hollowed, and darker patches of skin had spread across her cheeks like a black butterfly that had landed on her nose and slowly opened its wings. She occasionally repeated herself.

"You are not well," Jenny said. "Is there anything you should tell me?"

"Lupus," she said. They were at her office. "I've had it for some time, but it's catching up with me."

"Lupus? I've never heard of that."

"All the better for you. When you're at the library, look it up."

Jenny took her arm as they walked down the steps. The dentist's drill whined.

"Will that old fossil never retire?" Lurelle said.

She closed out her office near the end of 1960—the steps were too much—and dropped by Jenny's house not long before Christmas. She brought small gifts for the kids, and for Jenny, in case she had run out, a can of fresh lard.

They set about making biscuits and getting caught up. Roland watched from the side and said, "Miss Lurelle?"

"Yes?"

"You don't look so good."

"Roland," Jenny said.

"It's okay," Lurelle said. "It's true, Roland. I've got a sickness."

"Will you be all right?" Angel asked.

"Dear children, I don't think so," Lurelle said cheerfully. "There's a hellhound on my trail."

Roland's eyes widened.

"Are you watching how we make these biscuits?" Lurelle asked.

"Yes," Roland said.

"Because you might have a nice family of your own someday and then you can be the biscuit-maker."

"Roland cook? Ha!" Angel scoffed.

"That's the thing about family," Lurelle said. "You never know."

"I'm gonna be a farmer," Roland said. "Just like Uncle Emil."

"Let's hope not *exactly* like Uncle Emil," Jenny said.

"What's wrong with Uncle Emil?" Roland said.

"Come over here and punch this dough," Lurelle replied.

Roland hopped to it.

"Again," Lurelle said. "Like you mean it."

Roland drew back, gathered a fist.

Before she left, Lurelle did Angel's hair, never better, though her hands trembled. When she left, Angel cried.

Jenny did not hear much from Lurelle in the deep cold of January, though they talked occasionally on the phone, always social calls. "The colonel" was gone most of the time to the air base. Lurelle assured Jenny that she was doing "just fine," and always changed the subject. She inquired after the children, Angel in particular.

"She doesn't say much," Jenny said. "At least to me."

"Don't give up," Lurelle said. "Most of motherhood is just being there."

"I'm not her mother."

"You likely will be someday, if she wants to stay with you. And if you want her to."

"Of course I do."

"Okay. My point is, you don't need to talk things to death."

The winter ground on. With two teenagers in a small house, and John often home on weekends to make it three, it was hard to stay in touch with herself, let alone Lurelle. At the end of April, the phone rang. Angel picked up.

She held out the receiver and mouthed, "It's Miss Lurelle's husband."

"Oh dear."

The colonel got right to it. "I'm wondering if you might pay a call?"

"Of course," Jenny said. "It's been too long."

"She's been asking after you and Miss Angel."

"How is she doing?" Jenny asked.

The colonel paused. "Fair."

She and Angel drove to Grand Forks on Saturday, careful to arrive early afternoon so Lurelle did not feel she had to make either lunch or supper.

Caliste met them at the door. He shook hands, a hard, brief pump.

"My daughter, Angel. Angel, this is Colonel Stokes."

"Pleased to meet you," Angel said, and curtsied.

"And I, you, young lady." He returned a slight bow and a smile. "Miss Lurelle will be happy to see you."

"Miss Jenny?" Lurelle called from the living room. She lay on the couch, an orange, hot water bottle peeking from beneath a blanket and an open book face-down across her chest. She hardly made a shape under the blanket. "And there's Miss Angel too."

Angel burst into tears.

"Come here right now," Lurelle said.

Angel sat on the floor beside Lurelle's couch.

"Tsk tsk," Lurelle said, as she stroked Angel's hair. "We really must do something about this braiding."

"Yes," Jenny said. "We were in the neighborhood."

"Ha." Lurelle wheezed out a laugh.

"I called Miss Jenny," Caliste said. "Asked her to come for a visit."

"Don't ya'll worry about me," Lurelle replied. "This is one of my bad days."

"Most of them are bad." Caliste had gained frown lines across his forehead, and lost weight too.

"Well, I'm glad for company." With effort, Lurelle sat up and, with shaky hands, began to tighten Angel's braids.

"Lurelle and I have been talking," Caliste said.

"Let's not bother Jenny with all that."

"She needs to go home," Caliste said. "To Atlanta. The doctors there know more about Lupus."

"They do," Lurelle said. "The doctor in Fargo said one of the symptoms of Lupus is when your hands or feet get cold, your skin turns white. I told him I didn't think that would happen to me."

Angel giggled.

"But Caliste is right," Lurelle said. "I need better doctoring, plus there are things happening at home, the lunch counter protests and the marches for voting rights, that have been too long coming for me to miss."

"I can't take her," Caliste said.

Lurelle turned.

"I'm sorry." Caliste came over and sat beside Lurelle. "I've been trying to find a time to tell you. Things are coming to a head at the base. The planes are coming soon. They'll have the warheads, and I'm in charge of, well, most everything. I can't leave my men now."

Lurelle patted his arm. "Well, well. This is a pickle."

Caliste took her hand.

"I don't want to ride home on the mail train."

"I'll take you," Jenny said.

"And I'll come along," Angel said.

"Nonsense, you two," Lurelle replied.

"I have a few vacation days," Jenny said. "I've never been to Atlanta."

Lurelle laughed. "You never been nowhere, honey."

Angel said, "It would be educational for me."

"Maybe too educational." Caliste frowned. "This is not the best time to be taking a bus down south."

"That business with the Freedom Riders," Lurelle said.

"I'm not worried about that," Jenny said. "I'll have to speak with Edith and Roland. One way or another, we'll get you home."

"Glory be," Lurelle murmured. She reached to hold Angel and Jenny's hands, then closed her eyes. "I need to rest a bit and think about all this."

Eventually, when Lurelle dozed, they extricated their hands and stood.

"We should go," Jenny whispered.

Regarding the trip to Georgia, Roland, a senior in high school, had his father's conservative bent.

"Something might happen to you," he said.

"I'll be fine," Jenny said.

"And anyway, I'll be along," Angel said.

"You're too young to go."

"No, I'm not."

"She'll help me with Miss Lurelle," Jenny said. "It might take two of us."

"How long will you be gone?"

"A few days."

"What am I supposed to do?" Roland held up his hands.

"You know how to make biscuits," Angel said.

"Hush," Jenny said. "Aunt Edith will stay here."

"She's not my real aunt," Roland said.

"She's your honorary aunt," Jenny said. "Like Angel's your honorary sister."

***

Jenny, Angel, and Lurelle left by train early morning on May seventeenth, 1961.

Roland, on the platform, watched them with arms crossed.

"He'll be fine," Angel said.

For the trip Jenny had packed lap blankets and a large food bag. "It should get us a good part of the way," she said of the food. Lurelle had made a double batch of biscuits, a few of which they ate before the train hardly got halfway to Fargo. Soon afterward Lurelle fell asleep. Angel covered her with a blanket. Across the aisle, an older couple watched.

"What is it?" Jenny said.

They looked away.

Beneath the train, the rail seams went "chek-chek, chek-chek" as the cars rolled south and east through Detroit Lakes, Staples, Little Falls, Saint Cloud. Every fifty miles made a difference in the advance of spring with the fields showing a pale green fur of the new crop.

There was a long break in Minneapolis, during which they got off the train. Rather than eat down their own food supply, they had supper at the counter in the station. Angel sat between Lurelle and Jenny. Then it was back on the train and to their seats, which reclined most of the way—there was no sleeper car—for the overnight ride to Chicago.

Jenny dozed. The car grew chilly, and she shared her lap blanket with Angel, who drew in against her. Later, sleepless, she eased out to stand up and stretch her legs. At the rear of the car were four compartments, their curtains closed. In one of them, a woman giggled.

"Stop that now." She giggled again.

They arrived at Chicago early in the morning, a little before sunup. The filthy skylights high up in the grand old station gave no indicator of time of day. Angel and Jenny carried the three suitcases as they crossed over to the Greyhound station and bought tickets on the Atlanta-bound "Scenicruiser."

With its second level, the Scenicruiser looked a good deal like their train car, and while the view might have been better up top, the three steps up were narrow and difficult, plus the lavatory was midway on the lower floor. They settled in halfway back, Lurelle's choice. Ahead of them the passengers were mostly White; behind, mostly Black.

"Welcome to the south up north," Lurelle murmured to Angel.

She looked around at the passengers.

As the bus rolled out of the station and through concrete canyons and warehouses and hazy air, Lurelle told Angel about the "other great migration" in America. "Not the one east to west, but the one south to north. Black folks by the thousands went up to work in the Detroit auto industry and in the factories and packing plants in Chicago."

"That wasn't in our history book at school." Angel kept her nose to the glass.

The Scenicruiser passed through smoky, battered Gary, then into green, farm country and endless fields of corn, stalks already a foot tall.

Lafayette.

Indianapolis, and a one-hour stop for some kind of bus repair. Jenny hoped it was to the lavatory, which had begun to smell of urine. As they waited, a man with plumber's tools came and went.

Then, with a fresher smell in the bus, it was on to Louisville, Kentucky, outside of which the corn was knee-high, and there would be a half-hour break at the station. They debarked to stretch their legs. More passengers got on, mostly Black, though when they returned to the bus, a White couple was sitting in their seats.

"Pardon me," Jenny said, "those seats are taken."

"By us," the man said.

"They's open seats further back," the wife said, eyes on Lurelle. "We moved your things."

"You what?" Jenny said.

"We were sitting there," Angel said. "You can't just move our stuff."

"It's okay," Lurelle said, and tugged Angel's sleeve.

"It's not okay," Jenny said.

"Let's not have no trouble," the bus driver, a white man, said.

"We're not creating trouble… they are," Angel said.

"You make trouble, you're off this bus," the bus driver replied.

With effort, Lurelle pushed Jenny and Angel forward. As they passed down the aisle, most everyone averted their eyes. The only seats open were well back.

After they sat, Lurelle held Jenny and Angel's hands as if to keep them anchored.

"I'm going to complain," Jenny said. "Write a letter to the president of Greyhound."

Across the aisle, a tiny, white-haired Black woman leaned over. "Write one to that young President Kennedy too."

"He ain't doing that much for us," muttered an older Black man.

"Not so far," the old woman said right back. "But give him some time."

"That's what we been hearin' all our lives," the older man said.

Cincinnati.

Lexington.

The sun tracked low in the west. Their lunch bag shrank. The sun went down in Tennessee, and Jenny dozed until awakened by the lights of Nashville. Lurelle shared the last of their biscuits around the back. In the darkened bus she broke them in half, their whiteness passing one person to the next like the transit of planets. After Chattanoga, most all the passengers were Negroes, and the white couple up front now sat tight up behind the driver, as if he might protect them.

"Not long now," Lurelle said. "A couple of hours." She was sitting up straighter and had freshened herself with a lavender sachet.

"It'll be after midnight," Jenny said. Angel dozed under her arm.

"That might be good," Lurelle murmured.

The lights of Atlanta slowly lit the interior of the Scenicruiser. The dark shapes sat upright, faces to the front. The bus turned off the main highway and headed downtown, pausing now and again for a stoplight, then groaning forward. The interior lights of the bus came on bright.

"Atlanta," the driver called on his intercom.

"Glory be," Lurelle murmured.

The station was small, two storeys with curved front corners, a marquee over the main door, and a flat roof overhang on each side where a bus could park. The whole thing looked like an old gas station. Several cars and pickups waited out front. As the Greyhound pulled in, headlamps flashed on/off between three of the pickups.

"Oh dear," Lurelle said.

They leaned closer to the glass.

Men got out of the trucks.

"They here," a woman called.

"They never sleep," another voice said.

"Stick together," a Black man said. "When you step out, keep your heads down and don't say nuthin.'"

"No sir, we gone walk through this valley with our heads up." The old lady squared her shoulders.

Lurelle tugged a fellow's sleeve. "Young man, would you see if there's a wheelchair inside the station?"

He paused. "Okay."

"Can't you walk?" Jenny said with alarm.

"Here's a dollar for your trouble," Lurelle said.

He took it and followed the rest out.

"Everybody off," said the driver through the tinny speaker. He looked up to his mirror.

"We comin', we comin', Mister," Lurelle drawled. "An old lady needs some time." She had tied a scarf low across her forehead.

The young man came to the bus steps with the wheelchair, then high-tailed it to catch up with the others, who were passing through a gauntlet of men.

"Now listen," Lurelle whispered. "Jenny, you sit in that wheelchair with your suitcase on your lap. I'll push you."

"What?" Jenny asked.

"Don't ask, just do it," Lurelle said. "Angel, you carry the other two suitcases."

Lurelle stepped down first. "Look feeble," she whispered.

Jenny took Lurelle's hand, who shook Jenny's arm as if Jenny had the tremens.

"Is that one of them?" a man said.

"Into the chair," Lurelle whispered, and situated Jenny's suitcase.

"She a Freedom Rider?"

Lurelle hooted out a laugh. "Freedom Rider? What you men talkin' about? I'm her nurse. She come here to the city for doctoring."

"Doctoring," one of the men repeated.

"My mother's very ill." Angel stepped forward. "Let us pass."

Jenny tilted slightly in her chair.

"You heard her. You fellas go on and clear out." Lurelle pushed the wheelchair straight at them. "We goin' to the hospital."

The group of men parted, and Lurelle pressed ahead. She waved to a taxi across the street. Its light came on. "Praise the Lord."

When they were underway, the bus station receding behind, Lurelle patted Jenny's arm. "You a good actress. You looked mighty feeble."

"Thank you." Jenny took longer breaths.

Angel had turned to looked behind. "Are those men—"

"Oh yes," Lurelle said quickly. "They around."

"They don't come out so much in the daylight these days," the cab driver said, "but there's plenty of them."

"I thought they wore white hats and robes," Angel said.

"They don't anymore," the driver said. "But they's them."

"What about the police?" Angel said.

"They one and the same," the man said. "So, we got to look out for ourselves."

***

The Stokes family home, a narrow, two-storey house with a peaked roof, sat tucked close between similar houses on Auburn Street. Lurelle's older, unmarried sister, Bernice, lived there to help take care of their parents, who were lively though frail and no longer drove their car. Lurelle's arrival created great commotion, tears of joy, and some alarm at her appearance. Bernice and Lurelle were the mirror image of each other, though Bernice now looked the younger of the two. The sisters held onto each other hand-in-hand, arm-in-arm, always within touching distance as Bernice put together a late-night meal of cold chicken, hot collard greens and toast. The food calmed everyone, and they finally got to bed after two a.m. The little upstairs bedroom with a knee wall was familiar, and sharing a bed with Angel, whose elbows were always sharp, transported Jenny to her own youth and the farm in Skye. Pappa and Mama were downstairs, Mama in her long apron, and thick braids wound up on the sides of her head; Papa in his heavy pants and heavy wool sweater that smelled of horses.

"You're dreaming," Angel said, and moved out of touching distance.

The next morning, May 19th, Jenny and Angel woke up late, almost eleven a.m., to cheerful voices downstairs and the clink of coffee cups.

They freshened up in the little bathroom, brushed their teeth, then came down.

"Here comes the real nurse and her assistant," Lurelle said. A new couple was sitting at the table drinking coffee.

"Good morning," Jenny said.

Angel waved shyly.

"I was just telling the neighbors about our welcome party at the bus station," Lurelle said.

"Lurelle, she always the clever one," an older Black man said. He was short and handsome, with a wide and open face and big white sideburns.

"These are frightening times," his wife said. "We all need to be clever."

"This is Mr. and Mrs. King. Lonnie and Alberta," Lurelle said. "They live three houses down."

"Pleased." He shook Jenny and Angel's hands as introductions were made.

"We thank you so much for bringing Miss Lurelle back home," Mrs. King said. "We always worried she might freeze to death up north."

"Sometimes I had to put on all the clothes I owned, then jump up and down ten times," Lurelle said. She seemed rested and ten years younger.

Jenny felt underwater. Groggy. The warmth, the humidity of Atlanta, lay on her like a blanket that couldn't be cast off. "It does get cold in North Dakota."

"We'd best be on our way," Lonnie said to Lurelle.

"We'll mention you to Martin," Mr. King said.

"Is he home?" Lurelle asked. "If so, tell him to drop by."

"He's in Montgomery," Mrs. King said. "So much trouble there."

"We praying for him," Bernice said.

"How long will you stay?" Mrs. King asked Jenny, as if to lighten the subject.

"Just a couple of days," Jenny said. "A quick trip."

"Well, bless you for coming all this way." Mrs. King hugged Jenny.

After they left, Angel said, "The King family. Is that?"

"It is," Lurelle said. "We've known them forever."

Over the next two days, Jenny and Angel got a walking tour of the Sweet Auburn neighborhood and a drop-in to the King house, which, with a front porch, sharp stairway to the upstairs, and the kitchen in back, was much like Lurelle's house and much like the house Jenny had grown up in.

"We'd take you downtown for lunch…" Bernice said.

"But we might get soup on our heads," Lurelle finished.

Angel's eyes widened. Bernice, who had taken a shine to Angel, took her arm.

"Don't be frightening Miss Angel."

"I'm not afraid."

Sunday morning, they dressed for church.

"You need a hat," Lurelle said.

"I hardly ever wear a hat," Jenny said.

"Ya'll are honorary Atlanta ladies now."

Angel put on a blue hat with a yellow band. Jenny tried out a wide-brimmed yellow hat with a white band. She wore the only light dress she had brought along, one with short sleeves.

The Ebenezer Baptist Church on Jackson Street was an unassuming red brick building with two square towers and the main building, the nave, between. Inside, the great hall smelled warm, like a kitchen in which, over many years, there had been much cooking. Hats floated above the pews like a flock of large, many-colored birds.

"What I tell you about a hat?" Bernice nudged Jenny.

Lurelle, Bernice, and her parents headed toward the front. Angel and Jenny followed. There were smiles and nods to the family as they passed to an open pew where the Stokes family always sat. The choir wore long white gowns, and the singers soon swayed in song. The service, preached by Dr. Lonnie King, turned toward the power of God's love as manifested in Jesus's forgiveness of his enemies, his love even for his tormentors.

Jenny looked to her lap, trying to forget.

Lurelle nudged her.

"I know, I know," Jenny whispered.

Lurelle draped a bony arm around her.

King brought the message around to the "current troubles" without ever naming the white men, the ones who met buses, the ones who dumped soup on the heads of lunch counter patrons.

"They oppressed too," King called. "They been stepped on and beat down too. Only they don't know it, not like us, so we got to help them see."

"Amen," came voices around. People raised their hands.

Jenny touched her clammy forehead. The church warmed. The smell of it deepened, with a sharper body odor, not objectionable, strong, mixed with perfume and hair pomade.

King's voice rose. "As my own son has preached, 'Nonviolence means avoiding not only external physical violence, but also internal violence of spirit. You not only refuse to shoot a man, but you refuse to hate him.'"

"Amen."

"Tell it."

"That's right."

Jenny gripped the pew back with both hands. Took deep breaths.

Bernice and Lurelle were standing now, Lurelle braced against the pew in front. Both stood with palms in the air and eyes closed, both available for the Gift.

Jenny tugged Angel's sleeve, then broke for the door. Behind her the sermon continued, the voices of the congregants rising, calling out, praising. She headed to the front door and into the stale breath of Atlanta. She leaned against the brick wall of the church. Took off her borrowed hat. Breathed through her mouth. Inside, the choir started to sing, "There is a Balm in Gilead, to make the wounded whole... There is a Balm of Gilead, to heal the sin-sick soul."

She walked far enough to make the singing indistinct. Steadied herself against a tree, the base of which was littered around with cigarette butts.

A man and his wife paused. "Miss, you okay?"

"I think so."

"You leaning pretty bad," the woman said.

"I'll be okay."

"Take Melvin's arm. We'll stand here a minute with you."

"That's very kind," Jenny murmured. She took his arm in the steam-thick city air.

"Looks like you been to church," the woman said.

"Yes."

"That's why we out here today." The lady nudged her man. "I try to get Melvin walking past the church at least. Maybe someday he'll go in with me."

"We're doin' fine as is," Melvin said.

"One reason people go to church is to keep from being mad all the time." His wife gave him a look.

"I mad 'cause there's lots to be mad about these days."

"Or maybe you was just born mad," his wife said.

"I'm feeling better now," Jenny said.

"We'll walk you back to the church," the woman said. "Unless Melvin is afraid of getting too close."

"I ain't afraid."

"He worried that the Lord gonna reach his big old bony hand out the door and snatch him."

Melvin blew out a breath.

"You've been very kind… thank you," Jenny said to them.

"That's all we can do these days," the wife said. "Let our actions speak for us. Ain't that right Melvin?"

"I hope so," he said. "We need something. I know that."

His wife took his arm, and they walked on.

Back at the church, in the crowd streaming out, she found Bernice and Lurelle and Angel.

"What happened to you?" Bernice asked.

"This heat and humidity," Jenny said. "It's a bit much."

"Heat? Humidity? You wait till summer," Bernice said.

Angel's cheeks had turned pink as well.

"Or maybe the Lord was working in you." Lurelle gave Jenny another nudge.

"I'm not sure He'd have much luck."

"Never say that," Lurelle answered.

"Do you go to church up north?" Bernice took Angel's arm, and Lurelle Jenny's, as they headed to the parking lot.

Angel glanced at Jenny. "We don't, no."

"That's never no mind," Bernice said. "You both halfway to Glory for bringing Lurry home."

***

Early Monday morning Bernice and Lurelle drove Jenny and Angel to the station. A dusty bus, not a Scenicruiser but still a Greyhound, waited under the overhang, motor thrumming.

"Quiet here today."

"Fine by me," Jenny said.

"Don't forget your lunch."

"This will last us for a week," Angel said to Bernice.

"That old bus might take you that long."

Lurelle leaned close so that Angel wouldn't hear. "Don't forget what we been talking about all these times." She straightened Jenny's blouse collar, squared her shoulders.

Jenny nodded.

"No stalkin', no car burnin', no dirty tricks. None of that stuff."

Bernice's eyes widened.

"Miss Jenny, she light and wiry and pretty, but you don't want to cross her," Lurelle said.

Jenny hugged Lurelle's bony frame and then Bernice.

"Be sure to let the colonel know how it went," Lurelle said. "He's been calling."

"I will," Jenny said.

The driver tooted his horn. Jenny and Angel queued to board. Inside, they passed some white folks up front.

A woman smiled and caught Jenny's sleeve. "There's room up here."

"We're fine farther back," Jenny said.

"That's nice of you," the woman murmured, with a glance at her husband, who had nothing to say. Near the rear they took a window seat across from a young mother holding a sleeping baby. The baby's shiny hair was done up with pink ribbons.

"You sure you ladies want to sit here?" the mother said to them. "My baby girl going to squall and shout at some point."

"We won't mind," Angel said. "I can help with her if you want."

The mother looked her up and down, then held up her baby, whose wobbly face turned to Angel and smiled.

"Thank you, young lady. She likes you already."

As the bus pulled out, Jenny and Angel turned to the rear window. Lurelle spotted them, pointed and nudged Bernice. The two sisters raised their hands and held them high as if in church. As if to bless them.

Chapter Thirty-One
The Hats

After the trip to Atlanta, Angel carried herself as if she had shed a skin. She spent less time reading alone, more time riding her bike, sometimes with other girls. By August she was somewhat tan, even, and had grown an inch. She kept her hair up in "Miss Lurelle braids," which no one thought to comment on anymore. It was her style. She and Jenny did all right, much better than before the trip, though Jenny didn't push it.

In early October, the phone rang.

Angel picked up. Turned. "It's Colonel Stokes."

"Oh dear." Jenny accepted the receiver as if it might be hot to the touch. She listened. Then hung up and covered her face.

The next day, sunny but chilly, she and Angel waited at the gate of the Grand Forks Air Force Base. The hangars beyond were immense, the gate guards unsmiling in their sunglasses and bucket helmets.

A gray, military Jeep with a young airman at the wheel drove up fast to the other side gate. He spoke with the guard, who lifted the gate arm. Jenny drove behind the Jeep across acres of concrete, past rows of enormous planes to a quonset building. Across its front was the air force logo and "Headquarters: 22nd Reconnaissance Squadron." The airman escorted them inside. A secretary made a call. Colonel Stokes soon came out, his uniform crisp, his black shoes gleaming.

"Miss Jenny. Miss Angel."

Angel sniffled.

"I'm sorry." The colonel came over and put an arm around her.

"If we'd have known sooner," Jenny began.

"She didn't want ya'll to make another trip to Atlanta."

"We would have," Jenny said.

"Yes," Angel added.

"See? She had it all figured out."

Jenny dabbed at her eyes.

"I was with her at the end. Me and the whole family. It went as well as it could. The funeral at Ebenezer was overflowing. King himself, the younger one, did the service."

"We should have been there for sure," Jenny said.

The colonel went to his desk. "She sent a package for you."

Jenny accepted a good-sized box tied neatly with string. "Miss Jenny and Family," it read.

"I'll bet it's a book," the colonel said. "She was a reader."

Jenny clutched the box to her breast.

"She greatly valued your family," he said.

"And we her."

The colonel swallowed. Straightened. Checked his watch. "I promised you a tour of the base."

"You're busy, and I'd rather not," Jenny said. "Your planes scare me. I lost someone close to me in the war, a pilot."

Angel turned to Jenny.

"I'm sorry to hear that," the colonel said. "I'll see you out, then." At her car, he shook hands with them both. He wore his sunglasses though the day was cloudy. The top of his cheeks glistened. He wiped them.

"You'll stay in touch?" Jenny said.

"I'll try."

In their car, Angel opened the package. A Bible, Lurelle's. And two bright hats, the ones she and Angel had worn to church in Atlanta. Blue for Angel, yellow for Jenny.

At the exit booth, a young, Black female soldier in a bucket helmet leaned down to look closer. "Nice hats, ladies."

"Thank you."

Clear of the base, Jenny braked at the highway, then turned east.

"On the way home can we stop at the Dairy Queen in Grand Forks?" Angel asked.

"Sure," Jenny said. "We have time."

Angel checked her hat in the mirror. "And you can tell me about the pilot."

Section Four: Cold War

Chapter Thirty-Two
Government Men

In August of 1961, on a shimmering hot day under a cloudless blue sky, two men walked up the home farm lane. Their car had stopped before Emil's gate.

"Emil," Dag shouted from the porch.

He came to the machine shed doorway. The strangers wore white, short-sleeved shirts and black pants. Sunglasses. "Stop right there," Emil called and went to block their path. The men drew up. The tall one carried a clipboard. Both were sunburned. They didn't wear hats.

"Emil Haugen?"

"You missed the sign on the gate. The one that says 'No peddlers.'"

"We're not peddlers," the stocky one said.

"We're from the government," the other added. Their black shoes, low cut with heavy soles, came from the same store.

"I pay my taxes."

"You do, Mr. Haugen," said the short one. "We checked."

"What's it to youse?"

"Have you heard about the threat to America from Russia?" the shorter one asked.

Emil shrugged. "I read the newspaper."

"Their missiles? Sputnik?" asked the taller one. "The Russkies have a satellite orbiting the earth right now." He pointed a finger to the sky.

Emil did not look up. "The one with the dog in it? That was a damned shame."

"We don't care about the dog," the short one said. "We're worried about the missile that launched it."

"The missile that could reach all the way here," the tall one added.

"Because of that, our United States Government is developing a military response to this Russian threat from outer space," the short guy continued.

"And your farm has been chosen."

Emil stared. "Chosen."

"For a missile silo."

Across the yard a chicken squawked.

"You understand silos, I'm sure," the short one said. "But our silos are not above ground, and they're not for corn. We dig a deep hole into the ground, build a concrete ring around it, then put a nuclear missile inside."

"A missile silo," Emil said.

"We'll be installing dozens of them across North Dakota," the taller one said. "Including one on your farm."

"What?" Emil said.

"Once it's complete, you won't even see it," the short one continued, "and neither will the Russians. Though even if they do see it, even if they hit us way out here, they won't do much damage. Hardly anybody lives out here."

"*I* live out here."

Across on the porch, Dag stepped forward and shaded her eyes. "Is it my Watkins vanilla?"

"No," Emil called back. "Stay back."

"You'll get paid for your trouble, of course," said the short one.

"The government leases your land," the other continued. "Ten acres is all we need. Then once per year a nice check comes in the mail."

Emil took off his hat and stepped closer. "Listen. I don't care if you need a hundred acres or ten goddamned square feet. There's never gonna be a missile silo on this farm."

"We're sorry you feel that way, Mr. Haugen." The man leaned back but held his ground.

"Though what you think doesn't matter," said the short one. "If the government thinks a missile should go here…" He drew an X in the dirt with his foot.

"…then the missile will go there." The other one put his black shoe on the X. "Eminent domain, it's called."

"Either way, you get paid," the shorter guy said.

"Go peddle your goddamned missiles somewhere else," Emil said hoarsely. He pointed down the driveway.

"You're not patriotic, Mr. Haugen?"

"I got nothing against them Russians," Emil said. "They never held my family down. Not like the bankers and Cargill. Those guys are the real enemy."

"Whose side are you on, anyway?" the tall asked. "Russia or America?"

"I'm on my side," Emil said. "The Haugen side."

The government men looked at each other.

"Here's our card," the short one said.

Emil didn't take it.

"Then we'll have to come back," the tall one said. "Next time it will be with federal marshals."

"Those guys are way less friendly than we are," the short one finished.

"We'll give you a few days to think about it, Mr. Haugen," the other said. "There's a phone number to call. We'll leave our card in your mailbox."

"You do have a phone?" the short one asked.

"*Dra til helvete!*" Emil pointed down the lane.

The government men walked off and paused at his mailbox to leave their card. After its door clanged shut, they got in their dusty, white car and drove away.

Dag waited for him on the porch. "Who were those fellows?"

Emil exhaled. "Peddlers."

"They were nicely dressed," Dag said. "I thought they might be preachers."

"They weren't preachers."

"What were they selling?"

"Nothing we need."

"You're all red in the face," Dag said. "You'd better sit down."

Emil obeyed.

"I'll go get us a glass of lemonade," Dag said.

When Dag was gone, Emil squinted up at the blue, cloudless sky.

***

That same day Emil shored up his driveway gate, and the ditch around, with more stones. The government men did not return. Not the next week. Nor the weeks after. On September tenth, he and Dag were in the garden digging the last of the potatoes. Dag straightened. Cocked her ear to the west. "Whatever is that sound?"

"What sound?"

"Like tractors only bigger."

"I don't hear it."

"Your hearing's no good anymore." Dag continued to listen.

By turning his best ear to its best angle, Emil picked up the faraway rumble. "It's over on the Backstrom farm."

"I thought they already threshed."

"They did."

"Something's up over there," Dag said.

They drove in Emil's pickup around the south edge of the lake, most of a mile, to the Backstrom farm, which was as busy as a fallen bees nest. Three gray bulldozers, one behind the next, bored a plumb-straight line as they carved a driveway into a field. Black sod rolled up, torn and tumbled. The air smelled of fresh, prairie dirt. Government cars and trucks sat here and there. Men in military uniforms stood around as if guarding the bulldozers.

"What in the world?" Dag said.

Emil explained.

At home that night they ate cold leftovers for supper. "I can't even think straight." Dag fanned herself. "A missile silo."

"You better eat something."

"I'm too nervous," Dag said. "What if there's a nuclear war? What will happen to us?"

"The government don't care about us."

Dag blinked. "Those men a few weeks ago in white shirts and sunglasses. Were they from the government?"

Emil nodded.

"What did they want?"

"To put the missile silo on our farm."

"Our farm." Dag held onto the table as if to keep it from tilting.

"Have a drink of water." Emil held out her glass.

"What did you tell them?"

"*Dra til helvete.*"

As September continued, most nights after supper Emil and Dag drove over to watch the missile silo construction. A guard in a white helmet manned the worksite entrance around the clock. Behind him a black square grew across the wheat stubble. Bulldozers groaned and excavator tracks clanked and clattered. On wind-still days, pale-blue diesel smoke hung over the Backstrom farm like a ground fog. Most every night local cars lined the road, gawkers like Emil and Dag.

"I've never seen so much equipment," she said.

"It's a damned shame." Emil spit out his window. "Putting good farmland under concrete. Like that big, new air force base west of Grand Forks. A thousand acres, they say."

"I know, I know." Dag shaded her eyes. "There's even a kitchen. See where the men are lined up at that trailer? That must be where they cook."

A shiny Oldsmobile came along. The driver honked at the rubber-neckers and squeezed by.

"Why, that's the Backstroms."

Emil squinted. "They must have bought a new car with their free money."

Dag turned. "Free money?"

"The government pays to lease their land," Emil said. Centered in the new black square, two yellow excavators worked. Their claw buckets reached to draw up black dirt. Dig. Hoist. Swing the hydraulic arm. Release into a dump truck. The trucks rocked under each cascade of earth. Its box peaked up with black dirt, the truck groaned away as another truck pulled forward.

"How much does it pay?" Dag kept her gaze on the trucks.

"I never asked."

***

The next evening, they again watched the dump trucks come and go.

"It's a shame the men have to wait like that." Dag's gaze held on the cook trailer.

One worker received his tray, bent to smell the food. After only a few bites he hunched his shoulders, then dumped it in the trash with a sharp slam of his tray.

"Eddie Harjula always said army food was no better than hog swill," Emil said.

Dag was silent. She got out of the truck.

"Where are you going?" Emil called.

"Never you mind." She walked up to the guard at the gate.

Emil shaded his eyes to look. Dag spoke to the guard. The fellow, with low sun directly in his dark glasses, nodded as if Dag had said the right password. Stepped aside. Pointed. Dag walked on to the canteen, where she went up to one of the men who had a tray of food. They spoke briefly. He held out his tray as if happy to be rid of it. After a brief inspection of the food, Dag shook her head, then disappeared into the canteen.

Five minutes later, Dag came out and walked briskly, shoulders squared, back to the gate. She paused to speak with the guard. He smiled widely, then snapped off a salute.

Dag settled back into the truck.

"What was that all about?" Emil asked. She had high color in her cheeks.

She clucked her tongue. "It's a crime what those men are eating."

"What did you go and do?"

"I have a job, Emil." She turned to him with a shine in her eyes. "I'm the new Minuteman Missile Site head cook."

Chapter Thirty-Three
The Hole

Skye was booming. The Lyles' café, where Sally had worked decades ago, stayed open until nine p.m. seven days a week. Heavy-duty pickups, with license plates from faraway states, and dusty government cars clustered out front. The bakery now served box lunches-to-go and was cleaned out of donuts, Bismarcks, Kaiser rolls, and maple-logs before nine a.m. A Dairy Queen opened. The Prairie Hotel's orange light flashed "No Vacancy" full time. The new Wigwam Motel on the east side of town overflowed, with rows of travel trailers parked in back. And a new, hastily built tavern, the Dodge-In, went up on the east side of town just past the city limits.

"They say McConnell owns it and that son of his, Martin, runs it," Dag said. From her job at the Minuteman site, she was up on all the news. "He built it so his boy would have a job."

"He'll run it into the ground," Emil replied. "It won't last a year."

Soon after Thanksgiving, the first, thin snow turned the Minuteman site's black dirt greasy. Dump trucks slewed and groaned, their tires spinning as they hauled away excavated dirt and dumped it around. Bulldozers spread it in a wide, slow-growing circle around a hole. The site widened and swelled like a boil on the flesh of the prairie.

As the silo hole deepened, other excavators dug a sideways channel. "It'll all be underground," Dag said. "There's a tunnel that goes out to a bunker, and that's where the missile operators will live."

"Like prairie dogs," Emil muttered.

"They'll have screens they'll watch, and the button to fire the missile," Dag continued. "They say it takes two of them at once—"

"The Backstroms should have said no," Emil said without turning. "If we'd all got together and told those government men *dra til helvete…*"

"Too late now," Dag replied.

A few nights later, in addition to his government supper, Dag brought Emil an official government badge: "Minuteman Kitchen."

"What's this?"

"Now you can come inside the fence," Dag said. "But don't get in trouble."

Emil waited a few days before he approached the gate with his pass. The guard gave it a look, nodded, and then Emil was on the inside. His first stop was the kitchen trailer, where he poked his head in through the back door. In the hot, loud, steamy interior, Dag stood alongside one of the hired girls, hands on her hips. "Did no one ever teach you how to peel potatoes?"

"Sorry," the girl said.

Dag took the peeler and made skins fly. "And you," she said, pointing her peeler at a girl who watched. "Those carrots aren't going to peel themselves."

Emil ducked out.

At the shift change, men came and went on the gangplank toward the elevator. Emil slipped in among them. A diesel generator powered a heavy pump. Its arm-thick hose pulsed with groundwater drawn up and out of the silo's hole. Floodlights from the cylinder cast up a column of light into the gloaming sky. A man held open the elevator cage for Emil. Emil waved him off as if he had forgotten something. As the elevator clanked downward out of sight, Emil stepped to the side, to the viewing platform. Eighty feet below, encircled by a wooden form braced across by timbers, men wearing hard hats and welding helmets worked to prepare the silo's floor. A spider web of reinforcing bar spread to fit the circle like a woven, iron doily. Electric welders flashed. Grinders threw streams of sparks. The burnt smell of welding rods rose up the giant chimney.

"You wouldn't catch *me* working down there." An MP, a Black man in uniform, had come up behind Emil. He had a drawl.

"Me neither."

The guard's eyes went to Emil's badge. "You a long way from the kitchen, bub."

"Just wanted a look."

"Now you've had it. Move on."

That was fine by Emil. On the way home that night, he told Dag about the hole.

"What was it like?" She smelled like kitchen. Like cabbage.

After a long pause he said, "It gave me the Willies. You don't want to look down there."

***

By November, a cylinder of iron mesh reached ground level, then poked just above grade like a finely spun bird's nest. By December, the same rebar was sheathed top to bottom with plywood, ready for the concrete pour. The cement plant rumbled day and night. Concrete slurry flowed downward from a directional pipe like they were filling a real silo with chopped corn. When the base was set, the pour turned to the outer ring, the cylinder of concrete rising ever higher, as if the men were forging a giant gun barrel. Floodlights from the new little city on the prairie lit the land all the way to the Backstrom house, which at night was awash in light.

"I bet they don't sleep worth a damn," Emil said.

"I don't worry about that." After work Dag was too tired to talk.

As work progressed on the missile site, security grew tighter. When her shift ended, a guard escorted Dag to the gate. She often lingered a minute or two by the guard shack.

"Who is that guy?" Emil asked. He was hungry. Had been waiting in the truck long enough to melt the snow beneath.

"Dale Costello." She handed Emil his supper box, then held her hands over the truck's heat vent. "He works security."

"Does he have to walk you to the gate?" Emil put the truck in gear.

"No," Dag said. "He does it just to be nice. So the other men won't bother me, he says."

Emil blinked. "Does that happen?"

"*I'm not that old.*"

Emil put the truck in gear. "Maybe you should quit working there."

"What would you do without your government suppers?"

As winter proceeded, work on the silo paused only during blizzards, when snow swirled and blanketed the trucks, shacks and cranes and covered the bulldozers parked in rows as unmoving as bison. The cement plant slowed but never stopped entirely. Warmth from its internal workings, the giant mixers that throbbed, kept the cement plant's roof melted bare. On the coldest, wind-still days, white smoke rose from its pipe as straight as a rope. In deep winter, when the temperature dropped to thirty below zero, work ground to a life-and-death crawl. Then one day an ambulance from Skye arrived with flashing red lights. It left in no hurry and with no light.

"We lost a boy today." Dag talked as if the men were family.

In January came bright sunshine and with it, always, bitter cold. The air at thirty below zero was like breathing ammonia. "How do the boys keep warm in those little trailers?" Dag remarked.

"Maybe they got company."

Dag turned.

"I heard there's new ladies in town," Emil said. "They say someone's bringing them down from Portage Avenue in Winnipeg to the Dodge-In."

"You don't know that for sure," Dag said.

"It's what I heard."

Nightly, Dag spent longer and longer at the gate talking with Dale Costello.

"We need to get going," Emil said one night. "I don't want the fire to go out at home."

"You should meet Dale one of these times." Dag settled into the truck's seat with her bag of leftovers for their supper.

Emil's stomach growled.

"He's from Florida."

Emil turned onto the main road. "He came all this way for work?"

"Missile work is the best money in the country, he says. He worked in Alaska on the DEW line before this."

"Good for him."

"Look at this, Emil." She dug in the food bag. Put a big orange to Emil's nose. "A Florida orange."

The smell of it filled his mouth with spit.

She put it to her nose. "Dale had a crate sent to him from home. He says everyone has an orange tree right in their backyard, and they grow all winter. You just step outside and pick an orange."

"Ain't that nice," Emil said. "What else does Dale say?"

Chapter Thirty-Four
The Dodge-In

At the missile site, after grinding, fitful progress through winter, come March the cement plant thundered full time, its steam plume as steady as an awakened volcano. Spring came early. With planting, Emil was run ragged driving Dag back and forth. One day in May she said, "I'll drive myself to work today."

Emil stared. "You've never driven anywhere."

"It doesn't look that hard. And you're not using the truck during the day."

"You don't have a license."

"Who's going to check me?" Dag said. "Besides, I'm what's called an essential worker."

"Whose idea was this?" Emil asked. "You driving."

Dag colored slightly. "Dale said it must be a bother to you to drive me every day."

"'Dale said,'" Emil replied.

Dag had made up her mind, and, with surprisingly little grinding of gears, off she drove to work. She gave him a toot of the horn.

By May some of the heavy equipment was gone. George Backstrom had himself disced and seeded the ten-acre square around the silo.

"He probably got paid for farming his own land," Emil grumbled.

"They planted it to prairie grass," Dag said. "So it blends in from the sky. That way the Russians can't see us."

"Is that what Dale says?"

***

In the middle of June, on a warm night after work, Dag lingered outside the gate talking to Dale. Emil honked the horn.

She turned, glared, then walked to the truck along with Dale Costello.

"Don't you ever do that again."

"What?" Emil said.

"You know what."

"You must be Emil." Dale Costello led with his hand like a Watkins salesman. He wore a bucket helmet and sunglasses. Square jawed, wearing a private security company uniform with sleeves rolled up, he carried a holstered pistol on his belt. He looked to be well younger than Dag.

"That's right."

Dale shook his hand hard and fast, like it was some kind of contest. "Sorry for the delay. Dag and I got to talking. I just can't get enough of your sister." He flashed a big smile at Dag. He had lots of white teeth. And tattoos. One arm had a group of three faded roses beneath a sash reading "Mother." The other forearm had a grinning monkey wearing a sailor's hat.

"It's time to head home," Emil said. "My day ain't done."

She took her sweet time getting into the truck.

"I was thinking it'd be nice to drop by your farm sometime." Dale held onto the door frame. "See where you live."

Dag colored slightly. "We're a little hard to find. Plus, like I said, it's not much to look at."

"That's never no mind to me," Dale said. "Back home there were ten of us kids in a one room shack."

"What do you think, Emil?" Dag asked.

"Time to go."

***

By the middle of July much of the heavy equipment was gone, but the cement plant rumbled night and day.

"They're pouring the blast doors," Dag said.

"Blast doors?"

"The concrete lid on top the silo," Dag said. "It weighs ten tons and moves on rollers. Even a nuclear bomb can't smash through it."

"I doubt that," Emil said.

On a Saturday night in late July, with Emil's crops laid by and government suppers in their bellies, Emil and Dag drove into town for a cone at the Dairy Queen. Skye and Main Street was less busy these days. The action was at the Dodge-In, which they drove by on the way home.

"Turn in," Dag said suddenly. "Let's see if Dale's here."

Emil slowed for the Dodge-In parking lot and idled his pickup along the rows of trucks.

"Florida." Dag pointed to a dusty, heavy duty Ford pickup. "I'm pretty sure that's him."

They sat there, motor running. Dag stared at the tavern. She looked tired lately. "What are you wanting to do?" Emil asked.

"Could you go in?" she said. "Just a quick look?"

Emil parked so that Dag could watch the tavern's front. As he pushed through the door, noise hit him like a blast of hot air. A band played a loud country song, glassware clattered, people laughed and whooped. The din hung on a blue haze of cigarette smoke.

"What can I get you?" A barmaid passed with a tray of smudged, empty glasses. A plump daughter of the prairie, the top of her blouse missing a button.

"Nothing for me," Emil said.

"This is a bar, buster," she said.

Emil moved on.

"Wake up Irene!" the band leader sang. The fiddle player sawed and flapped like a rooster trying to fly, and the crowd whooped and careened around the floor. Emil slipped among cowboys, local girls, and "basers" from the Minuteman site. The only bar stool open was next to a big Black man.

"Evening," Emil said.

The Black man nodded.

They watched the dancers.

"You work at the base?" Emil asked.

"I do," he said. *Ah do.*

"You wouldn't happen to know a fella by the name of Dale?"

"Day-ale?" the man said.

"Works security. Usually at the main gate."

"Yes, Dale," the man said. "Everybody knows Dale."

"You seen him here tonight?"

The man pursed his wide lips. Gave Emil a side-eyed glance. "What you need Dale for?"

"Nothing, really. I think I saw his truck out front."

"'Cause I wouldn't want to get in the middle of anything," the man said.

"How's that?"

"Dale's quite the lady's man. Married, not married, it don't matter to Dale."

"I see."

"A joint like this, he'd for sure know where the back door is." The fellow took the last sip of his beer.

"Obliged," Emil said.

"What you drinking, buddy?" The bartender's hand slapped the smooth wood with a wet towel. Gave it a quick wipe with a forearm furred orange. He had a square face and carrot-orange hair. A roaring filled Emil's ears. It was the McConnell boy.

"I don't drink."

"You lost then?"

274

Some fellows laughed. "You tell him, Marty."

"Just looking," Emil said.

Marty leaned close. Pretended to wipe a spot. "All the girls are booked. Try next weekend."

"Say what?"

"No girls available tonight." He turned away.

Emil stared.

"Farmers," Marty said.

Men laughed.

Emil went to the far side of the dance hall. The band switched to a new song, "Are You Lonesome Tonight?" Throngs of dancers left the floor, stumbling and sweaty. Other couples headed out to dance the slow one. Dale appeared. At the far side of the dance floor, he led a young woman with a long, black ponytail held by a beaded clasp. She was way younger and way taller and slumped against Dale as they danced. Emil slipped close enough to make sure it was Dale, then headed to the front door.

Marty McConnell waved him over. He leaned toward Emil and tilted his head at Dale and the girl across. "The deal is, you take the girls out of here," he said, keeping his voice low. "That's what the goddamned back door is for."

Outside, Emil took a breath of fresh air. Headed back to the truck. In purple dark, the beer lights flashed brighter as the thudding beat softened behind. A deputy sheriff's car sat at the far side of the parking lot.

"Did you see Dale?" Dag asked.

He shrugged and started the engine. "Too many people."

"You were in there a while."

"Got to talking with another fellow from the base."

"Did he know Dale?"

"He said everybody knows Dale."

"He's just that kind of guy," Dag said. "Outgoing. Friendly. He must have loaned his truck to one of the fellows."

Emil drove around the rear of the Dodge-In. By the back door, silvery kegs of beer lay scattered as if kicked out the door. Barrels coned up with brown glass beer bottles lined the entrance. A straggle of cottonwoods, a former windbreak, stretched toward the road.

"Dale wouldn't be back here," Dag said.

"Maybe he's not the guy you think he is," Emil said. "Have you thought of that?"

"Maybe you're jealous," Dag said. "I've finally found someone, and you haven't."

***

The missile arrived in the fall of 1962. Main Street was blocked off for a celebration attended by politicians and military men from Washington, DC. Dag and Emil watched from the rear of the crowd. The military men carried more color, ribbons and medals and sashes, on their uniforms than rooster pheasants. The mayor himself, Doctor Robert McConnell, presented the general with a large, wooden key to the city, then droned on about Skye, its fine people.

"Goddamn troll," Emil muttered.

Faces turned. Dag nudged him.

The installation of the missile itself was not open to the public. There were pictures in the *Skye View* of a tall, shiny white tube being lowered into a silo.

"Look, Dag." Emil brought his newspaper to the kitchen table. "The photo ain't even from here."

She leaned closer. "It's a Minuteman missile."

"But that's not the Backstrom farm behind."

"Well, it's supposed to be secret," she said with a shrug. "Anyway, Dale was there. He said they screwed the warhead on top, then closed the blast door and that was that."

"Dale said," Emil muttered.

"You won't have to worry about him anymore," Dag said sharply. "He's going back to Florida."

Emil thought it best not to say anything else.

The next week, after Dale had left, Dag fell into such a funk that Emil found himself cooking his own supper. He served Dag too.

"You need to eat," he said.

"Not hungry," she muttered and stared out the window.

"We'll go for a drive after supper," he said. "We can get an ice cream cone in town."

On their drive, Dag wanted to go past the Minuteman site one more time.

The ground around, from the new seeding, had greened to match the surrounding fields. Except for a small, concrete building and the chain link fence, there was nothing much to see. Only a couple of construction trailers remained. Army trucks were hooking onto those even as Dag and Emil watched.

"There's nothing to guard anymore," Dag said. "Dale told me that all they need is a skeleton crew, the fellows underground who control the button."

A hawk drifted low along the fence, then flared up with a flash of red tail feathers to perch on the wire.

"It's a good place for birds," Emil said. "Meadowlarks should like it. Most of the fence lines are gone nowadays."

"You don't have to talk, Emil," she said and touched his arm.

He drove into town. Main Street was deserted but for three cars at the Dairy Queen.

"What would you like?" Emil asked.

Dag shrugged. "The usual. Vanilla cone."

"How about a banana split?"

She blinked. "What?"

"Have you ever had one?"

"No."

"Me neither."

Dag mustered a trace of smile, and Emil headed to the walk-up window.

Afterward, they sat in the pickup and with long, red plastic spoons ate the swimming scoops of ice cream, each a different flavor, from their little boats.

"Tasty," Dag said.

Mouth full, Emil nodded.

"Remember that time when we took Sally to Fergus Falls and we stopped at that DairyLand place?" Dag said.

"Yes."

"And you came back to the car empty-handed?"

"I didn't know about walk-up windows," Emil said. "It was a first for me."

"Jenny and I laughed like fools," Dag said.

"I'm sure."

By the time they finished their banana splits it was just them in the parking lot. The fellow inside the Dairy Queen put up a "Closed" sign and then turned off the lights, one by one, red on top, yellow down below.

"Well," Dag said, and took the last bite. "I believe the missile boom is over."

Chapter Thirty-Five
An Orange in Winter

After Thanksgiving, Dag packed her suitcase.

"Are you going somewhere?" Emil asked.

"Florida."

"What?"

"You heard me."

"It's that Dale, isn't it?"

Dag continued packing summery clothes. "I'm going for a visit. A vacation."

"A vacation?"

"It's what normal people do," Dag said. "Take a vacation once in a while."

Emil had no words.

"Goodness, I'll have to take this dress in." She held it up to herself.

"Dale Costello is a no-good."

"You don't know him."

"I know him enough."

"Doesn't matter, because it's all set." She held up a stub of paper. "I have my train ticket."

The following day, Emil drove Dag to Grand Forks to the train station. It was ten degrees, with thin snow falling. She had on a long coat, a modern hat, and a red scarf.

"You don't think I'll be too warm in Florida?"

"It's best to be too warm rather than the other way around." They drove on. Emil leaned forward to better see the road. "You can always take clothes off, but you can't put them on if you don't have them."

"Stop worrying."

Emil drove on in silence.

"I can take care of myself."

Emil had no reply.

Dag dabbed at her eyes. "What if I won't want to come back?"

"What?" Emil's eyes widened.

"What if I like Florida, and Dale pops the question. Then what?"

After a pause, Emil said. "I guess it will just be me at home."

"You'd go downhill fast," Dag said and clucked her tongue. "In a month you'd be walking around in your long johns and living on bacon."

"I like bacon."

At the depot, the train whistle hooted. People boarded.

Emil helped her with her suitcase. "Eat an orange for me down there."

Which set Dag to weeping. She hugged Emil hard. Bending low, he patted her back.

"You better go," he said. "Before you change your mind."

When her train's red taillight disappeared, Emil sat on the bench outside the station. It was soon as empty as the railroad tracks. He rolled a cigarette. Lit it. Took a deep draw. Above the ticket booth, the schedule read Fargo, Detroit Lakes, Alexandria, Minneapolis. In the cold air, he exhaled white—some smoke, some breath. They could not be separated.

"Miss your train, bub?" A depot worker rattled past with an empty cart.

Emil took another draw and stared down the disappearing rails. "It's hard to say."

The fellow paused, waited for more, then moved on.

***

At home Dag had left him a map with her route south, all the stops, taped on the ice box. There was food cooked and arranged in covered, numbered plates. Enough for a week.

Five days later the phone rang. Emil hurried to the wall.

"Collect call from Dagmar Haugen." The operator's voice sounded foreign.

"Yes," Emil said. "I'll accept."

"Mister Haugen?" a man's voice said.

"Yes?"

"My name is Cesar Rodriquez."

"I don't know anybody by that name."

"Wait, please do not hang up. Your sister is here."

"What? Where?"

"Here in Tallahassee."

"Florida?"

"Si."

"Well put her on."

"She will not talk to you," the man said.

"Why won't she talk to me?" In the background were children's voices, people speaking Spanish. The clatter of dishes.

"Because you will make her feel bad, she says."

"No, I won't do that. Is she okay?"

"Yes."

"That's the main thing," Emil said.

"I tell you everything, okay?"

"Okay," Emil said quickly.

"Tonight there comes a knocking on our door. My little girl says to me, 'Poppa, there's a white lady out there.' I go to see, and sure enough, here's a nice lady with a suitcase. She is wearing a wool coat. In Florida. Anyway, she says to me, 'Is Dale here?' I say, 'Dale who?' She says, 'Dale Costello.' I say, 'No. We are the Rodriquez family, and this is our house.' She says, 'There must be a mistake. I have the address.' She shows it to me, and I say, 'No, this is our house, and I never heard of no Dale Costello.' She looks at me, then says, 'I'm sorry to have bothered you.'"

"Goddamn him," Emil muttered.

"So, my family, we eat our supper," Mr. Rodriquez continued, "and we get the kids ready for bed. They say their prayers. We think they are sleeping, but my little girl comes out and says, 'Poppa, that white lady is still out there.'"

Emil stretched the curly black telephone cord toward the icebox and Dag's map. Put a finger on Tallahassee.

"I go to the window and sure enough, there she is," the man continued. "She at the sidewalk sitting on her suitcase. It's getting dark, so I go out there."

"Yes?" Emil said.

"To make the story short, she's here now, at our house. She ate an enchilada and orange—she asked if we had an orange tree. We talk to her, try to understand things, but she falls asleep on the couch. My wife, she covers her up and says let her sleep. But we did get your name and phone number from her."

Emil was silent.

"Hello?" the man said.

"Still here." Emil checked his watch (this was a collect call). "If she can stay with you tonight, I'd be obliged."

"What is *oblige*?"

"Thankful," Emil said.

"No problem," Cesar said. "Yes, no problem. We take her in."

"As long as she's safe."

"She safe."

"Okay, we'll sort this out tomorrow."

"Okay, Mr. Haugen."

Emil hung up quickly so as to stop the clock, then swore at himself. He forgot to get the telephone number in Tallahassee. Certainly, Dag would call him tomorrow.

Dag did not call the next day.

Nor the next.

Emil paced the house. Picked up the phone receiver more than once, then set it back in its cradle.

Three days later a local operator in Skye connected him with an operator in Tallahassee.

"Cesar Rodriquez?" the operator said. She had the same Spanish accent. "Do you have an address?"

"No." Emil listened to the "shuck-shuck" of phone book pages.

"There are over twenty listings with Cesar Rodriquez."

"Give me all their numbers," Emil said.

By the time she was done, Emil's pencil point was dull, and he had broken into a sweat at the cost of the call.

He gave matters another day, then began calling, in the evening, when the rates were lower. Sixteen long distance calls, each answered by someone speaking Spanish, and who quickly hung up on him. On number seventeen, a little girl answered.

"Hola?"

"Is Dagmar Haugen there? The American lady?"

The little girl giggled. "*Un momento.*"

After some clattering, and more laughter in the background, Dag answered.

"Hola?"

"Hola? What? It's me," he said. "Your brother."

"It's not like I have any other brother."

"Are you okay?"

"Yes. I'm here with the Rodriquez family. I'm helping out."

"And Dale?" Emil said.

"We're not talking about Dale anymore."

There was a pause.

"Are you coming home?"

"I would."

"You would?"

"I don't have money for a ticket."

"Dale got it all from you. How?"

"We're not talking about Dale anymore." She spoke cheerfully, as if children might be listening.

"Put on Mr. Rodriquez."

"They're both out," she said. "I'm babysitting."

"Can you stay with them until I send you enough for a ticket?"

"I'm sure I can. I've been helping with the children. There's four of them. We get along just fine. They're learning English at school. They call me '*Abuela*.'"

"What's that?"

"Grandmother," Dag said.

A child's voice chirped, "*Abuela*."

Dag laughed like a girl.

"Give me the address there."

"Get your pencil," Dag said.

After the call was over, he had a cigarette right in the kitchen.

The next day Emil went to the little house, unlocked the trunk, and took out a one-hundred-dollar bill. In the house, he wrapped it in two sheets of paper, then put it in an envelope. He held the envelope up to the light. After that he licked the glue and addressed the envelope to Dag in care of the Cesar Rodriquez family at their address in Florida. He drove into Skye to the post office and had the clerk weigh the letter to make sure he bought enough but not too much postage. He watched until the clerk dropped the letter into the mail bin.

Ten days later he got a letter from Dag thanking him for the money, saying she'd be there "for a little while longer" and to go ahead and have Christmas down in Crookston with Jenny and the kids. And not to over-water her African violets.

***

She arrived back in Grand Forks on the train on New Year's Day. Emil had shaved and wore his good coat and hat.

"Hello Emil." She paused on the steps of her Pullman car.

He held up an arm.

Dag shivered. "It's cold."

"It's twenty-two degrees," he replied. "A fine winter day."

"Feels cold to me."

"Your blood must have thinned out."

"I think that's an old wives' tale," Dag said. "I don't think it really thins."

In the truck, snow thrummed a steady note in the wheel-wells. They drove in silence for a spell.

"Turn up the heater," Dag said.

"It's on full blast," Emil replied. "Hold your hands on the vent."

She did. Flexed her fingers.

"So how did Dale get your money?"

Dag peered out at the white fields. "He said he was going to buy a house for us. Before I left, I sent him a check for the down payment."

"To the Rodriquez house?"

"To a post office box. He said that's where he took his mail."

"Bastard."

"We're not talking about him anymore."

Emil drove on. "Well, you're home now. That's the main thing."

"Yes."

"And I've had my fill of bacon."

"I'm sure."

They drove on.

"Rodriquez," Emil offered. "He seemed like a nice fellow."

"They're a fine family. Two little girls and two nice boys."

"I could hear them in the background."

"I almost forgot." Dag dug in her purse and pulled out an orange as big as a grapefruit. "Merry Christmas, Emil."

He hefted it. Held it to his nose. "*Gracias*, Sister."

Chapter Thirty-Six
The Funeral

The next spring, in mid-April of 1963, Emil called Jenny. "You'd better read the paper."

But there was no reason to go to the library for the *Skye View*. Arriving at the house, *The Crookston Daily Times* carried the article.

Two Killed in Late Night Rollover

Celie and Celeste DesMarais, seventeen and nineteen, from Saint Adolphe, Manitoba, were pronounced dead at the scene just south of Pembina. The driver, twenty-six-year-old Martin McConnell of Skye, North Dakota, was thrown clear and escaped injury. Alcohol was suspected as a factor in the crash. McConnell was released to the custody of his father, Doctor Robert McConnell, pending an investigation.

Jenny went to the backyard. Stooped to put her hands on her knees. Get her breath.

"Hey Ma, are you all right?" Roland, home from ag school for spring break, came onto the porch.

"I think so."

He hurried across the yard. "You don't look so good."

She let out a breath. "Just read some bad news."

"Like what?"

She straightened. "Two girls were killed in a car crash."

"Did you know them?"

"In a roundabout way."

At supper she made the announcement. "I have to go to a funeral on Saturday. I'll be gone up to Manitoba for the day."

"Can I come?" Angel asked.

"Not this time. It won't be much fun."

"I don't care. I don't want to be stuck home with Roland."

"You could do my homework," Roland said.

"If you pay me."

"Enough, you two," Jenny said without heat. With Roland coming and going from North Dakota State, he and Angel were doing much better.

"I'll stop at the farm too," Jenny said. "Check on Dag and Emil."

"Can I come?" Roland asked.

"You need to focus on your classwork."

"I hate college."

"You promised you'd give it a year."

Roland muttered something.

"I could help you with your English class." Angel made a money motion with her fingers.

"I don't need no help."

"Very funny," Angel said.

***

North of Crookston, early grain planting was in full swing. At Hallock, she turned east onto Highway 59. Wide, flat fields gave way, here and there, to upthrusts of gray stone bearded with scrubby brush. This was the leading edge of the Canadian shield and its pine forests that ran all the way to the Atlantic Ocean.

At the frontier shack on Highway 59, she had her driver's license ready. An older man emerged from a small store and café, the only other building, and ambled over to her car.

"Purpose of your trip to Canada?" Hand outstretched, he wore a brown shirt with a faded Canadian maple leaf flag patch.

"A funeral. In Saint Adolphe."

"Those girls from the reserve?" He handed back her license.

"Yes."

"I heard about that," the agent said. "Some drunken American was driving."

"I'm afraid so."

"I hope he gets what's coming to him." The guard lifted the cross arm.

She continued north on Provincial Highway Fifty-Nine, through Tolstoi, past a Ukrainian Catholic Church in Rosa and then along the Roseau River, which flowed north. Passing through Saint Malo, she turned west to Dufrost, then north from Saint Elizabeth to Saint Agathe. So many saints.

At the community center, a crowd mingled outside. Men smoked. Women wore traditional Indian dresses. Among them, chatting, was a youngish priest in a long black robe. He was the only other white person in sight. She drove past, to a parking lot crowded with older cars and pickups. Looked around for any car with North Dakota plates. Of course, the McConnells would not come. She rolled down the window. Sat for long moments with the car engine still running.

"Bonjour." A mother and her little boy passed. He had a crow's wing of black hair.

"Hello." She turned off the engine and got out.

The woman paused. "You came from Minnesota?" She glanced at Jenny's license plates. She had a soft, French-Metis accent.

The little boy said something in French that ended in "Min-ee-sota."

Jenny pointed south. "Yes. That way. Across the border." She got out.

"Are you from that family?"

"Family?"

"The driver of the car." The woman's eyes narrowed.

"No. Not at all."

"Then how do you know Celie and Celeste?"

SEE-lee-ah, Say-LEST. "I didn't know them. I read about the crash. I thought I should attend."

"Merci. Will you come with me?" She steered Jenny toward a much older Indian man with a strong nose and walnut eyes and a beaded leather vest. She spoke to him in French. The old man nodded, then leaned toward Jenny closer as if to see her better.

"Alphonse Beaulieau," the mother said. "Our tribal leader."

"Bonjour." Jenny introduced herself.

His fingers were strong, his grip soft. He spoke to Jenny in soft, mumbled French.

"He says for a stranger to come and share our grief your heart must be large."

Jenny had no reply.

"He welcomes you as an honored guest," the woman continued.

The chief gestured for her to proceed inside.

The hall, a square, concrete block building with a band of glass block windows high around the top, was warm and pungent at floor level. A smoky odor, sage or perhaps cedar, hung in the air, plus the deeper aroma of food. Two caskets, open, stood up front. The sleeping girls. Their family sat in the front row of folding metal chairs, eyes fixed forward.

Jenny had no choice but to join the line passing the open caskets. Close up, she looked at the girls for only a moment. In the side of her vision their faces, cupped by dark hair, floated as if on water or air. Sleeping girls, heavily made up, skin thick with cosmetics no doubt because of the crash. She focused on their dresses, their vests, their bead work, the tokens left alongside them in the coffin. A cassette tape… "Mix, Bee Gees, Donna Summer, Michael Jackson." A heart locket. A necklace with a tiny cross. A pen, chewed on top. The line continued past the DesMarais family. She shook their soft hands. They looked up with glazed unrecognition.

She took her seat. Near her in the front row sat the priest. He had short dark hair and wore a long, black frock and white clerical collar. He nodded to her, a gesture of kinship, of solidarity. She gave him the briefest of nods, then bowed her head.

After a very long time, the tribal chief came forward and made brief remarks in French. Four men carried in four round drums. When situated and ready, drumsticks in hand, they waited. The chief sat down. No one else rose. There was no further instruction.

Several minutes passed. Slowly, the last rustling and murmuring in the hall died away. When there was full silence, a woman in a jingle dress, its tobacco tins folded into little triangles and tinkling against each other, came forward with a small bowl. A younger man, weeping, hardly able to walk, followed with a second bowl.

The priest leaned over. "Food for their journey to the spirit world," he whispered.

When the bowls were situated inside the coffins alongside each girl, the carriers returned to their chairs. Silence resumed for several more minutes.

A drummer struck taut skin hard, then wailed a long, high note. The other drummers caught his rhythm and sang with him. The thudding, quavering song filled the hall. A hot flood rose in her throat. She shifted in her seat. On her left, a woman's brown hand reached over for hers. Jenny took it. Held on.

The fourth song was different in tone and beat. It rose beyond the first three—and ended when all four drummers hit a precise and final downbeat: "BOOM." As one, people rustled in their chairs, stood, and greeted one another.

Jenny looked about.

"That's it," the priest said. "It's over."

"I wasn't sure," she answered. "This is my first funeral of this type."

"They're quite moving." He smiled. He had nice teeth, an angular nose slightly bent to the left, and a scar, a full finger long, horizontal across his forehead as if grazed by a bullet. He had a dark beard shadow even though freshly shaved. "Every time I attend one of these I wonder if I'm on the wrong team."

She nodded politely.

"I'm Greg Garvey from Good Faith Church in Winnipeg."

"Jenny Olsen. Crookston, Minnesota."

"Mrs. Olsen." He bowed slightly as they shook hands.

"Jenny is fine." She paused. "What does one call a priest?"

"Many call me 'Father,' but how about Greg?"

The DesMarais family moved toward a long line of food tables. Garvey gestured the way forward. "May I join you for the lunch?"

"If you like."

They filled their plates. There were several varieties of wild rice hotdish and platters of meat cut to finger-food size.

"Venison or maybe moose," Garvey said.

"Both sound good. I'm rather hungry."

They found seats. He sat across the narrow table from her. "May I ask your connection to the family?" After crossing himself in the briefest of motions, he took a bite.

"It's complicated."

"Complications are what I do."

"I know the driver of the car," Jenny explained. "Martin McConnell. His family and mine are from the same town in North Dakota."

"Skye," Garvey said.

"Yes."

"I heard that McConnell had a bar and restaurant," Garvey said. "He promised the girls jobs, good wages, big tips. They were going down to check it out."

"It wasn't restaurant work," Jenny said.

The priest pursed his lips. "There are men who prey on girls from the reserve, and there's a special place in hell for them."

They ate and talked. He had good manners—patted his lips regularly with a folded napkin.

At length Jenny said, "I'd like to contribute to the funeral costs."

"There's a basket up front. Small donations add up."

"If I write out a check, could you make sure the family gets it?"

"Of course."

She dug in her purse. Found a pen.

The priest accepted her check, then coughed. "That's extraordinarily generous."

"It's the least I can do."

"The DesMarais family aren't wealthy, and funerals aren't cheap. But why would you give so much?"

"My family has a history with the McConnells, and not a good one. I'm here, I suppose, to offset their effect on the world."

He smiled. "I like how you think."

She shrugged. "Down in farm country, it's still how families pay for funerals. Or at least a part of the cost nowadays. People chip in what they can."

"With the size of your gift, would you like to meet the DesMarais family?"

"Isn't there something in your line of work about not making a fuss about one's charity?"

Garvey squinted. "Um, 'Be careful not to practice your righteousness in front of others, to be seen by them,'" he said. "Also something about not 'announcing it with trumpets, as the hypocrites do.' Matthew, somewhere."

"Yes to all of that," she said. They resumed eating in comfortable silence.

"Do you have a deadline to be back in Minnesota?" he asked.

"Not exactly."

"One of the things I like about funerals is how time slows down."

"That's true, I suppose."

"At every memorial I find myself thinking about my own life. It's one of the few times I can see it clearly." He looked across at the caskets, closed now. "Though, if it takes someone's death for us to reconsider our own lives, then maybe it's a devil's bargain."

"I'm not much for religion," she said. "It doesn't run in my family. And when it comes to Catholics, I'm quite in the dark."

"Catholics? Oh no." Garvey laughed. "I'm Anglican, an Episcopalian to be more precise."

"I see." She took another bite. "What's the difference between a Catholic priest and an Episcopalian?"

Greg Garvey's cheeks colored. "For one thing, we're not celibate."

***

A half-hour later, they arrived in two cars at his church on the south side of Winnipeg. He had promised a brief tour, and a cup of tea for her trip back. As they exited their cars, she checked her wristwatch.

"Don't worry. You're still on funeral time," he said. "Time out of time. I tell my parishioners it's the best excuse in the world to be missing or late. 'I was at a funeral.'"

"Dear me, what other things must you tell them?"

"They're used to me," he said. "Sometimes I think their main goal for coming every Sunday is to find me a wife."

"A wife?" She drew up.

"Um, it goes with that other thing I mentioned." Garvey said. "Episcopal priests can marry if they choose. There's a lot of rigamarole. Permission from the higher-ups, that sort of thing, but it can be done."

"But too much rigamarole for you."

He laughed again and steered her forward. "This way."

After passing through the gallery to the narthex, a new word for her, they stood at the center of the small, very old and very formal church. Stone arches converged overhead. On the curved ceiling were murals of angels and a Christ with a glowing head.

"Listen to this." Garvey raised his chin and gave an owl hoot.

It hoot-hooted back.

"That's remarkable," she said.

"The acoustics of a well-built cathedral are plenty enough proof of God," he said.

In his office, he filled an electric kettle from a small sink. "Canadians. We're big on tea." He took off his robe and hung it on a peg, his collar after. A nice, brown, wool pullover stretched squarely across his shoulders.

She looked away. He noticed.

"I suppose I seem like a different person without my vestments."

"Actually, yes."

He touched the black cloth. "I feel that. When I take them off, I'm just Greg Garvey, youth hockey coach and local boy who always liked church. An odd kid, I was."

Outside on the playground, children's voices rose and fell. A basketball thudded. As they looked at each other, the kettle whistled. He turned, found two cups, then rummaged for a tea bag.

"Whatever you're having," she said.

"English breakfast. Has a little caffeine in it. That's good for your drive home."

"Which should be soon."

"Tea needs at least six minutes. Please, sit."

She took a chair. Looked about his office. "Tell me more about your work here. What it is you do?"

"Okay." He took his chair behind his desk.

"Though I guess I'm not sure what to ask. Do Episcopalians have confession? Lutherans don't… that much I know."

"We do indeed have confession, though it's not so central as with Catholicism. There's no booth, no priest hiding behind a screen. It can be done anywhere."

"Here." She gestured to the chair she sat in.

"Certainly," he answered. "I often do it right here for parishioners. We have a sit-down chat. We get whatever is bothering them off their minds." He checked his watch.

"Well, Mr. Garvey, there's something on my mind."

"Shoot." He leaned forward, eyes on hers, amused, alive to the moment.

"Why did you invite me to see your church? Not to convert me."

"Certainly not. I'm not one to proselytize." Color rose in his neck.

"Why then?"

He paused. "I was trying, any way possible, to have a little more time with you."

"There. That wasn't so hard, was it?"

"It was, actually." Cheeks flushed as he smiled. "I see now how it is for my parishioners. Sitting in the other chair, I mean."

"Do you have more to confess, Mr. Garvey?" She stood. Checked the tea.

"As a matter of fact, I do."

She turned.

"You have bowled me over. With your beauty. Your manner. The way you think. Even the cut of your skirt."

"My," she murmured.

"I've been so busy lately I haven't been thinking much about women," he said, "and then you show up at the funeral and hit me in the gut like a hockey puck."

"Dear me, I'm sure I don't know how that feels."

"The air goes out of you, and you can't get it back."

"We wouldn't want that." She came over to where he sat. Put a finger to the scar on his forehead. Traced its line. "Is there someplace we could go? Certainly not here."

Chapter Thirty-Seven
Kerosene

She left Greg Garvey's rectory quarters late that afternoon with chapped lips and a humming body.

"Goodness me," she murmured. Driving, she touched her breast, then looked to the mirror and smoothed her hair. It was already four p.m. The plan all along had been to stop at the home farm to check on Dag and Emil. Pressing the speed limit, rounding up the calculation from kilometers to miles per hour, she soon enough arrived at the border. The American guard, a young fellow in sunglasses, leaned down quite close to ask about her day trip to Canada. It was their technique to get a look inside the car and sniff for alcohol.

"A funeral," she said.

"Where?" Face close alongside her, his nostrils widened.

"Saint Agathe. The two girls."

"I hadn't heard." He stepped back.

"You could look it up. It's in the newspaper."

"Any weapons, alcohol or tobacco?"

"No. Though I do have a knife in my purse."

He paused.

"A small one. For a lady."

"That's fine," he said, "but would you step out and open your trunk?"

"Do I look dangerous?" She swung her bare legs out of the car. He looked her up and down. "A little."

At Lancaster, she turned west and south into ever wider, flatter fields—the relief of open spaces. She soon crossed the Red River into North Dakota, with the home farm just a few miles ahead and the sun tracking lower to the west.

She entered Skye from the east and slowed by the Dodge-In. Built only three years ago, its ridgeline sagged, and the cheap, rough-sawn pine siding had mottled as if from skin disease. Neon beer signs flashed brightly. At five p.m., pick-up trucks packed the parking lot to the ditches, with some trucks parked along the cottonwoods behind. Into her head came the perfect DesMarais sisters in their funeral dresses. She stopped, watched for long moments, then accelerated sharply. A sheriff's car sat across the road. She cursed, sucked in a breath, and braked sharply. The officer waggled a finger at her, but did not turn on his red light.

At the home farm, Emil arrived in the yard on his tractor just as she drew up. He pulled an iron-wheeled grain drill. His dust mask handkerchief hung loose about his neck. She walked over to meet him.

"Dry," he said. The corners of his eyes ran dark, like the eye thread of black on big cats. Leopards. Lions.

"But good for seeding. The discs scour. No mud to deal with."

"You remember."

"I could start farming today."

"Better keep that town job, sister." He swung down.

She tugged his sleeve, which was their own kind of hug.

"How was the funeral?"

She could only shake her head sideways.

"The goddamn McConnell boy," Emil said.

"He's not a boy. He's twenty-five years old."

Dag called and waved from the porch. "Supper's ready."

Inside, Jenny caught up with Dag while Emil washed up at the porch sink. "Nice of you to go up for that funeral," she said. "What a tragedy."

"Martin McConnell should be in jail," Emil called through the screen door.

"So should his father," Jenny answered.

"Let's not agitate ourselves," Dag said. "I've cooked a nice pork roast for supper."

With Sally's chair empty, they ate. Jenny caught them up on family doings. John was with the rookie league of the Twins farm league.

"He'll make it all the way," Emil said. "You just wait."

"It's a long road," Jenny said. "And from what he tells, it sounds like a bum's life."

"And Roland?" Dag asked.

"He's still at the North Dakota State Ag School, but impatient with his classes."

"He wants to farm, not talk about it," Emil said.

"Don't I know," Jenny replied.

"And Angel?"

"She's doing well in tenth grade. Still a big reader."

They fell silent.

"Have you visited Sally?" Dag murmured.

"Two weeks ago, yes. She's gained a pound and has grown out her hair. They say they can't do without her at the telegraph office."

Dag dabbed her eyes.

Jenny patted her hand. "She's doing great. She won't be in Fergus Falls forever, they said."

"Then what?" Emil said.

They fell silent.

"If she comes back home, it'll be the same old ways," Dag said.

"For her and for us," Emil added.

Jenny nodded. "What's next for her will take some thought. We'll figure it out together."

"Well, *Den tid, den sorg*," Dag said.

After pie, Jenny glanced at the window. "Brother, can you show me your planting?"

Emil looked surprised. "Sure."

"Go," Dag said. "I'll do up the dishes."

In the yard Jenny said, "I'll drive your truck. See if I can still manage a stick shift."

They headed down the lane, then left on the county road. East of Skye she slowed past the Dodge-In. Came to a stop directly across. Neon beer ads flashed against the west sunlight.

"The funeral," she said. "You should have seen those beautiful girls."

"Ever since the missile came to town, he's been bringing them down from Winnipeg."

At the Dodge-In, two dusty pickups turned in. She parked across the road and turned off the truck's engine. They sat. Emil rolled a cigarette and, eyes on the beer joint, snapped off the top of a stick match with his thumb nail. It flared yellow with the sweet bite of sulfur. He drew on it. Two more pickups arrived.

"Another big night for Marty McConnell," Emil said.

She glanced his way, then to his cigarette. "Give me a puff of that."

"It's a bad habit. You don't want to start now."

She gestured for it. He shrugged and gave it over.

She took a short drag. Coughed and handed it back. Another truck pulled in.

"Nobody does anything," Emil said.

"We could something," Jenny murmured.

***

Dag was overjoyed that Jenny had decided to stay the night. Jenny made a call to Roland (the television was on loud), and afterward spoke briefly with Angel. Neither seemed interested that she would not be home until morning.

That evening Emil rustled his newspaper. Dag embroidered by lantern light. "The Rodriquez children write to me a couple times a month." She pointed to the small stack of envelopes on the desk. "That's how they practice their English."

Jenny paged through a couple of letters. "It's quite good."

"*Abuela*," Dag said. "That's what they call me."

"Rodriquez says he'll send us a crate of oranges this winter," Emil said.

"Wouldn't that be something," Dag remarked.

"We'll see if they come," Emil said.

"They will."

Jenny stretched out on the Chesterfield. The living room, warm from the kitchen, and with Dag embroidering and Emil reading his newspaper, was time out of time. That feeling again today. She looked across at Dag. "Do you mind if I have a little bath? It's been a long day."

"Mind? Heaven's no. There's hot water on the stove, and I'll heat more."

"I won't need much," Jenny said, with a glance to Emil.

His shoulders lifted and fell. Dag giggled.

After her bath, they had hot cocoa, and soon it was half-past nine.

Dag yawned. "I'm feeling the day."

Jenny blinked. "Me too."

"I might turn in myself," Emil said.

"Do you want to sleep in Sally's room?" Dag asked.

"I'll be comfortable on the Chesterfield," Jenny answered.

"I know what you mean," Dag said. "I can't go in there. I leave her door closed."

***

At two a.m., Emil tugged on her sleeve.

She started.

"It's time," he whispered.

She had been dreaming. Something about travel. A train.

They eased out the door and crossed the dark yard. The moon was high, half full, and bright. Emil had parked his truck facing down the driveway. In the bed was a dark can with a dusty beard of oil about its spout.

"Kerosene," Emil said. Without slamming their doors, and keeping the lights off, they headed down the lane. Jenny looked back.

"Now that Sally's gone, Dag sleeps like a stone," Emil said.

At the stop sign, he braked, then got out. Jenny slid over and took the wheel. Emil took the rider's seat. She turned on the headlamps and pointed them toward Skye.

The Dodge-In was dark except for a single, flashing beer sign. The parking lot was empty.

"Slow by the windbreak," Emil said.

"I know the plan."

Emil checked his gear—a candle and some stick matches.

She coasted, slowing without brake lights. Emil opened his door. Slipping out, he took the kerosene can without the truck coming to a full stop. She drove on well past the Dodge-In before reaching over to slam shut his door. She checked her wristwatch, then drove east out of town into full dark, bright stars. A waning half-moon bent inward, leaning like Greg Garvey's nose. Constellations hung naked, points of light to be connected by people with more imagination than she had.

Exactly eight minutes after dropping off Emil, she approached the Dodge-In from the opposite direction. The line of cottonwoods loomed. Slowing, she unlatched the rider's door. No Emil.

She drove on, then made a turn down a side street and then back past the Dodge-In. Slowing, she checked her watch.

No Emil.

She drove back to the open dark and then turned around once more. This time, as she slowed, Emil rose up from the ditch like a troll. Swinging the oil can, which clattered in the rear, he grabbed the door and swung himself inside. He smelled of kerosene. Kept his face to the front.

"What took so long?"

"Drive," he breathed.

"Are you okay?"

He rolled down his window. Spit. "I had trouble. With the candle." He reached for his breast pocket and his cigarette pouch. As she drove, he shucked out a rolling paper. Twice, tobacco trembled off its tissue. He gave up, crumpled the paper, and leaned back in the seat.

"But it's lit?"

"It's lit," he said. "We can't stop it now."

Back at the farm, truck lights extinguished, she coasted to a stop on the far side of the yard. She and Emil slipped into the house and went to bed.

**

She awoke to the telephone ringing and the smell of bacon.

"Oh dear, the telephone," Dag said. "I was trying not to wake you."

"It's fine. I have to get on the road soon."

The phone stopped ringing.

"Two longs and a short… that's the Backstroms," Dag said.

She went to the kitchen sink.

"There's hot water in the tea kettle," Dag said. "Emil will be in soon. He was up early. I didn't even see him. We'll have our *panakker* and then get you off."

Before she had finished washing her face, the phone rang again—a short and long.

"The Christensens," Dag said.

Emil came onto the cold porch. Washed his hands and then settled at the table.

"What's that scrape on your cheek?" Dag asked.

Emil touched it. "Turned into the barn door. Wasn't paying attention." He kept the side of his face away from his sisters.

"Did you sleep all right on the Chesterfield?" Dag asked Jenny.

"Just fine."

"I thought I heard a car in the middle of the night," Dag said. "I must have been dreaming."

Halfway through breakfast, the phone rang again—three shorts this time.

"The Harjulas." Dag looked to Emil. "So many calls this early. I wonder what's going on?"

"Nothing that concerns us," Emil said. "We're all here."

"Still." Dag's gaze went the to the black wall phone. She went over and eased up the receiver, covered the mouthpiece with her hand, listened. She turned to Emil and Jenny, then refocused on listening. Soon enough, very carefully, she replaced the receiver.

"They can still hear the click," Emil said.

Dag turned to them. "The Dodge-In burned down last night."

Emil cleared his throat. Did not look at Jenny. "Is that so?"

"To the ground," Dag said.

Jenny turned to Emil. "Well, you always said it might."

"They say the McConnell boy was in it," Dag said. "He was sleeping it off in the backroom."

Jenny turned to Dag.

"They're trying to identify the body," Dag said. "They're pretty sure it's him."

Emil continued eating as if in slow motion.

On her plate a yellow smear of the egg yolk. A brown trail of syrup. The cut of her buttermilk pancake, the honeycomb of tiny air pockets that gave it lift and lightness.

"More coffee?" Dag said.

"I should be getting home," she said. "Check on the kids." She pushed away her plate.

Dag, wearing an apron, accompanied her onto the porch.

"I'll check your oil before you go," Emil said.

"Wouldn't hurt." Jenny gave Dag a hug.

At the car, Emil lifted the Oldsmobile's hood. The shape of it shaded them both. He leaned with both hands on the engine.

"How were we to know?" Jenny said.

"We did know."

"What?"

"I didn't tell you last night."

"What happened?"

"The McConnell boy was in there," Emil said. "He must have been in the back room and heard me. He came at me out of nowhere. I had poured the kerosene and was just lighting the candle."

"Oh, Emil," Jenny breathed.

"We fought. He was like a bull. Kept coming at me. I took a chair and swung it. Knocked him backward. He slipped in the kerosene. Caught fire. He was mostly knocked out, but he wouldn't give up. He was swearing, fighting, his clothes were on fire, everything was burning by then. It was like the devil himself in the flames."

"Please." Jenny held a hand up to stop him.

Dag, thinking Jenny waved, waved back.

Jenny gave her a final wave and smile.

"We couldn't have saved him last night," Emil breathed. "I had to get out myself."

"Of course," Jenny said.

"What do we do now?" Emil asked. Still in the shadow of the hood, he held onto the car with both hands. He breathed through his mouth. "I never meant for this to happen."

"Nobody did." She glanced about, at the yard, the outbuildings, the grove, the empty fields beyond. "But it happened."

"Where do we go from here?" Emil asked.

Jenny met his gaze. "We go nowhere. We do nothing. It's not like there weren't rough characters coming and going from the Dodge-In."

"There were fights," Emil said. "The cops were always there."

"We go on with normal life."

"Yes, well…" he began.

"My oil, Emil," she said. "Dag's watching."

Emil pulled the dipstick. The shiny, metal wafer trembled in his hands. "Your oil is fine."

"We never speak of this again," Jenny said. "Not even to each other."

"Okay." Stepping backward into the light, he let the hood drop. The sound thumped off the face of the barn.

Section Five: The Past Is Never Past

Chapter Thirty-Eight
1981: The Letter

"There's mail," Darryl said. "It's on your desk."

Rosalie Rossi, forty-five, with reddish hair tucked up under a spring scarf, had just arrived at work. Rossi Clothing, her family's department store, stood midway on Broadway Avenue in downtown Fargo. She liked to walk from home, twelve blocks north, past the cathedral and then over the railroad tracks, a sixteen-minute trek, rain or shine. It kept her fit and also allowed her to try out women's clothing. Its comfort. Its fit. Today, below a light jacket and tartan skirt, she wore a pair of Keds casual sneakers. With white laces on gray, the brown rubber sole continued up the toe like a second tongue, an odd design but a solid shoe with good arch support. Her women customers were not eighteen or even thirty. Those shoppers all went to the new mall in West Fargo.

She passed through the women's section, straightening a dress on its hanger, on her way to the small back office. In the wire basket lay the mail. She took a breath and found her stiletto opener. On top, the light and power notice, still with a balance from the winter heating season. No matter how high the thermostat setting, their store with its high ceilings was chilly from November through March. Next, an overdue notice from Abelman's Clothiers in Denver, their wholesaler, with "VERY LATE" stamped in red. After that, the store's monthly real estate bill. Rossi's was on a monthly payment plan for last year's assessment, which was higher every year. A fat letter from First National Bank, which she quickly passed over. At the bottom of the pile lay a plain envelope without a return address, her name and the store address written in a shaky hand. She turned it over twice, then slit its top.

April 2, 1981
112 Maple Street
Skye, North Dakota

Dear Rosalie Rossi,

That's your maiden name, but likely you are married by now. There are not many in the Fargo phone book by the name of Rossi, so I'm sending this to the Rossi Department Store in hopes that it reaches you.

I have important information you might want to hear. I wonder if you know you were adopted? You have been raised since infancy by Mr. and Mrs. Rossi of Fargo, but you are the daughter of my husband, the late Dr. Robert McConnell, from Skye. I'm sorry if this information comes as a jolt to you. I thought you should know the truth about where you came from.

In 1933 Doctor McConnell had a fling with a farm girl named Sally Haugen. From that you were born in April of 1934. Robert was not my husband at the time, but that's no matter here. I write to you now, an elderly woman with health troubles, and not long for this world, with information about your real mother. I know where she lives, not so far from Fargo. It would be my dying wish that you meet her if only once, which would allow me to leave this world with a clear heart.

Robert was always conflicted about his "weak moment," as he called it, and the child, you, that resulted. But time marches on, he had his many patients to
attend to, and eventually we had a son of our own,
Martin, in 1936. He died too young in 1963. I enclose
a photo of your brother.

To the point, Martin died without wife or family. Now
that Robert is gone, and my own family too, I was
an only child, you are my sole heir. I am putting my
affairs in order. Please call at my house in Skye at your
earliest convenience. With my health these days, I
hope you won't wait too long.

Most sincerely,

Mrs. Robert McConnell (Dolly)

P.S. Enclosed find your father's obituary.

She read through the obituary, then stared at the red-haired,
square-faced boy in the photograph. Her free hand touched her own
hair. Darryl, her husband, popped in his head.

"Anything interesting?"

She slid the letter and picture out of sight. "Bills."

"Anything urgent?" Darryl had thinning hair and wore a
rather dark suit for April.

"I think I've got them covered," she said. But she knew she
didn't.

"You're a miracle worker."

When Darryl was gone, she read the letter again, then leaned
back in her chair. The small office window looked across the alley to
the dark, brick backside of another store. At the top, along its coping,
was "Fargo Mercantile." Faded, hardly legible these days, the colored
script had been bright when she was a little girl. Rainbow colored,

even. She squinted. Perhaps she knew the sign only from memory. Maybe it was not there at all.

She sat forward, tucked the letter in her purse, and went onto the floor. Darryl stood close by Stephanie, the part-time girl, supervising her as she dressed a new mannequin. Washed, flower-patterned jeans. Wide belt. A silky, square-shouldered white blouse with a high collar.

"What do you think?" Darryl asked. He stepped back.

"Let's do something about the nipples," Rose said.

"I thought so too," Stephanie said, and giggled. "But Mr. VandenEykel said they're the latest thing."

Darryl cocked his head at Rose. "Everything okay?"

"Yes, why?"

"You look like you've seen a ghost."

Chapter Thirty-Nine
Affairs In Order

A week later Rose arrived at the city limits of Skye. It was seventeen minutes until two p.m. On the east side of town, at a gas station with a line of mostly dead cottonwoods behind, she turned in to pee and freshen up. Gas was $1.12 per gallon, seven cents cheaper than Fargo. She parked her car, a 1964 Chevrolet Bel Air, at the pump, then went inside.

A young, plump woman with pimples sat on a stool behind the counter.

"I might as well fill."

"Okay."

Rose waited. "Is there someone?"

The girl pointed outside to the sign. "Self-service."

"I missed that," Rose said. She went first to the ladies' room, dimly lit, and lay down toilet paper on the seat. Afterward she washed her hands. The mirror over the iron-stained sink was cracked. No matter how she tilted her face, some part of it was missing. The endless-roll towel hung damp. She shook her hands dry as best she could.

Back outside, she ran her own gas, pausing to zip her jacket against a chilly breeze from the north. Spring had arrived on the high borderland but didn't seem happy about it. Inside at the counter, she handed over a ten-dollar bill. "I sort of miss the days when a tidy young fellow came out and filled the tank."

The girl rang up the gas, then squinted at the amount versus the ten-dollar bill. Reached for a pencil and a notepad.

"That's a dollar and twenty-three cents back to me," Rose said.

The girl did the math anyway, pinching the pink tip of her tongue for assistance.

In her car, Rose checked her watch, then her face in the rear-view mirror. She had a wide forehead with a frown line running straight up from the bridge of her nose. By habit, she pressed it flatter. She used lotion at night, but the wrinkle was there to stay. Tucking a strand of reddish hair beneath her scarf, she reviewed the map marked with colored pencil. After that, she touched her rosary beads that hung from the radio knob and started the engine.

Entering downtown Skye, she turned left, then right onto Maple Street. The houses were older, tall with shutters and porches, the kind not built anymore. Some were in decline, their height, their woodwork too much to maintain.

Checking house numbers, she slowed. Ahead near the sidewalk stood a wooden lawn sign, faded and with flaking paint: "Doctor Robert McConnell, M.D." Fastened beneath, faded as well, another sign read "Walk In—No Appointment Necessary." The house itself needed painting. A second-floor shutter hung askew. A small patch of shingles had blown off to reveal tarpaper underneath.

She parked, checked her hair once more in the mirror, touched her rosary, and got out. The McConnell lawn, green at the edge of the south-facing porch, had wide brown spots from winter-kill. She pushed the old-fashioned, mechanical buzzer. She was about to ring again when thumping came from inside. The door opened to an old woman with a cane. She squinted through wire-rimmed glasses. Her hair, walnut brown and pulled back, had a stripe of white roots down the part. "It's you."

"Rosalie Rossi, yes."

Dolly McConnell blinked with rheumy eyes against the daylight. "And right on time." Her voice had a rasp, and she hawked her throat to clear it.

"Punctuality is a thing with me," she said. "My children tease me about it."

"How many children?"

"Four. Two married, two still at home."

"I have four grandchildren, then," Dolly said. "Imagine that."

Rose paused. "I suppose, in a way, that's true, Mrs. McConnell."

"Dolly, please." She clutched Rose's hand and pulled her closer. She smelled strongly of pee. "Look at you. All grown up. And so nicely dressed."

"We own the clothing store. Being presentable is a requirement."

Dolly peered up. "Take that scarf off. Let me see your hair."

Rose untied the scarf.

"Shake your head."

Rose obeyed.

"Look at that," Dolly exclaimed. "Your father's beautiful red hair. Martin had it too."

"It used to be brighter, then along came the children."

"Oh, how I wish Robert could see you now."

"I'm hoping to learn more about him," Rose said.

"Well, we'd better get to it, then. I don't have long for this world."

Rose followed Dolly's thumping cane forward around wooden armchairs piled with magazines and past a heavy, cluttered desk still with a pen and ink set. A faded print of Jesus, in profile with His perfect nose and staring far away, hung on the far wall. A fine sheen of dust coated everything.

"This was the doctor's parlor." She gestured with her cane. "Patients waited here until he could see them. Sometimes it was so full that people sat out on the porch and down the steps."

"I see."

"This is where we met your mother," Dolly said. "I remember the day she came in with her toothache."

"I'm hoping to learn more about her too."

Dolly opened a door. "This was Robert's exam room."

A flat table with a folding back and dangling stirrups stood at center. To the side were glass cabinets with basins, bowls, a glass jar with cotton balls, small vials and bottles, and a mask-like contraption. Alongside it was a clear-glass flask with a conical top, as if to administer something by the drop.

"He saved many a life in this room," Dolly said.

Rose looked about.

"I was his nurse," Dolly continued. "Not a trained nurse, but I might as well have been for all I saw and did."

"You were a team."

Dolly gave her a side-eyed look. "We were. He couldn't have practiced medicine without me, and this town couldn't have done without him. It's a crime that they almost lost him."

"Lost him?"

"But that's another story." Dolly pressed on from the exam room and into the interior of the house, which was even more cluttered, dimmer still, and smelled of cat.

"Shoo." Dolly almost tripped over a large gray one, then whacked it with her cane. The cat yowled and ran off. She pointed to the only chair without dust, beside which a pile of novels, the potboiler kind, rose from the floor. "This is my spot. I'm a reader. Robert mainly read his medical journals."

"I see."

"I have photos of him. Many things to show you, if you have time."

"Some. But I won't be able to linger too long," Rose said.

"Don't worry. We'll get to my letter," Dolly said.

The doctor's study smelled faintly of pipe tobacco. Various plaques and awards covered the walls, which included a bookcase of medical texts and a large, faded photo of a seacoast and sharp hills.

"Isle of Skye," Dolly said. "The town was named after a Scotsman who was from there and settled here."

"It's the perfect name for a town up in North Dakota."

Dolly closed the door behind, as if for privacy. As if there might be someone else in the house. On the back of the door hung a wooden foot with straps and a kind of garter. With her cane, she hooked it off the wall and held it out. "This was Robert's."

Rose stared.

"Go ahead, take it."

"Was he in the war?" Rose turned it over in her hands and quickly returned it.

Dolly narrowed her eyes. "In a way." She restored the prosthesis to its hook. "He got a blister from a tight boot, then a callus that got infected. We took him down to Saint Luke's, but the infection was advanced. They had to take his foot."

"What bad luck."

"Not luck. It was them."

"Them?"

Dolly turned. "The Haugens."

Rose stared.

"Sit," Dolly said.

Rose took a wooden chair before the desk. Dolly took the doctor's chair, heavier and with arms. "I was there when that tall one, Emil, he'd be your uncle, came to the house," Dolly continued. "He wanted to cobble Robert a pair of shoes in order pay for his sister's bill. Henrietta fell for it. For some reason she took a shine to that Emil. It was strange. He was such a hayseed. Anyway, Robert went along with the shoe cobbling. He was far too accommodating to her and to all of his patients. The things they tried to pay him with."

"If you could slow down a bit. Who is Henrietta?"

Dolly blinked. "Robert's first wife. She was from Pennsylvania. They met down in Nebraska during college. They married, but when Robert had his foot trouble, she left him in the lurch. Packed up and headed back East while he was still in the hospital. She was no good for him—put on airs, never met his needs. No wonder he had his little fling with your mother." Dolly gave Rose a glance.

Rose waited.

"Anyway," Dolly continued, "after Henrietta left, it was me who cared for Robert and got him back on his feet. We married hardly a year later."

"That's quite a story," Rose said.

"It's all true," Dolly said. "And Robert's foot was just the beginning." She opened the desk drawer and withdrew a narrow notebook. "After the Haugen girl gave birth to you, her family got it in their mind to punish us."

"Punish you?"

"We never knew when or how it was coming." Dolly narrowed her watery eyes. "Nothing ever could be traced to them. Oh, they were sly. Robert wasn't sure who was doing it. I knew in my bones it was the Haugens."

"Doing it?"

Dolly pushed the notebook forward. "Read for yourself."

Rose took the notebook.

"Out loud," Dolly said.

"Tight boot, foot infection, amputation. July, 1935."

"Go on."

"Garden salt, 1936."

"I used to grow tomatoes," Dolly said, squinting at the window. "Big beefy ones. Better Boys, I think they were called, for the table and canning. After the summer of '36 nothing would grow, not even weeds. The neighborhood dogs loved the garden. They'd come around and lick the dirt. Robert had a professor from the ag college come up and test the soil. He said it might as well be the Utah salt flats."

"I don't understand."

"They salted it, don't you see?" Dolly leaned forward sharply. "Some night, probably raining at the time so it would soak in and cover their tracks, they came with a sack of salt. Did the lawn too. Go to the window and look for yourself. It's never been the same."

"I noticed that the grass was patchy." Rose closed the notebook and checked her watch. "I can't stay long. It's a drive to Fargo, and I have Lucy and Leo. You said you wished to talk to me about—"

"Teachers, babysitters, they'd just quit," Dolly continued. "Wouldn't work for us anymore. They'd never say why. It was like they were scared for their lives."

"Surely, you're not saying…"

Dolly pointed to the notebook. "And Robert's Packard. It burned in '42. I so loved that car. We used to take rides out to see his hunting land."

Rose opened the notebook and paged to a yellowed newspaper clipping with a photograph of a charred car.

"Vandals, the paper said, but I know better," Dolly said. "There's more things, more troubles, but skip ahead to the last page."

Rose opened an obituary. "Martin McConnell. 1936–1963."

"Robert's and my son. Your brother."

"You mentioned him in your letter. And thank you for the photograph. I'm sorry I never got to know him."

"Martin came late, but he was ours," Dolly said, leaning back and staring at nothing. "After he died, there were only the two of us. And you, of course."

"How did he die, may I ask?"

Dolly leaned forward abruptly. "The Haugens killed him, of course."

Rose drew back. "What?"

"It's all there," Dolly said, gesturing to the clipping.

Rose tracked her gaze down the faded newsprint. "A fire, it says, at the Dodge-In nightclub."

"We owned the Dodge-In. Martin ran it. The place sat where the new gas station is just as you're coming into town," Dolly continued. "It was a going business, especially during the missile years. Oh, but

Skye was lively then. Anyway, Martin worked there day and night. Sometimes he slept in the back room. One night it burned down with him in it. I know they did it."

Rose stood and returned the notebook. "I should go. Is there anything I might do for you before I leave? Would you consider a housekeeper? Someone to come in once a week or so and help? I could ask around."

Dolly caught her wrist. "I don't need a housekeeper. I just want the truth."

"The truth?" Rose pulled against Dolly's bony fingers.

"From the Haugens. That they killed your brother."

She freed herself from Dolly's grip and stepped back. "The newspaper said there was an investigation."

"Pfff." Dolly waved at the air. "The sheriff's department never liked the Dodge-In. They were happy to see it gone. Sure they 'investigated.' Nothing ever came of it. But Jenny Haugen's car was seen in town the night before the fire. It was in the police report, which they 'lost' hardly before Martin was cold in the ground."

"I really must go," Rose said. "It's a long drive. I'll come again."

"About the matter of my estate," Dolly said.

Rose paused in the doorway.

"Well, well," Dolly said with a cackle. "That got your attention."

"You did ask to see me about that," Rose replied.

"Yes. Thank you for making the trip. You are my sole heir, but I want something from you in return."

Rose paused. "If I can."

"I want you to worm your way into the Haugen family," Dolly said, narrowing her eyes. "Gain their trust. Get them talking. Jenny, she's the clever one. You won't get anywhere with her. But the tall one, Emil, he's less smart than he thinks he is. When he slips up, we'll have them."

"Have them?"

"For murder. There's no statute of limitations on murder."

Rose stared.

"If you do this for me, all this will be yours." Dolly gestured with both hands.

Rose looked around the dim, cluttered, cat-smelling house.

Dolly cackled again. "Don't let appearances deceive you. I never lived high on the hog. I managed Robert's medical practice, and I saved and saved. Money was not important to him, but it was to me. I grew up without."

"You're asking me to do a very serious thing based on lies and deceit."

"Everybody has their price," Dolly replied. "Want to see yours?"

Rose remained in the doorway. Dolly produced a ledger and opened it. With a skinny finger, she beckoned Rose forward.

She didn't move.

"You'll always wonder," Dolly said.

Rose swallowed, then came forward. She leaned to look over Dolly's shoulder.

"The house, Robert's parcels of hunting land, his Cadillac, plus our savings and investment accounts," Dolly said as she drew a bony finger down the line items. "It's all here."

At sight of the bottom number, Rose sucked in a breath.

"I thought that might interest you." Dolly grinned, her thin lips pulling away from yellowed teeth. "You'd be close to a millionaire. Think of what you could do for your family."

Chapter Forty
Department Store

Her drive home passed in loops of thought. She was in the doctor's study. She was in the store. She was driving. She was in the clouds looking down at her car inching along the flat, empty fields, the skinny ribbon of road. She found herself well over the center line and sharply corrected her steering.

Back in Fargo, she drove straight to the store and parked in the rear. Entering through the back door, she paused at the smell. Wool. Old carpet. Age. Time. Except for cat piss, Rossi's department store had the same odor as Dolly McConnell's house.

She passed along men's suits, straightening one coat on its hanger. Someone must have tried on the jacket. To the side was their bread and butter, rental formal wear. With winter formal dance, spring prom, graduation, and, of course, weddings, rental tuxedos and gowns were their largest source of income. It was seasonal but dependable. The downside was the odor of teenagers. She and Darryl dry-cleaned each gown and jacket upon return, but over time the embedded scent of high schoolers was impossible to steam away.

"You're back," Darryl called. "How did it go up north?"

She had, out of duty, shown him Dolly's letter; he read it once, twice, then said, predictably, "I wonder if this is on the up and up?"

"It went okay, but still some things to be sorted out."

"Well, you're good at that sort of thing."

She glanced about the silent store. Up front, Stephanie stood looking out the window. "How was the day here?"

"Slow, but spring formal is just around the corner."

She went to the till. A couple of twenties and some ones. "Credit card sales?"

"One or two."

She lifted a credit card slip and its carbon. "One. For eighteen dollars."

"Like I said, a bit slow."

"Where are the kids?" Rose asked.

"Lucy's at her guitar lessons, and Leo's working."

"Those lessons are so expensive."

"She has her own money from the bakery."

"Was there mail?"

"Not much. It's on your desk."

She retreated to the little office. Only one bill, "Third Notice!" from the plumber who had fixed a leaky heating radiator in late winter, along with a wholesale catalogue with all the latest "On-the-go" fashions for fall, 1981. Leg warmers were big. Purses were bigger. She turned it face down. Leaned back and looked out the little window.

Darryl leaned in. "Forgot to mention. Leonard from First National dropped by. Looked at a suit."

"That's promising."

"He mentioned that you had a meeting at the bank, but maybe you forgot?"

"I'll stop in and see him," she answered.

"As soon as you can, he said." Darryl shrugged.

"Sure," she said. "Me, the miracle-worker."

"Sorry," Darryl replied. "I wish I were better with the books."

Chapter Forty-One
Olsen Farms

A week later, on a bright, chilly day, Rose drove on gravel somewhere north of Crookston. A Minnesota map lay open on the rider's seat. Fields stretched flat in all directions. The sun, diffused in a low, white layer of clouds, gave no help with cardinal directions. She slowed, then pulled into a driveway where a farmstead sat tucked behind a windbreak. Small barn. Narrow and weathered house. Some wooden sheds, one of which had collapsed. A lilac bush struggling to bloom. The driveway carried wide tracks from heavy equipment. A giant digger of some kind sat field-side, its wings folded. Windows in the house were broken out, the door askew. A scatter of gray and blue pigeons circled, then glided in through the upstairs window.

Rose lay the county map on the hood of her car. She wore a light spring jacket, khaki skirt, and gym shoes. With her hair tucked under a scarf and tied at the chin, she turned the map ninety degrees, then squinted up the road that she believed ran north. Her eyes watered. Used to close reading, accounts and numbers, some muscle in them did not accommodate the distances surrounding her.

Back in the driver's seat, she touched her rosary and drove on. A mile ahead, a green tractor and a service truck sat near the road. The tall, John Deere with enclosed cab leaned on a flat tire, attended to by men on their knees. Behind the tractor was a wide-winged implement, a seeder perhaps. Much of the field was freshly black.

She drew to a stop. The men looked up when her car door slammed, then turned back to their work. She zipped her jacket and made her way down the ditch across the hard clumps of black dirt. The youngest fellow, straining against the long lever, swore at the tire. The nearest guy, with a brown face and a straw hat, stood. "Hello, Senora."

"Sorry to interrupt your work, but I need directions."

The other man pitched aside his iron lever and kicked the tire.

"And we need help," the man in the straw hat said.

"Me? No, I'm afraid I can't be of use."

He laughed. "No, I mean help is coming. Where are you going?"

"I'm looking for the Olsen farm."

"Si."

She waited.

"All of this," the man said and held out his arm to the fields.

A white pickup came fast up the road, a dust plume tumbling behind, and braked sharply.

"Mr. Roland will help you," the man said. "He's an Olsen."

A square-shouldered man in a seed cap and clean, work coveralls swung down from his pickup and hurried toward the tractor.

"Mr. Roland, this lady..."

"Be with you in a second," Roland said. "What's the trouble, boys?"

"There's one rock in the whole field," the man said. "I hit it." He shrugged and smiled at Rosalie.

Roland knelt by the tire.

"The bead is off the rim," the service guy said. He was young, sweaty, and red-faced. "It won't take air."

"Do you have carburetor spray in your truck?" Roland asked.

"What, like for cold weather starting?"

"Yes."

"Sure, but it ain't winter, and it ain't the carburetor that's the problem."

325

"Get it," Roland said.

With the spray can in hand, Roland turned to Rose. "You might want to stand back." He knelt, sprayed inside the tire until the can was empty, then tossed it aside. The mist, a drift of which came her way, bit inside her nose like hair spray.

Roland took a booklet of matches, leaned behind the tire as best he could, then tossed a lit one. POOMF! Fire flashed around the rim. The big tractor jolted upward, the tire's bead now sealed. The blast bowled over the tire fellow, which got a laugh from the man in the straw hat.

"You boys got to work smarter." Roland winked at Rosalie. "Let's get that tire aired up and this field finished, Carlos."

"Si, Mr. Roland."

Roland brushed the knees of his coveralls, which had an ironed crease. He was younger than her and had the bearing of an athlete or military man. "How can I help you?"

"I'm Rosalie Rossi. I'm looking for Mrs. Jenny Olsen."

"I'm Roland Olsen, and mother doesn't need Bibles, encyclopedias, or Watkins products."

"I'm not selling anything, I assure you."

He paused. "Does she know you?"

She paused. "I believe so, yes."

Roland looked her up and down. "Spring is our busiest time of the year. Maybe you could call her?"

"I was hoping to see her today. I'm passing. It wouldn't take long."

"Rossi."

"Yes. Rosalie. Rose."

"Let me get her on the radio."

She followed him to his truck. He sat inside with the door shut. As he talked into the hand-held receiver, he kept his eyes on the field. His mouth formed the "r" sound twice, and again, more distinctly. He turned Rose's way, then put the radio in its cradle. He opened the door. "She'll see you."

***

She drove behind Roland's truck and its tumbling dust and almost missed the driveway. A simple, aluminum mailbox. A small sign: "Olsen Farms, Inc." A long, straight, graveled lane led to a farmstead. Its big white house had a long front porch and a large, added wing on the side. Across the yard lay a ball diamond, sized smaller as if for kids, and beside it the curving boards of a hockey rink. Across, a complex of shiny grain bins rose up like a cathedral. A tower at the center with angled pipes connected all the bins. Beyond stood various white sheds, larger and larger the closer she drove. Roland parked and hopped out. He did everything quickly.

She drew to a stop. Rolled down her window.

"Wait here," he said.

She turned off her engine and stepped out. Roland's boots crunched gravel as he receded toward the center complex of grain bins. He disappeared into a smaller metal building. Across stood a white, metal-sided building with open doors wide enough to accommodate an airliner. Opposite the bins and sheds stood two identical smaller houses, the kind built somewhere else and delivered. Bright kids' toys scattered their front yards. A third trailer home had a small, fenced garden. A fourth, still-smaller trailer house had a chicken coop behind. Red chickens, a couple of dozen, ranged among the homes. Somewhere a lawn mower hummed. The grass around the trailer homes and the big house was manicured like a golf course. There were no shrubs, bushes, or landscaping. Somewhere behind the bins, hammers clanged and a motor hummed. From the road, the Olsen farmstead did not look large. Close up, it was a village.

Roland reappeared in the doorway and waved her forward.

Crossing the yellow gravel, she followed him into a garage-like building, inside of which was an office with an interior door and window. Jenny Olsen, medium height with salt and pepper hair curling from underneath a baseball cap, waited in the doorway. She wore a light-colored jacket with a European cut, matching lightweight pants, and fresh Nike sneakers, blue over white. With the cap, her look was light-on-her-feet. Athletic.

"This is the woman," Roland said.

"It appears so," Jenny Olsen replied. She didn't step forward.

Roland cocked his head at his mother.

"Thank you for seeing me," Rose said.

They did not shake hands.

Jenny turned. "Roland, meet your cousin."

"What?" He drew up.

"This is Aunt Sally's girl, Rosalie Rossi."

"Well." He took off his cap. He had full hair cut in a sharp flat-top. "I know of you, but that's about it."

"I should have called or written," Rose said. "I wasn't sure how this would work out."

"I guess it depends on why you're here," Jenny said.

"I'm not selling Bibles or encyclopedias."

Roland smiled.

"That's a good start," Jenny said. "Please... come in."

Roland glanced at his watch. "If you two are okay here, I should keep moving."

"We'll be fine," Jenny said.

"Spring is crunch time," he said to Rose.

"Of course," she said.

"I have my truck radio if you need me," Roland said to his mother.

"I'm fine." Jenny waved him off, then beckoned Rose forward. "Grain dust everywhere. But where would we be without it?"

To the side was a small, lounge area with comfortable chairs, a well-worn dart board and a pool table, its triangle of colored balls racked and ready. Skinny cues hung on the wall. Two modern desks anchored the center and corner of the office. One had a tidy ledger alongside the latest desktop calculator, a Texas Instrument with a small screen and power cord adaptor, and a Dictaphone. On the wall were charts, including the weight of wheat, corn, and other commodities. The capacities of grain bins. A blackboard with wheat prices chalked across the years in an up-and-down line. A similar, chalked graph with bank interest rates angling sharply upward to the current day.

"Today 16 percent and rising," Jenny said, gesturing to a chair. "Who knows how much higher it will go."

"It's a bit frightening," Rose said.

"Depends," Jenny said, "whether you're borrowing or saving."

"Do you use a computer yet?"

"No, but Roland is looking at them."

"I am too. I think they'd be quite good for our store… to keep inventory. My husband's against them."

"He'll probably have to change his tune."

They fell silent.

"So." Jenny steepled her hands. She wore the thinnest of golden wedding bands. "Why are you here?"

"To enquire about my birth mother."

"I suppose I could guess that."

"I was told that you'd be the one with information."

Jenny tilted her head slightly. "Told by whom?"

"A letter came to me." She dug in her purse. "Perhaps you could look at it and tell me if it's on the up and up?" She handed it across.

Jenny unfolded the page. Scanned to the bottom. "Dolly McConnell." She nodded.

"Do you know her?"

"I do indeed," Jenny said evenly. She took her time reading the letter.

"There's an obituary too," Rose said. "Her husband, the doctor, passed away a couple of months ago."

"I'm aware of that." Jenny gave the obituary a brief look. "Skye was my hometown. I still keep track of things there, obituaries especially."

"Did you know him?"

Jenny bit her lower lip briefly. "Everyone knew him."

"She sent a photo too," Rose continued and dug in the envelope. "She and the doctor had a son, Martin, who would have been my brother. Did you know him?"

Jenny did not change expressions. "I've met him, yes."

Rose lay the photo on the desk.

Jenny, letter in hand, gave the picture the briefest of glances. "That's him, yes."

"He died in an accident. A fire at a nightclub."

"I remember that." Jenny lay Dolly's letter atop the photo.

"Overall, then, what Dolly McConnell says seems to add up," Rose said, and leaned back.

"Have you met Dolly?" Jenny asked.

"Yes. I drove up to Skye and called at her house. She gave me information about your family."

"And now you're here."

Rose gathered the letter and photo. "I grew up in Fargo, but I've always known that I was adopted. My parents were as good as one could want. I was never much interested in where I came from."

"Until now."

"When the letter came, I felt I could hardly ignore it."

"Especially as sole heir."

Rose met Jenny's gaze. "I have four children, two still at home, and a family department store just getting by. If I can help my family, why wouldn't I?"

By the smallest degree, Jenny's manner softened. "Fair enough."

Rose tucked the letter and photo into her purse.

"You've kept your family name, Rossi," Jenny said.

"I have."

"You don't look like a women's libber."

"I'm not. My husband is a VandenEykel."

"Dutch," Jenny said. "Good people, but Rosalie VandenEykel is a mouthful."

"Exactly," Rose said. "Plus keeping the name has helped me more than once on the business side."

Jenny nodded. "I know Rossi's Clothing. I was there once as a little girl. My parents came down to Fargo to the mercantile store to buy some fabric. Maybe it was leather for shoe-making. Anyway, we went into Rossi's, but it was too rich for our blood."

"Well, thank you for looking," Rose said. "These days, most people go to the mall."

Jenny checked her watch. "So, what is it you want today?"

"If you can arrange for me to meet my birth mother, I'll have fulfilled my promise to Dolly McConnell. Then I'll be out of your hair for good."

With a trace of a smile, Jenny looked past Rose to the pool table. "Years ago, I learned to play pool. I still find it greatly relaxing. I also know that once you strike the cue ball, things happen down the table. Click, click. I am greatly protective of my family, and of my sister, Sally, in particular. I don't want disruption and trouble in her life."

"I understand."

Jenny nodded. "Good. And what Dolly says is true. Before the doctor married Dolly, he and my sister had a child together—you. That was in nineteen thirty-four. Sally was much younger than him. Afterward, you were adopted by the Rossis."

"That's all I know," Rose answered. "There's never been a reason for me to enquire further."

"Okay," Jenny said, as if that was the right answer. "Regarding my sister, she lives here. She's here today. But if you meet her out of the blue, it will be a considerable shock to her."

"I've thought about that."

"She's had her own health troubles over the years," Jenny continued. "She's delicate emotionally. Always has been, really."

"Thank you for telling me."

"It's taken her a long time to move beyond that particular time in her life," Jenny continued. "Beyond you."

Rose nodded. "Maybe if she has some time to think about seeing me."

Jenny met her gaze without seeing. She drummed her fingers, then blinked several times. "No. I think waiting might be worse." She produced a hand-held radio from her desk and pressed a button.

"Would you like me to step out?"

She waved for Rose to stay in her chair. After a beep, Jenny spoke loudly. "Dag? Round up Emil. He's mowing… and Sally too. I think she's back with her chickens. Tell them to meet at the house in a half hour. We have a visitor." She put down the radio.

"One more thing," Rose said. "What can you tell me about my brother, Martin?"

Jenny shrugged. "He had red hair like yours. He was wild at times, like many boys."

Rose waited.

Jenny frowned. "It was a long time ago."

"Of course."

Jenny checked the clock. "We have time for a tour of the farm, if you like?"

They went out the rear door to a waiting golf cart. Rose sat beside Jenny, gripped a dashboard bar, and away they whirred.

"We farm three thousand acres, give or take," Jenny said. "Some is rented… most we own."

"You and your husband?"

"Me and my family here. My husband lives in Winnipeg."

Rose glanced at her ring hand on the steering wheel, its small gold band.

"I married a Canadian," Jenny explained. "We could never figure out where to live so we go back and forth. He has his job there, heading up a church, and I have mine here."

"That must be difficult."

"It works quite well. We're always happy to see each other, plus I like Winnipeg and Canadians." Jenny drove on, across gravel into the mouth of the airplane hangar-sized shed. It had white-painted concrete floors and was immaculate. Across, the white spark of a welder burned near a farm implement, one wing up and folded, the other lowered and under repair. The welder's heavy cord ran to the wall and a bank of red tool chests and wooden racks, with forks and discs and tires and all manner of parts, everything tidy, everything in its place. Jenny beeped the cart horn.

The welder turned and tipped up his hood.

"Didn't want to sneak up on you," Jenny said.

"Gracias, Miss Jenny." He was an older version of the cheerful man she had met field-side.

"This is Cesar Rodriquez. He does all of our repair and maintenance."

"*Buenos dias*, Senora."

"Rosalie Rossi," she said.

"Red rose," he said. "*Muy buenos.*"

"Couldn't do without Cesar," Jenny said. "He runs our shop. Can fix anything."

"Runs the shop except when the snow flies," he said.

"Cesar and his wife are not much for Minnesota winters."

"We vamoose back to Florida," Cesar said. "Like the snowbirds."

"I wonder if I met your son? Out with the big tractor?"

"Si," Cesar said. "That's Carlos."

"Couldn't do without Carlos either," Jenny said. "But he's much tougher than his father. He stays here in winter too. There's always work."

Cesar laughed. "And I better get back to it." With a shrug, he dropped his hood.

They drove on past an enormous John Deere implement with a wide, jutting nose and tires so tall that a ladder ran up to the cab.

"One of our combines," Jenny said. "Cesar will have it ready to go in July." She drove out the other side of the machine shed and back onto gravel.

"How did your family get started farming?" Rose asked.

"In Norway, I suppose. A patch of rented land, which is why my parents came to America." Jenny drove on, then paused close alongside a grain bin. "These each hold twenty-five thousand bushels. We're sitting on last year's harvest, no thanks to Jimmy Carter."

"Jimmy Carter?"

"His grain embargo. No sales to the Soviet Union. It was supposed to be their punishment for invading Afghanistan. The only people punished were American farmers who couldn't sell their wheat. That and high interest rates are why you're seeing so many farm auctions. I never thought I'd vote for a Republican, but Reagan promised to lift the embargo."

"I see."

Jenny drove around back where a crew with a tall crane worked on an even bigger bin.

A boy waved.

"That's Tim, Roland's son," Jenny said. "He should be in school today, but he wanted to watch the bin builders. I'm annoyed with him for missing school."

"He looks about the same age as my Leo," Rose said.

Tim stepped forward to hook a cable to a wing of steel, then waved to the crane operator. The curved section, dangling by its thread, rose like an enormous silver butterfly.

"The new bin will hold fifty thousand bushels," Jenny said.

"Your family seems to be managing the farm crisis quite well."

After a pause, Jenny said, "I suppose so."

"Sorry, that's the bookkeeper in me. I don't mean to pry."

Jenny waved to Tim and the crew, then drove on. "They say to be a farmer you have to be an optimist. I'm a pessimist, and it's served me well. You have to expect that some year there won't be a crop, however that might happen. Including unforeseen events like having a good crop but not being able to sell a bushel of it."

"And other farmers?"

"Some weren't prepared, so there'll be fewer of them." Jenny turned the cart behind an older, smaller bin. On a space of grass, in orderly rows like a cemetery, stood a dozen monuments. Tin-peaked, elaborate, miniature cathedrals. Or witch houses.

"I've seen these," Rose said. "I should know what they are."

"Barn cupolas. They were for ventilating those big old hay mows."

"Of course," Rose said.

"Roland calls them my trophies. They're from farms we've bought," Jenny explained. "The barns we've taken down."

"Their design is striking, close up."

"There'll be no more of them," Jenny said. "The small, quarter-section farm is dead. These days, it's get bigger or get out. Someday there might be only one farm in the whole Red River Valley. If so, I want it to be me."

Rose touched the filigree metal on one of the cupolas. "What happened to these farmers?"

Jenny shrugged. "The father got cashed out. He got his nest egg. He and his wife could travel, but they hardly ever do. The sons now work part-time for me and other big growers and drive beet trucks for American Crystal Sugar. They'll never get back into farming."

Rose turned to the stretching, flat fields.

Jenny checked her wristwatch. "So. Are you ready to meet your mother?"

Chapter Forty-Two
Reunion

Rose followed Jenny up the wide front steps of the porch. It was swept clean, and the floor had a homemade boot brush, two broom heads nailed to face each other. Near them ran a long, trough-like sink with a water tap. By the sink was a linen towel dispenser, the endless roll kind common to gas station restrooms.

"We're here," Jenny called.

The house smelled of fresh bread and something spicier. To one side was the kitchen where two women worked, and across in the big dining room was a round table with at least a dozen chairs. A tall man, sitting with his cap tilted back over thick, gray hair, held a coffee cup. Across was a woman with a narrow face, kind eyes and a steel-gray ponytail. She wore a blue pullover zipped up to her neck, as if she might be chilly.

"The buns need to cool, but they're ready." A cheerful, stocky, short woman appeared briefly in the kitchen doorway.

Jenny drew up. "Everyone? Say hello to Rosalie Rossi."

For a moment no one moved. "It's you," the woman at the table said. Her voice was a dry whisper. She rose—she was quite tall—and with both hands steadied herself on a chair-back.

"*Gud i himmelen.*" The fellow in the cap lurched to his feet. He was even taller.

"Oh my, I have to sit down." Dag fanned herself.

"I'm sorry to just show up like this," Rose said.

"Just to be clear, I did not know," Jenny said to everyone.

"That's true," Rose said quickly. "And I think now I should have given you some warning."

Sally stepped forward. Took Rose's hands as if to steady them both. She looked her up and down. "No, this was best. I am… Sally." Her voice came out scratchy, like a radio station far away. She leaned closer. "It's you."

"It is."

"Can I see them?" Sally whispered.

"See them?"

"Your marks," Sally murmured.

"Those, yes," Rose said. "I'm clearly at the right house."

"Would you excuse us for a minute?" Jenny said to the others. She brought Rose and Sally down to the bedroom and closed the door.

Rose untucked her blouse in the back and turned the small of her back to Sally. "My children call them my tattoo."

"You can hardly see them anymore," Sally murmured. She touched them with her finger.

Rose flinched.

"Sorry," Sally said quickly.

"Your finger was cold." Rose retucked her blouse.

"It's not like I didn't believe you," Sally said. "I just wanted to make sure I'm not going crazy."

"You're not crazy, and you've never been crazy," Jenny said.

"I did it when you were one day old," Sally continued. "With a nib and a jar of ink. I knew they'd take you away. I knew I'd lose you."

"But now she's back," Jenny said. "And we have a few things to sort out." She steered the women to the door.

In the kitchen, Sally took the same chair, her chair. Jenny pointed to the chair across, which Rose took. Sally kept her gaze on Rose.

"Coffee?" Dag said, though she made no move to get it.

"Thank you," Rose said.

"I bring it. You all just sit," a smaller, cheerful woman called from the kitchen. She had dark hair and wore a bright apron smudged with flour.

"That's Luisa," Dag said.

"Hola," Luisa called.

"Look at you," Sally whispered.

Rose met her gaze. They looked each other's faces up and down.

"I always wondered what you'd look like grown up," Sally said.

"Well, here I am." Rose fixed a smile, after which she could not think of one word to say.

During the next half hour, Dagmar and Emil carried the conversation. Sally smiled or frowned or discreetly dabbed at her eyes with a hankie. Jenny observed, her gaze switching between Sally and Rose. Dag brought Rose up to speed on the family, who was who.

At length, Rose checked her wristwatch. "Thank you for the coffee. This has been very nice, but also a lot. I should go."

"Can't you stay for dinner?" Dag said.

"That's very kind, but no."

"We have *chilé rellenos*," Luisa called from the kitchen. "They're not spicy. Mr. Emil has a weak stomach."

"She tries to kill me with her jalapenos."

"He's gotten better," Dag said.

"Ask my bunghole later," Emil replied.

"Hush, Emil, we have a visitor," Dag said.

"She's family now, ain't she?"

The table fell silent.

"I've certainly heard worse from my kids," Rose said with a smile.

"Do they have your hair?" Sally murmured.

"Regular brown, and some lighter from my husband's side. But they're getting quite tall. I see where that comes from now."

"Do you have photos of them?" Sally asked.

"Not with me."

"Tell me their names again." Dag found a pencil and paper.

"Margaret and Mary Grace. Lucy and Leo are my two still at home."

"You being Catholic, I would have expected more," Emil said.

"For Heaven's sakes, Emil," Dag said.

Emil shrugged.

"Your family," Jenny said, her first words in some time. "Do they know?"

"That I'm reaching out? My husband and kids, yes. My parents, no."

"*Den tid, den sorg,*" Dag said.

"Excuse me?" Rose said.

"Cross that bridge when you come it," Dag said. "We still speak some Norwegian here."

"The time, the sorrow," Emil said. "That's what it really says in Norwegian."

"There was plenty of that," Sally said with a sideways look at Emil.

Outside, gravel crunched and doors thudded.

"The fellows are here for dinner," Dag called to Luisa and quickly headed to the kitchen.

"No problemo. We're ready," she replied.

Boots thumped on the porch steps. Men lined up at the outside cold sink.

"I really should go," Rose said.

"Too late," Dag said.

"Please stay." Sally came over and put a hand on Rose's arm. She had remarkably long fingers.

Rose paused. "If it's no bother."

"Are you kidding? We won't notice another setting," Dag said.

Roland, Cesar, and Carlos came in, followed by Tim and four fellows from the grain bin crew.

"No caps at the dinner table," Dag called.

"Sorry," one of the guys said.

"And that goes for you too, Tim."

"I know, Gran." His eyes went to Rose.

"This is Mrs. Rossi," his father said. "She's a, ah, relative."

"Okay," Tim said easily.

"You boys take the far end," Dag said to the bin builders. "Pull up a chair. Don't be shy."

The dinner moved quickly, with Dag and Luisa and Sally circling the table, replenishing the main platters of *rellenos* and beans. Side dishes moved around the table: tortillas, pickled herring, sliced cucumbers in vinegar, jiggly red JELL-O swirled in whipped cream. One of the rough boys from the grain bin crew rolled up red beans and pickled herring into a fat tortilla.

"Now you're talking," Dag said.

"How did we live without Mexican food?" Emil said.

"You didn't want me to go to Florida," Dag said on the move.

"I don't remember that," Emil replied.

"You don't remember lots of things these days."

"I remember." Cesar turned to Rose. "Many years ago, down in Tallahassee, one night we were just putting the children to bed."

"Not that story again," Tim said.

"Yes. Another time, Cesar," Jenny said.

"We don't want to bore everyone," Dag added.

"It is not boring," Cesar said, indignant. "It was a miracle."

Dag blushed. "Oh, Cesar."

"It's both," Jenny said. "But we don't have all day."

"What year did you go to Florida?" Emil frowned at Dag.

"It's okay, Emil." Jenny put her hand on Emil's arm. "Nothing to fret about."

"Then here's a story from today." Carlos told of the John Deere's flat tire, the spray ether, and how Doug the tire service guy got blown back on his *culo*. The men hooted. Dag clucked her tongue.

"Doug didn't think it would work," Roland said.

"It did, quite remarkably," Rose added. "I saw it."

Conversation moved to farm planning, with Jenny quizzing the grain bin team on their schedule and Roland and the field workers on planting progress. Parts were needed, and a list passed to Jenny, who would make the run to town.

"You're not eating," Dag said to Sally.

"Sorry, I'm staring," Sally said to Rose.

Who took her hand. Gave it a squeeze. "I don't mind."

For dessert there was apple pie (three whole ones disappeared) and coffee, after which the men abruptly pushed back their chairs.

"*Takk for maten*," Emil said.

"*Værsågod*," Luisa called from the kitchen.

"We're working on her Norwegian."

The grain bin boys and Tim headed for the door.

"What do you say?" the foreman said.

"Sorry. Thanks for dinner. Appreciate it," they called.

"That's better," their boss said and waved them out.

In the yard, doors thudded and engines started. The dining table was a jumble of emptied plates and bowls.

"Our noon dinners are fast and loud," Jenny said, "but we couldn't do without them."

"I'll help with dishes." Rose stood.

"I'd get out while you can." Emil rolled a toothpick in his mouth.

"And I should get back to work," Jenny said.

"We have leftover *rellenos*," Dag called from the kitchen. "Can I send a plate?"

"To be honest, Lucy and Leo will always eat."

Sally walked her to the door. "Can you come again?"

Rose, holding her plate-to-go, glanced at Jenny.

"We'd like to meet the children," Dag said.

"We would," Sally said softly.

Jenny said nothing.

"Maybe it's not the best idea," Rose began. "Let's think about it."

"Why-ever not?" Dag turned to Jenny.

Sally looked to Jenny as well.

"If you want to come out once with kids, that's fine," Jenny said. "But call ahead."

"Don't worry about that," Emil said loudly, waving Jenny off. "We're always home."

"Speak for yourself," Dag said.

"Yes, well, the one time we did leave home they burned us out, remember?"

"That's in the past," Dag said evenly.

"The past ain't ever past," Emil murmured.

"That's enough, you two." Jenny put on her jacket and turned to Rose. "I'll see you out."

As they crossed the yard, Jenny said, "Well, now you've met the family."

"I like them a great deal," Rose said. "This worked out well, I think."

They reached the car. "You'll have no trouble finding your way home?" Jenny asked. "These flat roads and square corners can all look the same."

"I know my cardinal directions," Rose said. "Most the time."

They shook hands, a brief pump at arm's length.

"You won't forget what I said about the pool table?" Jenny said.

"Click, click," Rose replied.

Jenny nodded, a trace of a smile in her eyes.

As Rose drove down the driveway, she watched Jenny in her mirror. She remained in the yard, arms crossed, watching Rose's progress. Only when the car turned left, and thus south, did Jenny turn away, as if to ensure that Rose was fully gone.

***

Heading back to the farm office, Jenny sat in her desk chair, staring. Emil came in. He took a chair without speaking. They looked at each other.

"What do you think?" he asked.

"About what?" she answered.

"Do you think she knows?" Emil asked.

"About how she came into the world?" Jenny shrugged. "Some. But clearly not the whole of it."

"Are we going to tell her?"

"Why would we?" Jenny replied.

Emil nodded.

They fell silent.

"She seems nice," Emil added.

"Yes," Jenny answered.

"Solid. Squared away," Emil continued.

"I don't want any more heartbreak for Sally," Jenny replied.

"Or trouble for us," Emil said.

Their eyes met. "She had a picture of her brother," Jenny said. "She wanted to know if I knew him."

"Jesus." Emil stood, came around, and put a hand on Jenny's shoulder. "I'm sorry about that."

Jenny briefly patted his fingers. "For now, back to work, I think."

Emil paused at the door. "Do you think we'll see her again?"

"I have a feeling we will."

"Well," Emil said, "She is family."

Jenny produced a sound short of a laugh. "That's the problem, isn't it?"

Chapter Forty-Three
Click Click

Three weeks after her first visit to Olsen Farms, Rose again drove across the Red River and into Minnesota.

"Why do we have to do this?" Lucy said loudly. She slouched in the back seat with her Walkman and headphones on and her little notebook that she always carried.

"Yeah," Leo said. "It's a little weird."

"The Olsens are family," Rose said. "I'd think you'd want to meet them."

"We already have a family," Lucy said.

"True," Rose said. "So do it as a favor. To me."

The teenagers glanced at each other.

"If it's too weird I want to leave right away." Lucy took off her headphones to check her teased hair in the side window.

"It's bound to be some." Leo, riding shotgun, glanced at his mother.

"We don't have to stay long," Rose said.

As they drove north of Crookston, Leo peered out the window. "Fields are huge here. You can hardly see to the end."

Rose pointed. "That's the Olsen farm ahead."

Leo leaned forward over the seat. "Wow. The buildings are big."

"Are they rich?" Lucy said loudly.

"Possibly," Rose said.

"Dad grew up on a farm, but he never liked it," Leo said.

"And now his brothers, the ones who stayed to raise potatoes, are the rich ones," Rose said.

"We have the store," Lucy said.

"But we aren't rich," Leo said. "Are we Mom?"

Rose parked in front of the house.

On the wide front porch, Jenny and Sally sat in chairs lined up in a row. Emil leaned on a post, smoking.

"They look like hillbillies," Lucy said.

"With your hair that way, you look like you got struck by lightning," Leo replied.

"Shut up."

"That's enough." Rose got out of the car, lingering a moment as if to look about, but really to wait for Lucy to put away her player. Leo stared at the giant sheds and grain bins.

Dag, Jenny and Sally came across the grass to meet them. "You're right on time," Jenny said.

"I can't not be."

"It's a thing with mother," Lucy remarked.

Dag stepped closer to inspect the children. Sally hung back and could only smile. She wore a nice blouse, long-sleeved, with a high collar buttoned at the neck.

"This is Lucy and Leo," Rose said. "Lucy's seventeen, Leo, fourteen."

"And I'm Aunt Dag. Cousin Dag? Well, who cares."

"I'm Jenny." There were hellos. Awkward handshakes.

"And I'm Sally." Her voice was low but stronger today.

Rose turned to her children. "This is Sally. Sally is—"

"Just Sally," she said, as if she had practiced.

Tim emerged in the door of the big machine shed. "Come over, Tim," Dag called. "Don't be shy."

Tim made an annoyed gesture but came across to shake hands with Leo, and, blushing, with Lucy.

"Won't you all come in?" Sally said.

"That's our brother, Emil, on the porch," Dag said to Lucy and Leo as they headed to the house. "Don't let him frighten you."

Lucy's eyes widened.

"She's teasing," Tim said.

"Sort of," Dag added.

Emil took a last draw on his cigarette, then stubbed it out into a coffee can. "Finally, we got some help around here," he called.

"These are Rose's children," Dag said. "Lucy and Leo."

"Where's the rest of the ball team?" Emil loomed over them to shake hands.

"They're off and away," Rose said. "Jobs, lives, children of their own."

"Well, glad to meet the last of the brood," Emil said as he pumped Leo's hand and then Lucy's. Lucy leaned back the maximum distance. "Though with Catholics you never know, right?" He winked at Rose.

"We have a nice lunch ready." Dag angled in between Emil and the kids.

"We can't stay long," Lucy announced.

"Long enough for a bite to eat, I hope," Sally said. "The food's all ready."

"I can show you around afterward," Tim said to Leo. He included Lucy in his look.

"Sure," Leo said.

"There may not be time," Lucy said.

"Hush," Rose said.

***

At lunch, Lucy and Leo sneaked glances at Emil, at the way he ate, fast and loud. Dag, a master at keeping the conversation going, kept asking questions. Jenny had little to say. Sally could not take her eyes off the children. Could not stop smiling. She ate hardly a bite and kept the dishes moving toward the children, especially Leo.

"I didn't expect to have Mexican food," Leo said. "It's my favorite. It's delicious!"

"Gracias," Luisa called from the kitchen.

"We have it a lot," Tim said to Leo.

"Try one of Roland's biscuits," Dag said. "He doesn't cook much, but he can bake biscuits like nobody else."

Just then Roland arrived. "Sorry I'm late." He settled in at the table. "Hi there. I'm Tim's dad."

"Does that make you my cousin, or something?" Leo said to Tim.

Tim looked to his father.

Roland scratched his head. "I'd have to think about that."

"It's no matter," Dag said. "Family is family."

Midway through lunch, a woman came in through the kitchen's back door. She was small-eyed, had sharply cut bangs, and was thick through the middle, a size twelve.

"This is Amy, Roland's wife." Dag handled the introductions.

"Hello." Amy did not come forward to shake hands. Her gaze homed in on the newcomers.

"Will you eat?" Dag asked.

"Already ate. I'm heading to town to the beauty shop."

"Well, I'm glad you got to meet the newest members of the family," Dag said.

Leo looked around. "It's going to take me awhile to figure out how we're all related."

"It's pretty simple," Amy said. "You've got your family… we've got ours."

No one said anything. Roland frowned.

"Shall we have our coffee?" Dag said.

"Let's," Jenny said, with a glance at Amy.

"Was there pie?" Emil asked.

***

After lunch, Tim took Leo in the golf cart "for a quick look around." They returned in time for goodbyes in the front yard.

"Sorry, Ma," Leo said. "Tim was showing me the big tractors and combine."

"Good," Emil said. "Leo might take to farming." He ruffled Leo's hair.

"We have to go," Lucy said.

"Indeed, we do," Rose said. She turned to Tim. "Thanks for taking Leo about."

"Sure," Tim said.

"You've got nice kids," Emil said. "With a good mom."

"That's very kind, Emil."

"I wanted to ask," Jenny said, "have you been up to Skye again? Talked any more with Mrs. McConnell?"

"No," Rose said. "How to say this? She's not someone I took to immediately."

"Ain't that right," Emil muttered.

"You mentioned her health," Jenny said. "Does she still live at home?"

"Yes, though she probably shouldn't," Rose replied.

"Well then," Jenny said, and checked her watch.

They all shook hands. Rose and the kids headed to the car.

As Rose drove out the long driveway, Leo looked back. "They're nice."

"They are," Rose said.

"Their farm is amazing. My cousin Tim said he could teach me how to drive a tractor."

"He's not really your cousin," Lucy said immediately.

"Yes, he is."

"Don't, you two. And anyway, who cares?"

"Amy does," Lucy remarked. "She didn't like us."

"That was uncomfortable," Rose said. "Roland wasn't happy about it."

"Seems weird those two are married," Lucy said.

Rose glanced over to Lucy.

"I mean, he's so… and she's so…" Lucy continued.

"Agreed." Rose shrugged. "Maybe she's the first woman he had sex with."

"Mother!" Lucy cried.

In the back seat Leo spit out a laugh.

"What?" Rose said. "Small town. Farms few and far between. When it's slim pickings, you take what you can get."

Lucy snickered. "What a horrible thing to say."

They drove on in comfortable silence. Rose patted Lucy's arm. "Thank you both for coming today."

"I'm glad I did," Leo said. "They're really nice."

"You said that already," Lucy remarked.

"So?"

"Sew buttons on your underwear."

"That's enough, you two," Rose said without heat.

They rolled across the unending table of fields. After a mile, Lucy turned. "Okay, Mother, what was this trip really about?"

Chapter Forty-Four
Lilacs

That same month, in a surprise to Rose, Jenny Olsen called.

"If you're free Saturday afternoon, there's something going on here that Leo might like."

"What is it, may I ask?"

"A surprise," Emil called from the background.

"He insists," Jenny said. She clucked her tongue once.

"Well, if you're okay with another visit."

"Not to our farm, but one close by," Jenny said. "If you've got a pencil, I'll give you directions."

Leo, from curiosity, could hardly get through the next couple of days, but come Saturday, with Leo holding the map and Rose watching the odometer, they arrived. A driveway, a tumble-down farmstead, windows out of the house, and a lilac blooming by a small shed.

"Ha," Rose said.

"What, Mother?"

"I've been here before. When I was looking for the Olsen farm."

Emil's pickup sat in the yard. Jenny leaned on the fender. She checked her watch. Emil and Tim emerged from the barn. There was no door.

Tim raced over to Leo. "You're here!"

"Yes. Why? What's going on?"

"You'll see," Tim said, hopping with excitement.

"You found us," Emil said to Rose.

"I'm learning the roads around here," Rose said. "There are no signs, but I'm getting my cardinal directions straight."

Emil turned to the boys. "We've got a little time to look around, but not much."

"Why? What happens?" Leo asked. He too began to hop.

"You'll see," Tim said and spun in place. "Right, Gram?"

"We will indeed."

Tim ran off to the barn with Leo close behind.

"Watch them, will you?" Jenny said.

Emil was already heading after them.

"I've bought this farm," Jenny explained. "It's one of the last quarter section farms in the county. We're going to take down the buildings today."

"Take down?"

"A fellow is coming with some heavy equipment. Emil thought it would be good entertainment for the boys." Jenny shrugged.

"Is there any use to the house?" Rose asked. "It's old, but carpenters can do amazing things."

"We prefer it gone," Jenny said. "We've tried that with other farms, save the house and rent it, but it was too much bother. We're farmers, not landlords."

"I see."

Jenny checked her watch. "Would you like a look inside the house while it's still here?"

Rose squinted across. "Okay."

The front door, without latch or handle, hung askew.

"It sat empty," Jenny said. She touched the door frame. "When that happens, people take things, even the door knobs. The old, ceramic ones are worth money, I guess."

"Who lived here?" She followed Jenny inside.

"An old fellow, Ole Olafson," Jenny said. "He died last winter. Never married, didn't like people, though he got along with Roland and Emil. Roland wrote out the land rent checks. Emil came over to play cards and talk Norwegian."

The kitchen had an iron-stained ceramic sink, a water pipe poking through the wall, a two-burner gas stove, and much trash. Tiny, black mouse droppings peppered everything.

"You didn't want to come in the house when Ole was alive," Jenny said, wrinkling her nose. "Once was enough for me. Emil never minded. He was the one who found him."

"I see," Rose murmured.

In the living room, cotton flowers bloomed from a chewed-up couch. A simple desk, more like a library table, lay overturned before a scatter of papers and narrow ledgers. Jenny, brushing aside a thick rope, shiny with use, headed upstairs. Rose followed. Halfway up, at a small landing, the stairs turned right, and the wall carried a smudged hand print, a left hand. The bedroom was narrow and peaked. Pigeons flapped out. An iron bed with some squirrel-chewed blankets remained. A pair of long-johns, stained yellow at the crotch, lay in the corner.

Jenny went to the broken-out window. "I wanted to see what our new grain bin looks like from here."

Rose joined her.

Below came the sudden voices of Emil and the boys, whose feet thudded up the stairs. "We found things in the barn," Leo said with excitement. "Uncle Emil said I could keep it." He held up a blue glass cone the size of a teacup.

"It's pretty," Rose said. "What is it?"

"A telegraph line insulator," Emil answered. "The wire wrapped around the glasses, post to post. If the wire touched metal or wood, the messages died."

"I suppose you can have it," Rose said.

"Look," Tim said looking out the window. "You can see our new grain bin."

Leo joined him. "It looks like a castle."

Jenny checked her watch. "We'd best head down."

On the first floor, Emil paused in the kitchen. "That's where I found him," he said. "Ole was at his kitchen table. He liked to look out south, down the road. He was slumped over, still had a coffee cup in hand. I thought he was sleeping, but he was frozen stiff as a board. Been dead about a week."

Leo looked wide-eyed to his mother.

"The undertaker fellows carried him out sitting up," Emil continued. "He wouldn't fit in the back of the hearse, so they put him right in the front seat for the ride to town."

"That's plenty of information, Emil," Jenny said.

A rumbling came on the road. "Lance is here," Tim shouted, and ran out. Leo followed, though not at full speed, with Emil after them.

"Sorry about that," Jenny said. "Though it is true about Ole."

Rose had no reply.

From the dust emerged a truck and long trailer carrying a yellow excavator, its long, jointed arm tucked up like a heron beak at rest. The driver down-shifted, his engine drumming louder off the face of the barn, and tooted his air horn. Tim waved excitedly. Jenny held up a hand. He parked on the road, hopped down from his cab, and went behind to lower the trailer ramps.

"Can I ride along today, Lance? And my cousin, Leo, too?"

"Talk to your granny." Lance, a big man, gave a head jerk to the women.

"We'll see," Jenny said. "Let Lance get organized."

Lance set about removing the excavator's tie-down chains. He wore a John Deere cap, a flannel shirt with the sleeves cut off at the armpits, and, bent over, had a substantial butt crack. Rose looked away.

"So, what's the plan, Miss Jenny?"

"Same as always."

"Anything in the house worth keeping?" He had filmy, off-colored teeth.

"Place has been stripped clean. Not that Ole had much to begin with."

Lance looked across the farmstead. "Old barn wood is worth money. People down in Fargo finish their basements with it."

"Not worth our time."

"Okey-dokey." Lance cranked over the Caterpillar's engine. Let it idle for a minute, then drove backward down the steel ramps. Leo stepped behind his mother. Peeked out.

"Don't be afraid," Tim called. "He's not going to tip over."

Rumbling toward the barn, Lance raised his toothed bucket high, then carefully punched holes in the roof around the cupola. Pigeons streamed blue and white out of the windows. With the claw-like teeth, he loosened the sheet metal flashing around the cupola. Nails shrieked on tin. He eased the scoop underneath, then lifted the tin cone up, away, down, and gently deposited it into the back of Emil's pickup.

"It's a nice one, Gran," Tim said. "Number thirteen."

After that, Lance dug a long trench, wide and not deep, along the south side of the barn, which leaned that way. The dirt came up clotted and black and smelled like coffee grounds. Then the excavator rumbled toward the barn. Like a giant claw hammer, the bucket smashed through the old roof again and again.

"Goodness," Rose murmured. Leo stared, wide-eyed.

Groaning, the barn's back broke. Lance reversed and swung the long arm against the side of the barn. Crunch and crunch as the walls gave way and then, like a big tree falling, the whole thing collapsed into the trench.

Tim clapped and cheered. Leo joined him.

"Not too close," Rose called to the boys.

"I got my eye on them," Emil said.

As Lance worked his excavator, Jenny walked over to the shed and the lilac bush. Keeping the boys in sight, Rose followed. Jenny broke off a branch with fists of pink. Put it to her nose, then to Rose's. "Nothing better than lilacs in spring."

"They're lovely."

Behind them, Lance pushed the excavated black dirt back onto the barn debris, gradually covering the splintered wood with several feet of soil. Afterward, he ran back and forth, compacting the dirt. Soon a low swell of fragrant earth lay where the barn had stood. He turned his excavator toward the house, then paused it. He stepped out onto a muddy, Caterpillar track.

"Tim? You want to do the house with me?"

Tim hurried over.

"I can squeeze your boy in too," Lance called to Rose.

Leo looked up to his mother.

"If it's safe."

"It's safe," Tim called. "I've done it before with Lance." He hopped up onto the track, then reached down to pull Leo upward. Into the cab the boys went, where they squeezed into the jump seat.

The house collapsed in a single blow. Rose followed Jenny's lead and took a seat on the pickup's end-gate to watch. In a half hour, the house wreckage lay buried beneath its own low rise of fragrant black soil. Afterward, the Caterpillar idled for a minute, then headed toward the windbreak. Tim was sitting in the driver's seat now, grinning, arms outstretched on the levers. On the way back, Leo got a turn at the controls. He emerged wide-eyed, face flushed, grinning.

"Did you see me, Mom?"

"I did," Rose said flatly. "It's a far cry from your basement train set."

"I could be a big work machine driver someday," Leo said.

"Or anything you want, really." Rose put an arm around him.

"All done, then." Lance looked back at the black, empty space behind. "You can farm right over it now."

"That's the idea," Jenny said.

"We should go," Rose said. She checked her watch.

"Do you want to stop by the house for coffee?" Emil asked.

"Thanks, but no," Rose said. "Enough for today."

"Come on, Mom," Leo whined. "Why can't we?"

"Please go to the car," Rose said.

Leo, hearing something in his mother's voice, blinked and headed away. "See you," he called to Tim.

"I hope this wasn't too much," Jenny said.

"Too much? No. Why?"

Jenny shrugged. "It was Emil's idea to call you. And then I came to think it might be fun for you to see how we do things out here."

Rose glanced back at the bare, dark earth. "Leo will have a lot to talk about at school," she said. "A show and tell item too."

"And here's one for you." Jenny handed Rose a bouquet of lilacs. "Something to take back to your family."

Chapter Forty-Five
Memorial Day

On April 24, 1981, President Ronald Reagan ended the grain embargo against the Soviet Union. In mid-May, Olsen Farms sold their last year's wheat crop, and Jenny Olsen decided to celebrate Memorial Day with a family get-together. The former Rose read in the *Fargo Forum*. The latter she learned from Dag.

"We're having a family reunion," Dag said on phone. "You and the children should come over."

"I don't want to wear out my welcome," Rose said. "And anyway, we're having our own gathering. My kids will be home, and Mary Grace has two little ones now."

"If you can break away even for a short visit, it would be an opportunity to meet everyone," Dag said. "We'd love to see you."

Rose paused. "Roland's wife never seems happy to see us."

"Ignore her. Amy was born crabby. Between you and me, I can't see what Roland saw in her." Dag giggled.

"Well, she has a nice boy."

"There's that, yes. Tim and your Leo get on like brothers."

"Leo loves to come because he gets to shoot a BB gun and drive the golf cart."

"Emil has taken a shine to Lucy too. He says she has hair like his."

"Wild? Unbrushed?" Sometimes Rose and Dag talked for half an hour.

"Anyway, Emil told me to be sure to invite you," Dag said. "It's hard to get everybody together these days."

"My parents will be here. We'll have a houseful. I'll see how things look."

When they rang off, Lucy popped her head in. "Who was that?"

"Dagmar. From the farm."

"Why does she call so much? Same with that old lady from Skye."

"They're family, sort of."

"I don't care," Lucy said. "We have enough family."

***

Memorial Day, Monday, May 25, was overcast and chilly in Fargo. Rose and Darryl hosted the family at their house on Seventh Street North, the house Rose had grown up in. With its small backyard and proximity to the church and downtown, the home had come to Rose and Darryl as a package deal in 1959. It was a kind of wedding gift, at a price the newlyweds could hardly refuse. The transaction allowed the store to remain in the family and her parents to move to the suburbs in south Fargo, near the country club. Arno and Helen lived only five minutes away, but they were late today. Her parents were always late. Mary Grace and Wayne were there from Minot with their little one, and Margaret and Bill from Minneapolis had brought their dog, a young, jumping black Lab. Louis, Rose's middle brother, dark like his father, worked in fashion in Kansas City and was unmarried. He tried to stay away from the dog and dog hair. Eventually, Arno and Helen bustled through the back door without knocking.

"So hard to find parking in the neighborhood," Arno said.

"Yes, well." Rose accepted his hug. He smelled, as always, like Old Spice aftershave, and a bit like hair coloring. He continued to dye his hair and narrow moustache. Never under-dressed, today he wore golf wear—patterned pants, white shoes, and a cashmere top.

Her mother, in a blue dress she often wore to family gatherings, smelled like peppermint, the candy-cane lozenges she always had on hand. As they hung up their jackets, Leo ran in to get a hug.

"Guess what, Grandma and Grandpa? We got to meet Mom's other family."

Helen's jacket paused halfway to its wall hook.

"Other family?" Arno said.

Mary Grace and Margaret glanced at each other.

"Oh dear," Louis said.

"We told you so, Mother," Margaret murmured.

"Yes," said Rose. "Haugens. But Olsen is the married name."

"We know," Helen said. "Believe me, we know."

Arno took her hand.

"They're really nice," Leo continued. "They have a big farm over in Minnesota, and when I go there, I get to—"

"Hey, let's go look at your train layout in the basement," Mary Grace said to her little brother. "Have you added anything?"

"Lots," Leo said.

Lucy, across the kitchen, was happy to hang around for any family drama.

"You went looking for them?" Arno held up his hands, dramatic, Italian style. "After all these years?"

"I did not 'go looking for them,'" Rose said. "A letter came to me out of the blue."

"From her, I'll bet. Sally." Helen steadied herself on a chairback. Her face had gone a shade paler.

"Not from her or any of the Haugens or Olsens. And now is not the time to talk about it."

"But you still went to meet them?" Arno pressed.

Rose gestured to the table. "Lucy, go call everyone up from the basement. It's time to eat."

"We did go meet them," Lucy said, passing by and stirring the pot. "Leo's been over there two or three times."

"Oh, honey," her mother said to Rose. "You don't know what you're getting into."

"Like with the store?" Rose said. "Selling it to us the year men stopped wearing suits?"

"Hey, let's not go down that road," Louis said.

Leo and the dog thundered up the stairs, chased by Lucy and Mary Grace, Margaret and the others close behind.

"Time to eat," Rose said as cheerfully as she could manage.

"After we pray," her mother said.

As a family, they rattled off the blessing and then it was burgers and hotdogs, plus potato salad and other sides dishes, a potluck affair. Helen did not eat much, though she had two glasses of wine. After the second, Rose nodded for Darryl to disappear the bottle. Following ice cream, Leo and his sisters and the others headed to the basement, from which soon came the sounds of a model train whistle. And the barking Lab.

"So, what are your intentions?" Helen turned to Rose.

"My intentions?"

"With your 'other family.'"

"I'm sorting that out," Rose said.

"Don't worry, Gran. We're your real family." Lucy gave her grandmother a hug, which set Helen to weeping.

"You might have told us straightaway," Arno muttered to Rose. "Look what you've done to your mother."

"I've done nothing. Maybe mother could cope better if she didn't start drinking so early in the day."

"I beg your pardon," her mother said. "And after all we've done for you. Took you in. Gave you a name. A home."

"That's enough, you two," Arno said sharply.

The family gathering soon tapered off, wrapping up at two p.m. Helen was first out the door. "I have a 2:35 tee time," Arno said apologetically, giving Rose an extra hard hug. "I'll speak with her," he whispered. Mary Grace and Margaret were eager to get on the road, Louis had a flight to catch, and by three p.m. everyone was gone. Lucy and Leo retired to their rooms. The house fell quiet except for Lucy and the muffled chords from her acoustic guitar.

"Well," Darryl said. He slumped in a chair.

"A deep thought," Rose answered. It was a Leo and Lucy joke.

"Well, it could have been worse, is what I meant."

"Not much," Rose said.

"It's behind us, and the kids had fun. Where do we start?" Darryl looked about the kitchen. The mess of dishes.

Rose glanced at the wall clock. "I haven't mentioned this, but the Olsens are having a family gathering today as well. They've invited us over."

"You're not thinking of going."

Rose shrugged. "A brief visit, if there was time."

"It seems a bit much for one day."

"You could come along. Meet them."

Darryl poured himself the last of the coffee. "To be honest, it's a little concerning how much time you're spending with them."

"Though you weren't adopted, were you?"

Darryl turned. "No. You're quite right. All of this for you… I'm sure it's a lot."

"It is. Anyway, if we went now, we could be back by suppertime," Rose said. "There are leftovers for the kids."

"I'm a little pooped. That dog drove me crazy. But you go, if you like. As long as you come back."

She stared.

"That was a joke."

She gathered herself. "I'll check with Leo and Lucy. See if they want to come."

Leo was an instant "Yes."

Lucy, guitar in hand and notebook open, was a quick "No."

"Then you have to help your father in the kitchen."

"Fine," she said loudly.

Rose turned to leave, then paused in the doorway. "Does your little thing tape-record too?"

"What?" She removed the headphones. "Little thing? You mean my Walkman?"

"Yes."

"It only plays. But you can buy the kind that does record. They have them at the mall."

***

The Olsen farmyard had a dozen cars, a softball game in progress, and a bonfire. Chairs ringed the flames. Adults held beverages. To the side sat a washtub with a silvery keg of beer. A Toyota and a dusty Volvo station wagon carried Manitoba plates. Rose parked her Ford beside a Volkswagen square-back with a Carter/Mondale bumper sticker and a University of Minnesota parking sticker. Dag came down off the porch, Sally close behind.

"So glad you could come." Dag wrapped her and Leo in a big hug.

Sally, smiling, hung back. "We have plenty of leftovers," she said to Leo.

"We ate and ate this morning," Rose replied.

"Is there Mexican food?" Leo asked.

"There is." Sally touched his hair.

"First, come and meet everybody," Dag said.

"I don't want to interrupt the ball game," Rose replied. Jenny was the pitcher and held the softball. She wound up and whipped it past a youngster.

"Strike three!" the home plate umpire cried. She was a tall, trim woman with quite white hair and a bright laugh.

"Thank you for that call, Edith," Jenny replied.

"That wasn't a strike, and anyway, Grandma pitches too fast," a small batter said. He flung away the bat.

"I can't hit her myself," called a guy in the outfield. He wore a light stocking cap and windbreaker with a maple leaf. "Maybe time for a break?"

The other players jeered. "That's because your team's behind."

"No matter," said a tall, blond fellow, also an outfielder. "We'll come down at Christmas—bring our hockey sticks and wipe the rink with you Minnesotans."

"No way. Forget it," voices called.

Jenny came over. She beckoned to the outfielders, who jogged over.

"I'm John," the tall man said. White-blond hair poked out from beneath a baseball cap.

"Pleased to meet you at last," Rose said.

"And one more Canadian," Jenny said, taking his arm. "My husband, Greg Garvey."

"Bonjour, hello." He leaned into their handshake with the easy manner of a people person. He wore a Winnipeg Monarchs stocking cap and had a trimmed, salt-and-pepper beard. "So nice to meet you, Rose."

"I wasn't sure I'd ever get to," Rose said.

"I trot him out on special occasions," Jenny remarked.

"And I her," Greg said, pulling her close. "It seems to work just fine."

Introductions continued with *"Tante"* Edith, the umpire. John's wife Juliette, petite with brown eyes, black hair and a French accent. Their three kids, Will, Genevieve, and Pascal, ranging from age sixteen to ten. Jenny's daughter Angel and her husband, Devon, a Black man wearing a tie, khaki pants and penny loafers, along with their two kids, LuRella and Malik, eleven and nine.

"It's a bit overwhelming," Rose said to Dag. "In a good way."

"I can hardly keep them straight myself," Dag said.

"We don't care what you call us…"

"As long as you call us for dinner," someone finished.

Chattering, the players headed back to their game.

"Come on, Leo," Tim called. "I've got a glove for you."

Dag and Sally took Rose inside to the warmth of the kitchen.

"John's a headmaster at a boy's school in Winnipeg," Dag explained. "He's lived in Canada since the Vietnam War."

"Jenny drove him across the border in the trunk of her car," Sally said.

"We had a family vote on the matter," Dag added. "It was unanimous."

"Not really," Sally said. "I was gone, remember?"

"Sorry, yes." Dag touched Sally's arm.

There was a moment of silence.

"We try to stay out of politics in my family," Rose said. "My father's quite conservative, my daughters far less so."

"We had another vote when Angel brought Devon home that first time," Sally said.

"That wasn't easy," Dag said, and clucked her tongue.

After a pause, Rose ventured, "I suppose that sort of thing could be a shock."

"It was a quite a shock," Sally said. "Imagine… an English professor."

The two sisters laughed until they had to lean on each other.

"Okay, okay, you got me," Rose said.

Alone in the kitchen, the women drank coffee and talked. Faint shouts and laughter, like geese calling far overhead, carried from the ballfield and soon drew them back outside. The late afternoon sky had brightened. A brisk breeze flowed from the north.

Dag shivered. "Fresh Canadian air, as Emil says."

"Let's head to the fire," Sally said.

Emil left his post as first base umpire. He took a seat by Rose and warmed his hands. The game continued, without direction, and soon without rules. Laughing, some of the adults, including Jenny, Devon, and Angel, gave up and headed back into the house for more food. Soon it was just Rose and Emil and Sally by the fire.

"Nothing better than a family picnic on Memorial Day," Rose ventured.

"Jenny says we need to observe the holidays," Sally said. "Otherwise every day is just like the next."

"I hadn't thought of farm life like that." Rose turned to Emil. "I'm still piecing things together. What year did you leave your farm in Skye and move down here?"

"In 1963. Me and Dag."

"And you?" Rose turned to Sally.

Emil looked at Sally.

"I was away then," Sally said. "I lived in Fergus Falls for a few years."

"I see," Rose said. "Did you have work? Or?"

Emil poked at the fire.

"I had a nervous breakdown," Sally said softly. "I was in the State Hospital from 1956 through '64."

Rose's eyes welled up. "Thank you for telling me," she said softly.

"It was a hard time for us," Emil said.

"It was the right thing," Sally said. "I see that now."

"She ran the telegraph office at the state hospital," Emil said.

"I did," Sally murmured.

"Then in the sixties, the state thought it was better for people to live at home," Emil continued.

"Home and with medications," Sally added. "They were useful at first. Now I hardly need them."

"When they let her out, we didn't think it would be good for her to go back to the farm in Skye," Emil continued. "It was pretty isolated up there."

"So, Emil sold the farm," Sally said.

"That was the homestead farm, right?" Rose said. "It must have been hard to leave."

"Had to be done," Emil said, his eyes on the fire.

"Well," Rose said. The fire snapped. "Thank you for telling me all this."

"I hope you won't think differently of me now," Sally murmured.

Rose took her hand. "I think better of you... for telling me."

On the porch, Dag rang a bell. "Pie and ice cream."

"I should go in and help," Sally said.

"We'll be along," Emil answered.

"I could come," Rose called to Sally.

"No, stay," Emil said. "There's plenty of help in there." When Sally was gone, he produced his cigarette fixings, then stopped. "Jenny don't like me smoking, and you probably don't like smoke blowing on you either."

"I don't mind the smell. My husband, Darryl, has no bad habits."

"I got enough for two men."

"I doubt that," Rose said.

"You don't really know me, though, do you?" He stared into the fire.

"I'm happy getting to know you. Leo too. He loves to come out here. His 'other family' he calls you."

"He's a good boy."

"Most of the time."

Emil didn't laugh. He turned briefly sideways. "There's things we haven't told you."

"I've had a sense of that," Rose said.

"About when you were born. And before that, when Sally was young."

"Maybe I don't need to know," Rose said. "After all, here we are now."

"I think about them a lot," Emil continued as if he hadn't heard her. "They don't go away."

"Perhaps I'm making them worse," Rose said. "Me just showing up like I have."

"No," Emil said quickly. "I'm glad you did."

"Thank you, Emil." She patted his arm.

"Well, you two are certainly getting along."

They turned. Roland's wife Amy had come up behind.

"Emil and I were just talking about family, I guess."

He nodded.

"Well, between the beaners and now you, it's hard to tell where the Olsens begin and end," Amy said.

"Beaners?"

"The Rodriquez family," Emil explained. "Amy don't like Mexicans. But if they weren't here, she'd have to get her ass in gear and do some work." He spit into the flames—made them pop.

"Jenny says to come inside," Amy said. "There's ice cream for dessert, plus she's got some kind of announcement."

In the crowded kitchen, Jenny stood at the head of the table. The space was fragrant with woodsmoke, beer, and sweaty kids. John tapped a spoon on his ice cream bowl. "*Mesdames et messieurs*, ladies and gentlemen, mother has something to say."

"First, what a fine day we've had," Jenny began. "Though too bad the Canadians are not better at softball."

There were jeers and hoots and laughter.

"Wait till Christmas on ice," Greg said. "You Americans had better sharpen your blades."

"We'll be ready," Roland said.

"Anyway, to the announcement," Jenny continued. "As you know, President Reagan lifted the grain embargo."

At his name there were boos and cheers in generally equal numbers.

"And we have sold last year's wheat at a decent price."

Cheers.

"We're going to reward ourselves accordingly," Jenny said. "With a family vacation."

"What? That'll be a first," someone said.

There was more laughter.

"Where to?" Tim asked.

Roland smiled.

"Norway," Jenny answered.

"Norway?" Emil frowned.

"I'm arranging a ten-day trip to Norway," Jenny said. "We're going to go back to the Stavanger area on the west coast and see where the family came from."

Emil drew back.

Dag turned. "Emil. What's wrong?"

He frowned. "It's a long trip."

"You may be turning eighty, but you're in perfectly good health," Dag exclaimed. "You've talked about 'going home' your whole life."

Emil had no reply.

"Showing up there and saying to old Sonder, 'What do you think of us now, Mr. Rich Man?'" Dag continued, in Emil's voice.

There were chuckles.

Emil shrugged. "The Sonders are probably long gone. The old farm too."

"You won't know unless you go there and find out," Dag answered.

"Anyway," Jenny said, reclaiming the conversation, "Emil and Dag were born in Norway. It would be nice to see where, plus tour around and enjoy ourselves for a few days."

There was clapping. Excited and overlapping voices.

"Who gets to go?"

"Everybody who wants to," Jenny said. "That includes Cesar and his family. Everyone's expenses will be paid."

Luisa clutched Carlo's arm in wonderment. "Norway!"

"When?" John asked.

"Sooner the better." Jenny's gaze flickered to Emil. "I'm thinking right after this year's crop is in the bin. Late August or early September."

John frowned. "I've got coaching then."

"We have the children," said his wife, Juliette, with a pained look. "The school year starts earlier in Canada."

"I'll be teaching then," Devon said. "Fall quarter at the 'U.'"

"Edith?" Jenny asked.

"That's very kind," Edith said. "You've included me in your family all these years, but this is your trip."

"She's afraid somebody will steal the books," Emil said.

"I hope they do," Edith said right back. "And I haven't seen you in the library for a long time."

"Words don't stick in my head anymore," Emil murmured.

"Well, I'm coming," Angel said.

"Me too," LuRella called.

Angel gave her daughter a one-armed hug. "We'll talk."

"Greg?" John asked.

"Maybe," he said. "Though it seems like a Jenny and family kind of thing. I'll see how my church calendar looks."

"I'm certainly not going," Amy said. "Norway is a socialist country."

"Social democracy," John said. "They're quite different."

"We'll try to have fun without you," Dag said to Amy.

There were titters.

"We do need someone to watch the farm," Jenny said to Amy.

"The last we all left home, they burned us out," Emil said.

Rose turned.

"We had a fire," Dag explained, "back when—"

"Let's stay in the present," Jenny said.

"I'm going to Norway," Roland said. "I wouldn't miss it."

"Sally?" Jenny said.

Sally looked to Rose. "I will if you go."

"Me? No." Rose answered quickly. "This is your family's trip."

"You're in it now," Sally said.

"Sally's right," Jenny said to Rose. "You're invited."

"Out of the question," Rose said. "I couldn't accept such a—"

"If you won't take Jenny's money, I'll pay for you," Emil said.

Rose stared.

"I've got a few greenbacks in my steamer trunk," Emil continued.

"Probably more than a few," someone added.

There was laughter.

"You could dust that old trunk off and use it on the trip," John said to his uncle.

Bigger laughter.

Emil turned to Rose. "I'll pay for you, and Leo and Lucy too, if they want to go."

"Can we, Mom? Can we?"

Rose drew in a breath. "I have the store. There's your dad to think about. I'm afraid it's impossible."

"It could work, Ma," Leo said.

"We'll talk," Rose said and waved off the attention.

"You go in my place," Emil said to Rose.

"*Hjemkomst*," Dag said to Emil. "Isn't that what you always wanted?"

Faces turned back to Emil.

"Wouldn't I have to get a passport or something?" He frowned.

"There's time. I'll help you, *onkel*," Angel said.

Emil bit his lower lip. Held it.

"It's a once in a lifetime trip," Dag said and tugged Emil's sleeve. "You're not getting any younger."

Emil swallowed, then hunched his shoulders and dropped his head. His trunk bobbed in small wheezes. Dag, Jenny, and Sally went to him.

"I'm okay," he mumbled and wiped his face with the back of his hand.

"No, you're not," Dag said and took his arm.

"Come on, Emil," Jenny said and sat him in a chair.

Conversation and eating resumed. The three sisters remained close.

"*Beklager*," Emil said. "I don't know what happened."

"You worry too much," Dag said. "Always have."

"Try to stay in the present," Sally said. "That's what they always told me."

"Look around you at all the good things," Dag said.

"They never last," Emil replied.

"Don't be a stick in the mud," Dag said.

"Okay, okay," he said. He waved Rose over. "I meant what I said, about the tickets."

"That's kind, Emil, but—"

"If you go, I'll go," Emil said.

The four siblings turned to Rose.

***

As they drove home from the Olsen farm, Leo slumped in the passenger seat but did not close his eyes.

"Did you have fun?"

He nodded.

"Get plenty to eat?"

"For sure."

She drove on, glancing his way on occasion. His forehead pinched together in that little wrinkle above his nose, the same worry line she had.

"Anything the matter?"

Leo turned. "What's wrong with our family?"

"Wrong? Nothing's wrong with it."

He looked ahead down the road. "In our family, nobody says stuff. With the Olsens, they just say it."

"Say it?"

"I dunno. How they feel, I guess."

She nodded. "I know what you mean. They take some getting used to. All families are different in their own ways."

"I wish we were more like them," Leo said. "They're more fun."

Soon enough his eyes drifted shut. She reached over and drew him down across the seat. Without complaint he lay over, his head warm against her leg, and slept. She stroked his damp hair and drove on.

***

They arrived home in Fargo at twilight. "Wake up, Leo."

Groggy, Leo sat up. She paused to let him out, then parked in the narrow garage. Passing across the backyard to the house, she paused midway. In fading light, the neighborhood had shrunk. Houses stood closer together, the Callahan's hardly a broom beyond the fence. Like Leo's train set, there was a scale to things. As quite a small boy, he had explained that scale was the ratio of the real world to the size of the model. Compared to the Olsens she lived at a lesser scale, in a neighborhood for three-quarter-sized people. She gathered herself.

Inside, Darryl and Lucy were lounging in the living room after supper, with the CBS Evening News on the television. Lucy, stretched out on the floor, wore her headphones.

"There you are," Darryl called.

Lucy waved briefly.

Rose came over and gave Darryl a hug right in his chair.

"Well," he said, surprised. He stood.

"Thank you," she said.

"For what?"

"For letting me go today." She went to hang her coat, and, out of sight, wiped her eyes.

"Glad it worked out," he said.

She went, automatically, to the kitchen and the sink and the dishes. Darryl followed, pausing in the doorway. "How was it over there?"

"Well, we met everyone," she said. "We had food. There was a bonfire. Leo had fun."

"That's nice."

"It was. Very."

Darryl glanced behind at the television, then back. "What are the Olsens like? In a nutshell."

She looked out the kitchen window. "They are, I think, a happy family."

"Do they have a lot of land?"

She turned to him. "Three thousand acres."

Darryl paused. "Well, we have a fine old store on Broadway. That's a good family achievement."

"It is, I suppose."

Darryl headed back to the television. Watching him go, Rose thought of the bills waiting for her at the office. "A store for now," she murmured.

Chapter Forty-Six
Hjemkomst

Jenny set up a personalized *Hjemkomst* tour with Bjerkness Travel Agency of Grand Forks, North Dakota, which specialized in travel "home" to Norway. As if saluting the family trip, the wheat crop that summer of 1981 ran sixty bushels to the acre, and harvesting went off without rain or breakdowns. On August twentieth, the family gathered in Grand Forks for the bus ride to the Minneapolis International Airport.

There were thirteen. Jenny, Dag, Sally and Emil. Roland and Tim. Cesar, Carlos, and Luisa. Rose and Leo. Angel and LuRella would meet them at the airport.

"It's too bad the reverend couldn't come," Rose said.

"Greg? We travel together in winter," Jenny said. "Plus, he's been to Norway."

"And Lucy," Emil said. He had gotten a town haircut (Dag usually cut it at home) and wore new, brown pants and a black vest over a white shirt.

Rose shook her head. "She'll regret it someday."

"We'll have fun without her," Leo said.

Sally wore a fresh blue skirt, a lightweight, gray turtleneck, and had her silver-toned hair pulled back in a ponytail.

"Don't you look nice," Rose said.

"A new outfit from Monkey Ward," Sally said. "Jenny's always buying me things."

"I hope you can come to the store in Fargo someday," Rose said.

"Is there a family discount?" Emil asked.

"For heaven's sakes, Emil," Dag said. She wore a yellow dress, sweater, and comfortable shoes.

Roland looked sharp in slacks, gray shirt and a lightweight, dark jacket with a school insignia over a Canadian flag.

"Nice jacket," Rose said.

"Gift from brother John," Roland replied. "He says if we get in any trouble on the trip, just say we're Canadian."

Other Bjerkness Agency travelers gathered. Ardie Bjerkness, a tidy woman of about fifty with prematurely white hair, full and sharp bangs, carried a clipboard. She checked in the ruddy-faced travelers, most of them older. The men were narrow-shouldered, trim, clear-eyed, clean-shaven, erect of posture, and wore their shirts buttoned to the throat. Their wives had round faces with bobbed white hair and wore sensible shoes. Emil looked around suddenly, then stepped over to look at the suitcases lined up and waiting. He moved a finger as he counted them. "Where's my trunk?"

"You didn't bring your trunk," Dag said evenly. "That was a joke, remember? There's your suitcase right there."

Emil nodded. "I remember now."

Angel, dressed rather darkly, including a black beret, though that seemed to be her style, took Rose aside. "Uncle Emil has changed a lot in the last year. We have to keep an eye on him. Usually it's Dag, and then mother after her. But it'd be nice for them to have a break on this trip."

"Of course… I'll help," Rose said. "It's the least I can do."

Soon a long shiny coach with tinted glass purred up. They climbed aboard and filed along the plush seats.

"Leo and I will sit with you," Rose said to Emil.

"And me," Sally said.

Emil glanced around.

"Dag and Jenny are across the aisle and back one row," Sally said.

"We don't want to lose nobody," Emil said.

"We're all here," Angel called.

"Speaking of..." From her purse, Rose produced a small, black secretary's Dictaphone. "Can we all say hello to Lucy? She asked me to record 'the sounds of Norway.' I think she's feeling bad about staying home."

"Hello Lucy, hello, hello!" everyone called.

"It's a shame she didn't come," Sally said. "I'd like to get to know her."

"There'll be time later," Dag said.

After the bus left Grand Forks and entered open farmland, Emil pointed out things to Leo. "See that field? How green it is? Those are sugar beets. The fellows will come along pretty soon and top them."

"Top them?"

"Cut off the green leaves with a big, pull-behind mower," Emil explained. "That stops the beets from growing. Then the fellows have to wait until the first frost to harvest them."

"Why?"

"Beets don't like heat. They need to cool down and then freeze in the pile. After that they go to the processing plant. Beet trucks run all winter, and those ugly old beets get turned into fine white sugar."

"That's where the bad smell comes from," Tim said, wrinkling his nose.

"That's the smell of money," Emil replied.

"He says that about manure too," Sally remarked.

For the first hour, the oldest of the travelers dusted off their Norwegian, argued over this phrase or that, and laughed a good deal. Ardie Bjerkness, in the front seat, checked her watch.

In hour number two, conversation faded in favor of gazing out the windows. Those who had gotten up early, and driven hours to be in Grand Forks on time to catch the bus, let their eyes drift shut. By hour five, lunch bags rustled, and the smell of potato chips and ham sandwiches wafted.

At the Minneapolis International Airport, Ardie Bjerkness herded the group to the Northwest Airlines check-in counter for luggage-tagging and then to the security station.

"Got some new passports here, I see." A cheerful Black man in a uniform checked them through.

Emil kept his head down.

Sally took Rose's hand.

"Nothing to be afraid of," Rose said and moved brother and sister along.

The flight itself, a DC-10 overnight to Amsterdam, carried over two hundred passengers. The center section was five seats wide, with two seats across either aisle. Emil drew the middle seat of the middle. Rose arranged that he trade with Leo, which put Emil on the aisle where he could stretch his legs and be next to her. Sally was with Angel just across the aisle.

"Seats are comfortable enough," Emil said.

As with the bus ride, the first hour was lively. People chatted. A Norwegian-looking stewardess paused to talk with Roland, her hand on his seat top.

After they finished a TV dinner of chicken Kiev or Salisbury steak, the overhead lights dimmed. Seasoned travelers, including Angel, had brought neck cushions and eye masks and tilted back in their seats. Leo leaned against Rose and slept. She closed her eyes. Next to her, Emil shifted restlessly. Once, she looked up to see him staring straight ahead, lips moving.

She awoke sometime later in nearly full dark. Around them, the others sat slumped and silent. Emil stared across at Sally, who was sleeping.

"Can't sleep?" she said to Emil.

He turned back. Shook his head. "My mind keeps turning."

"On what?"

"The past. After our parents were gone, I was hard on my sisters. Especially Sally when you were born. They were afraid of me."

"Now you're the closest family I've ever seen," Rose said.

"Too close, maybe," Emil said. "Maybe we should have all gone off on our own, like a normal family."

"There's probably no normal family."

"There are things keep me up at night," he whispered, as if to himself.

"You should have been Catholic, Emil. You could go to confession and get everything off your chest."

"Too late for that."

"Never too late," Rose said. "It's a question of finding someone you trust. What about Greg? He'd be someone to talk to."

"Greg's a nice enough guy," Emil replied. "But he's a little too close to home."

***

They landed in Amsterdam early the next morning, the North Dakota group full of strong coffee and wide-eyed at the size of Schipol Airport, not to say Dutchmen themselves.

"They're giants," LuRella murmured.

"The men have such big heads," Leo added.

Two security fellows approached. They carried rifles and radios strapped across their chests. Emil shied to the far side of the family group.

"They're no one to be afraid of," Rose said. "They're watching out for us."

Emil looked over his shoulder.

"Maybe in a past life the Dutchmen raided your village," Angel said to Emil.

The others laughed. Emil did not.

At Schipol, the full tour group broke up. Some headed to Oslo, another group to Stockholm. The Haugens and Olsens flew to Bergen on the west coast. On a mid-sized jet, two blonde stewardesses, broad-shouldered in their blue uniforms and wearing pert hats, moved along the aisle. They served dark coffee and white sandwiches, and spoke whatever language was needed: Dutch, German, Norwegian, French, English.

"*Tusen takk*," said Roland.

"*Værsågod.*" The stewardess gave him a nice smile. "Are you Canadian?"

From the airport they bussed to their hotel in central Bergen in time for lunch. It was one night there, then on to Stavanger for the Haugen/Olsen group.

"You're going to eat and then want to go to bed. The time change can be hard on us older folks," Ardie Bjerkness said cheerfully.

"I'm not tired," Sally said.

"That's the spirit," Ardie replied. "It's best to keep moving and be outside as much as possible to get acclimated to the time, to the light. You'll find the days quite a bit longer here. So, let's freshen up and meet back here in an hour. We have a fun afternoon ahead."

This included a walking tour of the harbor and the fish market, and many photos of the bright-colored harbor buildings with their pointy, steep roofs.

Gulls shrieked overhead. "*Måkene,*" Emil said, looking up. "*Eg husker dem.*"

"Not me," Dag said. "I was just a baby."

They rode the funicular up through low-hanging clouds as Ardie described what, on a good day, they would have seen below. At the top of Mount Fløyen they ate at a small restaurant and afterward walked on paved paths leading to a lookout and white fog below. Behind, stood the dripping, dark *Trollskog.*

"The Troll Forest," Ardie said, pointing down a path. "It's a favorite for children, but a bit wet for hiking today."

"That's fine by me," Emil muttered.

"Agreed," Dag murmured.

Then it was clickety-clack down the funicular to the harbor. Ardie kept them moving until early dinner at the hotel, after which they went to bed and stayed there.

In their room, after Leo fell asleep, Rose put the Dictaphone to her ear.

Not that way, mother. Laughter. Lucy's voice. She forwarded the tape.

After that they go to the processing plant. Beet trucks run all winter, and those ugly old beets get turned into fine white sugar.

That's where the bad smell comes from.

That's the smell of money.

She pressed "forward" again.

I was hard on my sisters. Especially Sally, when you were born. They were afraid of me.

And forward to Angel, who had sat with Rose for a while. She told of how she came to Jenny's family. Of going to Atlanta in 1961 with Jenny and "Miss Lurelle." How they had a near miss with the Ku Klux Klan and had visited Martin Luther King's house and met his parents. That her father had died in prison.

Silence and the whirr of tape.

Have you traveled? (Angel's voice again.)

Not much. I'm afraid my life in Fargo has been very plain. I've never had much adventure. Big ones, that is.

Are you kidding? You are *the adventure.*

Silence but for the whirring of the recorder. *I'm not sure I follow.*

Angel laughs. *Without you, the whole family would be on a different path. You changed everything. We'd be somewhere else right now, but not here.*

She clicked off the machine. Lay back in the dark with her eyes open. Across, Leo breathed in slow, deep sleep.

***

In the morning, the family gathered in the hotel lobby, luggage in hand, to wait for their rental van. Roland was the driver.

"You're on your own now," Ardie said.

"We've got our map, we've got our hotel reservations in Stavanger, we'll be fine," Jenny said.

"Emil speaks Norwegian," Dag added.

"The old kind," Emil said.

"It will get you by," Ardie said. She turned to Roland. "Remember, on the ferries, park tight up to the car ahead. They try to maximize space."

Roland shrugged. "I could park a combine in this hotel lobby."

There were guffaws.

"Roland's quite lively this trip," Dag murmured.

"I wonder why," Jenny said.

Dag and Sally tried not to laugh.

After five hours on the winding blacktop, a lunch stop, a long tunnel underneath a fjord, and two ferry rides, the group arrived outside Stavanger. Emil, riding shotgun, bent low to gaze up at the sharp hills. At the tidy, white farmhouses with fish-scale stone roofs, the little red barns.

"Every farm could be on a postcard," Rose said.

"Look at the little bitty silo," Tim remarked.

"They're all connected," Dag added, and pointed. "Barn, silo, house."

"That's how it used to be," Emil said. "You lived with your livestock."

Dag shivered. "Not for me."

They crossed a bridge into Stavanger *sentrum*. Passed down narrow, paving-stone streets with uniformly white houses close alongside. Reddish tile roofs, window flower boxes, the occasional Norwegian flag outthrust above a door.

Angel, directly behind Roland, navigated. LuRella held the map. "Turn left up ahead."

"Yes," Angel said. "Not so fast. What's the rush?"

"Some things never change," Jenny said.

Roland smiled and drove on.

Down near the waterfront, they found their hotel, The Victoria. Stavanger's oldest, built in 1905, The Victoria had four storeys, an elaborate red and white front, and a mansard roof with a small crown topped by a Norwegian flag. The building commanded the square.

"This will do nicely," Angel remarked.

"It had better," Jenny said.

Emil led the way inside and at the counter introduced the group in Norwegian. The young woman cocked her head.

He repeated.

"I'm sorry," the girl said.

Jenny stepped up alongside Emil. "We're the Olsen party from Minnesota."

"I understood the first part," she said. "I'm from Poland. We learn the Oslo kind of Norwegian, the Bokmål."

"That's a pity," Emil said.

Angel nudged him.

A somewhat older male clerk in a tidy, green vest came over. "Oslo has the Danish Norwegian," he said. "Here in *vesteland* we speak Nynorsk, which is the real thing."

"*Eg ble født her,*" Emil said. "*Min søster også.*"

"*Hallo,*" Dag said.

"*Velkommen heim.*" The clerk pumped and pumped their hands. He turned to Sally. "*Og deg også?*"

"*Nei,*" she said. "I was born in America. I don't speak much Norwegian."

"They didn't teach you?" He smiled. He had quite blue eyes, crinkled at their corners, and a bit of gray in his blond hair.

"It's my own fault," Sally said. "When I was young, I didn't want anything to do with Norwegian."

"That's quite common," the man said. "They say the first generation of immigrants remembers. The second generation is happy to forget. But the third generation comes back around."

"I'm not sure where I am on all that," Sally murmured.

"You're here," the clerk said easily. His gaze went to her ring hand, bare like his. *"Eg heiter Anders Vik."* He extended his hand.

"Sally Haugen," she said, and blushed.

"Well, well," Dag murmured.

Sally gave her a discreet elbow.

After lunch of *laks*, sliced cucumbers, potato salad, crusty *brød*, coffee, and berry tart, the group headed on a walking tour. Angel and LuRella lead the way, with Emil, Leo, and Tim close by. Cesar, Carlos, and Luisa were spread among the rest. Sally kept her arm in Rose's, and Roland brought up the rear, sometimes lagging behind a few paces as he took in the sights. The people. The Norwegian girls. An unsmiling old couple sat on the stoop, taking the sun. They gave the travelers an unblinking stare. *"Amerikanere,"* the woman murmured.

"You can tell by our map?" Angel said.

"None of that," Jenny said.

"Well, they shouldn't stare, then."

Emil paused, and in his back-throated Norwegian spoke to the old couple.

The old lady's eyes widened. Her husband smiled, said something sharp to his wife, and hoisted himself to his feet. He shook hands with Emil. They conversed, nodding, smiling like brothers. "Sondersgård," was the only word Rose picked up. There was more nodding and pointing. But the larger group was eager to move on, and it was up to Rose to disengage Emil from his new friend.

"I should have learned Norwegian," Sally said.

"It's in you," Emil said. "You just got to bring it out."

"Maybe Mr. Vik could help you," Dag said.

"Shut up," Sally said.

Dag giggled.

At the harbor, Emil paused on the cobblestones. Stared down at their smooth, square faces, then around to the red-roofed buildings, the quay, the custom house.

"Is this it?" Dag asked.

Emil frowned. "I'm not sure," he said. "It was so long ago. It's all different, but it's all the same." His voice cracked.

"What do you remember?" Jenny took Emil's arm.

"The steamship was over there. Or maybe there."

"Think, Emil," Dag said. "You can do it."

To the side, at a fish market, a fellow in a rubber apron pushed a wheelbarrow. Its iron wheel rang on cobblestones.

"Yes," Emil said. "This is it."

***

The next morning, they loaded out for the trip to Sondersgård.

"Are you nervous, Emil?" Dag asked.

"Wait till old Sonder sees us," Emil said. "He's going to fill his pants."

Tim and Leo giggled.

"If there's any Sonders left, they'll be younger, Emil. Remember?" Dag said.

Emil looked at her, then out the window.

Roland drove them from the downtown southward, then east past commercial buildings and warehouses, and finally into residential areas. Angel and LuRella read the map. As Roland navigated a roundabout, Angel said, "I think you're supposed to signal your turns."

"Okay, okay," Roland said.

"These traffic circles are nerve-wracking," Dag said. "Cars coming from every direction."

"They keep things moving," Emil said. "Nobody gets stuck at a light."

"They have them in Mexico City," Carlos remarked from the rear. "Most other countries have them."

"I doubt they'll ever come to America," Dag remarked.

LuRella pointed. "*Gamlevegen*."

"That means 'old road,'" Emil said.

"We're still in neighborhoods," Dag said. "There's no farms here."

"There probably used to be," Sally remarked.

After passing under a busy highway, they found themselves in a mixed-use zone of housing developments, densely built and tightly bounded, and the occasional small farm. Emil turned his head sharply. "There."

"What?" Roland said and slowed the car.

"That stone post. We stopped here for water."

Roland braked, and they all got out. A weathered, stone column with arrows and road names stood at an intersection before an upthrust of rock. Water trickled from a stony cleft into a catch-basin, which overflowed into a mossy rivulet stretching downhill. Emil leaned down to cup his hands and drink. He wiped his chin. "*Eg husker det.*"

Back in the van, Emil leaned forward as Roland drove them up a short hill and around a sharp bend.

"Yes," Emil said. "*Vi bodde her.*"

"We lived here?" Dag murmured.

Sheep grazed on small hillocks. Rust-red barns stood straight-backed on stone foundations. The driveway, a narrow ribbon of asphalt, wound past gardens to the commanding white house. Square and tall, with a shiny black tile roof and bric-a-brac woodwork across the gable peaks, it stared down on all who approached. To the side and behind stood several little houses, all painted white. Each had a vented, brick chimney capped by a piece of slate and a pointed anchor stone. In the center of the yard stood a square building on stilts with carved wood faces and figures around the railings, all freshly painted as if the owners were aware of its historical value.

"Talk about postcards," Angel said.

Roland stopped the van below the house. The Minnesotans spilled out, produced cameras.

"Hang on, everyone," Angel said.

"Yes," Jenny added. "We should ask, first."

Trimmed and sculpted shrubbery guarded the house, which had a sharply green lawn bordered by a bed of roses, pink astilbe, and lily of the valley. The most south-facing spot held a vegetable garden with a bumper crop of tomatoes.

"Is it coming back to you?" Dag asked.

Emil's gaze went to the building on stilts. "I remember being scared of those faces."

A woman came to the front porch. She was middle-aged, well-kempt in a Norwegian sweater and knee-length skirt. With half glasses on a shiny chain, she looked dressed for work at a fine office.

"*God dag,*" Jenny said.

Emil stepped forward. "*Eg heiter Emil Haugen. Vi er familen Haugen fra Amerika.*"

"I speak English, thank you," the woman said.

Emil blinked.

"Our parents, Karl and Petra Haugen, worked here," Jenny explained. "They left in 1906 to come to America."

"I see," she said. "Many have come and gone from our farm. And not uncommon for their relatives to return."

"Are you a Sonder?" Emil asked.

"I am Fru Kirsten Sonder. Our farm has been in the family for five generations."

"Can we take pictures?" Leo asked.

"For personal use, yes."

"Might you have any records of our family's time here?" Jenny asked.

"Of course we have records." She glanced again at her watch.

"If this is a bad time we could come back," Angel said. "Americans are not good at calling ahead."

Fru Sonder's gaze softened slightly. "Let us do this now. Wait here."

"Can we look around?" Tim asked.

"Don't go in the barns, don't pick any flowers, and don't eat anything from the garden."

"We're not stupid," LuRella whispered.

While Fru Sonder was gone inside, the Minnesota group took photos of the gardens, the barns, the little houses.

"We lived somewhere back here," Emil said. "It's blurry in my mind."

Fru Sonder came back out. Roland whistled for the family, who gathered again below the porch.

She carried a large ledger, the heavy kind of book Jenny remembered from her courthouse days, and laid it on the railing. Paged backward. "Karl Haugen. 1906." As she drew her finger down the page, Dag clutched Emil's arm.

"Here we are," Fru Sonder said. "Karl and Petra Haugen. Along with Emil and Dagmar, *barna*."

"The children, yes," Dag said. "That's us. That's me and Emil."

There was clapping from the group.

The woman leaned closer to the page.

"Is there anything more?" Jenny asked.

Kirsten Sonder straightened. Let her glasses drop to her breast. "Yes. Karl Haugen was a thief."

"Say again?" Jenny said.

With her glasses on, she leaned again toward the ledger. "When he left for America on June 18th of 1906, he stole *en skinke*, a ham, from the *stabbur*." She pointed across the yard, then to the page. "It weighed six kilos."

"That's a big ham," Dag said.

Emil let loose a burst of Norwegian.

The woman drew back.

"What did he say?" Tim asked.

"Something about being hungry," Fru Sonder said. "In a Norwegian dialect I haven't heard for a while."

"We were hungry," Emil said. "Your father worked us like slaves."

"Grandfather," Fru Sonder said.

"What does it matter?" Emil said. "It was your family that kept us down."

"Emil." Jenny stepped forward and took his arm. Sally took the other one.

Fru Sonder shrugged. "You had a job and a roof over your heads."

"That's true," Jenny said.

"And look at you now." Fru Sonder's gaze swept the group.

"Yes, look at us now," Emil called. "In America we farm three thousand acres. What do you think of that?"

Fru Sonder smiled. "I think you could afford to makes things right."

"Make things right?" Angel said.

"Pay for the ham, of course," she finished.

"*Dra til helvete,*" Emil shouted.

"Emil, that's enough," Jenny said.

Rose stepped forward, and she and Sally steered Emil back toward the car.

"*Beklager,*" Jenny said to Fru Sonder. "My brother is struggling a bit with age. We wanted to make this trip before, well." She stopped.

"I see," Fru Sonder said.

"But we can pay for the ham, and we will."

"We will?" Sally said.

"Yeah, why?" Tim asked. "That was like a hundred years ago."

"Quiet," Jenny said to them. She addressed Fru Sonder. "If you'll calculate its worth in today's dollars and send us that number, we'll make sure you get paid. We're staying at the Victoria Hotel."

"I was not entirely serious about the ham," Fru Sonder said.

"We are," Jenny said. "As a family, we like to have no debts to anyone."

"That speaks well of you," Fru Sonder said.

"Here's our card." Roland approached. Extended his hand.

Fru Sonder leaned down, took the card, and put her glasses back on. "Olsen Farms." She looked again at the group. "So, things worked out for you in America?"

Jenny paused. She turned to the family, to Sally in particular.

Sally looked down, then up, and held her gaze.

"There were hard times," Jenny answered, turning to Fru Sonder. "But yes. On the whole, things worked out."

Back in the van, LuRella was first to say it. "What a bitch."

"An old troll," said Tim.

Emil spit out the window. "Pappa told me he wanted to kill the Sonders in their bed. The whole family. He should have done it."

The van fell silent.

"Then we wouldn't be here today, would we, *onkel*?" Angel said.

***

The remainder of the trip was all fun, including a speedy boat ride up a fjord with a young woman captain narrating as they thudded along, spray shimmering behind. Mr. Anders Vik had arranged the excursion and even came along with the Haugen group "to make sure things went well." He had helped Sally with her rainsuit and oversized goggles. Made sure of her seating.

"Over 20 percent of Norwegians left for America," the captain shouted above the noise. "The emigration happened in three waves. It began in the 1820s and ended almost a hundred years later. Most went to Wisconsin or Minnesota, and some to North Dakota."

"That's us," Emil called.

And after the fjord ride, Mr. Vik walked them to a shop for tourists near the hotel. Dag held up a gray, wide-weave sweater with a patterned blue band across the chest. "This is you, Emil."

Emil hefted its weight. "I put this one on, I might never take it off."

"We'll bury you in it." Dag put the sweater in the basket.

Emil turned to Rose. "You should have a sweater."

"They're a bit rich for my blood."

"Pick one out," Emil said. "You, too, Sally."

"Oh yes, Miss Haugen," Mr. Vik said. "You need a Norwegian sweater. It will help you when you work on your *Norsk*."

"What a salesman you are," Sally said and clucked her tongue. "You must be getting a commission."

This time it was Mr. Vik's turn to blush.

And trolls. Most everyone bought some kind of troll. A troll figurine. A troll doll. A troll crossing sign. A carved troll.

"I can whittle you a troll just as good at home and save you a buck," Emil called.

"It's true. Emil's are much better," Sally said. She held up a lesser troll.

"But these trolls are from Norway," Dag answered.

"I'm from Norway," Emil replied.

"You're an American now," Dag replied.

"Emil? I'd say you're half and half," Mr. Vik said with a chuckle.

Angel leaned close to Jenny. "It's like he's part of the family now."

That evening, Roland turned up missing. Dispatched to look for him (Sally was having tea with Mr. Vik), Rose and Angel found him at a nearby café, sitting alone before a tall, almost empty stein of beer.

"There you are, Brother," Angel said. "What's up?"

"I'm divorcing Amy," Roland said.

"Oh dear," Rose murmured.

Angel waved for the barmaid, pulled up a chair, and pointed to one for Rose.

"Enough is enough," Roland muttered.

"You deserve better than her," Angel said. "I've always thought so."

"Women seem to like me," Roland said to no one with a slightly bleary look. "That nice stewardess. The ladies I see here."

"They do, Brother," Angel replied. "Why wouldn't they?"

"I got married too young," Roland said. "I shouldn't have been in a hurry. I should have looked around."

"I should head back to the hotel," Rose said.

"No, stay," Angel said and caught her arm.

"You're family," Roland added.

"So," Angel said, "all in favor of Roland divorcing Amy?"

Roland and Angel raised their hands.

They stared at Rose.

"I hardly know enough," Rose began. "This is such a personal decision."

"Come on," Angel said. "You've met Amy."

After a pause, Rose raised her hand.

"There you have it," Angel said. "It's unanimous."

"Tim," Roland said suddenly.

"We'll get him through it," Angel said, with a glance to Rose.

"Sure. He and Leo are good friends," Rose said. "I'll help as I can."

"There you have it," Angel said to Roland. "Time to think about yourself, for once."

***

By the end of the trip, the Olsens had exhausted her. Her real life—Fargo and the store, Darryl and the family—shrank away, shimmered out of focus. She had brought along her rosary, and though she and Leo said their prayers each night before bed, her faith thinned as well. The string of beads felt lighter, like a souvenir, a replica of something once real. In the middle of such thoughts at ten-thirty p.m., the phone jangled in the hotel room. Leo stirred but didn't wake. Fumbling, she grabbed the receiver before it could ring again.

"You have a phone call," said the desk clerk. "From America."

"Yes. Thank you. I'll take it."

After a click and a brief clatter, a faraway voice said, "Hi, honey."

"Darryl. Is everything all right?"

"We miss you and wanted to see how things are going."

The line whispered a faint, needling note. "That's very kind," she said. "Things are fine here. But these calls are very expensive, and I'll be home in just a couple of days."

"That's sort of why I called," Darryl answered. "Leonard from First National came by again. I told him you were in Norway on a little vacation. That seemed to set him off. He said if we have that kind of money to travel, then why are we so far behind on our loan payments? I said, what loan?"

"I have an arrangement with the bank," Rose murmured. "When I get home, we need to talk frankly about the store."

"He said we have six months. After that, he'd have to consider foreclosing on the store," Darryl continued. "I told him there must be some mistake. He was quite short with me."

"I'll be back soon. I'll deal with Leonard."

"That's a relief."

There was a pause, and that whisper again, as if every call had left its breath in the wire.

"Let's not linger," Rose said. "This is an international call."

After hanging up, she lay back open-eyed in the dark. Around her came the hotel sounds, a muffled laugh outside on the street, Leo's quiet breathing, and thoughts of Dolly.

***

In the airplane leaving Amsterdam for Minneapolis, she again sat beside Emil. As the plane broke upward from the low country haze, the oval windows flashed orange. Because of the sunlight, many passengers lowered their shades. After breakfast, more darkened their seat space and tipped back to doze. Soon it was twilight in the cabin. Day in night. Night in day.

Beside her, Emil slept, jaw slacked. On her other side, Leo slept too. She eased her little recorder from her purse and placed it on her lap. Waiting for Emil, she did not let herself drift off. After a long while he flinched. Looked about as he woke. "Dreaming," he said.

"What of?"

"I don't remember." He wiped his mouth. After that they talked some. Small talk. Sondersgård. The fjord tour.

She took a breath and readied the recorder. "Are you feeling better now after seeing the old farm?"

He nodded. "Some, I guess."

"It might be just the ticket for you," Rose said.

"The ticket?" Emil tilted his head.

"To not dwell on things from the past."

He was silent.

"On the flight over we were talking," she added. "You said there were things that kept you up at night."

"*Eg husker det*," he said.

"They can't be that bad." She pressed "Record."

After a long pause, Emil spoke. "I was the one who took you away from your mother," he said. "She didn't want to give you up, but I told her you had to go. I took you. From her arms."

Rose blinked. Took a breath. "But you got me to the Rossis."

"There's more to that story too."

"Maybe none of it's important now," she replied. "Look how things worked out."

Emil grunted, a kind of laugh. "For you, maybe." He glanced around at the sleeping passengers, then leaned close. "You want to know what keeps me up at night?" he whispered hoarsely. "Your brother. The sight of him on fire in the Dodge-In. Jenny and me, when we burned it down, and we killed him. We didn't mean to kill him, but we did."

Chapter Forty-Seven
The Tape

Her return home to Fargo found the kitchen sink full of dishes and frozen pizza cardboards in the trash.

"Sorry, I've been working a lot at the bakery," Lucy said.

"I've been at the store full-time and then some," Darryl said. "We haven't had much time to cook."

Rose let out a breath. "I should have a bath and a little sleep," she said and turned away. "I think I'm feeling jet lag."

"What time is it now in Norway?" Leo asked. He had slept on the bus ride from Minneapolis, then in the car on the way home from Grand Fork. He was none the worse for the travel.

"They're ahead of us seven hours," Rose said. "So, whatever that would be."

She awoke just after three a.m., wide awake. She lay there long minutes. Then more. It was no use. Easing out of bed, she dressed without waking Darryl and then made coffee and ate a banana. She kept the lights off but for the stove top and moved about the kitchen by habits, by steps. She could live in this house if she were blind. Its spaces, its countertop corners, its doorway threshold strips were inside her like north-south directions in ducks and geese. Which, it occurred to her, could fly with their eyes closed.

She leafed through the newspapers. Mark David Chapman had pleaded not guilty to murdering John Lennon. John Hinckley had pleaded not guilty to attempting to assassinate President Reagan. Voyageur 2 had taken images of Saturn's moon, Titan. She set aside the papers. Looked about the darkened, silent living room. The blank face of the television carried a silhouette, part of a face, her face, in shadow. She was a person without features. Crossing the living room, she cracked the curtains to check the weather thermometer outside the sliding glass door. The alley's streetlamp cast the backyard into a small dark square. She let the curtains fall shut, then sat again, staring. She heard herself breathing through her mouth.

At six a.m. she carefully locked the front door and headed to the store. There was no use sitting home.

Few houses in the neighborhood had lights on, and then only a yellow window upstairs or down. One person up, the others sleeping. On Seventh Street the lamp flickered, as always. Closing her eyes, she continued down the sidewalk, staying on the straight and narrow by feeling for the softness of grass underfoot. Eventually she slowed, shortening her steps for the curb at Sixth Avenue, which had to be close. Opening her eyes, it was still well ahead.

The east-west railroad tracks shone in the streetlight, and she stepped, as usual, across their iron. Nearby, the depot sat dimly lit and quiet. Broadway itself was deserted and lit only by the nightlights of stores, including Rossi Clothing. She paused at the window. The mannequins stared out with their own half features, their own non-eyes.

Unlocking the front door, the odor came at her. Wool, old carpet, heating oil, rental tuxedos, and prom dresses. Age, time, life in death. In her office lay a stack of bills bound by a rubber band. She was still sorting through them, triaging them, making a calendar of payments, when Darryl came through the back door at nine a.m.

"You're the early bird," he said.

"Jet lag," she replied.

"Well, good to have you back in the saddle," Darryl answered. "And I didn't get a chance to really ask you about your trip."

She paused. "Norway is a beautiful country."

"And the Olsens?"

"To be honest, ten days with them got to be a bit much."

"How so?"

She shrugged. "They can be exhausting. So many of them, so many of their stories, their issues. I found myself forgetting that I have my own family."

"I see," Darryl said.

"I've gone overboard with them, Darryl," she said, turning to him. "I need to focus on my own family. The Olsens will be fine. They don't need me in their lives."

Darryl came over. Put a hand on her shoulder. "I'm glad to hear that, because we need you."

"After this trip, I probably won't see them much," she said and briefly clutched his hand. "Maybe not at all." She turned away to look out the small window.

"It was probably something you had to go through," Darryl said.

"Maybe." She wiped her eyes and turned back to him. "I have business up in Skye with Mrs. McConnell that I've put off. I should head up there, even today."

"If it has to do with her estate, please go." Darryl winked.

***

Two hours later, driving north on Highway 29, Rose approached Grand Forks, slowed at the exit, then at the last second pressed on. Without a break she drove directly to Dolly's house.

No one answered the bell.

She buzzed again.

Going around the side, she stood on tiptoes to peer in a window. A gray cat thudded against the glass, a looming, snarling face. She jerked backward, then made a face of her own. "Get lost." Circumnavigating the house, she found all doors locked.

At the house next door, a youngish fellow answered the buzzer. He wore trousers but no shirt. In the hallway lay a scatter of toys. A baby cried.

"The old lady? Haven't seen her," he said.

His wife, a buxom, short young woman appeared. "I think they took her to the hospital. There was an ambulance here a few days ago."

Rose drove to the hospital on the west side of town, a small, modern branch facility of MeritCare in Fargo. Her first stop was the lady's room, then to the main desk.

"Dolores McConnell? Miss Dolly? Yes, she's here." The front desk attendant was a young Black woman with a commanding, cheerful manner. "Room 223."

"Thanks."

"If she's in a bad mood, just step out, then come back like you just arrived. It's a little trick the nurses use."

"Is she ill?"

"You are?"

"Family. Her stepdaughter. Rose Rossi."

"Yes, she's been asking about you. Dolly had a fall. The nurses can give you the details."

Rose arrived at room 223 just as a young male nurse came out. "Who-ee," he said. "Dolly's on the warpath today."

Rose introduced herself.

"Dolly tripped over a cat and broke her hip," the fellow explained. "A bad break. Living alone, it was lucky she got to her phone."

"How is she doing?"

He paused. "At her age, once they go down, it's a long road back up."

She tapped on the door frame.

From her bed, propped up halfway, Dolly peered across.

"It's me. Rose."

"Where have you been?"

"Working," Rose said and came forward. "Looking into what you asked me to."

Dolly's white skunk stripe across her part had widened, and her eyes had yellowed still more. "That's good to know," she said in a raspy voice. "What did you find out?"

"Quite a lot."

"Let's hear it." Dolly's eyes cleared, and her lips drew back in a grin. Her teeth needed brushing.

"First things first. How are you? How is your care?"

"No good, but I won't be here long."

Rose was silent.

"Back home in a few days, I think they said," Dolly added.

"That's good news."

"So, tell me." Dolly clutched her arm.

"You can listen yourself." She produced the Dictaphone from her purse. Arranged its earphone hoop over Dolly's head. She had cued the tape to Emil's voice. "Ready?"

"Have been since 1963," Dolly said and coughed.

She pressed "Play." "Can you hear it okay?"

Dolly nodded and waved her off. The clock's second hand turned. Dolly squinted as she listened. "The bastards," she shouted and jerked off her headphones.

A passing nurse popped in her head. "Everything okay?"

"We're fine," Rose said. She turned off the recorder. Gathered the wire.

Dolly's eyes gleamed. "We have them."

"It seems you were right."

"I'll take the tape." Dolly held out a bony hand, her forearm purple-blotched by needle pokes.

Rose stepped back. "I want some kind of guarantee."

"Guarantee?"

"You promised me certain things," Rose said. "This tape is going to create trouble. A lot of it for the Haugens and Olsens, and also for me. It's a terrible thing I've done." She kept the player out of reach.

"Worse than them Haugens killing your brother?"

Rose paused. "I need to make sure you'll hold up your end of our bargain."

Dolly pointed. "Open that little drawer. You'll find my house keys."

***

Back on Maple Street, Rose opened the creaky front door. The smell of cat slapped her. The gray cat shot past her and disappeared in the overgrown shrubs along the porch. Trying not to breathe, she passed through the mess to the doctor's office. His desk.

In it, as described, was a vellum folder and a document: "Dolores L. McConnell, Last Will and Testament."

She paged through it to the "Sole Beneficiary" page with her name on it, correctly spelled. Dolly's full name, typed above a blank and date, ended the document. Before leaving, she paused to look about. Opened a drawer filled with scalpels and silvery forceps and clamps.

They lay in order on black velvet. At the door she leaned close to the carved wooden foot and its harness. The leather, where it buckled around the calf, was dark-stained and shiny as a belt.

Back at the hospital, she went to Dolly's room.

"See? I told you," Dolly said and gestured for the vellum folder.

"It's where you said it was," Rose said.

"Sit me up more."

Rose pressed the bed's armrest button.

"Pen."

Rose handed one over.

Dolly squinted. "That's Robert's pen."

"It was the only one I saw."

"No matter. It'll all be yours when the sheriff gets here."

"The sheriff?"

"I called him. He'll be along soon. We'll need a witness to my will, then we'll give him the tape so I make sure he gets it. I don't want any funny business." Dolly raised an eyebrow.

"You've thought this through."

"Since 1963." She gargled a laugh. "I was always smarter than people thought. Everybody loved Robert. People would do anything for him. Robert, Robert, Robert. They thought he was God. But he was only a man. If people knew how I held things together." She coughed—beckoned for her water glass.

Rose handed it across.

"Ice," Dolly wheezed. "I need fresh ice. Why can't they remember that?" After a sip, she closed her eyes.

Rose went down the hall and found a cup of waiting room coffee, one sip of which was enough. As she headed back, the sheriff came around the corner. Wearing a short-billed hat with a gold star, he was older, not tall, and thick through the middle. On his wide belt hung a ring of keys, a small flashlight, and a handgun covered by a black holster. "Lars Torgerson" read his name tag.

He nodded. His eyes went to her red hair. He squinted as if he might know her.

"We might be going to the same room," Rose said.

"Dolly McConnell?"

"Yes."

"Then I'm happy for the company." He gestured for her to lead.

In the room, Rose tugged gently on Dolly's sleeve.

"About time," Dolly said even as she opened her eyes. "We don't have all day."

"Well, Dolly, what is it now?" the sheriff said.

"Ha," she cackled. "You never believed me, Lars. But finally, I've got proof."

"Of what?" The sheriff glanced Rose's way.

"You'll see. But first, meet Rose Rossi. She's Robert's and Sally Haugen's girl."

***

A few minutes later, headset on, Lars nodded to Rose, who turned off the Dictaphone.

"I told you." Dolly coughed again. "We've finally cornered those devil Haugens."

Lars turned to Rose. He had taken off his hat, which now lay on the windowsill. "How did you come by this?"

"It doesn't matter," Dolly said sharply.

"It kind of does," Lars began.

"What matters is the truth," Dolly said. "They killed Martin. They say so on the tape. Emil and Jenny Haugen. She drove him to the Dodge-In. He lit the match. He says they didn't know Martin was there, in the back room, asleep, but what does that matter? He burned to death because of them."

"In any case, I'll need to take the tape," Lars said.

Rose held onto the player. "Can you do one thing for us first?"

"What is it?"

Dolly beckoned Lars forward. "I need you to witness my will."

Lars narrowed his eyes. "What exactly is going on here?"

"It's simple," Dolly wheezed. "I asked Rose to worm her way into the Haugen family. Get the evidence of what I've always suspected. She did that. Now she gets her reward. She's my sole heir."

Lars pursed his lips. He turned to Rose. "Forgive me. I've only seen a photo of you, long ago, when you were a little red-headed girl child. Now here you are, a red-headed woman, yes, but there are many red-heads."

"For heaven's sakes, Lars," Dolly said, but he waved her off.

"You want me to prove who I am? Sure." Rose dug in her purse.

The sheriff gave her license a glance, then returned it. "Thanks. Due diligence. I'm sure you understand."

"I do," Rose said.

"Now that that's over, there's no law against me signing my will right here, is there?" Dolly asked.

"I guess not," Lars said.

"Then let me do it." Dolly gestured for the pen.

"You're not under any kind of duress or medications?" Lars asked.

"Medications, yes. Duress, no. I'm sharp as a tack," Dolly replied.

"Who is president?" Lars asked.

"Eisenhower." Dolly winked. "No, that fool Reagan, of course."

Lars glanced at Rose, then back to Dolly. "What day is it?"

"September fourth," Dolly said. "Nineteen-eighty-one. Who'd a thought I'd live this long?"

Lars shrugged. "Okay, then." He stepped forward.

They watched her sign, shakily. She handed the will to Lars. "Drop this off at the courthouse, and that will be that."

Rose ejected the tiny tape, let out a breath, and handed it to the sheriff.

"We've finally got them." Dolly let out a breath. Slumped back.

"We'll leave you be," Lars said.

Dolly's eyes drifted shut.

Lars turned to Rose. "We should talk," he said softly.

"I agree."

The waiting room was busy. A mother sat with a young boy, quite pale, who held one arm with the other.

"There's a little chapel off to the side," Lars said. "It's quiet there."

The chapel, in beige tones, carried an ecumenical glass mosaic of Jesus above a small altar and a box of tissue. The glasswork was colorful and abstract. One had to look to the side of it in order for

His image to come into focus. From habit, Rose dipped to one knee, then crossed herself.

"Are you Catholic?" Lars asked. He gestured for her to join him on the padded bench.

"I am."

"I'm something," Lars said. "Though I don't know what. Too long in this job, I guess."

"I'm sure you've seen it all," Rose said.

"No," Lars said, and mustered a smile. "That's the only certain thing."

She waited.

"So, tell me," he said, and held up the tape. "How did this all come about?"

She gave him the short version. Dolly's letter from out of the blue. Her trip to Skye to meet Dolly, and her trip to meet the Olsen/Haugens. "They all live together on a farm over in Minnesota."

"No surprise that they're all together," Lars replied. "They never let anybody come between them."

"I didn't believe Dolly," Rose continued. "After meeting them, I couldn't imagine that Emil and Jenny could so such a thing."

Lars shrugged. "People have surprised me so many times that nothing surprises me."

"I didn't want to gather information on the sly," Rose continued. "Especially with Emil in his condition."

"Condition?"

"He's eighty years old. He's in good physical health, but his sisters worry that he's getting senile."

"What's your opinion?"

"He has some issues, yes. But I believed his story. It seemed clear that he and Jenny did it."

Lars turned the tape over in his fingers. "This will never hold up in court," he said. "Nothing about it will withstand an attorney's challenge."

"Maybe that's a good thing. I never wanted to do it in the first place."

"Still, you did it," Lars said. "You know what they say about a rung bell."

"I do, I do," Rose said, beginning to sniffle. "But you don't know my family situation. The store. My kids thinking of college. Where's that money going to come from? And then, out of the blue, I get this letter saying I'm the sole heir to an estate, and I only have to do this one thing…"

"It's all right," Lars said, leaning forward. "You had a choice to make. Most people would have done the same thing."

"I've always liked to think I am not 'most people.'" She dabbed at her eyes.

Lars reached across for a tissue and offered it.

They fell silent.

"So now what?" Rose wiped her eyes. Gathered herself.

Lars's gaze went to the tape. "As I said, the tape won't hold up, but it does provide new information on an old case." He drummed his fingers.

"From the tape, could Jenny be charged?"

"We've got a new, go-getter of a county attorney," Lars continued. "He might well try to talk to her. Young guys in law enforcement want to make a name for themselves right away. Break the big case. Make the big arrest. She'd be okay with a good attorney, who'd advise her to say absolutely nothing. But it would be a can worms for all of them."

Rose blew out a breath. "This was all a horrible mistake. I never should have done it. I knew better." Her shoulders heaved.

"Tell you what," Lars said and leaned forward to touch her arm. "Let me think on all this. The wheels of justice move slow. I have some decisions to make, but nothing will happen right away."

She nodded.

"Shall we leave it there for now?" Lars took hold of his hat.

"You have good closure skills," Rose said, managing a weepy smile.

"It's a requirement around here," Lars answered. "With the old Norwegians, you never know when they're finished talking. They could be thinking. They could be done."

Rose glanced around. There was no clock in the chapel. "If you have a minute, can you tell me about my mother?"

Lars let out a breath. "Sally worked at the café in downtown Skye. I was a young deputy. I always took my lunch there."

"Was she a waitress?"

"She worked in back. A dishwasher. She was too shy to wait on people."

"That seems right. I mean, the shyness."

"They had fun back there," Lars said. "You could hear them laughing. Her laugh in particular."

"And the doctor?"

He looked at her.

"I'm trying to put everything together," she said.

Lars glanced about the chapel. "This is as good a place as any, I suppose. Or, you could read about it."

"Read about it?"

"In old *Sky View* newspapers from 1934, if they're still around. Or the *Fargo Forum*. That's where the trial was, in Fargo."

"The trial?"

"Of the doctor."

Rose stared.

"No one has ever told you?" the sheriff said.

"Told me what?"

Lars set aside his hat. "I was the one who took your mother to Doc McConnell that day. I was trying to do right by her and her toothache. She said Emil could pull the tooth, but I said no, you should see a real dentist. The dentist was out of town, so I took her to Doc McConnell. She was afraid—had never been to a doctor in her life—and so to fix her tooth he gave her ether. While she was out, he took advantage of her. Nine months later, you came along."

"Took advantage of her."

"Raped her," Lars said. "That's what he did."

The chapel was silent.

"I didn't want to use that word," Lars began.

She held up a hand, then rose and walked over to the glass-work visage of Jesus above the altar. Shards of glass came together, impossibly, to make His face, His eyes. The glass pieces had tiny air bubbles inside, little planets, galaxies of their own. "You've given bad news here before, haven't you?"

"None quite like this."

She turned. "It has been a long day. I should head home."

"If you need to collect yourself, we can sit a bit."

"Thank you, but no. I can manage."

Carrying Dolly's folder, the sheriff put on his hat. He walked her out. The air had chilled. The light had weakened.

"The days are so much shorter now," Rose said.

"Are you okay to drive?"

"It's straight south. It's not like I'll get lost."

He opened her car door.

She settled into the seat. Stared ahead through the windshield, then turned to him. "As long as we're doing this, tell me about my brother."

Lars shrugged. "Marty was a hell-raiser. Several times I had to call the doc to come get him at the station. He tried college. Got close to graduating… but bombed out at the very end. Didn't finish some paper or another. He came back home and did nothing but party. During the missile boom, the doc bought a business for him to run."

"The Dodge-In."

He nodded. "Worst possible place for Marty. He ran the bar and drank with the customers. He also ran call girls out of the back room. There was a car accident, and two of them were killed. Marty was thrown clear—he had that kind of luck. Anyway, the Dodge-In burned down right after that, with Marty in it. And now we know why."

She looked again through the windshield.

"At least today there's this for you." The sheriff handed her the vellum folder with Dolly's will. After a long moment, she took it.

"The Haugens and Jenny will survive anything," Lars said. "They always do."

"That's reassuring, I guess." She put in the key.

"Are you sure you're okay to drive?" Lars peered down at her. He kept his hand on the door frame. "My kids are gone. My wife and I could put you up at the house."

"The drive will do me good. Straight highway, open fields. It's a good time for thinking."

He held onto the door. "One last thing."

"Good news or bad?" She managed the smallest of smiles.

"I was sweet on your mother," Lars said. "In my mind back then, I had plans for us."

She patted his hand. "As if I hadn't figured that out, sheriff."

"I've thought about it a hundred times," Lars said, frowning. "What if I hadn't taken her to Doc McConnell that day? Everything would have been different."

"Wouldn't it though?" Rose said and started the engine.

Chapter Forty-Eight
Wheels of Justice

In the week after her trip to Skye, Rose occupied herself at the store and at home and hoped the phone would not ring. Fall clothes came in. Turtlenecks and crew necks were big for men, along with brown velvet jackets. For women, it was fur-lined puffer jackets and blazers. She gave the female mannequin a wig and, on a whim, crafted Elvis-style sideburns for the male. Finished, she stepped outside to look through the glass. She cocked her head. An older lady, passing, paused to look in, clucked her tongue, then moved on.

Sunday night after supper, the phone jangled. At the kitchen sink, she flinched. Continued with the dishes.

"Get that, Mother," Lucy called with annoyance.

"My hands are wet."

Lucy barked something, then hurried across. "Oh, hi." She covered the receiver and turned to Rose. "It's 'Aunt' Dag."

"Could you tell her I'm doing dishes?"

Lucy spoke into the receiver.

"No, I'll take it now," Rose said suddenly, wiping her hands.

"Are you back on North Dakota time?" Dag asked cheerfully.

"Mostly, yes."

"It's been a full week, but Sally and I still aren't right. We wake up at four a.m. Emil is worse. Seems like he never sleeps. He keeps asking after you. He worries that he talked your ear off."

"Tell him I'm fine," Rose said. "My ears are still attached to my head."

"I will. He'll get a lift from that," Dag said.

She hung on a bit longer, then faked a cough. "I did catch a little cold on the flight back."

Dag had advice (honey and tea), and soon they rang off. She replaced the receiver. Stared out the window to the street.

"What's the matter, Mom?" Leo asked.

"Nothing."

The waiting continued. Dag called once a week, as usual. Sometimes Sally came on the line. She was not the best on the phone. Phone conversations required rhythm. First one speaker. Then the other. Sally often paused so long to think, or perhaps to enjoy the news of the children, that when they started again, they spoke over each other. Closure, wrapping up a call, was another matter.

"Emil says hello," Dag said. "He wonders when you're coming over again."

"We're busy at the store these days," she said, "but I'll let you know. In fact, I'll call you next time, okay?"

***

She did not hear from anyone in Skye until early October, when the phone rang at two a.m. It was the care home where Dolly resided. They had found her on the floor, dead. After the call, Rose sat on the edge of her bed in the dark.

"Why did they call *you*?" Darryl asked.

She shrugged. "I'm it in terms of family."

"Seems like it could have waited until morning," Darryl mumbled from his side of the bed. "It's not like she was your mother."

She lay back, eyes open in the dark.

"Try to sleep." Darryl pulled her to him.

"I will."

He held her, a nice gesture, and she cleaved to his warmth. And gradually, more than cleaved. It had been a while. She sat up and peeled off her nightgown.

"Hello," Darryl said.

"You could help me get to sleep," she said.

"Well, okay then."

She crossed the room to lock the door.

Darryl watched her. "I'll take a midnight call like that anytime."

***

Halloween arrived. Their block in Fargo was a prime trick-or-treating neighborhood, with many little Spidermen and Smurfs.

"I wonder if they get any trick-or-treaters out at the Olsen farm," Leo said.

"No way," Lucy said. "Who'd go that far?"

"I guess that's one good thing about living in town." Leo hefted his candy bag.

"I'd never live out there," Lucy said.

There was no further news from up north until Monday, November 2, All Souls Day. The phone rang at the store. A secretary for a law office in Skye was on the line. By Dolly's request there had been no funeral, and her lawyer was moving ahead with the paperwork. Death certificate. Filing of the will. Probate of her estate. Signatures, in person, were required.

"Shall I come along?" Darryl asked.

"No need. All legal stuff right now," she said. "Papers for me to sign."

"Do you think she had money?" Darryl asked. "I mean, your father was a doctor."

"My father?"

"Sorry. You know what I mean." Darryl smiled uncertainly. With his thinning hair combed over increasingly, and his little potbelly more pronounced, he was suddenly a stranger to her. Should not one, even after many years of marriage, still look with some hope upon the other?

She turned away. "Whatever money comes from this will be mine. I'll listen to your advice, but in the end I will make the final decision on how we spend or invest it."

"As you should," Darryl said. "You've always been good with the books."

**

In Skye, Dolly's attorney was a stuffy, prematurely balding fellow named Bill Bauer, who directed his secretary to get coffee, open the documents, and hand them to Rose.

"If you'll follow along." He went down the list of assets, which included six, forty-acre parcels of land.

"Just hunting land," Bauer said. "Sloughs, low land, ponds, that sort of thing. Not worth much. Not like farmland. On the other hand, land is land."

"I see," she said evenly.

"There's the house on Maple Street. There's Dolly and the doctor's bank accounts."

"And the car?" Rose said. "I don't see the Cadillac on your list."

Bauer frowned, squinted closer, then barked for his secretary. "Of course you're right. Good help is so hard to find," he murmured, as if he and Rose were in this together.

When the list was revised, they went through it again. "In the end, a substantial estate," he said. "Dolly was a saver and a good manager. You're quite the lucky lady."

"The sole heir is sole heir," she said evenly.

Bauer coughed. "You're quite right. The law is the law."

"What's next?" Rose asked.

"The asset transfer. Probate is complicated. Usually takes a few months."

"I have my bank in Fargo," she said. "First National."

"That's a good start."

From her purse, she retrieved her checkbook, tore one out, crossed it through to void it. Wrote on it the name of her banker.

Bauer waved his secretary over to receive the check. "I can help with the real estate transactions, if you like. The house especially. I have a real estate license myself."

"I'll consider that. Thank you."

"And I do hunt the occasional duck. If you're inclined, maybe we can work out a little side deal on the smaller parcels?" He winked.

"We'll see. Anything else today?"

"Just some signatures."

***

Afterward, she sat in her car for long minutes, then drove to the sheriff's office. Lars Torgerson was sitting in conversation with a deputy. When the secretary passed him a note, he looked up through the glass and waved her in. The deputy nodded on his way out.

"Nice to see you again." Lars pumped her hand.

"Thank you."

He gestured to a chair, which she took. "How are you doing?"

"Thank you for asking. I have my children. My church. They don't know it, but they've been carrying me on their back lately."

"Last time was a lot," he said. "I worried afterward that it might be too much."

"I'm a big girl."

He nodded. "I heard that Bill Bauer is settling Dolly's estate. Is everything in order?"

"It seems so."

"Better it all goes to you than her damn cats."

She paused. "I came by about the tape. What you've decided."

He opened his drawer. Produced the miniature cassette. It was hardly as big as his thumb.

"You still have it," she said.

"The county attorney has been quite busy," Lars said. "As I said, legal matters can move very slowly."

"Which leaves me in limbo," she said. "Always wondering."

He paused. "I guess I can understand that."

"The Haugens call. We talk. Sally wonders when I'm coming over to visit."

"How is she? How did she handle the trip to Norway?"

"Well. She's at peace. Happy."

Lars tilted back in his chair—looked for long moments at the ceiling. Then he righted himself and leaned forward across the desk. "Tell you what. Why don't you keep the tape for now? It's so small. Things get lost here." With a finger he pushed it forward.

After a long pause, she reached for it. "If you're sure."

"I am. I've thought long and hard about it."

She put the tape in her purse. Snapped it shut.

"And made another decision," he said. "I'll be retiring this year. I'm sixty-eight. Been doing this long enough. Or maybe," he said, glancing at her purse, "I lost my way."

"I think every county should be so lucky to have a sheriff like you."

He shrugged.

"What will you do?"

"I like to tinker on cars," he said. "My wife and I will travel, some. In many ways, I've neglected her."

"I doubt that," Rose said.

He smiled. "I'll walk you out."

Streetside, the November sky had grayed. "There's weather coming in," the sheriff said. "It's good you get on the road."

"I think so too."

He walked her to her car. "One last thing?"

"Oh dear." She managed a smile.

"When I told you about your mother... how I felt about her," Lars said, "it occurred to me that you might think I've been a sad man all these years."

413

"That did occur to me."

"It wasn't really the case," the sheriff said. "I met my wife, we had our kids, we've had a pretty good life together."

"I'm happy to hear that."

"Still," he said.

She smiled. They had an awkward hug, after which she opened the door and got behind the wheel.

"Drive safe," he said, leaning down. "Watch for deer."

***

On the way to Fargo, she took the long way home, around to Olsen Farms. She drove not up to the house, but across to the office, where she found Jenny at her desk.

"Well," Jenny said, looking up.

"Sorry to just drop by."

"It's okay. The others have been wondering when they might see you again."

"But not you?"

Jenny gave Rose the smallest of smiles. "As I've said early on, I'm very protective of my family. To be honest, I remain uncertain about where this, with you, is going."

Rose took a chair. "You have good instincts." She opened her purse and produced the miniature cassette.

"What's this?" Jenny asked.

"You remember on the trip I had brought a recorder?"

"Yes. I thought that was clever. I'm sure you have some memories of the trip."

"Sort of."

"You have a player I believe."

Jenny stared, then opened a desk drawer.

Rose inserted the tape, clicked it on, then held it to her ear. At the right spot, she turned up the volume and lay the recorder on Jenny's desk.

Look how things worked out. "That's my voice," Rose said.

For you maybe.

Jenny looked up at Rose. As Emil continued, Jenny bit her lower lip.

"That's enough, I guess," Rose said.

Jenny looked across her office to the pool table. "Click, click."

"I didn't believe Dolly's suspicions," Rose said as she ejected the tape. "But I thought if I humored her, she would still follow through on her promise."

"Of her estate coming to you."

Rose nodded.

"And now you have it, yes?" Jenny said. "The estate and us. May I compliment you."

"You may not. I did this in a weak moment. Rossi's Department Store is not going to survive West Acres Mall. I've always felt indentured to that damn place, anyway. If there was to be money from Dolly, I saw it as my ticket to some different kind of life."

Jenny nodded. "What are your intentions with the tape?"

"My agreement with Dolly was to hand over the tape to the sheriff, which I did in her presence before she died."

"Lars Torgerson," Jenny said.

Rose nodded. "It was clearly a dilemma for him, which I felt bad about. But I've just come from meeting with him. He gave me back the tape. Said it was so small, and that things at his office so easily got lost."

"Lars," she murmured. Then she refocused on Rose. "So what now?"

"You have to tell me about that night. The night you killed Martin."

Jenny glanced toward the door, then went to make sure it was closed. She told Rose everything. The can of kerosene. The night stars while she waited for Emil, who only the next morning told her the truth—how Marty had come out of the back room and surprised him. How they fought.

Rose squinted away from that part, the fighting and the flames.

"I'd just come that day from the funeral of those two Canadian girls," Jenny continued, standing near the pool table now. "The ones from the reserve who died in the car accident. They were so beautiful. That was a big part of it, I'm sure. I was in a state. On any other day, I'd have had my senses about me." She hefted the white cue ball. "Plus, as it turned out, I met Greg, my husband-to-be, that day at the funeral. We had sex afterward at his place."

Rose laughed.

Jenny turned. "Yes. Shameful."

"Not really."

"Thank you." Jenny cocked her head at Rose.

"What?"

"That's the first time I've heard you laugh."

"I was always a serious little girl," Rose said.

"Me, too, I suppose."

They fell silent.

"I have a gift for you," Rose said. She held out the tape.

Jenny put down the cue ball. Accepted the tape.

"We need to start anew from this moment," Rose said. "Go forward from here."

Jenny, the tape in her pocket, went to her desk and found her two-way radio. "Dag? Tell Emil to come to my office." She put down the receiver.

"Yes, I need to talk to Emil," Rose said.

As they waited, Jenny ventured, "Have you ever played pool?"

"No."

"I'll teach you sometime. I think you'd be quite good at it."

There was thumping outside, then Emil came in wearing his old jacket, cap, and his new Norwegian wool. "Well," he said with a smile. "I *thought* that was your car."

"Nice sweater," Rose answered.

"I haven't taken it off since our trip."

"No kidding," Jenny said. "Dag wants to wash it. She's coming for it."

"Okay, okay." Emil kept his eyes on Rose.

"Rose came by to see us," Jenny said. "She has something to tell you."

Rose glanced at Jenny, then turned to Emil. "You told me about what happened to my brother. I want to thank you for being honest."

Emil began to speak, but Rose waved him off.

"I'm here to tell you that we have to move on. I see the full picture now. It's not a pretty one, but it's our picture. We can't go back, so for me, it's over and done. I want you to feel that way too."

Emil's shoulders slumped. He put a hand to his forehead, and his jaw quivered.

Rose went to Emil and hugged him hard. Gradually, his long arms closed around her, and his shoulders heaved. "Phew! Jenny's right," Rose said as she released him. "That sweater needs a good soak in Woolite."

"All right. I promise," Emil replied.

Crossing the yard to the house, Emil held Rose's arm. Or perhaps she held his. By the time they reached the front porch, he had mostly recovered himself.

"Why, Rose," Dag called. "What a nice surprise."

"I was in the neighborhood."

Dag hurried over for a hug. Sally came from the living room, still holding thread, a needle, and someone's shirt.

"Hello, Mother," Rose said.

Sally dropped her work on the table and took Rose in her arms. Held her for a long time.

"Will you stay for supper?" Dag asked.

Rose stood back, still holding Sally's hands. "No, but I can sit for a bit. Get caught up."

"It will take more than a bit," Sally said. "We have years to make up."

"We do," Rose said. "And I was thinking. We should start by getting together at Thanksgiving. All my kids will be home. Both of my brothers too. If you came down for Thanksgiving, you could meet everyone."

"That sounds fine," Dag said. "Jenny?"

"All right," Jenny said.

"I know where your house is," Sally said.

Rose turned to her. "You do?"

"I've been there," Sally said and looked away.

"As she was saying," Dag added. "We have lots to tell."

"Thanksgiving at my house in Fargo, then," Rose said. "It'll be crowded, but we'll make do."

***

As she left the farm, the snow picked up. The fine, slanting flakes were no trouble for the tires, but the graying light at 4:35 p.m. required headlights. On the straight road with whitening fields in all directions, she drove on. Her thoughts, like the snow, parting before her, swirling past, reforming behind. The money. The store. Lucy and Leo. Life with Darryl in the little house she had grown up in. Some things were going to change.

She slowed. The landmark for her turn west was a narrow windbreak of pines, which she might have missed. At an intersection she did not recognize, one with no stop sign, no signs of any kind, she braked. The angle of the snow seemed different. She gave its bend, its swirl, a long look, then turned right. She drove steadily forward, estimating, from minutes and average speed, the miles covered. When she believed herself heading to Canada, a warehouse loomed. Then the glow of lights. A familiar gas station. Her route home.

On the main highway south it was easy going, in the comfort of other headlights and taillights, all the way to Fargo.

Arriving at her house, the windows of which were brightly lit, she parked in the garage. She put the vellum folder out of sight in the glove box, then hurried inside.

Her family, at the supper table, had almost finished eating.

"There you are," Darryl called.

"Yeah, Mom." Lucy looked up briefly. "Where've you been?"

Rose passed by her daughter and smoothed her hair. "Working."

"You're always working," Lucy said.

"For you," Rose answered.

Leo gulped the last of his milk. "You want to go down and see my train setup, Ma? I think it's finally finished."

"You mean, you're too old to play with trains?" Lucy remarked.

"Shut up," Leo said easily.

"Yes, I want to see what you've done," Rose said. "It's been a while."

In the basement, supported by two sawhorses, the diorama blanketed a full sheet of plywood. A carpet of green, rolling hills with furry little groves of trees. A village at center. Rocky outcrops between which the railroad tracks ran. A blue lagoon with a siding and water tank for the steam engine.

"Is there a name for your town?" she asked.

"Just The Village." He shrugged. "It could be anywhere."

Rose leaned closer over Main Street. A fine, overhead wire ran street lamp to street lamp. Below, people came and went from the hotel, mercantile store, feed mill, and hardware store. A woman with a basket waved to someone across the street.

"I love your little people," Rose said.

"Uncle Emil is carving me a troll to scale." Leo held out his thumb and finger about an inch apart. "It will be about that big. And scary, he said."

"Where will it go?"

"He says it has to be hidden. Trolls can be anywhere, especially where you least expect them."

"That sounds like Emil," Rose said.

Leo laughed and clicked a switch. Tiny street lamps came on faint in the overhead light. He turned a knob on a controller, and the train came alive. With a whistle, it pulled its cars out of the station. "Everything looks best in the dark," Leo added. He extinguished the basement lights. The Village lit up twinkling.

"Wow," Rose murmured. "It's so real." Miniature people stood frozen in place yet still in motion. Hands outstretched to receive a box. A man, right foot forward as if walking. A worker with shovel in mid-swing.

"If you lean down close, it's like you're there with them," Leo said. Alongside her, he had, for the first time, the faintest smell of man.

She took his arm.

He turned to her. "What if they could look up and see us, Ma?" he said suddenly. "We'd be like giants in the sky."

"We would," she said. With a chuffing note the train grew louder.

"Get ready," Leo said. "Here it comes."

"Here comes what?" Darryl said. At the top of the stairs, backlit and faceless in dark, he held an ice cream bowl in one hand and a spoon in the other. In silhouette, his folded arms were stubby, useless wings. He threw on the basement lights. The Village reverted to a play town on old green carpet, and Darryl to Darryl.

"Change," Rose said, turning fully to face him. "Lots of change for us all."

-End-

Acknowledgements

I wish to thank friends and family who have, in ways large and small, made this a better novel. They include Jay Backstrom, Paul Benshoof, Craig Benson, Kris Cannon, Emily Enger, Dale Haugen (no relation to my fictional Haugens), Ian Leask, Gary Lindberg, Chris Marcotte, Marsh Muirhead, Malin Nøss Vangsnes-Weaver, Rick Polad, and Arlys Weaver (1920-2020). As well, a big thanks to all my workout pals at the gym, who keep saying, "Hey, when's that next book coming out?"

About the Author

Will Weaver grew up in northern Minnesota and graduated from the University of Minnesota and the Stanford University. His debut novel, *Red Earth, White Earth*, was published by Simon & Schuster and developed by CBS Television. His short story "A Gravestone Made of Wheat" became the award-winning indie film, *Sweet Land*, directed by Ali Selim, and starring Ned Beatty, Alan Cumming, and Alex Kingston. He is also the author of several novels for young adults, including the popular *Memory Boy* and *Saturday Night Dirt*. Returning to adult fiction, his novel *Power & Light*, the prequel to *Black Dirt, Bright Stars*, was a finalist for the 2023 Minnesota Book Award as well as the 2023 Midwest Independent Publishers' Award. He lives near Bemidji, Minnesota, on the Mississippi River with his wife, Rosalie.

www.ingramcontent.com/pod-product-compliance
Lightning Source LLC
Chambersburg PA
CBHW020830030726
47496CB00001B/172